MW00634658

More Than Alive

Death of an Idol

Fernando Torres

FIVE TOWERS
PUBLISHING

More Than Alive: Death of an Idol
By Fernando Torres

Copyright 2020
All rights reserved.

This novel is a work of fiction. All characters and incidents in this novel are fictitious. Any resemblance to persons either living or deceased is purely coincidental.

Published in the United States by Five Towers Publishing, Las Vegas
www.fivetowerspublishing.com

For all commercial inquiries, please contact:
comments@fivetowerspublishing.com

Library of Congress Control Number: 2020907399

ISBN-13: 978-1-7349506-0-1

Printed in the United States of America.

Illustrations by Tuyên Ngô Phạm

10 9 8 7 6 5 4 3 2 1

★ First Edition ★

FIVE TOWERS

PUBLISHING

"Our life is the light of the moon passing behind a cloud at dawn.
It is as lasting as morningtide's tears or a waning crescent.
Yet the night is not overcome by the stars,
nor the day absorbed by the mire.
What jealous cloud undertakes to deny, belies concealment.
What the sun bids to outshine, is nary overcome.
Day nor night obscures the shadow that endures.

Takuboku Yamamoto
(Reija 22)

DEDICATION

FOR DISILLUSIONED GHOSTS AND THOSE WHO
BELIEVE THAT THEY ARE
BUT THE MOONLIGHT AT DAWN,
BE NOT A SHADOW...BUT A LIGHT.

TABLE OF CONTENTS

CHAPTER ONE:

DEATH AND RESURRECTION
(MARCH 26, 2042, TAITO WARD, TOKYO, JAPAN)

In Japan, the word *kokuhaku* is synonymous with a love confession, but to Alice Suzuki, it defined a troubled heart. Devotion and doubt, as inseparable as sakura and spring, compelled her to clutch the letter like the pin of a grenade she had decided to pull. As frightening as falling for a childhood friend might be, it paled before the thought of another admirer overcoming any such reservations first.

Don't say it, Alice implored herself. *He doesn't have to know.* Unlike friends at school who protested the cluelessness of their love interests, she placed her faith in Keiji's total lack of awareness. Swinging a stick he had found on the ground; his imagination seemed primarily occupied with thoughts of being at-bat for the Tōkyō Giants, the championship resting on his shoulders. Alice's fingers rubbed the necklace Keiji gave her when she turned sixteen. Its angel pendant glistened from attention, and while the gesture was probably insignificant, perhaps it held supernatural properties to have so altered her view of their relationship. Alice was embarrassed that of all the boys at school, she had fallen for the one that embodied the most complications. She wished she could channel her feelings in a less precarious direction, but their gangly shadows overlapped like a pair of grease pencils, uncertain of the future they might draw.

Keiji's feelings were indeterminable, most of all, to himself. Oblivious to her internal turmoil, he only became aware that she no longer walked beside him when the *click-clack* of her heels fell silent, a clear sign she had stopped under the gnarled cherry tree they used to play beneath as children.

"*Suki desu!*" Alice cried, then covered her mouth in horror. Eyes wide, her small fingers failed to hide her astonishment at what she had done.

Keiji wondered if a bolt of lightning had suddenly flashed before his eyes. His ears rang as if caught inside a temple bell. While what she had said could be understood as, "I like you," neither doubted her actual intent contained a far more potent expression of affection.

"*Suki desu. Tsukiatte kudasai,*" she clarified. There had not been a day in the last month when those words had not tried to ram their way past her clenched lips. The pin had been pulled. There was nothing to do now but see if either of them would survive, shards of their friendship blown to the four winds.

Saturday was when Keiji would join Alice's family for a day trip to Hakone and ride the ropeway to where they sold the famous black eggs; ones said to ensure a long life. How a black egg performed better than a brown or white one didn't so much matter, as that it provided her courage with a deadline. Unrequited love was a prickly thing, and her feelings had developed beyond what their platonic relationship could embrace.

"Keiji-kun?"

The only reply was the wind whistling softly through the branches of the old cherry blossom tree. To Keiji, Alice had transformed into something that solicited both fear and desire. It was a simple high school confession, but to him, her words carried the weight of a marriage proposal.

"*Ano...*" he mumbled. "Would it be okay—can I think about it?"

"*Hai,*" she said, a quick response in the affirmative that was more automatic than sincere. Alice wanted the matter resolved immediately. It was like when her dad said he'd consider getting a kitten. She didn't want to bother picking out names if the whole matter was a moot point.

"*Gomen,*" apologized Keiji. He started to leave but realized the situation would become even more strained if he dropped any pretense of social protocol.

"*Mata na*," he said with a quick wave, his adolescent way of dealing with the ungainliness of the exchange. There was no point in making light conversation with the unavoidable truth finally breached.

Alice was a coin balanced on its edge. She watched Keiji run past a row of vending machines and wondered if the future would reveal her to be relieved or destroyed. Love, she had determined, was a cavity that signaled you were alive, but in pain. Whether it was worth the sweetness remained to be determined. She shook her hair and watched sakura petals fall like pink tears upon her black loafers.

A bright, gallows morning signaled to Alice that her day of reckoning had arrived. She opened her closet and selected an outfit appropriate for either light hiking beside Lake Ashi or total humiliation. Prepared for the possibility that Keiji might opt out of the opportunity to experience new frontiers of embarrassment, she struggled to determine how she might explain his absence to her parents.

"The car is here," her father shouted downstairs. "I reserved it for the whole weekend." Mr. Suzuki found it more convenient to subscribe to a self-driving car service than for the family to own outright. It arrived at their residence, like the autonomous cabs that salarymen ordered when they missed the last train. Only the affluent, hobbyists, or criminals retained a vehicle since autonomous car-sharing services had arrived.

"*Chotto matte*," said Alice, checking her vanity mirror one last time for any straggling messages. Unfortunately, the only thing displayed from behind the glass was a meme from Keiji that she was still trying to figure out. She wondered if Yuki had heard anything, but when she taped her avatar, a funny animation appeared that indicated that, once again, she wasn't available. Alice was seriously considering accepting applications for a new best friend, seeing as Yuki had been so persistently absent lately, not unlike her self-esteem. Alice clicked on Keiji's profile page to check his relationship status, but it remained unchanged. Not sure if she should be angry or relieved, she pretended to hit the mirror, which created a satisfying, shattered-glass effect. When she turned back again, it had already restored to its previous, undamaged form.

Running down the stairs, she almost slammed into her mom. "I guess Keiji can't make it. Can you tell dad we'll go on without him?"

"Are you okay, Alice-chan? He's already in the car." Mrs. Suzuki looked as if she had eaten a jar of umeboshi plums.

"Keiji?"

"Any other boys you were planning on bringing today? We can always cancel if you're not feeling well…"

Relief washed over Alice as she realized she had received a second chance, albeit one to humiliate herself. *Yatta!* She kissed her mom's cheek and skipped down the stairs. Being an only child, her parents had nothing, with which to compare her occasionally curious behavior. Additional cultural differences between her parents also kept them guessing, something of which she readily took advantage.

The door of the car flipped open to reveal Keiji grinning like the Cheshire Cat. He handed her a pair of augmented reality glasses; aware her parents considered AR contacts to be rude. "Did you download Smash Jumpers?"

"Hai," replied Alice. She couldn't tell if his arrival indicated deeper feelings or was merely a gesture of respect towards her family.

The mixed-reality game was something of a classic, and no longer one of the entertainment options that came with the car. Alice made sure it was available whenever they traveled further than the tonkatsu restaurant they frequented. "I get to be the kangaroo with the monocle." Unlike other girls, the request wasn't intended to appear enduringly immature.

A camera in the dashboard scanned Mr. Suzuki's face and matched his identity to his car-share account. He checked to determine if he had uploaded the route into the car's GPS. "Don't worry. There's more than enough charge to get to Hakone and back."

"I'm not pushing," said Alice, who remembered a trip to Nikko, where roadside assistance had to charge their batteries. That was the time they had reserved the car for a week, and it had completely slipped her father's mind. He was used to the batteries being topped off before the car arrived. Her mom's disapproving glare reminded her to refrain from making acerbic observations.

"Autonomous-drive engaged," said a soft, feminine voice through the speakers. The car pulled out of the driveway, and background music faded-up. The vehicle's intelligent assistant reported, "Estimated time en-route – one-hour forty-eight minutes."

The only sound they heard as they eased down the road was the patter of rain against the aluminosilicate windows. Alice's mom increased the tint level of the glass so she wouldn't strain her eyes as she read. Though she could just as easily project her novel inside her prescription glasses, she enjoyed the pleasure of turning the pages; the almond and vanilla-like scents the paper made as its compounds deteriorated with time. She called up the weather map. "I don't think the rain will last. The cell seems to be over Atsugi and Hadano. Well…mostly."

Alice and Keiji played their game as if the previous day had never occurred. It was reassuring to sit beside him, though Alice wondered what Keiji would do if she took his hand. Death from mortification seemed the most probable outcome.

The day Keiji gave her the necklace, was also the Wednesday that her friend Yuki hid in the school gymnasium. Being from Osaka, Yuki proudly embodied the brash personality found in comedians from that prefecture. She would do things at lunch, such as put chopsticks in her nose or place snails on her forehead until one day, a few of the girls decided to rob Yuki of her smile. The video they sent to the entire school featured Yuki's head on the body of a cow wearing a stereotypical Kansai leopard print. Keiji discovered her behind the bleachers crying with the same enthusiasm she brought to telling a well-crafted joke. When he walked her home in the middle of the day, he was nearly suspended. Seeing how he had risked himself for her friend, Alice discovered something new in Keiji. He wasn't remarkable because he played baseball, or scored well on tests, but for the way, he cared about people. She could not bear the thought of his attention wasted on one of her flighty classmates whose idea of culture began and ended at purkura booths.

Keiji paused the game, flipped up his glasses, and for a brief moment, they locked eyes. "Alice-chan," he whispered. "If you win the next game…I'll give you my answer." There was no need to provide any context. It was the first time he had addressed the unanswered question that lingered between them like an eye-floater of the heart.

Alice bit her lip. "*Un.*" She wondered if losing might not be the better option. Unlike other girls, her taste in fashion began with her school uniform and ended with gym clothes. Her voice brought a karaoke party to its knees. She didn't have any particular talent other than speaking English, which she had learned from her mother and visits to cousins in California. The more she thought about it, she could not imagine any particular reason Keiji would like her at all.

"Are we going the right way?" Alice's mother asked, tapping her husband's leg like a woodpecker.

Mr. Suzuki was quite content to let the car go down the highway unattended while watching the baseball game. "Those damn Tigers are just so good this year..."

"Father," Mrs. Suzuki pressed him again. They had met when she was an Army brat. Her plain-spoken personality had brought them together, although once married, her directness did not give him much room to maneuver. "Can you please check to see if we were supposed to get off at the last exit? This isn't the way we went last time."

Mr. Suzuki seemed unconcerned. "When are the Giants going to win? Can you tell me that? They actually lost to the BayStars. Does that even make any sense?"

"*Otousan!*" cried Mrs. Suzuki. "Did you update the maps?"

He gave an intentionally exasperated sigh and brought up the GPS database. "Of course. I did everything last night. It's probably just taking us on a shortcut. There's more than one way to get there, you know."

Alice looked out the window and saw they were on a bridge so new that the concrete looked bleached. "I don't remember this way. Maybe we're lost?"

"Let's pull over and check." Coming from her mother, it was more a polite command than a request.

Mr. Suzuki sighed, swiveled his chair forward, and hit disengage on the car's menu. The steering wheel emerged from the dash, but the vehicle accelerated. On its speedometer, the numbers advanced like a bathroom scale after Christmas.

"What's wrong?" asked Alice.

"*Otousan!*" yelled her mother. "Slow down!" The car's electric motors were silent, but she had an instinct for judging their speed based on the sound of the tires. It came in handy when her husband shut off the autopilot.

"I can't—must be the new OS." He tried to cycle through the menus, but his fingers bounced against the screen.

The time for a solution had already expired, as the car jerked violently to the left, and then crashed directly into the safety rail. Airbags exploded, and shoulders dug into seat belts. White powder and the smell of burning dust filled the air. The front half of the car dangled off the edge of the bridge, yet somehow managed to stay precariously balanced.

"*Okasaan?*" The silence scared Alice more than the sound of the impact.

Keiji was in a state of shock, but about to say something, when the car shuddered. They felt a sensation, not unlike going over the first hill of a rollercoaster, and Alice floated free of her seat. Their airbags already expended; it felt like they hit a wall, and immediately, a dark-green blanket enveloped the car's windows. There was a sound like coffee poured down a sink and a *thud* as they came to rest on the bottom. Water seeped in from the car's floor and bit at Alice's ankles, but no one responded when she started to scream. Alice threw her shoulder against the door repeatedly, but the outside pressure held it fast. In the stuttering light, she saw blood dripping from Keiji's hair. She kicked at the windows, but her loafers slipped on the sweating glass.

Within the murky depths, Alice could see a set of red eyes drawing nearer. When it finally reached them, a spectral black cloak passed through the front windshield and enveloped the cabin. Coronal filaments surrounded her father, as the specter worked unseen, before it shifted its attention to her mother, coaxing a tiny luminescent cloud from her gaping mouth. The dark water reached Alice's chest, as moisture violated the car's batteries. In the last flash of light, Alice saw a pale hand reach into the back seats. It grasped blindly between them, but then paused as if momentarily distracted. Outside, someone was attempting to force their way into the vehicle. Sensing help, Alice screamed, but the shadowy form increased its pace, moving their spindly fingers past her lips and pressing hard against the roof of her mouth. It tugged at something physically intangible, and Alice's consciousness peeled like the skin of an orange.

The phantom dragged her through the car's window, past her unknowing rescuer, and into the primordial darkness.

Immobilized by a metaphysical neurotoxin, Alice's panic quickly reached parity with resignation. When, finally, whatever it was that had been dragging her released its grip, her skin rubbed against porous stone until her progress abated. The first sign that she had regained control of her limbs was the realization that she could stand. The water's surface rose no higher than her shoulders, which led to the discovery that she had emerged in a Greco-Roman courtyard. Corinthian columns supported a portico adorned with beautiful glass mosaics, a foreign but reassuring reality.

As her vision cleared, she saw blurred outlines and heard a multitude of tongues from various lands, many of which she could not place. To her great relief, she spotted her mother, sitting on a carved granite bench, drying her father with a thick towel. "*Otousan!*" she yelled. He returned the kind of non-committal waves fathers are known to give. "Have you seen Keiji-kun? Is he okay?"

Her mom gave a bewildered yet sympathetic look. "Alice-chan. Where have you been? I've been worried sick. Don't you scare me like that again." She waved, palm down, for her to join them.

"Where's Keiji? Have you seen him?"

"I thought he was with you." Mrs. Suzuki looked around, concerned.

"I'll be right back. I promise." Not predisposed to imagine the worst, Alice set off with unwarranted expectations.

Racing to the other side of the courtyard, Alice apologized to a stocky lad wearing lederhosen over whom she had tripped. As success eluded her, she searched ever more frantically. An open door gave her momentary hope, but inside was only a slightly balding, silver-haired man who appeared prepared to attend a toga party. He gestured emphatically at someone she could not see, but his eyes telegraphed well his general displeasure.

To better understand the source of his ire, Alice leaned forward and caught a glance of a man who looked more out of his era and element than she felt. He wore a sharkskin suit, and his hands clutched a trilby hat. A loose bow tie hung upon his wingtip collar, and though he appeared only a handful of years older than Alice, he looked like he had just stumbled in from an off-strip casino. He offered a crooked grin before the older gentleman in the toga noticed they were being watched and slammed the door.

That is when Alice became aware that her environment had an odd hiccup as if time were a wheel that slipped from omniscient fingers. When she finally made it back to the bench, it was only to find it empty. All that remained was her mom's towel and a small pool of water where her dad had been sitting. Alice started to panic, but then she spotted her parents on the opposite side of the courtyard, being led through an imperial-looking door crowned with an archway of heavenly stars. Alice yelled for their attention and took a determined step forward, but then a hand reached out and blocked her way. Its owner had thin lips and placid eyes. "Those are my..."

"Oh, I'm sorry," replied the androgynous figure. "You won't be joining them—not yet." Their tone was sympathetic but firm.

"Why not? Where are they going?" Alice found her body afflicted by the same paralysis she had experienced earlier.

The door *hissed* as it sealed behind her parents.

"I believe they have something different planned for you."

"I'm ready to go home," she replied. "Why are you doing this to me?"

The Vegas lounge lizard's browbeating had apparently reached its conclusion. He came over to intercede, shooing away the guardian with an obnoxious clicking sound that implied he had the situation under control. "Hey there, kiddo. You've had a rough day, but remember...worry is like weeds." He picked at something caught in his teeth. "Tears only water them, am I right, doll?"

Alice was more confused than insulted. "This place isn't real. I'm dreaming. Right?"

His lack of eye contact served as his passive-aggressive response. "Have you ever wondered why zombie flicks are popular? Because people can relate." Something about her encouraged his tendency to ramble. "Did you ever see a movie where the actor has already adiosed in regular life? They're up there running from something, and you want to yell, 'Hey buddy. Take a breather.

You're already dead.' I don't know where I was going with that." On his wrist, two strands of beads, one side white and the other black, began to spin. They formed patterns that meant something to him because he appeared to protest. "C'mon. Seriously? Are you yanking my chain? Why do you hate me?" The beads cycled through various combinations. "That? Oh, I can explain that…"

"Who are you?" asked Alice. "What am I doing here?"

"Vegas Jack. Yeah, that's what they call me…Honest Jack. A few other things I'd rather not repeat in the company of a lady." He produced an old cigarette lighter and flicked its wheel a couple of times to no effect.

Alice dry swallowed and asked the question whose answer she feared the most. "Where's Keiji-kun?" Something told her that he'd know whom she meant.

Jack paused to consider what information he was at liberty to share. "That other kid? He's great…just fine. Never better."

A wave of relief washed over Alice. "Thank God."

"You, on the other hand," his eyebrows formed a wave, "are dead." He glanced back at his toga-wearing companion, who smacked his forehead. "The old guy in the dress says I'm supposed to work on something called bedside manners."

Alice had already assumed as much, but her current environment seemed designed to aide in the acceptance of such a conclusion. "But who are you?"

"Weren't you listening? Your ears must still be plugged up from the ride. I'm Vegas…"

"Jack. Yes, I know. What are you, though? Some kind of angel?"

The Rat Pack reject's eyes laughed a moment before his mouth. "That would be a big negatory. Look, you've had a hard day…you fell off a bridge. You died." He glanced over at the gentleman in the toga, who signaled for him to continue. "It's complicated. There's metaphysics and quantum mechanics to consider. I don't think I could explain it to you in a way you'd understand. Not that I'm saying you're stupid—just ignorant." He let out an exasperated sigh, rolled his eyes, and transmogrified into the wraith that she had first encountered in the car. Peals of smoke leaked from robes comprised of funerary shrouds, and his coal eyes smoldered red. Thin fingers, as pale as freshly marked gravestones, punctuated his every word. "Best soul harvester in the business, that's what they call me. Jack."

CHAPTER TWO:
CALL OF THE VOID

J ack's raven-black robes withdrew into the pocket of his smoking jacket, where it became his folded handkerchief. An attitude more appropriate to the Copa Room, circa the 1960s, returned along with a more suitably mortal form. He adjusted his cufflinks for no apparent reason. "Nothing to it. Merely one layer of the baumkuchen."

Alice shared the horrified reaction of the others in the courtyard who had witnessed his transformation. "You're that thing I saw in the car?"

Jack brushed some lint off his shoulder. "Hey, nothing personal doll. Just another gig to me." He hummed part of a tune that was running through his head. It occurred to him that he ought to register an objection to her insinuation. "And I'm not a thing."

Alice's heart worked its way back to something approximating a regular rhythm. "Maybe you shouldn't do that. You kind of freaked everyone out."

Jack waved dismissively. "Who, them? They're already dead."

Within the courtyard, a murmur grew as people reacted to Jack's proclamation. He rocked a couple of times on the balls of his feet and waited for things to settle again. Jack was about to say something in his defense, when there was an isolated scream, his faux pas having reached someone in the back.

"They're not supposed to know that yet, Jack," said the classical-looking fellow in the toga. "This place is a decompression chamber for people who have only recently crossed over." He gazed sympathetically at Alice. "Hello dear, my name is Clement, and I can see by your unsettled disposition that you've already met Jack."

"*Hajimemashite.* Alice *desu. Yoroshiku onegaishimasu.* Can you please tell me what I'm doing here? Why won't you let me see my parents? What's happening?" She was pretty sure she already knew the answer, but it was not the sort of conclusion that could forgo verification.

"Well, dear, I'm afraid you've passed." He was not especially apologetic, but his tone was more affable than his counterpart.

Even if she didn't like what she heard, Alice found it surprisingly easy to accept the conclusion, given her current state. "Then why am I still here?"

Jack's eyes narrowed, almost to the point he was cross-eyed. His head bobbed a couple of times, as if to say, *I've got this.* "How's about I told you that this was your lucky day, kid? Not mine, but what if you could find out who murdered your parents?"

"Murdered!" Alice cried horrified. "We drove off a bridge. The car malfunctioned."

"Very smooth, Jack." Clement did not have time to chastise his charge for every misstep, or eternity should be very long indeed. The philosopher and former teacher from Alexandria had been watching her as she reacted to Jack's foibles. When he paired up a team of harvesters, he looked for complementary weaknesses as much as strengths. "I know that all this happened rather suddenly, but I might have a solution to make your circumstances more agreeable." He noticed that Jack's eyes were imploring him to reconsider, but he plowed forward nonetheless. "It's not a path to be taken lightly. You see…most of the people who come out of that pool aren't upset that they're dead; they're relieved. Nothing takes more courage than facing another day. The future can be seen as either a blessing or an uncertain trial. It can be far scarier than even Jack. Well, more or less."

There were many unfinished matters that Alice had left incomplete back home on what had been the most fateful afternoon of her young life, but she didn't understand what she was being asked to decide. "I didn't even get to say goodbye to Keiji."

"Well, I'm afraid you can't do that," apologized Clement. "But you are allowed to find—well, a few answers. It's one of the perks, although the truth can be an unsettling reality. Also, unfortunately, Jack and closure are a package deal."

"See Clement; she's not interested." Jack tried to get the attention of one of the spirit guardians. "You know what? I don't blame her. Good choice, kid." He stuck his fingers in his mouth and whistled for assistance.

Alice wasn't exactly enamored at the thought of being partnered up with a second-rate lounge act, but being weighed down with so many unanswered questions was a torment of its own. "Am I being asked to be a ghost or something?"

"Nothing of the sort," replied Clement.

"How long have you been doing it?" she asked Jack, who appeared relatively young but gave off the vibe of someone who had enjoyed a senior discount or two.

"Two hundred and forty-eight years."

"Two hundred and forty-seven," corrected Clement. "And he can't retire until his replacement is trained and competent, a fact he would do well to remember." He rubbed the few white hairs that remained above his forehead. "Then, there is the matter of the outstanding demerits."

"I'm working on it." Jack buttoned his single-breasted jacket. "Everyone around here could stand to lighten up a little—or a lot."

Clement enjoyed annoying Jack, but it was rather tiring. "Why don't you tell her the good parts of what you do? Would that be too trying?"

Savvy to Clement's attempt to make him part of the recruiting process, Jack replied, "Well, it sure ain't working with you, cueball."

"Jack sometimes forgets you need intelligence to be funny." Clement regretted sending him to work on that comedian thread, a few years ago, but now he was stuck with the consequences.

"I bet you kill in the old folks home. The guy's a regular Don Rickles." Jack could tell that Alice was impatiently waiting for his explanation. "You get back whatever you lost when you died. Think of it as a witness protection program for the dead." He glared at Clement. "Happy?"

"So I could see Keiji? I could find out what happened to us?"

Clement knew that even sincere promises had their limitations. "Honestly, we just collect souls," he explained. "Erudition and Justice are entirely different departments, though Lord knows I've tried to get a transfer." He glared at Jack, the source of a great many of his woes. "But providing closure is always excellent training."

"C'mon Clement, cut me some slack. They went off a bridge. It's an old story. Seems pretty cut and dry."

"Autonomous cars don't simply drive off bridges. Could be something there. I want you to look into this thoroughly. I might not even see you for months…"

Jack didn't like it when Clement competed with him at being a wise guy. "Cars were dangerous enough when someone with a noodle was at the wheel. You'll never catch me in one of those robot-driven contraptions."

"Our Jack doesn't trust technology," said Clement. "He went on for years about how the telephone was a harbinger of doom."

"See that guy over there?" Jack pointed to a man drying himself off on a bench. "Just fell off a cliff checking his messages. Ask him how happy he is with his provider."

Clement was in the inevitable position of having to convince two people this time around. "So what do you think? Sound intriguing?"

Before she had the chance to respond, Jack pushed his way between them. "Look, I'm sensing hesitation, and I need help like I need an enema."

"That can be arranged. Krakatoa, perhaps?"

"C'mon, Clement. I don't need some dame, cramping my style. Can't you see she's wishy-washy? Probably on account of all the water she recently swallowed."

"You've been alone long enough. If you had been a little more careful, we wouldn't be having this conversation now, would we?"

"She just wants to see her Romeo. She doesn't care about the job. This is serious work."

"That comes in time." Clement had reached the limit of how much of Jack his patience could handle for one day. "Alice, I'm trying to offer you a door." He pointed across the pool to a gateway that stood in contrast to the one through which her parents had departed. "There are some who would kill for such a chance, or at least die for it. All you had to do was run afoul of Jack's incompetence. Not uncommon, but quite fortuitous, I'd say."

"One of these days, old man." Jack bit the palm of his hand, though he lacked the bile to add sufficient bite to his threat.

"But there is a cost."

"So, all I have to do is walk through that door?" asked Alice. "The one with the silver globe. Is that what you're saying?"

Jack had seen Clement's routine before, undoubtedly influenced by the origin stories of Greek heroes he had once known. "I've got quirks. Lots of quirks."

"But Keiji's on the other side. Are you saying he's wrong?"

"Clement?" huffed Jack. "No, he wouldn't *steer* you wrong." He made a driving gesture. "What? Too soon?"

The Greek philosopher stuck his thumbs in his belt-cord and exhaled quite forcefully. "Alice, the people who work for me are individuals who ended up here for unforeseeable reasons. Wouldn't you like a chance to untie a few knots? I believe Jack could use someone who understands the modern world. For goodness sake, he still misses ocean liners."

"I like shuffleboard," replied Jack defensively. "It's relaxing. Is that some kind of crime around here?"

"You've been a little too relaxed, and the threads don't involve lamplighters or video rental shops anymore." Clement's fashion choices might have looked antiquated, but he was quite informed concerning the modern world. "We had a thread involving singularity, and he thought it was about dating."

Jack squinted like a gunslinger, but he couldn't volley over things he didn't understand.

Alice wondered what made her different from the other people that emerged from the pool. She wanted to regain something that approximated control, but not if it was only an illusion. "So, I have a choice?"

"If you didn't, we wouldn't have a job." It was the sort of philosophical postulation that Clement posed for his entertainment. "Experience with free agency is why only mortals are called to this position. You see, we can't know precisely when a soul needs to be harvested. It's your job to prevent supernatural interference. Well, without creating threads of your own. Basically, don't *jack* it up."

Jack sniggered, sarcastically. "Clement of Alexandria, everyone. He's here all week – and the next. And the century after that." He waved goodbye to Alice with the top of his fingers. "Well, this has been super. Bye-bye now, I work alone."

Clement stood protectively behind Alice, his hands on her shoulders. "I think we both know what this is really about. I liked Hiro as much as anyone, but he isn't coming back." He remembered well the many times he'd been in the middle of resolving the differences between Jack and his old partner. Time had erased the more problematic memories and left his reflections more favorable than was warranted.

"So is that what's happening here? She's Japanese, so I'm supposed to think she's like Hiro?" asked Jack. "Well, I can tell by looking at her, she's no Hiro."

Alice wasn't the type to be easily offended, so she collapsed on a bench, next to an elderly Eastern-European woman, more out of frustration than offense. "I can't believe I'm dead."

The woman looked at Alice, horrified.

"Hey, doll," admonished Jack. "Keep it down. You're going to scare someone."

◆ ◆ ◆

The stacks of boxes rising from George Okada's desk mimicked Shinjuku's equally indifferent skyscrapers. Having to do his new job while waiting for his old one to get filled meant he would unpack as the need arose. His new cubicle was closer to the center of the room, but it made his growing mess more apparent. The chair's former occupant had departed in such a sudden and unexpected manner, that George spent half his time searching for clues.

"Okada-san," yelled a curt voice, which nearly separated him from his skin. It was Izumi, the director of ergonomics. Her hair was drawn up tight in a bun, and she had an eye patch from an infection she apparently lacked the time or desire to get treated. The ergonomics pirate had already driven one of the office ladies to tears, scolding her for twenty minutes on the correct procedure for resting her wrists when she typed.

"Izumi-san, *ohayou gozaimasu*. How is your eye?" George knew that he had no choice but to endure whatever chastisement awaited him. If his shoulders remained characteristically hunched over, it was from being berated at home and in the office. Still, everyone feared the ergonomics director and George wasn't any different, so he immediately corrected his posture.

"It itches now, thanks to you." She looked around his cubicle and pushed around various items for no apparent reason. "We have noticed that your chair moves over beside Abe-san's desk every Monday at 9:05 a.m."

It had slipped George's mind, but all the furniture had sensors so that the Ergonomics Department could study employee workflow, or at least that was the justification.

"Yes, well, it's only polite for me to greet my neighbors when I arrive."

The answer was about what she expected from a newly minted middle manager, and it was her sacred duty to put him in his place before he ascended any higher in the ranks.

"This happens shortly after you check the weekend sports scores on your company-issued desktop." She looked at her tablet as if to confirm what she already knew. "Ergonomics is not merely about ensuring that our employees stay safe. It's about how motion affects our use of time."

George knew better than to argue. Izumi was looking for someone to spar with, and he didn't plan on being her opponent.

"And you do an excellent job Izumi-san. Don't worry; I'll ensure that my chair no longer wanders off without me. Especially at that particular time."

Izumi knew his response was nothing more than workplace judo, where the opponent only appeared to submit. A veiled threat would be necessary.

"Please see that it doesn't." Her foot moved like a rabbit scratching an itch. "I would hate to have to forward this to Employee Monitoring for a more thorough examination. Especially now that your career is finally starting to show a pulse." Everyone knew that her ergonomics title was nothing but a justification to allow for more invasive employee surveillance. She was Employee Monitoring.

A frozen smile remained fixed on George's face until the tight bun on the back of her head passed out of sight. Then, he kneeled next to his desk and peeled the sensors off from underneath his chair. Re-stuck on the floor, beneath where he sat, the ergonomics mat would cover them quite nicely. George rolled his chair over to Abe's cubicle.

"So did you see that game last night? *Saiko desu!*"

♦ ♦ ♦

As Clement droned on about his many shortcomings, Jack wandered through his considerable library of memories; early-morning walks in Paris during the Belle Époque, adventures in the American West, and his favorite, afternoons spent at the Great Exhibition in Hyde Park. It was not until he realized that Alice had given them the slip that he attempted to interrupt Clement's laborious monologue concerning his inadequacies. Unfortunately, it only came across as yet another challenge to his criticisms, so the philosopher raised his voice louder to be heard over any perceived objections.

On the other side of the courtyard, Alice's hand rested upon the door with the celestially adorned tympanum. The only thing that stilled her hand was the uncertainty of Keiji's fate and an inexplicable call to leap into the void. It was the same curious sensation she felt whenever she peddled her bicycle beside a ravine. Her eyes drifted over to the door with the silver globe; its filigree darkened gray from age. If Keiji was behind the mysterious gateway, then perhaps the call was not without reason, nor could it be easily ignored.

Jack attempted one more time to interrupt Clement, grabbed his wrinkly pink head, and cranked it towards where Alice stood in the open frame that led to the earthly realm. The erudite philosopher skidded upon his words, but Jack could not help but grin as Alice stretched out her arms and dove into the unknown.

Alice's vision permeated with the radiance of dying stars as she flew through interstellar clouds and chromatic fields of plasma. Stellar winds whipped her coal-black hair until an auroral vapor surrounded what she understood, relatively, to be her being. When, finally, the details of the terrestrial world resolved, she found herself in Akihabara, or Akiba, as the Tōkyō electronics district was commonly called. Named after the deity that protected against the hazard of fire, towering signs competed like carnival barkers in an illuminated wonderland. For a second, she considered that it might have all been but a dream, save that a group of light stick-wielding otaku walked right through her, proving she lacked the physical substance to embrace that theory. Alice watched them enthusiastically wave their light sticks at a holographic idol set up in front of the train station until a nearby crane game caught her attention. Testing her materiality, she passed her hand through its transparent cabinet, in an attempt to touch the prizes its 3D printer produced.

"Lesson one…never play the crane game." Jack enjoyed watching her jump out of the skin she presently lacked. "Over the last thirty years, I've only won four times."

Alice withdrew her hand as if slapped. "What are you doing here? Are you stalking me?" She walked away, uninterested in his response.

Undeterred, Jack dangled his black and white beads in front of her face. "These give me the coordinates for the next thread. More a hint than a target, but all I had to do was look for your abnormal energy fluctuations—child's play. You really should be more careful."

"Leave me alone. I have a lot I'm working through, in case you didn't notice." Alice abruptly reversed and walked right through him. "Stop following me."

"Look, sweetheart, when you walked through that door, you entered a whole different ballgame. We're not the only side in this tug of war. There is darkness out there, so dark—well, let's just say it's dark."

Alice pretended to join the gathering of otaku cheering along with the holographic idol. The projections shone from the floor of the small stage, but the effect was more lifelike than Pepper's Ghost. "Please go away."

"You're lucky I found you."

"I find that hard to believe."

"If I didn't, someone else would. Someone who lacks my rosy disposition and forgiving nature." Jack knew that without training, she was nothing more than harvester chum. Because he had a physical presence, however, it was making it difficult for him to keep up.

"I'm going to look for Keiji. Don't try and stop me." Alice wondered where the otaku boys learned the chants that accompanied the performance they were watching. They didn't even seem to care that the subject of their devotion was basically a digital apparition.

Jack had already concluded that she was trying his patience. "Look, kid. As your handler, I can disperse you any time I'd like. The sooner I train my replacement, the quicker I get Clement off my back. Let's be clear…I'm not all that attached to you."

Alice had no idea what he was talking about, but she wasn't going to be reeled in by someone who was a cross between Edgar Allan Poe and Dean Martin. "You wouldn't disperse me."

"What? Are you saying I'm bluffing?" Jack was a bit concerned that she might already have his number. "I'll send you through the first door so fast you'll get splinters. Right through the tenth dimension." Despite his attempt to conceal his bemusement, a tooth peaked from behind his thin lips. Still, he knew spirit would only get you so far in their line of work. One wouldn't last long without wisdom, and he had always relied on his former partner. He knew to fulfill that part of the equation wouldn't be easy. A girl dressed in an obnoxiously frilly dress walked up and handed Jack a sheet of e-paper that displayed a short video advertisement.

"How can she see you?" asked Alice.

"Oh, I'm totally solid," replied Jack. He watched the rather clumsy performance on the flyer and was surprised to discover it featured actual living performers. "I didn't know they still did that. Real idols, huh? I guess everything comes around again. I always wanted a mullet—said no one ever." Jack enjoyed his humor the way a cook fancies their cuisine.

Idol music had once been so popular that the elections to determine member status, garnered more votes than those for the politicians who actually ran Japan. For a while, there was even talk of limiting the influence of such groups. Too many men of marital potential had been substituting a fantasy that required less effort and commitment than an actual relationship. The legislation never went very far as there were too many people in the government who were idol fans themselves.

Alice didn't want to admit that there might be a few bits of knowledge she needed to acquire before she set off on her own. "If I promise not to run away…will you take me to the bridge?"

"What bridge?"

"I think you know which one I'm talking about."

Jack thrust his hands deep inside his pockets. "C'mon kid, give me a break. What do you want to see there?"

Alice realized that she recognized the song the holographic idol performed from a soda commercial. "Clement said you would help me, and aren't you the reason I'm here? *Ne.* Take me to the bridge, and I won't make you look all over Tōkyō for me. Deal?"

Jack wasn't used to his mistakes hanging around long enough to debate him. "Let's say I take you there, and we find nothing? There'll be no more recharging this guilt trip. Capiche? Also, rule number one—stay out of my way. I work alone, and as far as I'm concerned, you're nothing more than a glorified intern."

"Fine," replied Alice. She didn't care what Jack did as long as it involved as little of her as possible. "Alright then, let's go."

"One condition. If Clement comes around, you pretend like I'm all about training you, coolio?" He stuck his finger through where her head would be if she were physically manifested. "Hmm. I guess we better get you solid, and no can do if anyone's around, disrupts the normies' reality. We need someplace private." He tapped the flier for the idol group. "Also, it looks like we've got a little show to attend."

"You know, just because I'm sixteen doesn't mean I have bad taste in music." She took a closer look at the flyer. "The Genki Girls? Never heard of them."

He dangled his beads in such a way that she could watch them spin. "Apparently, they're our next thread."

◆ ◆ ◆

"Okada-san. Can you step inside my office for a moment?" Fujisawa had been George's boss for three years, but they had history, having worked together before in a different department.

"Hai, *fuku-shachou*." George liked Fujisawa, but he knew a call into his office meant there was a one-in-three chance his day was about to be ruined. Today would be no exception.

"Have a seat," said Fujisawa. "So, you were feeling a little under the weather yesterday?" He opened a pillbox and swallowed enough medication to constitute a fourth meal.

"Yes, a bit of a head cold, I'm afraid."

"But you still went out for sushi? We retrieved a video clip from your company car. Human resources asked me to clarify."

George had signed off on the right to be monitored during work hours when Tokuji-Tech Pharmaceuticals hired him, but it wasn't like he had a choice. It was a standard procedure for most companies. "I was feeling better, so I thought…"

"There's no record of you signing onto your business account from home. You didn't even check your messages. You can understand why HR is saying you might have taken a mental health day?"

George shifted uncomfortably, producing an inappropriate sounding squeak from his chair. "Fujisawa-san, please appreciate that I really was sick. I would hope the company might be concerned about my health."

"Of course, Okada-san. That's why we downloaded the data from your smartwatch's health app. They noticed an increase in your stress levels."

"Isn't that a bit…personal?"

"We only look at such things because your well-being affects the company as a whole. You acknowledged that in your terms of employment agreement."

George gazed longingly at the door. "Well, I appreciate your concern, but I have a few things—"

"Look, you think I don't feel stress? My doctor says that I'm one idiot away from another coronary episode." He took a moment to swallow his last pill and screwed the cap back onto the bottle. "Okay, I'll make an excuse for you this time, but you can't just take a day off because you get wound up a bit tight.

We're all feeling it from Suzuki-san's passing, but if anything, it means we need to work a little harder. You're a Senior Project Manager now – my number-two man. I need you here, not at home watching baseball in your underwear. While you were out, there was a timeline question about the new drug. Oh, and the inspector from the PMDA came by asking about some inventory discrepancies." The Pharmaceuticals and Medical Devices Agency was not an arm of the government Fujisawa had any intention of wresting. After all, he had not risen to where he was questioning policy, but by enforcing it.

It irked George that he was the only one taking up the slack, but he wasn't in any position to object. "I feel great now, chief. I'll have no problem catching up from yesterday."

"That's good to hear. Oh, that reminds me. Your health app says your hydration is low, and your heart seems to have a murmur. We made an appointment for you with the company physician. They're also going to run a battery of psychological tests to help you pick out a hobby. You know, for your stress. We can't have you getting sick on us—now that you're doing two jobs."

◆ ◆ ◆

Orange cones marked the spot where the car had tumbled over the side of the bridge. The barrier appeared recently repaired, evident from where they had poured the new low-carbon cement.

Jack ascended from beneath the surface of the water and sat on the bridge next to Alice. "They've already taken the car away. I'd guess they probably used a barge with a crane. Anyhoo, we should probably go. I haven't been in Japan for a while. It might be nice to get some ramen. Shio...or miso? What's your poison?"

Alice wasn't sure what she was looking for, other than that it was the last place she had seen Keiji. "Wasn't the barrier supposed to stop us?" She summoned her courage to look over the edge. The same peculiar urge she felt in front of the door returned.

Jack squatted so he could take a look at where the vehicle had jumped over the curb. "It's the way they make cars these days. Autonomous—puh-leeze.

Anyone impressed with how smart cars are these days has never owned a horse."

Alice wasn't interested in Jack's musings on the retrograde consequences of technology. "He was about to tell me if he liked me."

"And you can't feed them carrots."

"What?"

"Never mind. I think we're done here. Maybe some sukiyaki? How about that?" He wasn't sure if it was better to tell her to let go or have her come to such a conclusion on her own.

"There was somebody in the water," remembered Alice. "I think they were trying to rescue us."

"One of those hero types. Happens all the time. We get a lot of them in the waiting room. They come out saying, 'Did I save them?' And I'm like, 'Sorry. The shark got them,' and they're like, 'But we were in the desert,' and I say—"

"Sand shark." Alice wasn't in the mood for dad jokes. "That's terrible, Jack. Just awful."

Occasionally, Jack's age showed, no matter how he chose to look. "I only did it four or five times. Once, if Clement asks you."

Alice leaned down to pick a hydrangea that grew beside the bridge. "We were going to take a trip to Hawaii. Mom was happy because my dad never takes time off. He thought if you did, it meant you weren't needed." She threw the flower and watched it settle on top of the water.

"No reason we can't head over there sometime."

"Where?"

"Hawaii."

"I don't want to go to Hawaii. I want to be alive." Tears rolled down her cheeks, compelling her to hide her face as it interfered with any attempt to appear strong. "I want to see Keiji."

Consolation had never been Jack's forte. "Sheesh. Who doesn't want to go to Hawaii? Closure is overrated. You know what isn't? Hawaii."

Adults might dismiss her feelings for Keiji as nothing more than a schoolgirl crush, but she had already fleshed out their future in her imagination. Perhaps such dreams were meant to disintegrate with time, but living through their loss was an integral part of acceptance. The shock of surrendering them all at once had been devastating; it completely exposed the temporality of her existence.

It was apparent to Jack that they wouldn't have much of a chance to complete the thread if she was weighed down with more baggage than an international flight. Hiro had taught him that emotions had consequences, and it was better to leave them out of the equation. "When you hit that barrier, did you go straight through?"

Alice could remember the airbags going off, the seatbelt grabbing her shoulder, and then the smoke. "I thought we were okay, but the next thing I knew, we were falling—then we hit the water."

Jack allowed his heels to lead as he tried to deconstruct the accident site. A car passed through him, but he was too absorbed in thought to notice. His finger rose as if ready to announce an observation but then went back to slowly stroking his chin. It didn't make sense why they would accelerate when the barrier had already done its job. With the airbags expended, nothing remained to soften the blow.

Alice visualized the car's path over the side of the bridge. She remembered that seemingly eternal pause as they hung between terra firma and eternity, the smell of the fumes and the taste of powder from the airbags. "Look over here. Those are skid marks, and they're not even near the railing." She wondered if it suggested more a struggle than an accident. "We didn't brake…"

CHAPTER THREE:
BECOMING WEIRD

aori Okada set the lacquered bento box on her husband's desk. Her hair, loosely braided to one side, seemed to direct his attention down to her handiwork. "*Anata*. I brought you lunch," she said, her face beaming. When they were dating, she had called him George, but after they married, both titles and roles changed. Then after Yuki was born, she had become *okaasan*, or mother, and even hearing the sound of her name made her blush. The rumor around the office was that she had selected their quaint domicile more for its proximity to Tokuji-Tech Pharmaceuticals than her daughter's school. She unwrapped the blue cotton furoshiki and set down a black bento box. Its automatic cooling and heating system kept her husband's meal at the optimal temperature during the four-minute walk to his office.

"Do you always have to use the food printer to stylize my food? It's embarrassing." The fish, rice, and pickled vegetables resembled a pond with a small pier. During the national election, she had shaped his meatloaf to mirror the various candidates. George stopped to consider whether the tiny fisherman, cut out of a radish and a small sausage, was supposed to be him.

"But, you like fishing." She handed him a pair of casting rod chopsticks.

He was quite aware of the humiliating glances from his co-workers.

Sometimes she even sat with him as he ate. "Okaasan...I'm level two with the company now. If anyone sees this..." George covered it with the lid, but he couldn't ignore the tears that formed in the wells of his wife's eyes. "Never mind. *Sugoku kawaii. Arigatou.*"

Her radiant smile returned, and she proudly handed him a flyer on which a short video clip looped. "Did you remember your daughter has a performance tonight?"

During the company picnic, a young producer forming an idol group had stumbled upon their talent show. His wife had somehow convinced him that it would help their daughter's self-esteem. Because several other co-workers' daughters filled out the rest of the line-up, there was little choice but to acquiesce.

"Is that tonight?" He sucked his teeth from the side of his mouth. "Six o'clock..."

"Can't you leave the office early, just this once?" Mrs. Okada's eyes watered again.

"*Chotto*...it's not a good time. Suzuki-san left so much work behind. There are some very serious matters I still have to resolve." There was one area he knew she'd understand, the pocketbook. "In a few years, Yuki-chan will be going to college. Where are we going to find the money?" He shoveled the food in his mouth to expedite the conversation.

Mrs. Okada's eyes glistened. "But you were just promoted—and I've been taking small jobs to help. Won't you please come? The other girls' fathers will all be there. It's practically a company event."

That his wife had persuaded Tokuji-Tech to sponsor the Genki Girls, with a few token donations, did not make it a company event in his eyes. He bristled when people joked that they had an official idol group, especially since the group seemed to focus around one particular girl who wasn't even the daughter of anyone at the plant.

Mrs. Okada leaned over his shoulder to retrieve the empty bento box. She could often be found in the employee kitchen cleaning out loose pieces of salmon before exiting through the warehouse. People often returned to find their containers gleaming from her unexpected attention.

"Just this once, don't you think you could slip away early?"

George thought for a moment, but now it looked like he was the one who would cry. "Okaasan, I can't even have a bowel movement without them knowing."

◆ ◆ ◆

Alice could tell from the rolling green mountains that Jack had transported her to somewhere decidedly, not home. "I thought we were going to Tōkyō? This isn't Tōkyō, is it Jack?"

"Tenryū-ji Temple? Nope. Nice, though, right?"

"Where are we? Chiba? Kanagawa?"

"You're getting warmer—Kyōto."

"Kyōto? We're supposed to be in Tōkyō. Zap us back, or whatever it is you did to me." She had been to the old capital before, but her family went by bullet train, not Sin City psychopomp. All he did was place his hand on her shoulder, and a journey of five hundred kilometers was over before she could protest, no doubt in line with his intentions.

Naturally, he didn't weigh her protests seriously. "I've got some errands piling up. What? You got plans or something?"

"The police might scrap the car. We need to go see it before it's gone."

Jack washed his hands in a small fountain. "I'm sure it's fine. Besides, I think this will do you some good. Get a whiff of that fresh air. Don't you feel your head clearing?"

"I can feel my annoyance growing." Alice grabbed his bracelet. "Where do those things say we're supposed to be at, anyway?"

"Hey—hands off the goods." Jack lightly slapped her hand away. "We're taking a fiver. Is that okay with you, peaches?" He had decided long ago that if the beads were going to be approximate, any attempt to follow them would be likewise.

"Isn't it part of your job to teach me how to read those things?"

Jack brushed a leaf off his shoulder. He knew she was only trying to lean in on his ability to lead. "Know any binary languages?"

"That's not exactly an elective at my school."

It was pretty much the response he had anticipated. "Look. These are synchronicity beads. They're black on one side and white on the other, kind of like zeros and ones. Hip to what I'm saying? Hip? Not hip? Kind of hip? Haven't you ever seen a number like twenty-two, fifteen times in the same day? Well, these help you sort out those types of coincidences." He scratched his back. "See, the universe…it's, well, like a big computer program. We're basically the tech support."

"The world is scarier than I thought." Alice only wished that she was kidding.

"Sweetheart, you haven't even begun to see scary."

"I don't know. I've seen you."

The landscape garden at Tenryū-ji had been designed to make use of the natural environment it embraced. At its center, Sōgen Pond mirrored the Arashiyama Mountains, and the gravel lines of its karesansui garden provided a tastefully drawn border. The late spring branches reminded Alice of the sakura tree near her school and the vulnerability she felt as she spilled her heart to Keiji.

Jack had seen his first dry garden during the period of the warring states, roughly thirty years before the arrival of Commodore Perry. Japan was still closed to the outside world, meaning he was unable to physically manifest as a Westerner. His mentor Hiro thought it was hysterical to watch villagers react in astonishment at his inability to use chopsticks. Jack could tell that Alice was similarly annoyed. "Look. We can't go to the police yard until its dark anyway, so why don't you just chillax for a bit? It won't take long."

Alice sulked while Jack sat and appreciated the dry garden, her bored teenager expression well-practiced. She wasn't going to admit any appreciation for the site's beauty, though it was undeniable. Maybe if she didn't take an interest, Jack would get the hint and bring her back to Tōkyō. Alice almost didn't notice when he bent over and scooped up a handful of gravel that he then placed in a small velvet bag. On his wrist, his beads violently spun in protest. "Jack."

"What?"

"You can't do that." It was hardly possible to say whether she was more stunned or offended. "Put that back."

Jack was nonplussed. "Shhh. Keep it down. Someone might hear. We're material, remember?"

"I don't care if we're made out of mochi. Put it back!" She began to slink away, in an attempt to appear unaffiliated with him.

Jack tucked the gravel inside his pocket. "I don't think anyone saw us."

A bucket-hat wearing tourist had been eyeing them, though. Alice gave the man a pained look to indicate that she had no excuse to offer and started to leave. To her great disappointment, Jack quickly caught up. "So do you ever actually harvest anyone, or do you just go around giving foreign tourists a bad name?"

"I harvested you, didn't I?" Even with only the back of her head to go on, he could sense that he hadn't helped his argument. "You know how many people will die today...138,625. I'm only responsible for two to three hundred a year."

"Maybe they don't trust you." She noticed that the tourist had found a fossil of a monk and pointed angrily in their direction.

This seemed to offend Jack as he stopped in his tracks to make sure Alice appreciated his point. "Au contraire, sister. The buzzards put up the big numbers. You know, the losers assigned to work hospitals, battlefields – all the creepy joints. They can pick up more souls in a day than I can in five years."

"So why aren't you a buzzard?" She hoped the question would prompt him to start moving again.

"Because I don't suck. Trust me. That's the last thing you want. It's the worst gig in the celestial dimension. Don't worry though, if you screw up this gig, that's the party you'll be attending." Seeing the monk headed in their direction, Jack resumed his progress towards the exit. "I'm a specialist. I keep the fabric nice and tight. When a soul leaps, that's where things get unraveled. You know how I said this universe is like a program? Well, free will is the operating system. That's where we come in. What we do is like walking between raindrops, thus – limited workload."

"So, your hobby is stealing?"

"No, gardening." Before he could justify himself any further, he noticed that the monk had grabbed a wooden rake. "Also – run!"

Sandals *click-clacked* behind them across the little wooden bridge, like a pair of kendama. Outside the temple, Jack picked up Alice and threw her into a cluster of green and yellow bamboo.

The monk arrived and thrust his rake's thick wooden tongs in the area where they had both leaped. He yelled some rather salty phrases he had acquired in his former life as a soldier in the JDF until he became aware of the perplexed tourists who were watching. Deeply bowing, he waited until everyone lost interest before he prodded the area where the barbarians had last been seen. To his great astonishment, no one was there.

Fortunately, Alice and Jack re-materialized inside a bush not far from Shinjuku Station in Tōkyō. Alice spat out a candy wrapper and pulled several pieces of trash from her disheveled hair. It gave her the appearance that she had awoken after a particularly difficult night on the town. Jack brushed off his beloved sharkskin jacket to find a silver-haired woman staring at them; her disapproving eyes pinched tight against her nose. She rested a wrinkled forearm against her cart and scowled.

"It's not what it looks like," said Jack. "I swear. She's actually my cousin." Realizing that Alice was half Japanese, he added, "Twice removed."

"What if we'd been caught?" Alice was still annoyed. "We could have been arrested."

"Not for what you think," Jack added, for the benefit of the old woman, who was still listening. "She's talking about a totally different crime." He prodded Alice to start walking. "To answer your question, I'm not a thief. Not everything is as simple as that schoolgirl existence I saved you from."

"We could have been hurt."

"Do you think I'd put you in any danger? I mean, other than our job, which will probably kill you—again."

"Isn't taking things from a temple, like, against rule 714 or something?"

"No. Rule 714 is, 'No scary manifestations around people with heart conditions unless previously cleared for harvest.' Been there, broke that. We're going to have to take some time to study when things slow down."

"Why, Jack? Help me understand. What's it for?"

"You're not the only one with unanswered questions, doll, and I'm nearly out of time."

◆ ◆ ◆

Akari Kawabe had the chestnut color hair favored by most of the fashionable girls in Tōkyō. She had no interest in being blonde, but in her mind, the group was more of a solo project, and featuring the other Genki Girls was to be discouraged. She perceived the group to be a vehicle that could transition her into commercials, movies, and even modeling. The three years that separated Yuki and Akari represented the difference between a twenty-year-old who hung out in Ginza bars and a schoolgirl.

"I'm the center," said Akari. "Blonde hair makes Yuki look like she's the center."

It was the last thing Haruto needed. As their producer, he tried to play the role of the adult, though he was barely twenty-five. Boyish features like a small nose made him look more like a freshman in college. It was difficult to tell that he had already enjoyed a brief career as a record company executive. Back then, he wouldn't have respected a producer who couldn't meet his payroll, which is what he had become. Slight though they were, all of the proceeds from the group's performances went towards wardrobe and advertising. Keeping the girls happy was a matter of survival, at least until they secured a recording deal. What had seemed such a novel idea, to forgo holograms and bring back real idols, had become a migraine in lace petticoats. Holographic pop idols didn't have explosive egos. They didn't pout or push back when they encountered something they didn't like. Still, he knew that the industry had forgotten something essential when they replaced physical artists. As people's lives became increasingly digital, it only increased the value of what was real that remained. A handshake could be quite potent to a generation starved for human interaction, especially in a world in which physical contact was discouraged.

"And one more thing." Akari paused to consider whether she wanted to pursue the argument she had laid out within her head. "That doughnut song is stupid. We need something that'll wake up the clubs—get bottles popping!"

"Otaku don't hang out in clubs," replied Haruto. Quitting his job at the record label was starting to look like a fast lane to the unemployment office. When Akari had auditioned at Flavor Beats Records, he had been the only one to encourage her when she was denied a contract. He never imagined it would lead to him submitting his resignation and starting a group that featured her in the center position.

Earlier in the century, Akira's grandmother had been a member of one of the last great idol groups. The idea that people once appreciated you, instead of your avatar was an intoxicating notion. Even though she was ranked fifty-eight, pictures of her grandmother still occasionally turned up in antique stores. Akari's mother had also been an entertainer but in a less honorable context.

"Ms. Ito," said Haruto, trying to move things along. Real-time English translation apps had normalized the use of Western honorifics, especially in the entertainment industry. "Ms. Ito, maybe we should go through the moves one more time before we head over?"

"*Mina-san*," shouted Ms. Ito. "The gig is in an hour, and we need ten hours of work." She had been his assistant at the record company and now doubled as his choreographer, marketing department, and anything else he couldn't afford. "And it's your right fist held to your chest, not the twelve o'clock position."

All nine members of the Genki Girls groaned, more from exhaustion than because their music was insipid. Haruto had to write all the lyrics, but he knew that if they could only become more popular, the songwriters would beat their way to his door. Until then, he stuck to the timeworn themes of doing your best, and having the courage to confess to the person you loved, areas in which their otaku fans were not exactly experts.

"One, two, three—kick! Turn and knee bend." The music was lively but predictable. Momoko! More dancing, less crying!" Ms. Ito threw up her hands.

"Saori, you're in my zone again," snapped Akari, seeing that her second had encroached upon her space.

"*Sumimasen*," Saori apologized. Since she had finished high school, the other girls wondered if Saori would graduate from the group to focus on college. Her glasses gave her an aura of intelligence, though it was standard procedure to correct one's vision in childhood. Frames continued to be a popular fashion accessory, as some fans preferred girls who wore them. Saori rarely challenged Akari's authority, but a sliver of her spine peeked out on occasion.

Akari saw the incursion as a blatant attempt to usurp her position. She intentionally missed her turn and checked Saori hard. "That's it. I want her moved!"

Haruto signaled for Ms. Ito to pause the music. "Okay, ladies. That's enough for now. Nice work, everyone. Let's all get dressed, and we'll walk over together in say, fifteen minutes. Sorry. There won't be time to change before we go on stage." The girls groaned. He took Akari aside. "Akari-chan, I need your help on this one. She's your number two, and I can't keep shuffling people around, not right before a gig. They're not professionals like you. They can barely remember the moves, as-is."

"She's trying to outshine me." Akari did her best to appear vulnerable, but she was too tough for it to play authentically.

Haruto had been in the business long enough to know how the game was played. "Akari-chan, that's not possible." He took a second to see if flattery was the appropriate tool. Sensing the effort had failed, he switched gears. "Well...I could always bump Yuki up to number two—"

She was well aware he was giving her the less-desirable option. "Just remind Saori that she works around me. M'kay?"

"Wait until you hit that stage. All eyes are going to be on you. You're going to sparkle." As she stormed off, he reflected on his life and the mountains of instant ramen he had eaten to pay for the concert fliers.

Not far away Saori watched, her face a green tint from either jealousy or because she was going be ill. "Gag. If he didn't kiss her ass all the time, she'd be easier to manage." She leaned in to better examine Yuki's blonde locks. "Gene therapy or dye?"

"Dye." Going blonde hadn't even been her idea. Her mother wanted her to go permanent, but dyeing had been the compromise. "I tried to tell her it wasn't my fault."

Saori lowered her glasses and pursed her lips. "It looks *mecha* good. Tell her she can spin on a yakitori stick."

Yuki had no intention of running afoul of Akari; she had enough problems at school. "She didn't even bother learning my name until she needed to yell at me. There's a dance crew performing before us. Let's go check them out."

Saori cleaned a smudge off of her glasses. "As long as she's around, we're never going to do anything more than open electronics stores." There was no getting around that she would have to put up with Akari's diva complex to be a part of the last real idol group in Tōkyō, but she didn't have to like it.

◆ ◆ ◆

"Let's stop at this bakery; I want something." Jack was surprised to see Alice's thin eyebrows scrunch up. "What? You don't like sweets?"

"I'm not hungry."

"Of course not. You're dead." Jack opened the door, which produced a cheerful jingle.

"*Irasshaimasu*," said the person behind the counter.

Jack looked at the trays of melonpan, tea marble loaf, and red bean rolls. "How's it going? Let's see. No. Nopety…and nope. Do you have any birthday cake?"

The employee behind the counter smiled. "We have chocolate cake, also a nice strawberry. First harvest."

"Okay, great, but do you have birthday cake?" Jack thought he had made his request clear.

"Well, you could use any of them. The 1000 Yen store has candles—"

"But what you are saying is that none of these cakes were explicitly made to be used for the occasion of someone's birthday. They're not *real* birthday cake." Though Western, Jack knew his Japanese was without fault, although he did sometimes fall into an archaic form of Kyōto-ben.

"How about a nice matcha roll?"

"You disgust me." Jack's words dripped with indignation as he slammed the door. The bell signaled his departure with the same cheerful tone as when he had arrived.

"Is it your birthday? *Tanjōbi omedetō.*" Alice didn't realize that one still marked such an occasion after you had died."

"No—of course not. What gave you that idea?" He seemed more perplexed than was warranted.

Alice hadn't eaten anything since dinner the night before the accident. She had been too distracted to grab breakfast before getting in the car, and it only now occurred to her that she hadn't been hungry since. "You're like me, right? You don't have to eat..."

"When we are physical, we're technically alive. It's usually only for an hour or two, so I haven't even had to use the bathroom in thirty-seven years. I mean...I've been in them. I'm that guy that just kind of stands there."

"Thanks for that."

"If you stayed solid long enough, and didn't change forms, eventually you'd have to eat."

"So, you're hungry?"

"No. I like birthday cake. Is that okay?" His stomach growled. "Now that you harp about it, I am starting to get hungry."

Alice thought she might like to grab a bite, not that she had any money. "If I hang around you...am I going to get weird or something?" It was a sincere question, having been raised on the Japanese proverb, that the nail that stuck out was the first to get hammered.

Jack's answer was not the one for which she might have hoped. "You can't visit as many places and see as many things as I have and not pick up a few quirks. Yeah, you're going to get a little weird, but you'll probably find it's the best thing about you." Tōkyō lights cast a luminous glow upon his face. "Look at this—Akihabara. When was the last time I was here, the 1950's? 'Course back then it wasn't much to see. Hiro needed a vacuum tube for something. It was mostly just some small shops with radio parts." He stopped to look at a display for the latest VR headsets. "Want some advice? Don't fight it."

"Fight what?"

"Getting weird." Jack found he had to raise his voice to overcome a grinding metallic sound. It was like a factory's heavy machinery had been appropriated for a courtship ritual. "Great googly moogly. What is that racket? C'mon. Let's go see where it's coming from and what it'll take to make it stop."

Around the corner was a small stage with a rather sad looking banner advertising an electronics store that had taken over the Hayashi building, formally known for a ramen shop that one foodie described as using mop water for broth. A dance troupe of unnaturally muscular guys produced copious quantities of sweat as they attempted to match the frantic, pulsating rhythm of their music. They all sported the type of electro-charged tattoos whose luminescent and conductive ink became visible whenever a special bracelet signaled for them to pulse in time with the music. There was something unintentionally comedic about the level of swagger they projected considering the modesty of the venue.

To the side of the stage, the Genki Girls watched in awe. They pointed at the male dancers with a look that signaled appreciation and concern at having to follow them. Finally, the sound of anvils struck at 190 bpm ceased, and they took their bows. Several flexed their muscles, which caused their tattoos to illuminate one last time to the appreciation of the forty or so people in attendance.

"Thank you, Superflat," said the announcer. "Now, for the act, for which you've all been waiting. Tokuji-Tech Pharmaceuticals is proud to present…the Genki Girls!"

A sound that was a mixture of techno and frosted sugar cubes blared from the speakers. With smiles as bright as the previous group's electrically activated tattoos, the Genki Girls came out and began a routine explicitly designed to mask their limited dance and vocal abilities.

"Ugh, I hate idol music," groaned Alice. "Are you sure I'm not in hell?" She did a sudden double-take. One of the girls looked suspiciously like her friend Yuki, but she couldn't be sure with her recently bleached hair bopping up and down so fast. "*Chotto*…is that Yuki-chan? *Nande?* That's my best friend up there." Alice covered her face with the flyer. "Jack, we have to get out of here. Now."

If he was concerned, Jack didn't give any indication, tapping his suede shoes as if he heard Mack The Knife in his head. "Relax. Wear this." He produced the type of surgical mask people wore to fight hay fever or go in public without makeup. Unfortunately, it also digitally displayed an animal face that synced with your mouth, via embedded sensors. "You know, this music kind of swings. I think I'm feeling rather *genki*."

"Great. A non-grim reaper." It was definitely Yuki up there, only blonder. "She colored her hair? I'm dead for like five minutes…"

"Harvester!" Jack yelled over the music. "Soul harvester. There's a big difference. I don't kill people," aware of the skeptical look he received; he added, "on purpose."

"So, basically, the only difference between you and the grim reaper is that you make mistakes."

"There's no such thing as grim reapers, shinigami…whatever you guys call them. Judges have black robes. Why don't you think I'm a judge? They deal in life and death."

"Well, judges do make mistakes."

Jack hated it when people misinterpreted his role in the universe. "Do I carry a scythe? I'm not even skeletal. Reapers are skeletal."

"Whatever. I don't care, but if you don't want to be mistaken for a pirate, don't wear the hat."

His eyes narrowed. "I can see hanging with you is going to be a real treat."

"So, where did you get that look?"

"What? This?" Jack adjusted the handkerchief in his smoking jacket.

"No, not that. The one that doesn't look at all like a reaper?"

The truth was, Jack shared more in common with Akihabara's otaku inhabitants than he cared to admit. "It was around the 1870s. Hiro and I were in England on this serial killer thread. Yeah, we did a lot of those back in the day. Must have been around the holidays, 'cause I went to a reading of this new book by this cat…Dickens. The part that grabbed me was when the Ghost of Christmas Future appeared, black robe, but *not* a reaper. Gave me the willies. Of course, I gave it my own spin."

Alice couldn't disagree that it was working. "Well, you do have that in common, I guess." She took a moment to watch her friend dance. She seemed to be concentrating too much to be genuinely having any fun. "I don't think I've ever been to a real concert. Just VR."

Jack guffawed. "It's not a concert if you can't get your tooth knocked out by an inebriated hooligan. This is basically a recital."

"What's so great about losing a tooth?"

"It makes you feel alive."

"I used to *be* alive. Guess whose fault that is?"

"So touchy."

Yuki's dancing was passable, for someone who had never really tried before. When they used to go for karaoke, Yuki copied the moves in the videos, but that was the extent of her experience. It was hard to feel betrayed at seeing her so transformed, especially as Alice was on a journey of her own. The song itself was terrible, something about sharing doughnuts with your *senpai*, the sort of tripe for which idol songs were known. Yuki made the shape of a doughnut with her hands and then bent her fingers inward to form a heart that she pretended to throw out into the audience.

"So, you actually like this?" asked Alice, seeing Jack bounce in time with the music. She was starting to wonder about the character with whom she'd been saddled.

Jack had stopped caring what people thought, at least a century prior. "It's not bad, but the lyrics make me want to harvest whoever wrote them." There was one fan in the front row, however, who seemed especially enthralled by the performance.

Taka Masui had initially been a VR otaku, or votaku, as they called the geeks who hung out in Akihabara's virtual reality cafes. Most of the VR cafes started as karaoke facilities but converted, as people asked for the option to sing virtually with their favorite artists. As they added games, it became a place to both harmonize and play with your friends. A votaku could not bear the thought of even one graphic feature being grayed out, and the cafes served that niche by providing equipment unparalleled by the home experience. In his definitive paper on the subject, sociologist Yoshitomo Murakashi noted that VR cafes allowed people with limited social skills to participate in a communal environment, with technology providing a cushion for their interactions. Recently out of college, Taka made his living online, so he had almost entirely eliminated the need to interact with actual people.

One day, Taka was leaving his usual cafe when he saw the Genki Girls attempting to hold a handshake event. It was an archaic thing to do, and a bit of an escapade. Handshaking events were in vogue during the Heisei period but had fallen out of favor for a variety of health and safety concerns. There was something both nostalgic and thrilling about attempting to revive the practice. The girls had decorated their collapsible tables with homemade posters, but without any fans, it had devolved into a "check the messages on your phone event."

"Ne. Over there." Akari called out to Taka, who had stopped near their booth to blow his nose.

He lowered his handkerchief to discover someone who seemed to take fashion as seriously as an anime fan might the debate over subbing versus dubbing. Akari seemed to sparkle under the mid-day sun, mostly in part to reflective nanoparticles in her hairspray.

"You…with the black backpack." It hadn't occurred to Akari that she had described almost every otaku in Akihabara.

Taka pointed at himself and walked over to her table.

"Well…shake my hand," she demanded.

"Excuse me?" said Taka. He was not comfortable with any physical contact that involved the opposite sex. Point of fact, he was not comfortable with any physical contact at all.

"It's a handshake event. You're supposed to shake my hand." Akari was aware that the other girls were now giggling, but she would not let them have the satisfaction of seeing her fail. She had told Haruto no one would know what to do, even if it had once been a staple idol activity. "Put out your hand."

Though uncomfortable with the suggestion, Taka was not equipped to dismiss such a specific request from a girl. Despite his objections, he found his trembling hand reaching across the table.

Seeing he was not going to make it, Akari reached forward and grabbed it. Putting on her best-rehearsed smile, she shook it for far longer than for which he was comfortable. In a cartoonish voice, she said, "A pleasure to meet you…"

"Taka," he replied.

"I'm Akari-chan, and these are the Genki Girls. Won't you tell all your friends to come and see our show this weekend?"

"Hai," he replied, awkwardly, aware that the only friends he had, were known by their gaming handles. Before he was allowed to leave, Akari convinced him to buy every last piece of merchandise on which she was featured. Over the next few months, however, Taka faithfully attended every performance they gave in the Tōkyō area. In that way, he became the Genki Girls first, and only, fan. Now, in the front row filming them with his personal VR camera, Taka was a fully converted idol otaku. He waved his fan, made of e-paper that displayed a loop of Akari striking different poses, and sang along with every ill-conceived lyric. He was keenly aware when the words changed, as their young producer sought to improve his craft. The Doughnut Song had somewhat improved since it was first performed, an unimaginable thought.

Taka had once liked a girl, but when she rejected his confession, he withdrew into the type of VR relationship games where you could simply start over again. Now he had discovered a fantasy world with some basis in reality. Even though the girls were real, there was no risk of rejection. Today, he had finally summoned the courage to approach Akari with the hope of increasing their connection. He would be there when she stepped off the stage, present in hand. As the last song wound down, he positioned himself near the steps.

"Akari," he called out, as she accepted her towel. Taka gulped hard and choked on the words he had carefully practiced. "Akari-chan. I was wondering. Would you like to…" He handed her the gift, still working up his courage.

She could read the social cues well enough to anticipate what he was about to ask. Heading him off was the only way for them both to save face. Still, in character, Akari said, "Taka-sama, thank you so much for coming to see me again. Stay, genki!"

He watched her glide away, but with courage, he had gained from the idol lyrics he recited like sutras, he yelled, "Would you go to karaoke with me?"

Akari's reply was swift. "Taka-sama is so sweet, but I need to rest my voice. Stay genki!"

Several of the girls hurried to form a barrier around Akari so she could escape into the room where their after-performance refreshments awaited them. One of the girls, however, considered him with genuine sympathy. Momoko may not have been the most popular member, but she often performed in

Taka's direction, as he was a familiar and friendly face. She started to say that she would be interested, but Nana, their youngest member, dragged her inside before she could make the offer.

It was of no use anyway, as Taka basked in Akari's fading radiance like a Jizo statue. Then his smile sagged until it mirrored the flatness of the horizon. *Karaoke? How could I be so stupid? She just finished singing.* Akari always seemed happiest when she sang, but it was undeniable that he had traded one fantasy world for another.

Jack watched the awkward exchange from a distance. "Did that otaku just ask that idol out? What's he doing? Doesn't he know they're not allowed to date? They're like Japan's very own Vestal Virgins, for crying out loud."

"You know way too much about this stuff," observed Alice.

Jack watched the otaku and glanced at his synchronicity beads. "Well, if you add it up, I've spent thirty-one years in Japan. That's almost twice as long as you've been alive. Hang around long enough, and eventually, you're going to find yourself an expert in Swahili mating rituals."

"Yup," Alice said, with apparent resignation. "I'm going to get weird."

CHAPTER FOUR:

VIRTUALLY DEAD

Boss Mori, kumichō of the Kurome-gumi, had led the yakuza clan since before vice was virtual, and the hostesses of Kabukicho were valued by the elasticity of their synthetic skin. A government crackdown nearly ended the role of such criminal syndicates in Japanese society. Still, they were saved by the discovery that people who abstained from recreational pharmaceuticals in their everyday life were not opposed to enhancing their virtual ones. Boss Mori was chairman of the Kurome-gumi clan and patriarch of the most powerful of the three remaining families. He wore a pinstripe suit intended to make him look like a CEO, but the effect was more that of a Chicago gangster. At any rate, the way he fended off competition was classic yakuza.

Head low to the ground, Sho Kowabe attempted to display contrition and regret but felt neither. Though barely more than a foot soldier, he had technical skills of benefit to the clan that he hoped would keep him above the ground. Sho believed there were times when loyalty to your values eclipsed any obligation to your sworn family, but he understood there was a price for such misplaced fealty.

"What am I to do with you, Sho-san? It is no secret how you refused even to play oicho-kabu with Jiro-san. When I saw what the sharks in Sagami Bay had done to him, I was very displeased." Amber whiskey swirled within the crystal glass his saiko-komon had given him for his fifty-third birthday. Boss Mori didn't understand the surveillance and drone technology in which Sho specialized, but he could read a police report. It suggested that the death of Sho's aniki—Jiro— had been an inter-family dispute. "When I sent the two of you on that job, it was my hope that the scales might be scrubbed off the fish, and you would come to see each other as brothers. If it is as you suggest, that the Ankōshoku clan had him killed, it is a matter of grave severity—even war. So I ask again, what was the cause of Jiro-san's death?"

Sho lifted his eyes, their whites tattooed in the manner favored by his yakuza brothers, and they glistened like black marbles. The sign of permanent allegiance had become a popular trend among wannabe gangsters until the Kurome-gumi started gouging empty the sockets of any non-family members who dared to appropriate the kurome-gumi look. "*Oyabun*, I am sure you remember the drone that shot up the Satō family's massage parlors? We had only just finished...that certain matter you sent us to do. Heading back, it was not unpleasant between us. Then, there was a sound like a rock hit our rear window. I looked, and Jiro-san's blood covered the dash and window. I drove into a gorge, in case the drone returned, but it was too late. I realize my answer is insufficient." His bow became so low that he nearly lost his balance. "*Moushiwake arimasen deshita.*"

Honorifics like aniki and oyabun were meant to foster the impression that the Kurome-gumi was more a family than a business. Still, the price of failure brought consequences that exceeded any such arrangement. Once again, Sho lowered his eyes, as a sign of contrition, knowing well, it was unlikely that he would be leaving the room unscathed.

Through the many cut edges of his glass, Boss Mori considered Sho's story. In his rise to power, he had heard so few genuine expressions of truth, that he could not retire his cynicism. Additionally, Jiro occupied the position just above Sho in the family. "You ditched the car, and who but you are qualified to tell me if the Ankōshoku clan has finally found a way through our drone jamming defenses? The convenience of this outcome has not escaped my attention."

"I only thought of protecting the family, my brothers, and my kumichō."

Boss Mori had a wakizashi that he had purchased at an antique auction, as he lacked the family lineage to have any such an inheritance. Such a blade was favored for committing seppuku, an appropriate apology for taking action against another member of the family. His thick fingers placed it on the table in front of Sho. "When have I ever needed to be protected? Everyone always speaks highly of how you perform your duties, and I assume this was a private matter between two brothers. Still, if I value my product, how much more do you think I valued Jiro-san? He served me well for many years. It was my hope that he would one day lead a family of his own. Much saké was shared between us."

Sho knew that when the wakizashi was produced, its blade always tasted blood. Only then would it be restored to its place of honor. "If there had been a problem between us, I definitely would have brought the matter to you."

Boss Mori took a sip from his glass, its contents reminiscent of sunlight reflecting off the surface of the Kizu River. "This is why I have offered you this blade as a gift, but if I find your story at fault or your loyalty in doubt, you will not find my love for your brother lacking."

Sho grabbed the wakizashi and immediately brought it down on his left pinkie. He wrapped a towel around the remaining stub and held up the severed member as a token of his loyalty and remorse.

For a pregnant moment, there was no indication if the act of yubitsume had been sufficient, but then Boss Mori tossed a small bag of pills on the table. "You have been lowered to shatei until you prove yourself, nothing more than small deliveries for now. In the meantime, I will accept this as your apology for not protecting your brother."

Sho backed out of the office, clutching the wet rag glued to his disfigured hand. Severing one's pinky had not held the same weight since digit regeneration had become a commercial enterprise, and had actually led to a resurgence of the ritual. However, having a finger regrown was something for the type of clinic that charged twice as much but asked half as many questions. Sho considered the bag of pills and its accompanying list. At the top was a name that made the family's message most unambiguous.

◆ ◆ ◆

"*Tsukareta*," whined Yuki. It was a relief to be back in her favorite pair of old sweats with the worn-out waistband. "My calves are on fire."

Her mom eyed her stage costume for signs of wear as she placed it back on its hanger. "Yuki-chan. Are you listening to me? I could tell you were counting. Half the time, you moved on the down-beat." She didn't mind being the only other mother in the dressing room.

"You were happy when I learned to count." Yuki's attempt at humor wasn't well received. Trying to be funny was how she had ended up in the Genki Girls in the first place. Her stomach growled. "Can we stop for bubble tea on the way home? I'm starving."

Before her mom could answer, she spotted the Genki Girls' producer attempting to make his retreat. "Haruto-sensei. Oh, Haruto-sensei…"

The young producer cursed his lack of stealthiness. Keeping the parents happy was an essential part of his job, but he found it more challenging than writing half-decent lyrics. "Mrs. Okada. A fairly good audience today." It was the sort of absurd distortion of reality that went along with the job.

"The girls' costumes are starting to fall apart. In my day, idol groups were known for their different dresses and cute styles. Honestly. They look like they work at the mall."

"Why do you think the outfits were so cheap?" Haruto cleared a frog in his throat. "Hmm. Okay, well, I'll go home and think about that."

"Did you see the boys that came on first?" she asked.

Haruto was fairly sure Mrs. Okada wasn't about to suggest they ink her daughter with electro-charged tattoos. "Yes. They had considerable flair, much of which they perspired on those of us in the first row."

"I think we might be able to make some outfits. Maybe we could buy some old kimonos – take them apart and give them a modern touch." She fixed a snag in Yuki's hair.

The last thing Haruto wanted was to have the parents contributing creatively. Exploitation was something best left to professionals. "Or maybe Tokuji-Tech could—"

Mrs. Okada knew she had already fished out that particular stream. "Or we could make them ourselves. Okay, good talk. *Jaa ne, bai bai.*" She grabbed Yuki's hand and dragged her away.

"See you later. Nice hair Yuki." Haruto was aware that he was losing control, but without the resources to fight back. Yuki's mom made the bento lunches for the girls, and she had orchestrated the sponsorship grant that funded what little style they currently enjoyed. Lacking the carrots of fame and fortune, his grasp on authority waned.

"Nice hair?" Akari was a master at lingering out of view until ready to make her point. She had changed into her usual short denim skirt and t-shirt that read, Get Genki!

Haruto spun around startled. "Akari-chan! Great show! Saikou desu!" There was little chance she was going to let him change the subject. "Just keeping everyone happy. That's what I do…"

Her foot tapped faster than the bass line of Superflat's last song. "You're supposed to keep me happy. Remember me…your center?" She lowered her sunglasses so he could better appreciate her displeasure. "Speaking of happy—"

Haruto cringed, aware that he had more bad news to deliver. "Sorry, I couldn't score the pills this time. What do you need those for anyway? Your whole life is a fantasy." He felt enhancer was a harmless vice, but he was reasonably sure that she had drawn him into her supply chain to ensure he couldn't hold her accountable.

Akari huffed, not the least bit surprised. "No money. No pills. Crappy music. What kind of producer are you? Do I have to do everything?" She let him hang for a moment and then leaned over to reveal a small bag stuffed in her bra.

Haruto knew her interest in him extended only as far as he could propel her career, but they were co-dependent in a way that made him feel uncomfortable. "*Ja*…okay then."

Akari grabbed his shoulder to stop him from leaving. "Wait. You're coming, right?"

"What about the other girls? Doesn't Momo-chan usually hang out with you?" Momoko only spent time with Akari for the same reason as Haruto, to avoid being a party to her wrath. All of Akari's friendships were built on a foundation of control, toxic relationships being the only type she understood.

"She had to study for some stupid test." It was an excuse she knew better than to believe. "I reserved the Oni room." Akari reached down her shirt and hard swallowed one of the pills.

Haruto didn't like VR cafes, but it was his job to keep Akari out of trouble. A couple of times he had made excuses, only to regret it later. "*Okkē*. I have a couple of things to finish up; then I'll stop by. Just for a minute or two."

"Don't make me drink alone," she warned him. "Oh, and Yuki goes back to a brunette on Monday."

The line on Haruto's forehead rippled like the *Great Wave off Kanagawa*. He felt trapped from every side.

◆ ◆ ◆

"So why exactly are we following this guy? Need advice on your anime figure collection?" Alice dodged a group of teenage boys whose dolls creepily turned their heads to track Jack. Distracted, Alice walked through a holographic maid, directing people into a cafe. It was getting more and more difficult to remember who was solid, and who wasn't.

Having one eye on his beads and the other on Taka made Jack look cockeyed. "Northeast. Three degrees. Soul collection—fifteen minutes—my money is on that cat with the plushies pinned on his backpack."

"Which one?"

"That one," he said, pointing at Taka.

"Are you going to turn into that thing again?"

"You know it's rude to insult someone for how they look."

"But, your ugliness is a choice."

Jack had been under the impression that a new partner should be more like a sponge than a stone. "I don't have time to spar with an amoeba, so listen up. Harvests go south. Threads get tangled. Just stay out of my way, and we'll all be copacetic."

Alice looked around for Taka, but he had disappeared. "Where'd he go?" She hopped, like a pogo stick to see above the sea of people with pink hair and animal ear headbands. "Wait…a VR café. Maybe in there?"

Seeing a purikura machine, the type of photo booth that printed a short selfie video on digital sticker paper, Jack pulled her inside. It was the type popular with girls Alice's age, as you could also download the clip or post it on social media.

"Do we really have time for this?" asked Alice.

"Time to go ethereal. Haven't you ever read a comic or seen a superhero flick? I guess people burned out on those after the hundred and eighty-seventh time." He could feel the beads rolling against the small hairs upon his wrist. "Eight minutes."

The Kira Kira was one of many VR cafés that had sprouted up around Akihabara. The paint had been recently freshened, and its ten rooms were equipped with omnidirectional treadmills only a couple of generations old. Friends could play competitively or cooperatively, but the café's income came primarily from marked-up snacks and drinks. The Kira Kira was also famous for its backdoor that allowed patrons to arrive incognito. Law enforcement had a growing concern that the back rooms were meeting places where transactions were less virtual than vice. Due to its location, it was also a popular hangout for people in the entertainment industry, although star sightings were few and far between, by design.

"Talking is okay," said Jack. "No one can hear you, so sing if you want."

"I thought you said we didn't kill people."

Jack liked her spirit but wasn't sure how it would wear, although he wasn't one to talk. "Give me a regular old jazz bar any day over one of these places; black coffee…the sound of a needle being dropped onto freshly-pressed wax. All right. Enough jibber-jabber. Time to suit up."

"I told you. I don't do cosplay."

"It's called metamorphing, and it's one part imagination and two parts spiritual refraction. Really. There's nothing to it. It's a—"

"Piece of cake?"

Jack gave his best slow-burn glare. He transformed into his harvester manifestation and popped his head into the first booth. Inside were two high school age boys running along at a good clip on their treadmills. They were playing a shooter game where they had assumed the role of space marines. Multi-tentacle aliens devoured one of the players while his friend tried to fend it off with his railgun. When the gamer's character died, Jack appeared ready to take his soul, before concluding he was in the wrong game. "Sorry. My bad."

One of the players asked, "Do you remember a reaper in this game?"

"No," replied the other, his next life spawning. "*Kakkoii!*"

Alice emerged from one of the booths in a bleached white kimono, charcoal eyeliner bleeding down her porcelain skin. A monochromatic maiko of death, her obi was tied in the tateya musubi style, and her wareshinobu hairstyle hinted that she hadn't lived long enough to achieve the full status of geisha. "Nothing in the rooms I checked."

"Yūrei meets teahouse. Nice."

"I used to want to be a geisha," she said, adjusting the white triangle below her weeping wisteria hair ornament. "That was before I found out I couldn't dance."

Jack's beads spun frantically. "There must be another one down the hall."

"Death before beauty."

"I'm not Death. That guy's an a-hole."

They passed through the door to find someone smoking their omnitread, in a state of apparent distress. The girl with the Get Genki! shirt either took the game too seriously, or she was genuinely terrified. Alice reached over to pull off her VR goggles, but Jack wagged his finger. Upon a small table, amid half-eaten rice crackers and lukewarm sushi, was a pile of gray pills. Jack tapped his beads to indicate they were in the right place. Four minutes remained.

The red six-fingered hand gripped a thick tree trunk sized club peppered with iron spikes. It *whooshed* past Akari, who leaped out of its way, shattering the hand-fired tiles where she had been standing. The embroidered cranes on her furisode kimono took flight as she ran up the oni's club, and onto its hairy arm. Her heel focused itself between his two horns, and the monster's head jerked back violently, silhouetted by an aizome sky.

"What's the attraction with these things?" asked Jack, uneasily surveying the virtual environment. "This isn't my idea of relaxing. Again. No jazz. Haven't you guys ever heard of poker?" His natural-sounding voice created a bizarre juxtaposition to his otherworldly manifestation.

"I'm starting to think you're some kind of gothic hipster. Oh, and in case you didn't notice, it's not 1965."

"Maybe to you, it's not." Jack spotted a bronze bell flying in their direction. "Duck!" The oni hurled a torii gate at Akari, but she skillfully rolled up her body and tumbled clear of the threat. "See, she just made my point. Not relaxing."

"It's a game. Don't you like games?"

"Depends on the stakes. What's the point if you can't lose your shirt or buy the farm? Sorry, I keep forgetting you're worm bait."

Alice glared.

The oni had finally taken notice of them, and its tiger-skin loincloth flapped like a flag as it ran over. The demonic-looking ogre rested the spiked club against his muscular neck and stroked his chin with freshly sharpened claws. "Jack? I didn't see you there. How long has it been? You're not here to cause me any trouble, are you?"

"Saul?" answered Jack, noticeably surprised. "I thought you were dead." It had been years since he had seen the shadow demon, in any form, but there had been rumors.

"I've told you," he replied, "don't call me that."

"Such a small world," said Jack. "Maybe you should leave?" He was aware that the shadow demon's real name was Solak, but he had personal reasons to annoy him.

"Funny, you should say that," replied Solak, but then he realized that Jack had no idea of his plans. "You'll laugh later. How did you know it was me?"

"Your face kind of looks like a hannya mask. It's disturbing."

"Who's the larva? Don't tell me they made you a trainer?" Solak fiddled with a small lead mirror that hung around his neck, checking to see if Jack had a point about his appearance.

While he knew they weren't ready to challenge the shadow demon, Jack wasn't sure if any other viable options existed. "Don't worry about her; I'm your problem."

Solak's burnt orange eyes became wild. "Stay out of my way, or you'll be next." He addressed his twisted horns towards Akari, who was using the reprieve to catch her breath.

"What say I don't," said Jack. He elongated his jaw to unnatural proportions and blasted Solak with the residual dark energy of souls he had recently reaped.

Caught unaware, Solak flew off his feet and traveled through a stone wall, its debris filling the gaps in his pointed teeth. The shadow demon sprung back onto his beastly feet, without even using his hands. "You're just full of bad decisions. Aren't you, Jack?" He emerged from within the lingering veil of dust and tackled Jack with his thick red arms.

Akari, unaware of the supernatural conflict that had intruded upon her game, prepared to re-engage her opponent. Solak animated two wooden Niō guardian king statues, one open-mouthed to symbolize birth and the other closed-mouthed to symbolize death. The one known as Agyō, sprung to life and grabbed Akari from behind. She wrapped her arms behind the statue's neck and lifted herself backward onto its shoulders. Untying her obi, she flung it around its neck and jumped. Unable to counter the leverage, the Niō statue collapsed.

Alice was so enthralled at the sight of Akari reversing her fortune that she failed to see the second guardian statue smash through the chicken wire and grab her like a sack of flour. "Jack," she gasped.

Her partner had problems of his own, however, as he was pinned against the ground with Solak using him for batting practice. They were not making a particularly good showing in their first engagement. Using the cobwebs—he had collected during midnight strolls through forsaken graveyards—Jack created an iridescent shield that shook like Christmas pudding as Solak beat upon it. More elastic than robust, it held, but each blow from the club reduced its strength. Jack hoped Alice wasn't watching him receive such a beating, as he was supposed to be the one giving the lesson not getting schooled.

Either Solak could not perceive that the silk was ready to collapse, or he had more pressing matters with which to contend. Seeing Akari occupied by the Niō statue, he said, "We'll catch up later," and dismissively walked away. It pleased him to see his old associate in such a submissive position, but it had become an unnecessary distraction. His club dragged a line in the dirt as he lumbered towards Akari.

Alice was not doing much better, the other wooden guard handily throwing her into the temple gate. When it arrived to finish her off, she pushed one of the torches into its face, and the guard's head ignited. It blindly grabbed her wrists in an attempt to draw her into its combustible gaze.

Forced with the choice of helping his partner or preventing Solak from completing his task, Jack ripped a bronze lantern off the temple eave by its chain and used it as a flammable mace. Already weakened, the statue collapsed into a pile of glowing charcoal embers but still managed to set the temple gate ablaze.

Akari blocked a strike to her ribs and countered with a knee to the statue's left shin. She swept its legs and prepared to perform a finishing move, but Solak had loaded up his club and swatted her into the flaming Niō-mon gate on the other side of the courtyard.

"Looks like you're going to have another ghost." Solak laughed, knowing that Jack would have to retrieve her soul before her brain cells died, and the metaphysical bridge collapsed.

"Alice! Water attack!" yelled Jack. He put his wrists together as if to demonstrate something, but she only looked back bewildered. "Well, can't let the house win." Jack formed a barrier with the howling visages of a thousand wailing spirits and placed it between Solak and Akari's remains. "Anytime doll. Anytime."

Alice placed her wrists together and was surprised to see a trickle of water spurt from between her hands. Shocked, she allowed them to separate. She looked over at Jack for additional help, but his attention was occupied with Solak, who had almost broken down his spirit-shield. It was apparent that he had picked a fight he couldn't win, which made her wonder why he had started it in the first place. Once again, she joined her wrists and flexed her forearms. A blast of water sprayed at the fire causing the flames to subside, but the blackened wood was already frail, and the beams collapsed in on themselves.

Jack's barrier shrieked with every blow of Solak's club, but somehow it held. "You know, I thought you might be alive."

"I had completely forgotten about you," Solak replied. "So you're in Japan? I guess I figured you'd be stinking up a booth in some casino."

"Harvest her!" yelled Jack. "Harvest her!"

"How?" asked Alice. "What do I do?"

A two-handed blow from Solak's club exhausted the last bit of resilience left in Jack's barrier. Shrieking ghostly faces scattered across the temple courtyard as it collapsed. As Jack was thrown aside, he clasped a net of skeletal hands onto the shadow demon's back to slow his progress.

"Can't hold him much longer..."

Alice found Akari's lifeless body pinned under a termite-infested support beam. Akari's contact enhanced eyes gazed vacuously, her neck oddly askew. Mimicking Jack's hand placement from when she had been harvested, Alice pressed her thumb against the roof of Akari's mouth and dug her middle finger against her forehead. To her astonishment, Akari's soul locked on, and her incorporeal essence gently eased from its mortal coil, a pulsating red fog that stretched like spun sugar. Having forced his way free of Jack's ghoulish net, Solak grabbed ahold of Alice's wrists and pulled them towards his chest. The light of Akari's soul vanquished the shadows, as they struggled, neither willing to yield.

"Do you have it?" cried Jack.

"I think so. Get me out of here!" Alice tried not to look into Solak's eyes; his demonic gaze more terrifying than she was ready yet to accept. "Do it, Jack!"

At that point, the environment collapsed, and she found herself back in the private VR room at the café. Akari hung in her omnitread limp, still wearing the clothes she had changed into after the concert. Unlike in the game, she was pale, but not disfigured.

"Jack...I think she's dead."

"Of course she's dead. Good job."

"Did I kill her?"

"Don't be ridiculous. Solak killed her. I'm not sure how, I mean it's just a game, but we can figure that out over a highball or two. Oh, right. You can order a melon soda and pick at the snack mix. See, that's why it's good to look at least nineteen."

"Look," said Alice, who noticed the bag of pills next to the plate of warm sushi. "Maybe these had something to do with it." She tried to pick up one of the gray pills, but not being materially configured; it passed right through her hand. She heard the door *creak,* and there stood the Genki Girls' producer. For a moment, Alice instinctively froze before she remembered that they couldn't be seen.

A chill passed through Haruto's spine at the sight of Akari hanging like a puppet in her VR rigging. His concern was both personal and professional. It was not the first time he had participated in the longstanding industry practice of reviving overdosed talent. "Akari! Oh shit. Akari! Can you hear me?" He noticed a flat, moving line scrolling upon the face of her watch. Her health app flashed an alert indicating that medical personnel had been notified. Haruto gathered the pills off the table and slipped out the back exit.

"Hey, wasn't he at that idol show? He was like an agent or a producer?" Jack's finger tracked him as he ran outside. "The Guppy or Grungy Girls—"

"Genki Girls. Let's get out of here."

Jack peered under Akari's dangling head to see if he recognized her. "She's not looking very genki now."

Alice's patience with Jack's whit had long since been exhausted. "Isn't there somewhere we're supposed to go? Somewhere with no corpse?"

Jack pondered his options, not the least bit in a hurry. "Now that I think about it, there is something I need to do."

"Good. Let's do that then." Still, it seemed inconsiderate to leave Akari in such a state. "What about…"

After the first fifty years as a harvester, Jack had begun to see the remains of his work as little more than degenerating cells, which was pretty much how he viewed the living. "What?"

"Her. Shouldn't we do something?"

"Don't you think you've done enough?" Jack snorted. "C'mon. That was funny. Great. I'm partnered with a square." He became momentarily solid and cracked open the door. "Help!" he yelled, using Akari's voice. "Happy? Okay, buttons. Let's jet." He grabbed Alice and pulled her through the wall.

Taka arrived to find Akari hanging in her harness like a scarecrow; her VR glasses pointed at the floor, arms draped like withered branches. He unlatched the omnitread, and she collapsed against his chest. Taka rocked her back and forth, consoling her with words she could no longer hear. Then the paramedics burst into the room and reluctantly pulled Akari from his arms, leaving him witnesses not only to the end of a life but a dream.

◆ ◆ ◆

"There has been a seven percent growth in our line of neurotransmitter medications that utilize the synthetic glutamate N-43." Fujisawa looked at his notes. "Speaking of which, Okada-san is now overseeing Neuroko, in addition to his previous duties. Any questions you might have had for Suzuki-san, concerning that drug, please forward to his attention."

George had been sleeping during the meeting with his eyes half-open. He stood and gave a slight bow. "Please be patient with me as I get up to speed. Onegaishimasu." There was no question that he was being set up to fail, so his co-workers' mercy was the only thing that could forestall disaster.

"Don't take too long," his boss replied. "Neuroko XR is in Phase III clinical trials. When it's approved, things are going to start moving around here."

"So it looks like it will be approved?" asked Abe, who liked to repeat other people's statements as questions, solely to imply he was participating.

Fujisawa looked around the room to emphasize that what he was about to say was strictly confidential. "Look. We all know that Neuroko is about to go generic, and it represents most of our sales. The stock is already down, and Neuroko XR just extends our patent. N-44 is pretty much 43 with some minor molecular tweaks. Trust me. It'll clear."

George liked his boss well enough but hated how he acted like the department's purse strings were his own. "Fujisawa-bucho. Is it possible we will be growing our department?"

His boss had no intention of bothering his superiors for additional monies, especially when their regard for his managerial abilities was based primarily on how tightly he controlled such resources.

"Okada-san, how many times must I tell you? Our pockets are empty. Even the investors know it. Why are you the only one in this department who's always looking for a way to sink the budget?"

"Oh, well, I thought if sales were up—"

Fujisawa shared a different train of thought. "If anything, it is a call to work seven percent harder. It is why we must ensure that we are keeping the inventory projections and research timelines accurate. Speaking of which, Okada-san. Have you clarified the discrepancies we discussed?"

"Not yet, chief."

"And why not?"

He wasn't sure if it was the time to complain, but he could hardly help himself. "This is my fourth meeting today, not counting an impromptu one with ergonomics." Left to his own devices, he could probably handle the work of three positions, but satisfying the company culture hardly left him the time to fulfill one.

"It might not even be a discrepancy," offered Abe, attempting to aide his friend. "N-43 atomizes barely above room temperature. It's remarkably unstable. That's why 44 was developed."

George gladly accepted the logic of his co-worker's reasoning. "Hai. When we're done, I'll immediately go to the warehouse and verify."

"There's no time for that now, Okada-san," replied his boss. "We meet with marketing in ten minutes."

◆ ◆ ◆

Alice would have assumed the reason that Jack liked to slip out of Tōkyō was to get away from all the noise, except he was from Vegas. Kyōto seemed the antithesis of the martini-slinging casino rat, but maybe it was because they both embraced the older way of doing things. Jack certainly had an undertaker's indifference about what they had just gone through with Akari, but as for Alice, she was still shaken. "So any idea about those pills?"

"Ginkgo biloba? How should I know?" Jack lifted a lanky leg over a bamboo fence that separated the path from the forest. "So, where'd you get the idea for that ghost-geisha deal?"

"When I was a little girl, my parents brought me here…to Kyōto. We went to see the spring dance, the one where all the maiko and geiko perform. That's what they call—"

"Geisha. You know, I saw that dance before they had electricity and, technically, maiko are apprentices, sound familiar?"

The thought hadn't occurred to Alice, but maybe the manifestation chose the person, seeing as Jack's reflected what a horror show he was. "I would have given anything to be that beautiful."

"Now, you can look any way you want."

"Yeah, but it's not really me."

"You think the girls at your school actually look like that? Let me tell you something. Being invisible, you see a lot. Wait. That didn't sound right."

Alice's mouth accidentally found a bamboo leaf. "How did you know I could do that thing with the water?" Alice had played VR games with mechs and kaiju, but something about what they had experienced felt different. She couldn't tell where the game ended, and the incorporeal world began. Alice felt spent. Like she had gone for a run up the steep steps of a temple; emotionally wrecked.

"Our bag of tricks is limited to whatever the situation requires. Nothing more. Nothing less. We call it 'powers of convenience,' but you can call it 'getting your ass kicked while you figure out what you can do.' There's nothing worse than trying to put out a fire and realizing the only power you have is more fire."

"So…how am I supposed to know?"

"Experience. Once you've seen enough, you'll get the hang of it. Anyway, relax. You're just a trainee. Don't get your neutrinos in a bunch." Jack stopped abruptly as if a critical thought had stopped him in his tracks. "Oh, and don't forget we can't strip people of their agency by letting them see beyond the veil. If you have powers in front of someone with a pulse, ten to one, their gig is up."

"So, I couldn't do any of that in real life?"

"I don't even understand the question. Real life? What's that? The soul is the only thing that matters, kid. Are you less real if you lose a limb? 'Course not. No percentage makes you less real."

"What about VR?"

Jack was surprised she had beaten him to the punch. "Say, you're pretty sharp."

"For a girl?"

"For someone younger than the gunk between my toes." They had played nothing but defense during their first engagement. The genetic makeup of the team was the least of his concerns. "Oh, and listen up. Sometimes your powers are more a manifestation of who you are and where you've been, as opposed to what you need."

"Great. Well, that explains it."

"Explains what?"

"You know how some people are afraid of clowns? That's how I feel about oni."

"I'm afraid I don't follow."

"Haven't you heard of Setsubun?" If Alice thought she was going to give Jack a lesson in the local culture, she was about to be disappointed.

"Spring festival, well, technically the day before spring, where kids throw roasted soybeans at—"

"Oni." Alice waited for the light bulb to appear above Jack's head. "Yeah. You think sitting on Santa's lap is scary? Try having your dad chase you around your house dressed as a demon."

"Sounds fun to me. Usually, I'm being chased by real demons."

Jack stopped in front of a small wooden arch with a precariously hanging weathered seal embossed with kanji characters. "This is what we came back for…it's my old partner's pad. Now I take care of it. No comments on how I'm doing." Most of Jack's expenses went to maintaining the multitude of residences he had acquired over the years. There was no common denominator about them, except neglect.

On the other side was a rocky pathway lined with traditional stone lanterns, but it was apparent that they had not been lit for many years. In the distance, Alice could hear the gentle knocking of a shishi-odoshi as it emptied its water. They reached the end of the path, overgrown with tall grass and above the foliage peeked the rooftop of a late Edo period villa. Its straw roof dappled with moss; its wood beams were well-aged from the ebb and flow of the seasons. The rising terrain formed a barrier from the wind that whistled in through the mountains.

Amber light filtered through hole-riddled shoji doors to reveal a room frozen in a state of abandonment. Tatami mats dusted with grayish-green mold paid tribute to one too many humid Kyōto afternoons. A black ink kakejiku of a dragon, its three claws extended over a crashing wave, hung on the northern wall of the room. Jack opened up the screens at the back of the house to reveal a partially finished Zen garden. From his coat, he produced his velvet bag and poured the gravel he had gathered onto a bare spot of dirt.

"So how long have you been stealing from temples?" asked Alice, her words a potent amalgamation of sarcasm and vitriol.

"You're going to learn there are a lot of things that don't fit in that little box of yours. I've got toilet paper older than you. Seriously. In a house, I own in Fresno. I never go there." He slid open one of the room's fusuma panels to escape from her into the next room. "Why don't you take a nap or something?"

"Can I do that?" She felt simultaneously wide-awake and exhausted. Her physical compulsions were a phantom limb.

"Physically, you reset every time you metamorph. What's going on in your head...I don't even know what's going on in mine. That's an entirely different kind of tired." He attempted to close the panel, but she stopped it with her hand.

"Was that really an oni?"

"Saul is like us, which means he can look any way he wants to. He once showed up as a goat. Didn't even realize it until I tried to get milk for my coffee. Now he's the lapdog of Erklikhan—the god of death—a shadow demon. That's as high as a human can reach...or as low, depending on one's perspective. His real name is Solak. He used to be a salt merchant. Puts it all over his salad when he eats. Weird—right?"

"But that wasn't just a game, was it?"

"Context is king, I always say." Jack leaned against a cabinet upon which a katana and a samurai helmet rested. The wakizashi was positioned in a manner that demonstrated its owner was ready to fight, but it had sat undisturbed for quite some time. He remembered how he used to place a piece of paper in his mouth to keep moisture from hitting the blade whenever he studied its otherworldly craftsmanship. "Taking care of Hiro was Saul's initiation rite…to join the other side. Well, let me tell you something. Where I'm from payback is a bitch, and I'm the county dogcatcher." Jack talked a big game for someone who had just been beaten like a blanket. He ran his finger over its ray skin handle. "A sword carries a warrior's soul. Don't dust or touch it. That goes for the helmet too."

Alice didn't care about Jack's precious relics. "Fine, but remember to stay away from my stuff." Not that she had anything other than the necklace Keiji had given her. She noticed that there wasn't enough gravel to rake lines around the garden's larger standing stones. "You know you can buy gravel."

"I can't use any gravel. Don't you get it? No, I suppose not." Jack's voice had started to mirror her whine. He grabbed a decomposing orange and threw it high up into the hillside. "If it were up to me, we'd wrap this gig up. Kyōto is the city that always sleeps. I'm like a shark. I've got to keep moving." For the first time, it occurred to him that she would probably have to accompany him after they left Japan.

Alice didn't know how long they would be at the villa, but she was already making plans to wipe the tatami mats with a damp cloth, at the very least. They smelled like samurai dander. "Doesn't it seem like demon shadows should have better things to do than hang out in VR cafes?"

Jack grabbed a rag and wiped the orange residue off his hand. "And I don't? The way I see it, we got this thread so that you can learn the ropes. Why else involve someone with my illustrious credentials? You can't figure on Saul. He's the type that goes into people's dreams and pushes them off cliffs. That's how he gets his kicks."

"He can do that?"

"You still don't get it? The mind is a physical inter-dimensional interface. It knows what's real and what's not…the lock on the gate if you will. Ever watch a movie? It doesn't matter how good it looks; there's that little voice in your head that tells you it's not happening."

"But what if you couldn't tell?"

"Then, the virtual world would be wide open…like dreams." Jack paused to study his reflection in Hiro's katana. "Great googly moogly! We've got to get back to Tōkyō and find those pills."

◆ ◆ ◆

Yuki dropped the incense into the bowl, said a quick prayer, and bowed towards the portrait of Akari. It was a fresh-faced picture from when the recently deceased idol had first joined the Genki Girls. Yuki plopped next to Saori, who was studying people from over her glasses, a habit that only served to remind everyone they weren't necessary.

"Is there even any family here?" wondered Saori. The wake was thinly attended and mostly by family members of the group. One of the few exceptions was Taka, who sat beside Akari's portrait, sobbing. "It makes us all look bad; I'm just saying."

"I saw her brother," said Momoko. She was wearing a gothic lolita dress that, with its matching black gloves and parasol, might not have been as appropriate a look as she thought. "He's over there. The guy whose head looks like a cute potato with sunglasses."

Yuki craned her neck and saw a shaved-headed gangster a handful of years older than they were. "He's the one who took all the envelopes. He does kind of look like her, I guess." She looked around to see if anyone else had left. "Well, that's the end of the Genki Girls. At least I won't have to hear her say 'stay genki' all the time. She was the only one who could say it like it was a threat."

"What are you talking about?" asked Saori in disbelief. "We're not done. I didn't do all those electronic store openings to give up over Akari."

"Um, Saori…Akari kind of was the Genki Girls," replied Yuki. "We were her extras."

Saori wiped a fingerprint off her glasses. "Maybe she thought so. Have you seen the news? They're actually talking about us. No one had even heard of us before. This is the chance we've been waiting for—to start over."

"Have you dropped all your pachinko balls?" asked Yuki. "You can't be serious. We sucked even with her around."

Saori's voice was intentionally loud. "I think Akari would have wanted us to go on. I don't know what your prayer was, but I made a promise. A promise for us to keep going and stick together." She walked over to Taka, whom she made a point to sit beside and comfort.

Momoko twirled one of her twintails with her parasol. "I don't get her problem. She was going to retire anyway."

"She was going to be center," said Yuki. "She'll get over it. Best part. Maybe now I won't fail algebra. Thanks, Akari!" Then something occurred to her. "Uh...I totally forgot to offer my condolences to her brother."

Though not the usual custom, Sho had already started for the door during the last sutra. Yuki sprang to her feet, afraid she wouldn't have time to intercept him. As he reached for the handle, she grabbed his jacket, agitating him enough to glance back. His sunglasses slipped, and Yuki gazed into his eyes for the first time. It was an emotionless, onyx stare.

"I'm sorry," said Yuki.

"Not as much as the people who did this are going to be," he replied.

CHAPTER FIVE:
OFFICE SAMURAI

Haruto gazed skyward at his old Flavor Beat Records office. A stylish woman, whose purse was worth more than he had made producing the Genki Girls, waited for him to show some initiative and enter the Roppongi headquarters where it had all began. Haruto longed for more time before he emasculated his pride, but the woman cleared her throat to indicate that he was preventing the progress of people whose time actually mattered. After an unnecessarily extended apology, Haruto took his first steps into the glass tower since he had quit in a manner that had become the stuff of legend. Hardly an industry party was held in Tōkyō, where the story of him releasing a box of pigeons was not acted out with theatrical precision, especially the part where he had told them to, "Fly free!"

The last week would have been enough to kill a more broken man, but Haruto was already dead inside. In a sense, he was returning to his grave, the place where his soul had been hollowed. Still, a lack of spirit did not forestall the onslaught of hunger pains, nor the need to pay one's rent. Akari's passing, and the media onslaught that ensued, had driven Haruto to his cousin's house in Nagoya, at least until his landlord had managed to track him down. One saké-fueled night, Haruto called his old boss at Flavor Beat and pleaded for a meeting to discuss even the most meager of opportunities. Now he sat across from the man who had given him his start in the industry, trying to remember the terms on which they had parted, and considerably more sober. He could only remember the pigeons and a lunch with a nearly lethal amount of alcohol.

"So, how have things been?" asked Haruto, shifting in his seat. "You look...good."

Genjirō, the Senior Vice President of Artists and Repertoire, sat behind a translucent desk intended to mimic a Late Baroque sensibility. His gaze was brushed aluminum cold. Gold records hung from his walls, even though no artist had released a single on such a physical medium in decades. There was a recent photo of the group Superflat signing a contract, apparently not realizing that such an event merited wearing a shirt. "I was wondering when we'd hear from you, but you left so...dramatically."

"*Etto...*" mumbled Haruto, trying to find the right words. "It seems I was given the wrong prescription. Maybe I should sue the pharmacy? Irresponsible of them, don't you think?" The framed image of Superflat caught his eye, as it changed to a short clip of them flexing their muscles.

"You called Flavor Beat a prison and said we should stay in our cages until you cleared the watchtowers." His old boss had no intention of letting him off easy. The aftermath had inflicted a poisonous effect on morale, not to mention a substantial quantity of bird droppings. The label was always concerned about their employees striking out on their own, or poaching artists. When Genjirō had learned that his former protégé had founded an idol group, he understood the lengths he was willing to go to get out of his contract.

Haruto appreciated how the situation appeared, but he had run out of alternative means of self-flagellation. "Apparently, there was an interaction with another medication I was taking. Does anyone even read all those tiny instructions? I mean...you practically need a microscope." He squirmed in his chair. "I was hoping maybe we could work something out? For old times' sake."

For a while, Genjirō eyed him coldly. "Yes, I know why you're here, so you can cut out the pleasantries. What's it going to cost me? Do you think I care that you made a nuisance of yourself? Bad behavior is the oxygen of this industry. We're just used to the artists being the assholes."

"Well, I have been trying my hand at lyrics..."

Sour-faced, he was well aware of Haruto's attempts. "Yes, someone hung them in the lunchroom so we could all have a laugh." A gleam appeared in Genjirō's eyes, or perhaps it was a reflection from the neighboring office building. "Look, we're not exactly cranking out Handel's Messiah here, but I've been watching you. Well, I've sent people out to watch you—an intern actually. You've somehow managed to lower the bar for idol music. A lot." He inhaled deeply to obtain the oxygen required to override his scruples. "Okay. I've got about five minutes of patience with your name on it. I can do forty-five, and that's all. I would have offered you forty, but my time is worth more than the company's money. Take it or leave it – I really don't care."

Forty-five million yen was fifteen percent less than Haruto had been making before he left Flavor Beat, but he was relieved that his former boss was even willing to consider the notion of his return. He had a fuzzy memory of calling him 'hell's warden' as he collapsed drunk outside his door. *Maybe he wants to re-hire me, so he can make a point of publicly letting me go? What if this is some plot for revenge? I wouldn't hire me.* "Ano...forty-five—"

Genjirō looked up from the desk toy he had been playing with, two small sumo bots you could control by tapping your fingers. "What? Forty-five isn't enough? I thought you knew how it works around here? If the single does well, you'll have an option. And touring – you'll go out with our other artists. I don't have to tell you that's where the real money is." He watched the sumo bot with the green mawashi get tossed out of the ring. "You're not sitting here because of old times or because I believe your bullshit story. The new trend is for real artists. Everyone is scrambling to put actual groups together. Those Superflat boys have more abs than brains, but anyone who's got an actual pulse is getting a look. That's what people want now. Holograms are so last week. You'd better get on board while you can. It's probably some sort of retro fad. Next week it could be singing cats." He took a moment to ponder the possibility.

Haruto tried to discern if they were both tracking the same conversation. His impression had been that the meeting was to discuss his return as an A&R Director, not to sign the Genki Girls. Touring was indeed an area in which he had some expertise, but he was always paid a salary, never by the single. "I'm afraid I don't understand."

"Sure, you don't. Okay, you want to say you won? Is that it? You want to be the big man? Fine. Forty-eight million but stop insulting my intelligence. I went to Tōkyō University." It was something he reminded his subordinates about a bit too readily. "Do you think I never saw you pull this whole act when you worked here. You can't buy press like you've been getting. I get it. Remember, though, there are no guarantees anyone will care in a month when Akari's still not producing carbon dioxide. I'm the one taking the risk here. Flavor Beat doesn't owe you anything. Not after how you left."

"You want to sign the Genki Girls?" The young producer had assumed that without Akari, his group was finished. Once he secured his old job, He planned to call a meeting and officially disband the Genki Girls. For most of the night, Haruto had lain in bed, parsing the various ways he might break it to them.

A blood vessel slithered across Genjirō's forehead. "Fifty?" The bewildered silence with which Haruto responded to his offer caused him to seethe. "Fifty, isn't enough? Is that what you're saying? I'm starting to wonder about some of those rumors, but you know what? I don't care – you do whatever it takes to stay in the news. Fifty-five, and that's my final offer, but I want that track while the news cycle still cares. And make it something sad. Tragic sad. Not the type of sad you've been doing. Good sad."

Within the halls of Haruto's comprehension, the light of understanding flickered. The thought of not being forced to return to his former position as a white-collar slave instigated a laugh he could not suppress. His old boss could only see through his own perverse calculations and had assumed Haruto arranged the meeting to take advantage of the coverage generated by Akari's death. It had launched a firestorm of media attention on the safety of VR cafes, with the story of Akari's tragic demise framing the debate. Such behavior was encouraged in their industry, but Haruto had never been inclined towards such maneuverings, at least not intentionally. "Hai…I think I understand."

As he whistled on his way back to the elevators, Haruto ran into his former colleague, Wataru, who worked in Marketing, from the floor below where he had been in A&R. Haruto had even been dragged to lunch with him a couple of times, out of obligation.

"Haruto-san, nice to see you. I heard you were here to get your girls signed? Between us, you have them by the short hairs. Your group is so hot right now. *Atsui dai yo*!" Wataru looked like a typical salaryman in his white shirt, black slacks, and thin tie. His fashion sense and air of desperation kept him firmly fixed to the same desk since Haruto had been an intern.

"*Sou desu.* Looks like I'm going to be making a single for you guys." Haruto found himself falling into the old habit of making social pleasantries with a department he could ill-afford to ignore. "How are things in Marketing since I left, Wataru-san?"

"Damn depressing. Say, you don't have any enhancer on you, do you? C'mon don't hold out. I know you always carry for the talent." Wataru's pleading was never attractive. It carried the same air of desperation as the office workers who passed out beside him on the train ride home.

"I don't think I have any," Haruto lied. The gray pills had accompanied him since the day of the accident. To cleanse his conscience, he had even taken one while he was staying with his cousin. It had caused him to order a pallet of robotic cat ears headphones, but other than that, there were no ill effects.

"C'mon," pleaded Wataru. "I know you can help me. You were right when you called this place a prison. I need to escape. Hey, I think my new secretary likes me. Help me out. I'll hook your group up real good."

Without giving it much thought, Haruto shoved the plastic bag of enhancer into Wataru's shirt pocket. "No more than one at a time. And you didn't get them from me."

"Well, all right!" Wataru pretended to shoot off a couple of celebratory rounds with his fingers. "I'm going to do everything I can to see your new single is treated real nice. You just leave it up to old Wataru-san."

Haruto was relieved to see that his elevator had finally arrived. "Don't forget what I said. One. They might be stronger than those other ones I used to get." Haruto felt relieved to have finally put the entire episode behind him.

◆ ◆ ◆

Alice looked skeptically at the dented metal door, unmarked except for where its number had fallen off. Not even a potted plant warmed the hallway. It was the type of subsidized apartment the government promoted as a way to provide affordable housing in Tōkyō. "Are you sure this is the guy we saw at the cafe?"

Jack furrowed his forehead, disappointed that his young charge had so little faith in his abilities. "It's Akihabara adjacent. His name is Taka, and he runs a Genki Girls blog. A simple IP address search and voila! Am I good, or what?"

"I think you're creepy even when you look normal."

"Hey, I'm of the opinion that all of this technology is b–a–d, bad, but it used to take me days to track down a lead like this. Now people leave so many digital breadcrumbs I'm thinking of getting a new hobby. Maybe I'll take up extreme ironing."

"Whatever. Let's get this over with so I can go see Keiji."

"Cool your jets. When every soul on this thread has been harvested, then maybe I'll take you."

Alice pulled her hand back from the doorbell and began to walk away. "Later."

Jack flipped up his collar. "Sullen teenager doesn't work with me. I'm death's umbra. I've watched empires fall. I may look twenty, but that doesn't mean we're from the same wheelhouse."

"Let me guess. That's how old you were when you died?"

Jack's furrowed his brow. "No…I was nineteen." He gave a quick double take that made it clear such a conclusion should be obvious. "You want to see how I really look?" He transformed into his rotted-out likeness and tossed out a maggot that had found its way into one of his eye sockets. "I'm two hundred and sixty-six years old."

Startled, Alice screamed. "Don't do that again. Like, ever."

"Relax," replied Jack, returning to his ring-a-ding persona. "You're going to see worse in this gig, that's for sure."

Though breathing heavily, Alice didn't want it to appear like he had rattled her cage. "Okay, so why not nineteen then?

"I always wanted to be twenty." Recognizing his role in Alice's eternal adolescence, Jack felt something that approximated guilt. "Alright. So, I was thinking. Maybe after we're through here, we'll go to the police yard and poke around a bit. How's that grab you?"

Alice exhaled any remaining apathy she retained. "Fine. What are we supposed to be doing here, again?"

"We're reporters. Remember? From the local college." Jack looked her over and realized he had forgotten to make the necessary physical adjustments to her appearance. "Hey, chicken dinner. He'll never buy you looking like that. Time to age you up a bit."

"I like how I look."

"I'm not talking about surgery. Remember what I said? We have the power to look any way we want. A little different than you is not you. Just enough for them to say, 'Hey isn't that—um no, because she's dead.' It doesn't take much. People are basically idiots."

Alice was keen to avoid another close call with someone she knew, the last time having been traumatic enough. "Fine. What do I have to do?"

"Inhale, but focus on your hair."

She took a deep breath, and her straight black locks retracted.

"Now, stick your thumb in your mouth and blow."

Alice felt ridiculous, but she followed the lead of his suggestion, and her proportions altered, ever so slightly.

He parted her bangs and stretched her eyes larger with his fingers. "Whoa, too big. You look manga-y. And how about brown?" Jack returned them to a more manageable size. Next, he used both of his hands to push down on her head, which lowered her height by around four centimeters. "Not bad…like you could be your own cousin, but without the inbreeding."

"Did you have to make me shorter?"

Jack adjusted his handkerchief, which was sitting akimbo in his pocket. "Taller never works. Don't ask me why—something to do with eye contact. For the record, there wasn't really anything wrong with you. It's occupational. I wouldn't have changed a thing, except, maybe your personality."

"You're kind of like a grotesque fairy godmother."

Before Jack could protest, the door opened, and there stood Taka, low-shouldered, his eyes underlined with blue splotches from too many hours of playing video games. He wasn't used to finding a high school girl and a foreigner who looked like he had escaped from a host club standing in his hallway. "Did I hear yelling?"

"Sorry for the hubbub. I'm Jack, and this is…my cousin." It wasn't wholly implausible as Alice's mother had been a Westerner.

"Alice desu. Hajimemashite. We're reporters," said Alice, in an attempt to prop up their story. "Well, It's more like a blog—a music blog. Yoroshiku onegaishimasu."

Fortunately, awkward was the only type of communication to which Taka related. "Look, I don't have anything else to say. You guys are the third group to come around since last night. Why can't everyone just leave me alone?" He began to close the door, but Alice blocked it with her foot.

"We're not like those other reporters. It's an idol blog." She found the words distasteful but still managed to spew them for his consumption. "And I really love the Genki Girls."

"You do?" replied Taka astonished.

"So very much," Alice lied. "You're like their biggest fan, right? My cousin only came because he has trust issues."

Taka took a moment to weigh Jack's opinion of him. "Oh, I get it. You think otaku are dangerous. People put on knickers and golf, but that's not weird?"

"Hey, buddy. I'm not here to judge your proclivities, no matter how distasteful. I just don't want her alone in the big city." Jack had assumed Taka would find Alice a suitable foil, and he was not disappointed.

Alice made a half-baked attempt to imitate the sweet as honey attitude some of the girls at her school used as a weapon. "I hear you know more about the Genki Girls than anyone. Can't I just ask you a few questions?" She swallowed hard. "Senpai."

"An idol blog? Is it one I know?" It just happened to be the one subject on which Taka didn't mind conversing at length about. Still, something about Jack made the hairs on his neck stand on end. "You look familiar. Have I seen you before?"

"Had any near-death experiences?" It occurred to Jack that it might be better for him to remove himself from the equation. "Say, you kids have fun. I'm going to get some air. Smells like yakisoba in here."

Taka motioned for Alice to follow him inside. "Taka desu. *Douzo*," he said, and closed the door behind her.

The small studio apartment was plastered with pictures of Akari, homemade fans, and Genki Girls souvenirs. His computer was open to his blog, which he had been updating with the latest news about Akari's death. Several bottles of green tea had met their fate nearby and were strewn about the floor.

"Everyone is saying she killed herself, but that's a lie. Akari would never do that." Taka recited Genki Girls lyrics like an otaku monk. "She sang about taking chances and never giving up. She would never have killed herself. It was against everything she believed."

Alice mumbled inoffensive agreement knowing that such lyrics were as much a staple of idol music as short skirts and petticoats. She would never admit to it, but she had listened to a playlist of such corporately tested encouragements before confessing to Keiji. "What do you think happened?" She unfolded her phone into a larger tablet to take notes.

"How much do you know about VR tech?" He was encouraged to have found a sympathetic audience.

"I hooked up everything at home and guess who has to download all the content from our cloud?" No one was as technically proficient as a bored teenager.

"Do you know anything about enhancer? Dropping 'E?' The VR pills everyone is taking?"

She remembered seeing them scattered on the table next to Akari. "I'm not really into that sort of thing."

"It causes virtual reality presence-levels to achieve true parallel reality. When they achieved three-millisecond latency and developed variable focus recognition to solve vergence and accommodation issues, they thought they'd done it."

"Done what?"

"The problem was you could use the smoothest omnitread in the world, but in the back of your mind, you still knew it wasn't real—that it was just a game."

"I'd ask you to repeat that, but I'm pretty sure it wouldn't help."

Taka attempted to use terminology a sixteen-year-old might understand. "It turns off the part of the brain that says 'this isn't happening.' The technology was never the problem. Suspension of disbelief was."

"So Akari was using enhancer?" She was confident she already knew the answer.

Taka had broken a few laws to gain access to her autopsy report. "None of it makes any sense. It can rot your will to live, but it doesn't kill you." Taka used an app on his phone to change the pose of one of his figures. "Do you know where it comes from? The yakuza. They control the flow of enhancer in Tōkyō. All of Honshu, actually."

Alice nonchalantly looked around the apartment, hoping she would see something that would prompt a question. "Well, the yakuza wouldn't care about Akari, so maybe she just had a bad heart?"

"Have you ever seen those creepy dudes with the blacked-out eyes that hang around Kubukichō?"

Apparently, Jack had gotten bored of waiting outside, as Alice saw him pass through the apartment door and rejoin them. "My life is a cornucopia of creepy."

"That's Kurome-gumi; full-on yakuza. There's one that shows up at Genki Girl events. He was even at Akari's funeral." Taka pulled up various images of the yakuza and displayed them on his wall.

"Maybe he just wanted to see Superflat?"

"Seriously. Ask yourself. Who had the most to gain, and it wasn't me. I loved Akari. She was the Genki Girls' center. Maybe someone else thought they could do a better job?" Taka held up a fan with Akari's smiling face. He had glued tinsel around its border, and her name was written in glitter. "I've seen people passed out like that before, but they always come back. Always. Someone saw to it that she didn't. I'm going to find out who."

She noticed that Jack appreciated the care that had gone into Taka's stalker collage, or maybe not, as he drew a couple invisible circles around his ear. Fortunately, only Alice could see him. "Does anyone think you were behind it?"

"They say they don't, but I've caught the police following me online." Taka noticed that his 3D printer had finished. He removed a plastic figure of Akari and placed it in the shrine he had been making. "I want to know who did it more than anyone. Right before you knocked...I'd already figured out the addresses."

"The addresses?" Alice thought, for a moment, that she had bumped into Jack. She made an odd flailing motion, as she passed through him but tried to play it off as an unseen bug.

"Of all the Genki Girls. Now that you're here, it won't look weird when we show up where they live. Let's go. *Ikimashou ka?*"

Alice looked over at Jack and mouthed *help*.

Jack, however, was too distracted by his synchronicity beads. "Something's stirring. You kids have fun. Tell me if anyone looks guilty—besides Taka. Ciao."

◆ ◆ ◆

"Wataru-san. You're not seriously still working on that press release, and for the Genki Girls?" Tsubasa peered over his shoulder and watched him delete a word that seemed utterly inconsequential. "It's seven o'clock. Izakaya time."

Wataru looked at his secretary, still feverishly at work. "Naomi-san and I have to finish this project. Maybe in an hour or so...gyoza is on me."

Tsubasa noted that Naomi's face had acquired a bit of color. "I think I know what you want to finish up, you old raccoon," he replied. "I guess somebody wasn't paying attention during the sexual harassment seminar or took all the don'ts for tips and suggestions."

"Haruto-san is my old friend," protested Wataru. "I told him I would see that everything on our end is right. I'm not leaving until this press release makes people want to kill for the next Genki Girls single."

"Seems like you have a handle on that group." Tsubasa laughed a bit maniacally. "All right, well, don't take too long. Don't keep Naomi-chan here too late."

"Yeah. Yeah." Wataru watched a couple of his co-workers exchange knowing glances, as they gathered their purses and bags. He had never cared before what anyone thought, and he wasn't about to start the habit now. "Are we clear?"

"*Yokai*. We're all alone," confirmed Naomi.

Wataru sauntered over to her desk. "I have something special for tonight." He pulled out the bag of pills Haruto had given him.

"What are those?" she asked innocently.

"Enhancer. Our game will feel completely real once we take these. Total immersion."

Naomi used a more vulnerable voice than during work hours, which could be mistaken for courting behavior. "I don't know, Wataru-san. I've never taken anything like that before. Is it dangerous?"

Wataru popped one in his mouth. "They're totally safe and non-addictive. I use them all the time and look at me. I'm fine." He placed the plastic bag of gray pills in the palm of her hand. "Keep them in the drawer with the glasses."

Naomi hesitated but finally swallowed a pill. She gazed back with large brown eyes that indicated she knew how to keep a secret.

He reached into her desk, where they kept a pair of AR glasses. "So, what shall we play?"

"Bunny Wars!" shouted Naomi. She could tell by Wataru's disappointment that it was not the answer he was expecting. "Office Samurai!" she cried, attempting to match the enthusiasm of her first choice.

Wataru initially seemed not to embrace her second selection, but then yelled, "*Yoshi!*" He ran to the other side of the office and adjusted his glasses.

A digital overlay of a Fourteenth-Century Japanese Castle rendered over the copying machines, filing cabinets, and workstations. The castle appeared to continue beyond the ceiling tiles, into a digital azure sky. Ten warriors materialized beside Wataru, smartly attired in lacquered black armor. Each wore a helmet, shaped to represent a different creature like a rabbit or a seashell. They wielded single-edged blades that glistened under the virtual sun. Wataru locked eyes with Naomi, who had traded her demure office attire, for a magnificent crimson suit of armor. Ten similarly outfitted samurai, including one with a sashimono banner attached to his chest, awaited her command.

Wataru took out an iron war fan and shook it aggressively. "The White

Heron Castle will fall. Your defense of it shall be your downfall. It is my birthright!"

Naomi drew her katana and gripped its stingray-covered tsuka with both hands. "I would sooner die than let it pass to a tyrant such as you!"

Gunbai raised, Wataru's warriors leaped over the cubicles to meet Naomi's crimson-clad samurai at the center of the office.

"I see your men are using the Two Heavens As One technique," yelled Naomi.

"You can tell from how we both defend and attack," cried Wataru as one of her warriors was slain. "Soon, will I be at your gate!"

Naomi blushed and rushed into the fray, exchanging blows with one of his kuro samurai. "Not if I can help it, Wataru-san." Her feet fluttered like a butterfly.

Wataru swiftly thrust at his opponent's neck, where their armor had left them vulnerable. The warrior grabbed his blade, but Wataru stabbed him with his tanto, a particularly capable dagger for such close engagements.

Naomi recognized the increasing futility of her position, with but four remaining warriors to his seven. She raised her gunbai and out stepped a colossus of a samurai, two hundred and forty centimeters tall. His helmet had two massive horns, and his lacquered menpō was in the likeness of a hannya mask.

The fierce-looking giant tossed Wataru's warriors as if skipping pebbles across a stream. The meek advertising manager summoned his courage, raised his katana high, and charged. An enormous sword greeted Wataru's blade, cutting a deep notch into it as they embraced. Within the shower of sparks, he gazed into the savage, orange eyes of his enemy. The enhancer had reached full potency, but the euphoria, fear, and adrenaline were real. The AR glasses he wore now forgotten; his only reality was that he was from the Age of Warring States. The graphic overlay took into account every object within the office, and if it was actually there, he felt its reality. Cubicle walls now formed the foundation of the castle, and as Wataru jumped back onto someone's desk, he failed to realize that they would discover his footprint in the morning.

The giant samurai grabbed Wataru's sword and hurled it aside. Wataru produced a sickle weapon, called a kama, and threw it into his opponent's chest armor.

Naomi laughed with delight at his skill and resourcefulness. "How did you learn to use a kama?"

"My family is from Okinawa," replied Wataru.

Unbalanced, the titan stumbled back, the sickle protruding from his chest. Wataru produced its partner and sprinted to close the distance between them. As he threw himself against the samurai, there was a sudden snap, and they dropped through where the floor of the castle should have been. With nothing to actually stop them, they fell until they hit the pavement six stories below. The window had been capable, but the frame that held it, less so. It landed in one solid piece beside them and shattered.

The AR overlay quickly dissipated, lessening the effect the drug had upon Naomi's cognition. She knelt beside the window's edge and looked down at the street below. Wataru's outline was visible, but naturally, she could not see Jack, who had arrived in time to retrieve Wataru's soul, an activity beyond mortal sensitivities. Panicked, she took the remainder of the pills from her pocket and tossed them into a trashcan, crying hysterically as she fled the building. The next day she would insist that she had only stayed a few minutes after the others had left.

One combatant, however, remained after the digital overlay had dissipated. The hulking samurai brushed the glass off his shoulders, not particularly surprised at the supernatural form draped over his victim. "Jack? Where's your shadow?"

"I thought I was looking at him. Who sent you Saul? What's your game?"

Solak smirked devilishly from behind his mask. Black eyeliner made his titian eyes appear wild. "Was I that obvious? Hannya menpō too on the nose?"

Solak vanished before Jack could address his lack of respect, or at least get pummeled trying. Fortunately, Alice wasn't there to see how little regard the shadow demon had for him. Jack looked at the sign on the door. *Flavor Beat Records*, he read to himself. *How much do you want to bet this is the Genki Girl's label?*

◆ ◆ ◆

"Tails" was Momoko's nickname because she wore her hair in the popular twintails style. It was popular with girls emphasizing their "kawaii-ness," an attribute she had refined to nuclear-grade levels of potency. Though already out of high school, her small features, and narrow face, made her appear younger than Alice. She was more likely to be mistaken for an autonomous doll than a mathematical prodigy, especially as she smelled of perfume bought in a toy store. "Akari was more like a frenemy, who knew I wouldn't fight back. The only one she really liked was Haruto-sensei. He's the producer of the group. Say, you kind of look familiar. Do I know you?"

"Nope," replied Alice. "How well did they get along?"

Momoko employed her primary skill, which was pretending to have the maturity of a teddy bear. "Akari once made me bring her clothes over to her place. From outside, I could hear her brother yelling at Haruto-sensei. You know, the bald guy with the glasses?"

"That's her brother?" asked Alice.

"Yakuza, as if we didn't know. Usually watches from the back," said Momoko. "He really blends."

"Did Akari see you as a threat, because you're so kawaii?" interrupted Taka.

Momoko twirled one of her ponytails and beamed. "Taka-kun is so sweet! Saori was the one she couldn't stand. Akari couldn't sing as well as her. Dancing was Akari's thing."

Alice brought the Genki Girls' profiles up on her tablet. "Saori was the number two position in the group, wasn't she?"

"Why do you think Akari wanted her out? They were too close in age. When we hung out, all she did was complain about her. And those glasses—"

"Glasses?" asked Taka.

"She was always trying to get Haruto-sensei to make her stop wearing them. She knew Saori looked like a thumb without them." Momoko giggled childishly.

Conducting the interview in Momoko's bedroom made it difficult for Taka to focus, and the way she kept looking at him was equally unsettling. Fortunately, Alice was there to serve as a buffer. "But isn't Saori going to graduate soon?

What's it matter if she's going to college?"

Momoko held her hand over her mouth and giggled. "Glasses don't equal smart, silly." She leaned close enough that Taka could smell her strawberry-scented shampoo and whispered, "Not smart enough to get a scholarship—no money to afford college…"

Taka shared a look with Alice, who replied, "So becoming center was all she had to look forward to?"

"I hadn't thought of that," replied Momoko, her eyes as wide as doughnuts. She held her unicorn-painted fingernails over her mouth in mock surprise.

◆ ◆ ◆

Sho placed the plate of sashimi next to the urn containing his sister's ashes. His family's butsudan was one of the few objects that had survived their childhood. The small wooden shrine was a hundred and twenty years old and held the memorial tablets of his parents and their ancestors before them. His trembling voice caused the incense smoke to shudder as he addressed the portrait of Akari. "Our one chance to be better." He had tried not to soil her by association, even as he attempted to lift her high on his shoulders. "You would have gotten the pills from someone. You would have, wouldn't you?" Sweat collected on the stubble near the back of his head. "I thought they were safe if they came from me." Sho stumbled back from the cabinet and slammed against his kitchen counter. His hand reached for a bottle of cheap sake, but before it met his lips, he hurled it against the wall. There was no point in killing Akari. Nothing made sense. His funerary obligations might have bought him some time, but he had also failed to secure an alibi. Perhaps it was already too late. Leaving him alive to suffer the results of his mistakes seemed too cruel even for the yakuza. If he wasn't careful, his grief might get him killed.

◆ ◆ ◆

Flavor Beat Records' night janitor swept the pieces of a broken monitor into his dustpan as he hummed a Hokkien pop song. The marketing department looked like a typhoon had passed through it. Even worse than when a disgruntled employee had released a bunch of pigeons in the A&R offices. Leaving his girlfriend in Taipei, for the glamour of Tōkyō, was starting to appear a most questionable career decision. It wasn't like Roppongi's sashimi could hold a candle to his mother's braised pork rice, anyway. Why someone would hurl themselves at a window was a matter best left to a psychologist. All he knew was that he was the one responsible for putting everything back in its place. The wind took one last opportunity to blow debris across the room. The janitor's callused hands grabbed a wastebasket, and as he tipped it over, out fell a half-eaten apple, some tissues, and something he couldn't exactly place. *Well, what do we have here?* He stopped humming as he considered the small plastic bag with three gray pills.

CHAPTER SIX:
BECOMING GENKI

There was no need for Alice to read the brass numbers on the faux brick wall, her internal alarm had started ringing three blocks away. "Taka, I'm pretty sure this isn't Saori's house." Hardly a humid Tōkyō summer day passed that she couldn't be found at Yuki's house, watching Korean dramas and nibbling on soda-flavored popsicles, until their lips turned blue. Because their dads worked together, they had practically been friends from inside their mother's wombs.

"*Sugoi!* You can see that?" Taka assumed she was reading the address off of his phone. "Saori hasn't been able to pass her entrance exams. I'm not saying she meant to kill Akari, but she might have wanted to find a way to make sure everyone knew she had a problem; bump herself up." He pointed at the Okada nameplate posted next to the front door. "Yuki was third behind Saori. If this were a science experiment, think of her as our control. Then, when we go talk to Saori, we'll have something to compare her against."

Alice thought it must have taken a lot of practice for Yuki to place so high in the group, or perhaps it was more a reflection of the quality of the other members. "She's really third position?"

"Well, I hear her mom has a lot of pull. They haven't exactly held a fan election, so that probably has something to do with it. Until then, it's all pretty arbitrary."

Nervous that Jack's extreme makeover might not have been enough, Alice started to squirm like ants had crawled up her legs. Even girls at her school used makeup tape to lift their cheeks and prosthetic makeup to alter the shape of their noses. Yuki didn't make any friends when she would put tape on her face to make fun of those girls. Alice grabbed the Genki Girls hat Taka was wearing and pulled a surgical mask from her pocket. "Hay fever."

The hat was rare, one of only a few made. Haruto had given it to him after a gig, no one else attended, and it was the pride of his collection. "I'm getting that back, right?"

Notified that she had guests, Mrs. Okada appeared on a small monitor wearing a frilly apron imprinted with a bunny whose cartoon bubble said, *Oishisou!* She had a habit of closing her eyes whenever she smiled. "Oh—kids! You must be Yuki's friends. Oh, dear. Why didn't she tell me? I could have made something."

Taka's backpack knocked Alice aside as he nudged closer to the camera. "Hello, Mrs. Okada. We have a small music blog, and we were wondering if we could ask Yuki a few questions about the future of the Genki Girls?"

"Oh, how wonderful. I'm sure she'd love to!" Mrs. Okada knew how difficult it was for Yuki to form positive relationships with kids her age. She recognized Taka from various Genki Girl functions, but not well enough to remember his name.

"No, I wouldn't," shouted a voice, somewhere off-screen. A door slammed.

Her mom disappeared, and there was some unintelligible back-and-forth before she reappeared. "I'm so sorry; she's been through a lot lately. It can't be helped. Won't you please come in?" There was a *click* as the door unlocked.

Taka sat on the couch, nervously dampening his enthusiasm with the small towel he had bought at one of their events. For a second, the unmistakable sound of him geeking out escaped, but he grunted to cover the slip, feigning that something had become lodged in his throat.

Mrs. Okada asked Alice, "Would you feel more comfortable if I took your hat?"

"No, thank you." She snuck a cookie under her mask and was surprised to discover she could still find pleasure in such things. She never noticed the way salt made the sugar taste sweeter. Between the familiar smells and tastes, it almost felt like she had returned merely to study geometry with Yuki. Jack's penchant for cake almost made sense. No, she decided. He was still weird.

"I'm sorry, they're a couple of days old," apologized Mrs. Okada. She looked up the stairs, wondering what might be taking her daughter so long. "Such a shame. The other mothers and I just finished the new costumes for the girls. We sewed the cutest little lights in the hem. They were going to flash with the music. I'd probably have to take in Yuki's now, the poor dear. She hasn't been eating." Her hair was tied in a motherly side plait that rocked slowly as she whispered, "Her best friend died."

"Akari?" asked Taka.

"No, goodness, no—her best friend. It's going to take some time." She poured tea in Taka's cup until it overflowed. "Where is that girl? Yuki-chan!"

As if on cue Yuki plodded down the stairs, disheveled, wearing grass-stained sweatpants and a shirt from an anime program that had ceased being kakkoii years ago. Her blonde hair was tied back, and bloodshot eyes made it clear that she hadn't been sleeping. Yuki's once cherubic face had narrowed, a casualty of her lingering depression. She looked nothing like the would-be idol Alice had seen on stage and bore only a passing resemblance to the girl who had once been her best friend. Alice pondered, which of them had changed more.

"Yuki, some friends came to see you. Isn't that nice?" Mrs. Okada knew an opportunity to get her daughter out of her room when she saw one. "Here, dear. Have a cookie."

Yuki looked at her mom like she was a wheel short of bicycle. "That's Taka, Akari's fan. Don't you recognize him from the handshake events?" Next, she considered Alice, who was rigid as a chair. "And I've seen you…somewhere. Don't you go to my school? What's your name?"

Alice was about to stammer her cousin's when Taka filled in the blank for her.

"Alice," he said, attempting to be helpful.

Yuki momentarily grappled with a bout of cognitive dissonance, then sunk within the crevice of the couch.

"Oh dear," replied her mom, who picked up their used napkins and rushed to the kitchen.

"Hajimemashite. Yoroshiku onegaishimasu." Alice attempted to play it off as a coincidence. She wondered if she could harvest Taka, or if that sort of retribution was frowned upon.

Yuki grabbed a cookie and ate it like a squirrel. "My friend's name was Alice."

"I'm so sorry. We heard. That must have been terrible. Were you close?"

"She wasn't like you. She hated idols. I never even told her about the Genki Girls." Yuki hard swallowed the cookie and reached for another.

"Why not?"

"Bad enough, everyone else was disappointed in me."

"But being in the Genki Girls is *meccha kakkoii*," objected Taka.

"Maybe to you. Everybody else thinks we're a joke."

"I don't think she would have laughed," said Alice. "I can tell you miss her. She couldn't have been like that."

"No one wants to see us," said Yuki. "Taka was the only fan we had. Everyone else was there out of morbid curiosity. At least we were good at something. Sorry if I came off a bit bitchy. It's not like three other girls at our school aren't named Alice. It must have been a trend."

"Gomen," Alice apologized, anyway.

Relieved not to be recognized, Alice asked, "You're going to perform again, right? I'd really like to see you guys again."

Yuki saw her mom peeking out from the kitchen, no doubt, to verify that she was managing to keep it together. "Do you know why my mom made me join the Genki Girls? I got picked on one too many times at school. She thought I'd make friends. Like people didn't judge me before."

Taka was shocked to hear his passion being talked about so negatively. He had placed the group on a pedestal, even above the convenience store egg salad sandwiches he loved. "Don't you realize being real is what made the Genki Girls great? None of your fans are perfect. Did you ever think that might be because we need each other, just a little bit?" He realized he had been a bit too honest and became quiet.

Yuki threw aside her cookie in favor of a celery stick. "Maybe too real. People say there's nothing wrong with being yourself, but perfect is what they buy."

There had been so many times Yuki had made herself unavailable, Alice couldn't help but feel a bit slighted to discover that she had been spending all her free time with girls who were twice as cool as she could ever be. "Were you and Akari friends?"

"It's hard to get close to someone who calls you the 'marshmallow girl.' She had an image for the group, and I wasn't it. I don't know if I hated her more for what she said or because it worked."

Taka assumed it would be safe to talk about the most apparent change. "Your hair color. That's different, too, right? Did Akari say anything?"

"What do you think? Everyone had to know she was the center. Her outfits always had little extra bows or a train. The hair wasn't even my idea, and now I'm stuck with it for a month. I look like a yolk."

"As if," said Alice. "You rock that look." She realized it was the same stupid expression she had stolen from an old movie they used to watch, an inside joke of sorts. Alice wondered if she'd made a fatal slip and became as quiet as Taka.

Mrs. Okada reappeared to refresh the senbei crackers, humming as she arranged them in the shape of a fan. Her daughter's close-lidded expression revealed how much she was annoyed by the habit. There was a soft ping, and the living room monitor indicated they were receiving a video call.

To everyone's surprise, the Genki Girls' producer appeared. Haruto had been in hiding since their last performance, and some wondered if he would ever re-emerge at all. Counter-intuitively, he seemed more relaxed than he had in quite some time. "Hello, Mrs. Okada," he said as if nothing of great importance had occurred since they had last spoken. "*Hisashiburi. Genki datta?*" He saw Yuki slouching on the couch, trying to appear invisible. "Yuki-chan. Just the person I hoped to catch."

"I'm fine. Why can't everyone just leave me alone?" She thought she had seen the last of Haruto and his musical sweatshop.

"Sorry, I didn't mean to disturb you. Glad you are doing well. It's been difficult, right? It's just…" Haruto tried to make it appear like he struggled with the request he was about to make. "There's something I have to ask you, but I'm not sure how. I've been calling everyone because Flavor Beat Records…well, they've asked us to record a single."

Mrs. Okada perked up, like a hamster hearing pellets placed in its cage, and clasped her hands in abject joy. "*Subarashii!* Did you hear that Yuki-chan?" She was annoyed to see her daughter playing with her phone.

"Yes, apparently there is more demand for us now than ever," continued Haruto, "by which I mean—there is some. But I don't know what to do. What would honor Akari?" As a producer, he was well-rehearsed in projecting his reservations so that he might appear more compassionate than manipulative.

"Giving up never honored anyone. I think Akari would want us to do this. Yuki-chan would be delighted."

"*Nandeyanen?*" said Yuki, realizing her attempt at disinterest had backfired.

"What kind of song?" Taka was enthusiastic at the prospect of seeing his favorite idol group re-form.

"I'm not sure yet, something that pays tribute to Akari, of course. That's the only reason I would do it." Haruto was aware there would not be a single unless he could gain the support of all the girls and their families. "Everyone knows how much I cared about Akari-chan." It occurred to him that his words could be misconstrued, so he rephrased himself. "I would never do anything that wasn't a tribute to everything she worked for."

"It seems you just got an exclusive," Taka said pointedly, to Alice.

"Yuki, forgive me. I didn't realize you had friends over." Haruto never liked to conduct business in mixed company. Taka, however, was practically an ancillary member of the group. He could be counted on to appear at even the most insignificant event, and Haruto often pulled him aside to gauge his opinion.

"Alice desu," she replied. "I have a small music blog—nothing important."

Haruto's face filled the screen as he sized her up. "Have you ever seen us perform?"

"I was at the last concert." She struggled to frame the experience in a positive light. "*Tanoshikatta. Very genki.*"

Haruto's producer instincts, as integral to him as his circulatory system, roused at the awareness that he might have discovered a solution to an unaddressed problem. "How old are you?"

"Sixteen. I was going to be seventeen—I mean, I'm going to be next April." She realized she sounded a bit flighty.

"And how tall are you?"

"Um, I'm not sure." Alice tried to estimate how much her measurements had changed. "About 167 centimeters." Now she felt like a complete idiot.

Haruto didn't seem phased by her lack of self-awareness, but Yuki's head tilted like a Border Collie. "That's good, very good. You would fit in nicely." He cleared his throat. "You might have heard we've had a recent opening? I wonder if you could take off your hat and mask, just for a moment?"

Alice was getting ready to offer an excuse when Yuki used the opportunity to knock it off her head and flick her mask from her ear. Mrs. Okada gasped, but Yuki's disappointment confirmed that Jack's handiwork had been sufficient.

"Yuki-chan! What are you doing?" Her mom handed Alice her things back. "I'm so sorry, she hasn't been herself lately."

Haruto, however, was pleased with what he saw. "No, that's fine. Yes, I can see it. Say…you wouldn't consider auditioning for the Genki Girls, would you Alice?"

"*Muri! Muri!*" she cried, indicating that such a thing was impossible. "I can't sing. I can't dance. I can't…idol."

As their number one fan, Taka wanted nothing more than to see the Genki Girls reunited. "When you're an idol, you don't want to be too good. People want to root for you to get better. That's what makes the Genki Girls better than those fake, holographic groups. Even when they try and program them to slowly improve, well, real people can get sick or catch a cold. Sometimes you might have a case of the Mondays."

"Taka-san is right." Haruto was a bit ashamed that he could not make his case half as well. "Say, Taka. You'd make a fine assistant producer. No pay, of course. Your first job is to bring her to rehearsal tomorrow."

"Tomorrow?" asked Mrs. Okada. "So soon?"

"Yes, I still need to write the lyrics, but that should take about half an hour, maybe forty-five minutes. I really want to give it my all this time."

Alice gave a full-second blink. It was about what she had expected after hearing them perform his song about curry bread.

"Okay then, I'll send you all the details. Yoroshiku onegaishimasu."

"We'll be there," said Mrs. Okada, not the least bit concerned that her daughter failed to share her enthusiasm.

"*Ojama shimashita.*" Haruto bowed several times, and the monitor returned to the family photo that had previously filled the screen.

"Well, that's great," said Yuki, sarcastically, "and by great, I mean awful. Maybe you'd like to sign me up for an intensive gum cleaning. Why don't we make sure all my shots are up to date?"

"Maybe you should ask your friends to stay for dinner?"

"No, thank you," replied Alice, "although I suddenly have the strangest craving for curry and doughnuts. We should go." She wasn't sure if she could stay any longer without making a heinous slip, though Taka appeared quite disappointed to have his opinion decided.

"Well, I thought that went pretty well," said Taka, when they were close enough to the train station to hear its departure melody. He stopped at a vending machine to buy a hot can of coffee, unaware of Alice's dilemma.

"I can't be in the Genki Girls," she cried. "Have you heard penguins mate? That's pretty much how I sound." Killing an argument through absurdity was always a sensible choice.

Taka assumed she was only modest. "It can't be too bad, or we wouldn't have any penguins."

"What does that even mean?"

He mistakenly threw his coffee can into the wrong recycling bin. "Don't look at me. You started it. And now we don't even have to bother visiting Saori. You can interview everyone at practice—incognito."

"I. Can't. Sing." Alice waited for the idea to sink into the udon noodle wrapped within his head.

"I think I know what this is about."

"I guarantee you don't."

Taka grabbed his hat back. "To you, music is something you listen to on the train or maybe when you're out for a run. You probably thought writing a blog would help get you a college scholarship, or something. Music isn't just a hobby for me. You're probably not even a fan."

"Well, I guess you caught me. I better go find another group that wears roller skates in their video."

Just then, Jack appeared behind Taka and tapped him on the shoulder. "Hey, shruggles. She'll do it." It pleased him to see Taka nearly jump out of his skin, from having been surprised.

"No, I won't," replied Alice, so loud a crow took flight behind her.

"Won't you excuse us for a moment." Jack pulled her aside. "You want to see Keiji, right? Well, this is the gig. I need you to find out why Saul cares about some two-bit idol group, 'cause I don't."

"Maybe I could sing life-affirming idol songs if I wasn't dead."

"Are you still sore about that?" Jack was already over it.

Alice growled as they walked back over to Taka. "Fine. Send me the info."

"Honto ni?" asked Taka. "Okay. Great. I'll see you there. Three p.m.?"

She let out a sigh of resignation. "Don't get too excited. Once they hear me sing, they're not going to want me anyway."

"See, if you were a serious fan, you'd know that's not a problem. Besides, all you have to do is fish around and see if anything looks out of place to you."

"Mission accomplished."

For the first time, Taka grinned. "Very funny. You know what I mean. See if anything smells weird."

She glanced over at Jack, who self-consciously leaned into his armpits.

As Taka turned to leave, he yelled, "You know…I guess this means I have a new favorite idol."

Alice pointed at herself. "They haven't even accepted me yet."

"Not you—Momoko. Wasn't she cute?"

Alice surmised that she had just been insulted. "Ja—later, Taka."

Jack's lighter may not have worked, but he liked how the grooves of its spark wheel felt when it rubbed his finger. "Nice kid. Terrible taste in music, but not entirely a bad cat."

"I can't join the Genki Girls, Jack. I'm dead. I'm the opposite of genki."

Jack shook his lighter as if he expected it to come to life after fifty years. "It'd make for a great Halloween single. Like I said, this is what we do. We get close to the thread. We learn, react, and fix, if necessary."

"Are you insane? My best friend, Yuki, is a member. I ended up at her house. I was so scared there's probably a stain on her couch."

"But she couldn't tell it was you, could she?"

"She was definitely weirded out."

Jack smirked. "Then, there you go. The hard part is to get people to look beyond what they see." He did a boomerang toss with one of his cards and caught it with the tips of his fingers. "See kiddo? No one's going to know it's you."

"When are you going to take me to see Keiji?" It seemed like the right time to press the issue.

"It's a long road to that taco shop, so you might as well relax and enjoy the ride." Jack's stomach growled.

Alice had an attention span commensurate to her age. If the thread were a game show, she was ready to solve the puzzle. "What else is there to know? It's Solak, and he's using enhancer to get inside people's heads. What am I missing?"

Jack had once been a simple sort of guy, but he found himself in a job where cause and effect played out in both the material and spiritual planes. "Any buzzard could figure that out, but what is this really about? Saul doesn't do small jobs. If he's here, it must be important." It wasn't the answer she wanted to hear. "Look, I get what your itch is, and it's not like I've been sitting on my thumbs. Did I mention I found your family's car?"

"Really? Can we go see it?"

"I don't know. Are you going to be a Genki Girl?"

Alice exhaled so forcefully that her hair grew back a bit. "I don't look like this because I'm planning to become a hostess."

"Well, okay then. Let's saddle up."

◆ ◆ ◆

The vehicles in the police impound lot had been seized for reasons as minor as illegal operating system modifications, all the way up to yakuza family associations. Sho's cleanly shaved head shimmered under the moonlight. Before him sat a family sedan caked in black mud, its mildewing interior appropriate for having been retrieved from the bottom of Sagami Bay, but it wasn't the right color. He glanced at his phone to confirm that he was still jamming the yard's cameras. It was easy enough to prevent the upload to the police department's cloud, but pausing the live feed was a project that had taken the family three years, and a considerable amount of bribes to achieve. A timer showed him how long he had until the security program would repair the error he had introduced. *Four minutes, plenty of time.*

There were more cars than Sho had expected, but fortunately, what he was looking for practically reached out and bit him. It was black, like all proper yakuza vehicles, and of the same make and model preferred by criminals and politicians, not that there was much of a difference. Sho popped the hood to see if the autonomous drive module had been disconnected. That was the easiest way to confirm a vehicle had an illicit past. Yakuza didn't like their cars telling them where they could and couldn't go, especially if the police triggered the automatic pullover feature. He ran the serial number and confirmed that it was registered to the Kurome-gumi, not that he had any doubt. It was definitely the car he had been in with Jiro the day their differences had been resolved. In contrast to the story he had provided Boss Mori, there were no visible signs that the vehicle had been attacked. He addressed his pistol at the rear window and validated his alibi.

Sho thought he saw something, a shadow in his peripheral vision, almost like a ghost. At two in the morning, the yard should be as quiet as a matsuri after the takoyaki vendors had all packed up and left. He squatted yankii style and waited. *A moon passing behind a cloud.* It was from a poem he repeated to himself whenever he was feeling edgy. The pistol had been muzzled, so it was unlikely he had been heard. There was only a gentle *crack* as the glass broke. Satisfied that his imagination had gotten the better of him, he straightened his legs only to discover that a similarly garish pair of shoes pointed back.

An antique hannya mask, the type you'd find on the wall of a bar or inked into the back of a made man, stared at him with its crooked gaze. Its weathered white paint was capped with two gold horns and fangs jutted from its leering grin. The wooden facade's savageness stood in stark contrast to its owner's well-tailored black suit and narrow tie. Sho did not need to ask what he was doing there. Only a yakuza associate would protect their identity, and if they were from a rival family or even his own, the welcome would prove no more agreeable. The mask's pinholes revealed nothing of its wearer's actual eye color, but Sho knew the appropriate response. The man had seen him alter the car's narrative, and such a re-write was punishable by death. Sho raised his gun, but immediately a backward grip was applied to his wrist as the man circled behind him. The nozzle rotated back towards his face, and Sho had no alternative but to allow his body to topple, or his wrist would be broken. A whistle of breath escaped from between the sharpened teeth of the grinning mask. Then, the pressure on his wrist released, and his opponent was gone. Something had alarmed them sufficiently enough to expedite their exit. Anything causing such a fearsome adversary to flee was worthy of consideration. Sho cleared the front gate just as the police department's computers resolved the errors he had introduced into its system.

"Did you hear something?" asked Alice. "I think I heard the gate."

"Eh, so what," said Jack. "It's not like anyone can see us." He passed through a service truck, not wasting his time with the pathways the police had made between the vehicles. "You know I have my own car back in Vegas. I don't get to use it much, but let me tell you, it's fast as hell, and it'll take you there if you don't watch your speed." He smiled at the memory. "We don't have to make them semi-autonomous like you do over here. Land of the free, as long as you're brave, don'tcha know."

"What's so great about driving? You don't even need a car. You can go wherever you want."

He looked at Alice like she had a cumquat growing out of her forehead. "Don't you get it? It's about freedom—the journey. Maybe I see a place that sells banana date shakes. Maybe I'll pull over? Maybe I won't."

Alice thought she saw her car, but it was too light a shade of blue. "Sounds boring."

"That's 'cause you're used to limited freedom, kid, and limited freedom isn't real freedom at all." Jack floated inside a dark-blue sedan, his head just outside of its roof. "Wait a second." He re-enacted a few moments with his hands. "I'm pretty sure this is it."

Alice's washed-out expression revealed that she had reached a similar conclusion. She drifted into the backseat, her last moments with Keiji a persistence of vision overlay. An iridescent tear ran down her face that cracked like plaster of Paris.

"I'm going to have to pop the hood to get at the black box. That should give us the information we're looking for, usually." Jack could tell that Alice wasn't listening, but he continued anyway, if for no other reason than to help distract her from her memories. "I'm going solid. I'll use an electromagnetic discharge to knock out the cameras, but we'll only have a minute before somebody notices. Well, they'll notice, but it should only take a couple seconds." He watched Alice's hand reach out towards where Keiji's eyes had last smiled back. "Um, you stay there. Don't break anything." He placed his fingertips together, and blue electricity forked between them. There was a crackling sound, and the yard lights flickered and subsequently failed. Jack solidified and popped open the hood of the car. There was a plastic access panel covering the black box, really nothing more than a fuse-sized solid-state drive. It was an aviation term adopted when lawsuits necessitated a removable form of stored memory for all autonomous vehicles. He placed the component into his pocket and gave it a quick pat.

Jack looked inside the car to find that Alice had already disappeared from the back seat. His head swiveled like a stick puppet until he spotted her standing beside the car parked next to them, a black sedan whose rear window had been shot out. She was fixated on its front bumper, which appeared to have struck something blue. Jack noticed a similar spot of color missing from the vehicle her family had shared. "I wonder why the police put these two vehicles together? Maybe we should get the box out of that one, as well." At that moment, the overhead floodlights came back to life, and Jack noticed a light within the office. Realizing he was on borrowed time, he passed his hand through the door, so he could release the car's hood. Unfortunately, not being material, his arm was unable to work the latch. "Bombsville. Only one thing to do." He allowed his arm to achieve materiality, and it was immediately sheered off by the door's structure. Jack bit his shoulder to stifle a scream, but it had fortunately started Alice awake. She floated to the front of the vehicle, briefly materialized, and opened the hood. Having already regenerated his arm, Jack fumbled in the general area where the other car's black box should be found. "It's gone. There's nothing there."

"Maybe the police took it?" Alice saw that an officer had appeared and was shining his flashlight around the yard.

"I don't know. It's just missing." The officer's beam reflected through a nearby car. Jack vanished as the flashlight passed through him. "Either the police or—"

"Or what?"

"This car is yakuza. No time for chitchat. Let's skat."

The officer's flashlight discovered the pair of vehicles with their hoods inexplicably wide-open like a pair of alligators' mouths. Alice and Jack were long gone, so the cameras simply resumed their normal function for the second time that night. The officer shook his head and slammed the hoods closed. The nightshift was getting a little too spooky for his taste.

Alice preferred not to admit that she had been rattled at seeing the last car in which she had ever ridden. "So, where do you get the energy for that EMP attack?"

"My last few harvests."

"You mean like…from the people?"

"That's right." Jack wiggled his fingers to confirm that their functionality had been restored. "So?"

"That was me!" she cried and stormed off.

"Hey. Where you going? It wasn't personal." He bent his elbow a couple more times. "You should be like, 'Thanks, Jack. I'm glad my energy didn't go to waste." He looked around the corner, but she was gone. "Great googly moogly,

I lost her again."

◆ ◆ ◆

Keiji's house hadn't changed, and that was more than a little reassuring. The box hedges had recently been trimmed, and his bicycle rested securely on its stand. Out of habit, Alice started for the front door, but then she remembered that death had its advantages and opted to pass through the outside wall, its frame, the interior gypsum board, and an anime banner that hung on the other side. With any luck, Alice hoped to find Keiji in his bed, snoring as he did in class. Though it was the middle of the night, his bed was empty, its sheets stretched as tight as a schooner's sails. His class ID rested upon his desk, and the leather bag he always carried hung eerily on his chair. The room was unnervingly static. Preserved.

Alice didn't care what Jack would do when he found out where she had gone, as being sore at him was her intended excuse. She hovered above Keiji's bed, and being emotionally spent, her consciousness regressed to a spiritual approximation of sleep. She dreamt that the accident had never happened and that they had spent the rest of the day in Hakone, riding the sightseeing boat around Lake Ashinoko. Stopping for tea and rice cakes, they gossiped about their teachers and shared dreams of a future that would never come. "I'm going to be an idol," she told Keiji. He laughed, but Alice didn't mind one bit. She thought it sounded just as crazy.

As they walked among the rows of cedar trees, Alice summoned the courage to hold Keiji's hand. She was too happy initially to notice, but then it occurred to her that his fingers were a bit too large, and the texture of his skin had changed to leather. Reflexively, Alice pulled back her hand and discovered they belonged to an impeccably dressed man wearing a white hannya mask. "Solak?" she stammered.

"In the flesh. Well, not really. More palatable than that oni manifestation, wouldn't you agree?" Expelling no effort to conceal her spiritual emanations, the girl had been quite easy to find.

"Where's Keiji? What have you done with him?"

"That boy? Nothing. You do know this is a dream, don't you?"

"You know that mask is female?" Alice wasn't pleased to have such a pleasant fantasy so unceremoniously destroyed.

Solak was equally insulted at her attempt to usurp his role as the teacher. "Do you even know what it stands for?" Her silence pleased him. "Jealousy." He enjoyed the theater and was in no mood to be instructed.

"I know who you're jealous of—Jack."

Solak folded his arms and laughed. "You haven't been paying attention. If anything, he wants to be like me. I can do whatever I want. He has to be told, but I choose. Now, which is worthy of jealously?"

"Can you choose to be good?"

Solak recoiled at the suggestion. "I am good. Jack is the one who abbreviated your life, and now he's using your love for that boy as a bridal to lead you around Honshu. But I can help you find your lost love…it would be my pleasure."

Before Alice could register her response, Solak tilted his head and vanished, leaving her standing alone in the avenue of cedar trees, their falling pine needles suspended on their journey to the ground. Alice searched for Keiji, hoping that he would return, but the dream had already started to fracture, leaving only the dark silence of a spiritually anabolic state. She had never felt more alone.

CHAPTER SEVEN:
WATERLOGGED

The windows dancing in their frames stirred Alice from her dream. On Keiji's bookshelf, an anime figure was brought to life by the seismic waves that passed through Tōkyō. Through the window, she could see Keiji's parents, standing outside with the rest of the neighborhood, in their robes. For a moment, Alice panicked until she remembered that she couldn't be held accountable if she wasn't visible. Still, there was one more mistake she planned on making.

The house where Alice had lived was only a couple of blocks further up the road. So, she silently thanked Keiji's unknowing parents for their hospitality and continued on her ill-advised journey through memory lane. She gazed back only to see if Jack lurked within the shadows, as he certainly seemed more interested in curbing her freedom than the shadow demon. It was reassuring that her kindergarten teacher's house looked the same, and across from it, where the old lady who taught her how to tie her shoes still lived. Alice turned the corner and was surprised to discover a for-sale sign fastened to the gate of her house. Her mother's roses had been trimmed so that the notice could be more visible, and their window frames had been touched up with fresh paint. Alice clutched her angel pendent, the last memento from her former life. *They're selling our house?*

Where am I supposed to go?

◆ ◆ ◆

George spun the holographic spreadsheet to view it from another angle, but his conclusions remained the same. There were clearly unaccounted fluctuations in the inventory levels of N-43. While not so much that it could affect production, apparently enough to trigger a call from the PMDA. "That's right, I'm Suzuki-san, well, his replacement," he said to the investigator. "But don't worry, I've got all of his files. I'm sure it's nothing. I'll just need some time to go through everything. Hai. Hai. *Wakarimasu. Kashikomarimashita. Shitsureitashimasu.*"

Accounting for resources at home was also becoming a concern. His wife spent every yen that wasn't glued down to enable their daughter's self-esteem to "flourish." They had suffered a miscarriage early in their marriage, and the effects had persisted long after she had given birth to Yuki. Increased pressure at work had manifested in the form of stomach issues and a doughnut pillow for his chair. The pharmaceutical industry was tightly regulated, and middle managers always made a suitable sacrifice. He checked his schedule and noted that there was still enough time to squeeze in a site visit before his next meeting.

The raw materials warehouse was a frigid, sterile place not far from the cleanroom where the crystallization vessels were located. If one was not careful, you could get run over by an autonomous forklift taking supplies to the insertion bots over in manufacturing. Breathing personnel were considered secondary to maintaining a tight production schedule. George recognized the warehouse supervisor from his trademark yellow hardhat blazoned with the blue Tokuji-Tech logo. "Yagi-san. A word, please."

Yagi's attention remained fixed on an AGV forklift in the middle of deftly retrieving a barrel. He logged the transaction before looking up to see who had distracted him from directing his delicate ballet of autonomous co-workers. "Okada-san. I didn't see you at our daughters' last concert."

"Mrs. Okada recorded it for me. I'll watch it—someday. Maybe. Say, I'm here because I need to ask you about something." A sweeping AGV stopped short of his toes before identifying the obstacle and spinning away. "I was going through the inventory spreadsheets, and well, I noticed a little problem."

"That's strange. Let me take a look." Yagi gave a gesture to his tablet, and the information from George's screen appeared on his own. He grunted as he thought. "*Naruhodo*. I see what you mean. N-43. Barely measurable, though, a fraction of a percent."

"It's an ongoing problem. Any idea why?"

Yagi removed his hardhat and wiped the sweat off his forehead with the back of his sleeve. "Well, those barrels are usually stacked on the corners. We've been having problems with the forklifts bumping into them. They seem to be having a disagreement with the sweeping bots over who has the right of way."

"I see," replied George. "The thing is Suzuki-san never mentioned a problem, so I'm trying to get a handle on all the variables. I wouldn't want people to think I'm not thorough. Perhaps temperature fluctuations in the warehouse?"

"Doubtful. Humidity and climate conditions are closely monitored, but you already know that. Give me a second. I'll check the numbers myself." Yagi rarely saw George's predecessor and hated problems being brought to his perfectly controlled environment. "Hmm. It's relatively minimal. I'm not sure I'll be able to account for this before I send my End of Day summary."

"I see…it's just that I received this call…"

Yagi noticed that George was not wearing his company-issued smartwatch, but rather the type of antique timepiece his grandfather had favored. His love of mechanical objects got the better of him for a moment. "Say, that's a nice watch you have there. A real windup!"

George's hand moved to instinctively hide it before his pride relented. He had stopped wearing his smartwatch after it prompted a colonoscopy that seemed to be company-sanctioned intimidation. George removed it from his wrist so Yagi could have a better look. "Yes, well. No GPS. No camera or heart monitor."

"So, what is it for? Fashion?" Yagi raised it to his ear and listened to the watch softly tick, like a feather flicking. People often laughed when they visited the warehouse only to find him talking with his autonomous assistants. Here, however, was a device that spoke to him on an emotional level. The whirring gears reminded him of being a child, resting against his mother's chest, the sound of her heart during a thunderstorm. Any object that was not inert, he concluded, could not be completely dead. If it contained energy and purpose, perhaps it was alive; the breath of life wound into its springs by its creator. "Sugoi!"

"You wear a watch like that," observed George, "to monitor your world, not so that it can monitor you." He placed it on Yagi's wrist. "Are you sure there isn't some way we can justify this discrepancy before the end of the day?"

At first, Yagi appeared conflicted, but then he stammered, "Ano...I don't know, Okada-san." As his own smartwatch found its way into a nearby drawer, he felt an unexpected wave of relief. It felt rebellious to be so unencumbered. "Well, we did have an earthquake this morning," he said, forming his rationale. "Between that and the problems with the forklifts...I suppose it's probably just breakage?" He held the watch to his ear. "That's the right column, I think. Breakage."

George's eyes gleamed from the warehouse lights as he patted Yagi on the back. "Sounds reasonable to me. Keep up the good work." He had fulfilled a manager's most important duty.

As he left, Yagi shouted, "Oh—and thank your wife for the cookies."

◆ ◆ ◆

"You'd think they would have put up some decent street signs in the last two hundred years." Jack took out the smartphone that Clement had forced him to buy, an obnoxious reminder that even he was not immune to technology's barnacles. Still, its ability to locate even the most obscure back alley had caused him to, begrudgingly, add it to his arsenal of tools. Jack shook his beads. "If you weren't such a crumb, maybe I wouldn't need this mechanical abomination." They whirred back indignantly. "Well, that wasn't very polite."

Lined in the alley was a menagerie of small booths, their tables draped with wire harnesses and aftermarket car parts. Punkish toughs sifted through the components like junkyard pickers. Black-eyed yakuza slithered through the crowd, bumping against each other in the narrow passageway. Jack paused at one of the booths to ask a question but was pointed to an adjoining table.

Behind the counter, feet crossed, was a handsome blasian gentleman who wore the type of newsboy cap Jack used to see in London, back when he had a hundred and fifty years less on him. It had been ages since he had seen anyone wear a bow tie, especially someone only around twenty-five. "Hey there, are you, Matthew?"

Beneath a tweed brim, a pair of soulful eyes looked up. "The jazz bar is down the street. We don't serve martinis, and I'm not interested in being Sammy to your Dino."

Jack had not expected to hear such archaic references tossed about so cavalierly, that was his job. "Am I dealing with a hipster or a smart-ass?"

"A bit of both," replied Matthew, "but I'm guessing you're not here for my personality."

"The dark web says..." Matthew's fingers muffled the rest of Jack's words.

"First, I like to know a little bit about my clients. That will determine the nature of our association." A metal arm projected a grid over Jack's face. Matthew's horn-rimmed glasses reflected the scrolling database, his eyes bouncing behind them as he read. "Hmm, well, that's interesting."

"What?"

"Should I be surprised you don't exist?" He flashed a UV flashlight into Jack's eyes. "Your whites have never been inked, but if you've served time, you definitely would have been registered." Matthew wasn't sure which box to place Jack into, and that made him cautious. "Don't worry, I serve people from all the offices, but it'll cost you a bit more. If you've been erased, that means you can pay, am I right?" He waited for Jack to confirm his assumptions. "I'm Matthew." He slid a scanner in front of his customer. "That's what you feed to get more."

Jack held his smartphone over the card reader. "Crypto, fine?"

"Top five only. No shitcoins. Matthew generated a temporary key to begin the transfer. "So, where did you get the box?

"From a car that was in an accident. I'm trying to find out what happened."

"Friend of yours?" asked Matthew. "Enemy?" He used his fingertips to insert the storage device into his reader, but all it returned was an error message. "Seems to be damaged." He retrieved some cleaning swabs. "I'll see what I can do, but no refunds. You're paying for my time, not the results."

"Might be a little waterlogged," said Jack. "The car took a dip. So, what else do you sell here?"

"A bit of everything." Matthew inserted the small SSD box back into his reader. "This isn't my bread and butter. I'm better known for pharmaceutical solutions, but I don't do lethal. That's not my bag, so don't ask." Backward kanji projected across his glasses, and a toothy smile spread across his face. "Well, there you have it."

"What?" asked Jack. "What do we have?"

"This car went off a bridge."

"Yes, I know." Jack watched the counter draining decimals off his wallet. "But why did it go off the bridge?"

Matthew's voice lacked any sense of inflection. "To avoid the school children." He reached to unplug the black box, but Jack grabbed his arm.

"School children? I don't remember any kids." Having been under the water, he couldn't be entirely sure, but it wasn't like they could have left the accident scene that fast.

Matthew leaned back and locked his fingers behind his head. "AMH."

"AMH? What's that?"

"Autonomous Moral Hierarchy." Someone approached the booth, and Matthew shooed them away. "Scat. The drift booth is next door."

"Interactive moral what?" He had begun to wish he had brought Alice, who was a bit more up to date on her tech, but he wasn't sure what secrets the box held. If he discovered her father had been responsible, he had already resolved that she would never find out.

"Autonomous vehicles have to make judgments too, right? Sometimes there isn't time to switch to manual. It's like their inner-morality. The manufactures don't like to talk about it. No, they don't."

"What kind of judgments? They're machines, right? It's not like they have values..."

"Uh, yeah, they do, but they're different. Integrity for a machine means consistency and reliability. Like...how they respond to their programmed values."

"That can't be right. Small kiddos wear those yellow jackets. No way I'd miss that."

"Doesn't matter," replied Matthew. "The car thought they were there. That's integrity. It had to decide who was more important, the people in the car or the kids on the road. I think we know who it chose."

Jack didn't like machines even before they could think, but Autonomous Moral Hierarchy, that was every nightmare he'd ever had. "People can't even make the right call. How are machines supposed to?"

Matthew was more than happy to pontificate. The longer he talked, the more he was paid. "When a corporate lawyer faces a jury on behalf of an autonomous they're responsible for, it had better have made the life or death decision most people would agree with. You know how they determine what an autonomous will choose, don't you?"

Jack tried to think about the material world as little as possible and the mechanical one, even less so.

"Focus groups. They run mock cases based on potential hierarchies. I mean...they can't win them all, but they don't have to, only enough to be profitable. The AV's AMH adjusts its values based on where it is at the time—through its navigation system. You know, small changes based on how jurors in that region would react."

Jack snatched a stool from the booth next door. "How often do those things fail?"

Matthew rubbed his narrow chin. "Damn near never. They're set at the factory. Hard-wired. Most over-the-air updates are for things like the entertainment systems or suspension profiles."

Jack stopped the transfer of tokens. "Thanks for your time. I think you've given me enough nightmare fuel for one day."

"Sure. Hey, if you or your family ever need a box wiped clean or your autonomous drive system disabled—I'm your man. Drones too!"

◆ ◆ ◆

Momoko clutched her panda purse, a childish affection that resembled a gutted stuffed animal. It suited her adopted style, a movement the fashion blogs referred to as *baka-kawaii*, a trend that took cute to an aggressive, even hostile, level. It had started as a rebellious parody of Japanese society's love of kawaii culture, but the very people it sought to criticize had appropriated it. The irony was lost on Momoko with her three-dimensionally printed cartoon character shoes and makeup that gave her the porcelain sheen of a Victorian doll. Her fashion efforts had never been intended as a knowing commentary, but rather a calculated attempt to solidify her position as the cutest member of the Genki Girls. "Did you feel the earthquake?" She gave an exaggerated shudder, to underline how traumatized she had been by the experience.

Saori was not the least bit amused by such posturing, but she had long ago given up protesting Momoko's feigned immaturity. "I don't get out of bed for anything less than a five. Make that a five-point-eight."

"Saori-chan is so brave," squealed Momoko. She squeezed her panda purse until its large eyes appeared they might pop.

Ms. Ito interrupted their discussion to hand out the lyrics to their new single. Her patience was measured by the amount of sleep she had the night before, divided by the number of hours she had to spend with the Genki Girls.

"Is this the Akari tribute song?" asked Saori, wiping a smudge from her glasses. Her lips moved as she read the lyrics. "Did Haruto-sensei actually rhyme death and dress? Honto ni?"

"Just learn the lyrics," snapped Ms. Ito. "Maybe you should work on your delivery?" She gave Saori a piercing glance and returned to where Haruto nursed his coffee. He had a bandage on his forehead from where a picture frame had fallen on him during the earthquake.

"Okay, girls," shouted Haruto. "This one is for Akari so—"

"Pretend we liked her?" asked Yuki.

"Too soon. We record on Wednesday, so start memorizing those lyrics. Relax. I'm not going to change them this time...much." Haruto noticed everyone's eyes had drifted towards the rehearsal studio door.

Alice had assumed idols always appeared the way they did on variety shows and in music videos, so she was dressed to give a concert. It hadn't occurred to her that practice meant sweats and t-shirts. Apparently, she wasn't the only one able to transform per the occasion, albeit with help from wardrobe and makeup. Alice had trouble even placing the girls she had met with Taka. Of course, Yuki was easy to spot, though her bleached hair was hidden under a baseball cap. "Alice desu. Yoroshiku ne." When no one responded, she singled out the Genki Girls equally mystified producer. "You asked me to join you for rehearsal?"

Haruto racked his brain as he struggled to remember when he could have met her and if shochu had been involved. He had recently placed a notice on their landing page for the vacancy Akari had created. "Ano…where did you get that outfit? That's one of ours, isn't it?"

It hadn't occurred to Alice that she had metamorphed into the one she had seen at their gig in Akihabara. "I made this myself. You don't remember? I was at Yuki's house." Everyone looked over at Yuki, who seemed embarrassed to be unwillingly dragged into Alice's story.

Fortunately, it was enough to jog Haruto's memory. "Oh—right. When I called Yuki the other day. I remember now." He leaned over to Ms. Ito and whispered, "Cancel the auditions. She'll do."

"Don't you want to see if she can sing?" She was well aware of his tendency to settle. It was one of his defining characteristics.

"I'm a producer. I have instincts and pitch software." His smile countered her cocked-eye skepticism. "She's even got the outfit. Go ahead and put her in the number nine position, and let's see what happens." He cued the music, and the girls began to sing.

If I captured a sacred crane,
Do you know what my wish would be?
I'd wish to be alive with you,
And not dead eternally.

Alice thought *warui*, but she was there as a harvester and not an art critic. If the thread was keeping her from Keiji, she was determined to see it through and as fast as possible. Learning why Solak was involved in Akari's death was more important than whether the Genki Girls' next single was going to be any good.

Clap. Clap. Clap. From the back of the hall, sarcastic applause echoed. Sho's heavily tinted glasses certainly made him look like a producer, though his cleanly shaved head gave away his actual vocation. The similarity was appropriate, seeing as both industries treated people as commodities.

"Okay, girls," Haruto announced. "That's all for today. Tomorrow. Same time. Good job." He nervously hurried them out of the room to deny his visitor the opportunity to embarrass him any further.

Alice probably stared at their guest a bit too long, and they locked eyes before she could feign disinterest. He had the same intensity she remembered seeing in his sister, though that was to be expected under those circumstances. She showed herself out before anyone could object.

Sho paced back and forth like a caged puma. "That was craptastic. I'm actually glad Akari wasn't alive to see that. She might have died from embarrassment."

Haruto clutched a microphone stand, both to hold himself up and to have a potential implement to use for his defense. "Sho-san, you know how dear Akari was to me. Can't you see how hard I'm working to honor her memory?"

"And who exactly was that last girl? The one who didn't know it was Casual Friday?"

"Who—Alice? She replaced…" Haruto realized some questions were better left unanswered, so he pivoted back to Sho's first objection. "About the song, if you just tell me what you don't like…"

"Why weren't you at the funeral? Guilt?"

Haruto tried to hide behind his music stand but awkwardly knocked it over. "I wasn't in town." He began to organize the chairs nervously. "I wanted to be there. Family obligations."

Sho grabbed the lyrics Haruto had been shuffling nervously. The e-sheet sensed the warmth from his fingers and activated. "I'm a ghostly butterfly, soaring towards the Tōkyō sky?"

"It's poetic, don't you think? Maybe it's just not something you would under…" Haruto bit his tongue, not about to insult the gangster.

"What's that? You don't think I know poetry? Is that what you were about to say?"

"No, I would never say that. You wouldn't be here if you didn't love—the arts."

If Sho hadn't joined the Kurome-gumi, he would have liked to study Japanese Literature, one of many dreams that died when he took his place in the criminal underground. "There's a lot you don't know. Maybe I should open a hole in that head to help get it all in there?" He turned one of the chairs backward and sat, his arms resting on its back. "Our mom worked in the water trade; our dad was a street thug. I wasn't going to let that happen to Akari. Have you ever done that? Made a promise with every ounce of your being?" He picked up the chair and flung it across the room. It made a terrific sound as it shattered a mirror. "She was the one who was going to make it." Sho collapsed the chairs that Haruto had been stacking with a strong kick. "Akari was going to be better. Better than me."

"Sho, it was an accident. Look, I didn't always agree with your methods, but the way you watched out for her…well, no one ever did anything like that for me." Seeing that the gangster had settled, he added, "She thought the Genki Girls was her idea—just like you wanted. Akari was living her dream. What could be better than that? There was nothing else you could have done."

Sho picked up one of the many condolence cards that had fallen on the floor and placed it back where Haruto had made a small display. "Lucky for you." His words were dark, but like a thundercloud that had passed. The group remained his sister's last remaining legacy, the only positive contribution his family had ever made. He didn't know enough about music to offer any improvements, but he was a specialist at applying pressure to those who could.

"The song—it's a tribute to her life. When people remember how great she was, they won't care how she died. Trust me, I've had lots of artists…" Haruto cut himself short, not wanting to underline his record. "If it wasn't for Akari, I might not have ever become a producer. I want this song to be great. Maybe as much as you do."

Sho was the one who had compelled Haruto to release a box of pigeons on the day he quit. It had helped erase any bridges to Haruto's previous life. When the young executive initially wavered, Sho used a small drone to fire rubber bullets at him whenever he left the building. It was his way of shepherding him onto the correct career path. "I might have been a bit rough, you being a civilian and all."

"I still can't walk around corners." Haruto had long dreamt about forming his own group, but it had taken bodily threat to make it a reality. "I flinch every time I see a delivery drone. I soiled myself at the summer fireworks display." Seeing that Sho still appeared unsympathetic, he added, "I was on a date."

Sho helped himself to a poster of his sister, which he tucked away in his jacket. "So, where are they?"

"What?"

"The pills. You were there when she died, but they were gone when the police showed up. I need to know if it was an accident."

Bug-eyed, and sweaty, Haruto stammered, "Sho-san. You should have told me. I gave them to a friend, but…he died. Don't you know where they came from?"

"He died?" Sho was glad the police weren't able to trace the pills, but he had assumed Haruto was still holding. For a moment, it seemed he might erupt, but he was too emotionally spent to follow through. Instead, he collapsed on a chair. "They came from me. I supplied them."

"You what?" Haruto was glad he had been too busy to help Akari that day. It didn't make sense that someone of Sho's rank would be involved in such a petty transaction.

"One of my brothers died on my watch. They made me a pill pusher because that's how they found me. I need to know if that was the only lesson they were trying to teach me."

"Sho-san, if there's anything I can do…"

"You can start with that stupid song."

It wasn't the answer the young producer had expected. He was artistically bruised, but his concerns were primarily practical. "It's our next single. Once it's released, I can pay you back. Isn't that what you want?" Haruto had negotiated with people worse than yakuza before, namely lawyers. "I haven't forgotten your investment. You don't have to worry."

"Don't lay down a single track until you hear from me. I'm going to take care of it." He hated the way his sister was being talked about online and in the media. More than that, he felt responsible. "She deserved better."

◆ ◆ ◆

Above Boss Mori's desk floated the avatar of his saiko-komon, a hannya mask. In the yakuza world, it was common to protect your identity during video calls, and even civilians used holographic avatars that resembled popular animated characters or emojis. Since the crackdown, it had become an essential precaution if one was to thwart the police's facial recognition software. The devilish mask was easily recognizable to anyone within the syndicate, and the kumichō's loyal advisor always used the horned avatar whenever he called. Through a series of mysterious successes, his status had risen, second only to Boss Mori.

"I followed Sho to the police impound lot." The mask listed to the left as if cocking one of its wooden ears.

"So was our car there?" Boss Mori was most expectant of the answer. Jiro had been his wakagashira, his first lieutenant. He had hoped he would serve as his point man for his plans to expand their distribution of enhancer into Kyushu. Sho, on the other hand, was the family's prime drone and surveillance expert, but his story smelled like rotting horse mackerel. Sending disputing family members on a job always carried the risk that one would use it as an opportunity to secure an alibi. It had been tried often enough that returning alone ensured the survivor would be held in suspicion.

The holographic mask danced. "All of our cars are clean. They could impound our entire fleet and discover little more than our taste in enka music."

The large ball of ice rolled in Boss Mori's whiskey glass, for no other reason than that he liked the sound. "So was it a drone? Was the back window blown out?"

"Oh, it was blown out."

An alcohol-infused sigh escaped Boss Mori's thick lips. "And I assumed Sho was lying."

The hannya mask hovered within a whisper of the kumichō's nose. "Sho went to the impound lot and shot out the rear window himself. It would appear that he sees the truth as being quite malleable." The mask bounced as if made of rubber.

The glass slammed against the desk. "What?"

"He most certainly killed Jiro and tried to cover it up. At least he had the decency to wait until the job was completed. Quite the professional."

Boss Mori's antique chair creaked as he leaned forward, his nostrils opening and closing like factory vents. His instincts tended towards anger, which is why his saiko-komon's primary job was to persuade him to pursue more practical solutions. "What would you recommend? Zetsuenjō? Something more permanent?"

The mask rocked like a metronome, but its maniacal grin held firmly in place. "There are other factors to consider. Right now, we have to play the media carefully if we are to get the most advantageous response for our other endeavors. No one has even heard of Sho, but if they discovered he was the brother of that insipid idol…her death would be seen as merely a yakuza matter. Uncertainty drives the market, and this family's future depends on timing. Best to keep Sho both loyal and alive. For now, that is. For now."

Boss Mori was well aware that the family had reached a critical juncture. The last thing they needed was a bunch of *marubo-dekka* poking around their office. "Housewives took enhancer like aspirin before that bitch's death was in the news. Then that record exec smashed through an office window. The older vices were safer, even syabu. I don't understand how killing our own business makes us richer."

The mask spun three times to the left, and three times back again. "Before I arrived, the clan's finances had shriveled like grapes under an Okinawan sun. Now we have a long-term strategy, but if we waver, we will lose both the present and the future. You're like a man complaining his feast is too small. The dip in demand is temporary and necessary for us to increase our position."

"I have a *yokozuna* appetite." Boss Mori pointed a fat finger at the levitating hannya mask. "If we can't maintain our revenue today, how will we buy a large enough stake tomorrow?"

The mask rotated so that the carve marks on its back became visible.

"Business is like a roller-coaster. The dips are the most enjoyable part. What is worthless today is tomorrow's treasure, and it's best found where nobody else is looking."

◆ ◆ ◆

"Scary, right?" asked Saori, seeing Alice trying to listen through the door to the practice room.

"Who?"

"Akari's brother. I didn't think we'd see him around anymore." Saori knew from his leather trench coat and dark glasses that he was trouble, but not dull. The group's rules about dating had kept her libido in check, at least up to this point, but she wasn't dead.

"What do you think they're talking about?" asked Alice.

"Probably about money," replied Yuki. "Let's just say we get sent outside a lot."

Momoko twirled one of her twintails. "Let's go for ice cream. What do you think, Yuki-chan?"

Yuki searched for an excuse to decline until, conveniently, her mother's car pulled up. "Sorry, my ride is here. Mata ne."

Alice didn't like the feeling that she was unintentionally creeping people out. That was Jack's job. "Yeah, I'm busy, too, I guess."

Saori watched Alice grab Taka and walk him around the corner. "Only a Genki Girl for a day, and she's already locked up Akari's old fan club."

Momoko squeezed her stuffed animal purse. "Taka-kun is kind of cute." She had thought so before but wondered if it was only because he was one of the few guys outside the school she saw regularly. "They're probably just friends. Right?"

"So, how'd it go?" asked Taka, wondering why he was being pushed.

Alice considered it a minor triumph to have even passed herself off as someone who could sing. "Well, they want me to join."

"*Suge!* Did you talk to Saori?"

"Some. Well, she did ask me to get out of the way." There hadn't really been an opportunity that wouldn't have felt forced. "Sorry. I'm not very good at this."

"You're doing fine," he said supportively. "It's probably better to take things slow. Earn their trust. Maybe someone knows who gave Akari those pills." Taka saw Jack leaning against a streetlight, shuffling his cards. "Jaa, you're cousin is here. You did great. Really. Anyway—see you."

Like a teenager caught lying about a sleepover, Alice knew Jack was there to ask how it had gone. "Hi, Jack. Mad?"

"Annoyed. Perturbed. Why do you even bother to try and give me the slip? I'm like a root vegetable. I always turn up." The power to tell jokes had apparently not been retained from his time in the Catskills.

Alice had already formulated her excuse for ditching him at the police yard. "I had some things to take care of. You don't always want to babysit me, right?"

"Look. I'm trying to keep you from getting hurt. There are people out there, and I use that term in the loosest form of the word, that would put you in a shredder and make metaphysical confetti out of you." Jack felt the telltale sensation of spinning on his wrist. "Harvest in twenty-two minutes. We'll talk about this later."

"Where is it?"

"Somewhere near Ueno Station."

"No problem," said Alice. "I'm all about that area."

Jack wasn't about to tell her that he had been there when the train station had opened in 1883. "Just don't go running off anymore. I don't need the paperwork."

◆ ◆ ◆

"Excuse me, sir. Do you have a reservation?" The maître d' could tell that the man was yakuza from the sunglasses intended to obscure his tattooed eyes. Paired with a carefully shaved head, it was a tipoff that he wasn't the sort of patron his establishment wanted to accommodate. He pretended to search the seating chart for a table, preferably at another restaurant.

"I don't need reservations. I'm here to meet someone…Takuboku Yamamoto."

The maître d's left eyebrow parted their hair. "I'm sorry. Do you actually know Yamamoto-sensei? The poet and national treasure?"

"If I didn't know any better, I'd say you were questioning my character. Why doesn't anyone think I can appreciate poetry? Is there something about me that looks stupid?"

"No, sir, not at all. It's just that you don't seem—how should I say this…"

Though he didn't grow up in a house that emphasized an appreciation of the arts, Sho had been making up for the lost time. He once waited two hours in line for a Hokusai exhibit, only to miss the person he was supposed to be trailing. "Don't bother to tell me he's not here. I've got a little business proposal for him. Trust me. He'll want to hear this."

The maître d' searched the room for his manager, intent on settling the matter without involving such an esteemed regular. He scrunched his lips. "I'm sorry…is he expecting you?"

Sho could only conclude that he was not being taken seriously. "Here's the deal. Either you take me to meet my new friend or tomorrow, I show up with some of mine."

The maître d' found Sho's counter-proposal quite compelling. "Right this way, sir."

Japan's greatest poet, a distinguished-looking gentleman known to often enjoy the Emperor's company, sat in a booth enjoying the attentions of a beautiful, and markedly younger, female companion. He was busy sharing a story with her about a prank he had played on a famous kabuki actor involving fugu sashimi. Sho hovered nearby, pretending to participate in their conversation. He laughed along, before sliding next to them in their leather booth. Awkward intimidation was his trademark.

Yamamoto met so many people, he wondered if Sho might be an acquaintance, or perhaps an autograph seeker with, particularly bad manners. "I'm sorry, can I help you with something?"

Initially, Sho gave the impression of a star-struck fan, as he tried to recall one of Yamamoto's poems. "Our life is the light of the moon passing behind a cloud at dawn."

The poet often heard people quote his verse back to him, but never by someone who looked like they enjoyed mixing drinking games with violence.

"I can't remember the next line. It's about dew or something. How's it go?" Sho gripped the poet laureate's shoulder like an old friend.

"I'm very flattered, but as you can see—"

"How's it go?" Sho's tone was set like concrete.

Yamamoto gulped, wanting to satisfy his unconventional guest if only to be rid of him. "It is as lasting as morningtide's tears or a waning crescent."

Sho mugged. "See, that wasn't so hard." He winked at Yamamoto's date and threw some stationary on the table.

Yamamoto looked around the dining room, but the service staff had made themselves notably absent. "Oh, you want—I see. Whom shall I make this out to?"

"It's not for an autograph. I need you to write one of those famous compositions of yours for my sister, you know, like a tribute. She recently passed away."

The poet did not wish to seem rude or abrupt, but it felt like he was on one of those shows where famous people were placed in humorous situations. "I'm quite sorry for your loss, but I'm afraid all requests go through my agent." He patted his pockets, searching for a card.

"That won't be necessary," replied Sho. "A nice artsy guy like you shouldn't associate with those types anyway. Am I right? Why don't the both of us go for a little walk?"

Sho moved his hand to the scruff of Yamamoto's neck and dragged him, toes down, over to where the restaurant kept its fish tanks. "That poem is so beautiful. I must have read it like a thousand times while waiting on jobs. There's a lot of downtime in my line of work. Do you like lobster?" He palmed Yamamoto's head and shoved it a millimeter short of the chilly water where his diner had originated.

Yamamoto's voice assumed a touch of reverb from the walls of the tank. "How did you find me?"

"Nothing to it. I hacked the dining app you used to make your reservation. Thanks for letting me know the exact time and place of where you'd be. So what do you think of my proposal?"

"Well, as much as I would like to..."

Sho thrust Yamamoto under the water before he had time to prepare himself. It was bitingly cold.

Returning to the surface, the poet coughed saltwater from the cilia within his lungs. "What do you want from me?"

"I need you to write some lyrics."

"I'm not a lyricist. Don't you know who I am?"

Sho was offended that Yamamoto doubted his enthusiasm for his work, so he dunked him again. He was always handing out copies of the poet's collected works to bewildered colleagues. This time he held him under a bit longer.

"What type of lyrics?" Yamamoto gasped when he finally came back up.

"It's for an idol song."

The poet was horrified. "Not even if there were piranhas."

It was an admirable display of resistance, but Sho had already taken notice of another tank that held enormous red crabs brought in from Hokkaido. The poet's heels drew wet lines upon the floor as Sho introduced him to his discovery. The cries from Yamamoto were so loud that the rest of the restaurant could not possibly ignore them, but the level of courage required to intervene was lacking. As he held the poet underneath the water, Sho displayed his appreciation for his work. "Yet the night is not overcome by the stars." It occurred to him that the source of his admiration could not hear him, so he pulled him back up again. On the other side of the restaurant, the manager spoke urgently to someone on his phone, no doubt the police. "More people hear even the stupidest pop song than a work of genius like that." The poet did not seem impressed, so Sho dunked his head back under again. "I'm not saying it's fair. Baseball shouldn't be more popular than kabuki, but here we are."

"Cold…so cold," Yamamoto cried, a pincer attached to his left ear. Sho's palm increased its pressure, as he readied to dunk him again. "Wait. Wait! Does it have to have my name on it?"

Sho took a moment to consider his counter-proposal. "I suppose not, but I want it to be good—like that moon poem."

The award-winning poet gazed deeply into the tank, aware that he had failed for the last twenty years to match his most shining moment of creative glory. Every time Yamamoto sat to commit his thoughts to paper, he felt like an imposter, a fraud. The king crabs gazed up at him in giddy anticipation of his return, so he did the only thing he could. He lied. "Of course. Better even. Much better. I'll have it done by next week. Good?"

Sho dunked his idol so hard against the bottom of the tank that the poet's forehead butted one of the spiny shells. "I guess we're still negotiating."

◆ ◆ ◆

"This place is disgusting." Alice tried to pick up the stem of a rotting banana, but her fingers passed right through it. There was a black fungus in the process of colonizing some pineapple cakes that appeared ready to walk away. At least she couldn't smell anything in her current form.

Jack peaked his head through the refrigerator door, but it was empty save for a couple bottles of Oolong tea and a partially used container of miso paste. "Why is there never any birthday cake? One in three hundred and sixty-five odds, and nothing!"

On the stove was a pot of ramen that had boiled over, only to be abandoned. It gave Alice the heebie-jeebies, not unlike Jack. "Why are we here again?"

"You know the odds are actually better than that. People usually get a few days out of a cake. So, statistically speaking—"

"Jack!"

Though Jack might have trouble seeing how everything connected, he was generally there when the action went down. Furthermore, he was usually early. "Let's see...what should I tell you? When you're on a thread, don't go off appearances. You never know how it's all going to fit together. What we do is more like jazz than science."

"And this song is over when exactly?"

"A day—ten years. Who knows? And the next one might not even be in Japan. I was in Greenland for a year, but that might have been Clement giving me a time out." Jack passed through a cabinet filled with second-hand plastic dishes and the paper-thin wall behind it. "Bloody hell. Come and take a look at this mess."

"I'm not waiting ten years to see Keiji. Hear me, Jack? Not waiting." Alice passed through the other side and was similarly taken aback at what she saw.

Sprawled upon the floor, toes to the sky, was what appeared to be a corpse. A line of drool had dried itself upon a face that was open-mouthed and gaunt.

Their VR headset softly pulsed indigo blue, and he wore it like a condemned man might a blindfold. For a moment, it appeared that they were too late, but then the body twitched as if from a cramp.

Jack leaned down and smelled the man's breath. "Extreme dehydration. I've seen this plenty of times in Vegas, but usually because of the drink prices on the Strip." He chortled but realized Alice might not be in on his joke. "Tough crowd."

"Why is he twitching?"

"Something to do with sodium levels. Gets all out of whack in the blood." With more than two centuries of experience, Jack had done the equivalent of a medical residency. In the last hundred years alone, he had delivered three babies and performed CPR seventeen times.

"Why doesn't he drink something?" Alice reached for a bottle of water, but Jack stopped her short.

"Whoa, now hold on, sister. His marker has been called. You want to create a loose thread? I don't need that kind of help."

Alice had not achieved the tradesman's indifference that Jack wore like a cheap suit. "Are you sure you're human, or are you pretending to be that too?"

"Hiro and I worked the opium dens in Hong Kong; different century—same story. This guy punched his own card." Alice's look of disapproval came as a surprise. "What? I didn't tell him to flush his life away."

"You're a real humanitarian."

"Yeah, well, it's a living." Thinking some helpful factoids might alter the tenor of the conversation, he dipped into his vast reservoir of experience. "He probably sweated for a couple days before his kidneys started to fail." Jack squatted next to the body. "He was probably already exhausted when he plugged in. A long day at work, maybe—"

"Jack!"

"Yeah?"

"Maybe you can sit here and watch him die, but I can't."

Jack read his beads. "It's only a few minutes more." For him, it wasn't so much a lack of compassion, as a deeper understanding of the universe. Like a simpleton who had spent a hundred years observing a chess match between immortals, he had gradually gained an appreciation for the game. "All right. If it'll make you feel better, why don't you go in and see what's so bee's knees that he abandoned some perfectly good ramen?"

Alice looked for a spare VR headset. "Maybe, I will."

Jack grimaced at her inexperience. "Hey, earth to Alice. You don't need equipment. Just dive in."

The virtual rabbit-hole, the dehydrating man had fallen down, was a baroque world of noblemen, ladies, and courtesans. Alice appeared underneath a Foscari Arch and was overwhelmed by Venetian surroundings that would have warmed the heart of Bacchus. Concealed by their lavish ornamental masks, she could not determine which of the guests were avatars and which were merely NPCs. Powdered guests perused a massive cinquecento table that overflowed with floral and gastronomical delights. They raised their goblets beneath statues of Mars and Neptune, symbols of Venetian power, and a party to their whispered secrets. Finding a neglected papier-mâché mask, Alice held it over her face to obscure her identity.

"Can I have this dance?" asked a man in an Arlecchino mask. It had an enormous red boil that stood out from its forehead. His trousers and coat were a patchwork of colorful fabric, their boundaries delineated by intricate patterns of gold embroidery.

Alice was both surprised and embarrassed. It was a question that she had never had posed before. "Sorry, but I'm looking for someone."

"He's over there," they replied. "The only other person not speaking Italian. This is all quite realistic, isn't it? You should see the lancet arches of the arcade. They're quite stunning."

"Solak?"

The lower half of the mask opened, like a puppet, when he talked. "You are much sharper than your partner, but so is that fruit bowl over there. I thought we might continue our conversation. Shall we?" His thin, almost feminine, fingers pulled her onto the gleaming ballroom floor.

Alice's first thought was that she ought to resist, but the banquet's opulence made it seem safe not to object. "I don't know. Are you going to try and kill me?"

"Why would I do that? I'm already in control. Do you like my mask?" he asked. "I couldn't wear my usual one. Not culturally appropriate, but did you see my walking stick?" The flickering candlelight revealed its figural handle was crafted in the shape of a hannya mask. "I used to visit the Venetian Empire quite a bit back in the day, but of course, I was on the other side. Youthful indiscretion."

Alice had many questions for the shadow demon but remained concerned for her target. In his virtual state, however, he seemed to be having a most wonderful time.

"Where is Jack? He didn't care, am I right?" Solak took her silence as confirmation. "He's always been that way. Me? Well, I'm here to save him. Do you know from whom?"

This time she filled in his thoughts. "Jack?"

"Well, my oh my. They did find a bright one. Not that they get a terrible amount of say in the matter.

Alice saw her mark twitch. "Is he going to be okay?"

"Only if we work together."

The thought had never occurred to her. "You want me to help you stop Jack?"

"Isn't that why you're here? You could have sat outside and watched. You're not like him, are you? He isn't in a hurry to help anyone, is he?"

Alice was undoubtedly aware that Jack wasn't in much of a rush to reunite her with Keiji. He didn't seem to care about her feelings at all. Before she could dwell on the fact, her target regained his composure and began to laugh. "Isn't he supposed to die? It's his turn, isn't it?"

Even with the mask, Solak's disappointment was unmistakable. "That's Jack talking, isn't it? He hasn't told you that there might be some discretion in such matters? If there wasn't, why exactly would you be here?"

Alice was not sure whom to believe, but she was surprised at the extent to which his conclusion resonated. "You killed Jack's partner, didn't you? And what about Akari? You killed her, too, right?"

Solak laughed, which triggered someone dancing next to them to join in. "Is that what happened? Are you sure? How did you get here, I wonder?"

Alice was aware of the role Jack had played in her transition to a less-material lifestyle. She supposed that she ought to be grateful for having been given a position where she could at least cross back and forth, but it was true that he had ruined everything. Her future plans had all been dashed, and that did not exactly place Jack in the hero role.

The demon shadow sensed that he had successfully planted a seed of uncertainty. "Consider this. If he has so little regard for whether people live or die, how can he possibly be on the right side? I preserve life, and that is why he resists me. I'm not afraid to push back, and from your appearance, I would say, neither are you. The only question is…whose perspective are you going to choose?" He led her off the dance floor to the table where her target made merry with some well-endowed, courtesans. "I've been absolutely begging this man to eat and drink. No matter what I offer him, he simply will not listen."

Alice watched her target grab one of the ladies and pull her onto his lap. She squealed with delight, even as he twitched. "You're not giving him real food. Of course, he's dying."

The man looked into her eyes, as if he had become aware of his condition and convulsed violently. The well-coiffed ladies, who had, previously, been so enthralled by him, shrieked and retreated as if what he had might be catching. Horsehair screeched, as violin bows stuttered to a sudden stop. The only sound was the silver rattling as the man's knees knocked hard against the table. Already his ghost pushed forward from his body, halfway liberated. A strong wind blew through the gallery arches and whipped Alice's hair as she assumed the ghostly persona of a maiko cut short in her prime. The cords that hung from her obi animated like serpents and peals of lighting filled the ballroom. If Jack hadn't quite convinced Alice of the value of her role, the shadow demon had yet to sway her otherwise. Seeing that she had resolved to fulfill her duty, Solak slammed his walking staff into the ground, and the lagoon underneath the marble floor was revealed. Water seeped from between the seams of the tiles and crawled up their feet. The festive mood immediately turned to panic as the water pressed around their ankles.

Alice's last memories of life were triggered, and she began to hyperventilate. Her target became lost in a riot of satin, powder, and feathers. Pushing aside her memories, she placed her hand on the water's surface and froze it solid. The man's ghost had wholly broken free of his mortal coil and was already headed for the door.

"I'm not an agent of chaos, but of purpose," yelled Solak. "We will come to an understanding."

At that instant, the courtyard doors blew open, and in its threshold stood Jack, manifest in the vestments of his calling, his robes snapping like the black sails of a haunted galleon. His fingers drew a toroidal vortex, a vacuum of necrosis, and the man's soul stretched like the truth in a courtroom. Jack was more annoyed than relieved, as his palm collected his prize. He looked over at Alice, slack-jawed and immobile, and asked, "How'd he even go runner?"

"What? Didn't you see..." she looked for Solak, but only his Arlecchino mask remained on the marble floor. Alice felt guilty over having become so clouded. "I'm sorry. I'm still trying to figure this all out." It wasn't fair that she was expected to perform like a veteran. "Why were you so late? Any idea who he was?"

Jack transformed back to his, supposedly, suave persona. From the inside pocket of his smoking jacket, he produced a gray pill and a security card. It played a brief profile animation of how the man had appeared before they found him. Upon it, in holographic ink, was printed, "Custodial Services: Flavor Beat Records."

◆ ◆ ◆

The robe Haruto grabbed had been taken from a hotel where he stayed on a business trip to Osaka. He groggily stumbled to the front door in its matching slippers. *Is it really one in the morning? If they're not here to kill me, I'm definitely going to kill them.* Outside he discovered a yellow envelope resting lazily upon his doormat. Haruto assumed that the record company must have sent a messenger to hand-deliver the Genki Girls' contract. It seemed rather old fashioned, as digital conveyance had long been the norm. The envelope had no address, but inside he found some tea-stained stationery. The kanji strokes were wildly drawn, and the characters blotchy, like an ink wash painting. At the top of the paper was a title, "Remembrance." It occurred to Haruto that this was not a contract, but lyrics:

Winter came with the rushing of wind,

Casting shadows…over all of our sins.
Hush the trumpets, the things that we said.
Still, kill the quiet…silence amplifies our regret.

Long after you have gone,
I will remember.
Long after your voice is quiet,
I will still hear you.
Though your face may fade,
I still see you.
Though feelings may change,
I love you.

When Haruto was at Flavor Beat, he had become quite familiar with the lyricists they employed. As he read on, he realized that this was artistry beyond what was even accessible to a commercial operation. Financial leverage was not enough to entice artists capable of such craftsmanship. The lyrics went right to the line of what was artistically appropriate for a commercial endeavor. No matter how remarkable a Shakespearean sonnet, set to music, it would be commercial death. Haruto had assumed that the entertainment industry had long ago rendered his heart inert. Still, as tears ran down his face, it was apparent that such an organ yet existed and was not without its vulnerabilities. His relationship with Akari was not unlike the path of their careers, a wave of lost potential. Though she had made him feel trapped, he also accepted that her success was his salvation. Haruto reached the end of the lyrics and searched for a name or signature that might reveal the author of such timeless lamentations. Curiously, it was unsigned, but within the stationary, there was an embossment. It was the insignia of the Kurome-gumi.

CHAPTER EIGHT:

REMEMBRANCE

Saori's glasses shuffled over the new lyrics like a typewriter carriage. Around her, sniffles of approval indicated that Akari's legacy had inexplicably been preserved. "Alright," demanded Saori. "Who wrote these?"

Haruto had earned his place as the patron saint of e-paper for his habit of wirelessly updating revisions ad nauseam. It was the reason they were all hesitant to commit any new lyrics to memory, which only contributed to their unprepared reputation. Once again, without apology, he had relegated the previous version to the digital trashcan.

"What makes you think I didn't write them?" The inference hurt more than his talent merited. For a moment, Haruto had even considered affixing his name to the file, but the document's apparent connection to organized crime gave him pause.

"In one of our songs, you compared love to a crane game." Saori had begun to adopt Akari's acidic observational skills. It was the only example she had of how a center should behave.

Haruto had always been proud of "Crane of Love." The aspiring lyricist could hardly believe what he was hearing. "It's a metaphor. You know…sometimes, love is like a prize that passes through your fingers." He looked to Ms. Ito for validation, but she was busy taking a phone away from one of the girls, who had been texting. "I thought it was good."

"It's a simile. Guess how I can tell you didn't write this?" Saori shook the e-sheet until the words scrambled. She had been studying for her exit exams, determined not to fail again. Momoko's nose was making a sound like sandpaper. "What are you blathering about?"

Momoko pulled a tissue from her panda purse. "Akari would have loved this."

"Definitely not," said Yuki, blotting the lyrics before the paper short-circuited. "She doesn't have any lines."

A couple of the girls giggled into their hands, relieved that somebody had deigned to make light of the one many felt least worthy of such a tribute.

Saori gazed sternly over her red frames. Having finished parsing the lyrics, she yelled, "Haruto-sensei! A word, please."

Haruto winced and leaned in so their conversation wouldn't spread. "Yes, Saori?"

"I'm the center now, right?"

"You know you are."

She waited to see if Haruto would pick up on the source of her irritation. "Why do I have fewer lines than Yuki? She's my second."

"It's an arrangement issue. I promise you'll be very prominent in the choreography. Isn't that right, Ms. Ito?" A closed-lidded glance indicated that she was not entirely receptive to the idea.

Saori had heard such a line fed to Akari many times before. "I even have the same number of lines as Momoko. What does she contribute other than twintails?"

"Would you like one of her lines?"

She ran her finger over the lyrics. "Momoko's part follows mine. I can't echo myself. I'd look stupid."

Yuki's mom would definitely notice if he trimmed her part, leaving sparing with Saori as the preferable option. "I'll give you the first line of the third verse, but remember. We're doing this for Akari."

Saori knew there were a lot of reasons, but Akari was the least of them.

◆ ◆ ◆

George never gave much thought to his daughter's musical development. He only cared about her education and assumed that his wife would ensure he'd be the last to know if there ever were a problem. While the long hours he worked appeared sacrificial, he was happy to avoid the drama of child-rearing. It was not possible, however, to ignore the quarterly company-wide meeting about inter-departmental synergy. Idol lyrics were veritable philosophical treatises compared to the bureaucratic double-speak he had to memorize, not that he cared about either.

Fujisawa, sat next to him as a matter of protocol, but also because George would endure his ramblings. "You know what this is about, don't you, Okada-san? The stock is getting hammered. People are hacking our drug, but it's the doctors who should be more careful. Don't you think?" He waited for George to grunt in agreement. "Anyway, the exchanges are afraid the government might get involved. Imagine if they found out the PMDA has already been here. It's not like we can control what happens after our drug leaves the factory, but if the stock goes any lower...I'll be retiring when they carry me out the front door."

Izumi turned around to share her best librarian, shush. She had been jotting down every word their president uttered and was one of the few people not in a catatonic state. His pronouncements were like manna from heaven that she could creatively interpret to her ends.

For George, zoning out during meetings was an art form, especially ones that took place in the company's auditorium. Their president seemed quite worked up over the threat of governmental interference and the need for everyone to conduct business to the highest ethical standards. All George could think of was that if they could package the droning of his voice, they could produce an entirely new category of sleep aid. "Did he just say to avoid VR clubs and pachinko parlors?"

Izumi increased the potency of her glare by a few more degrees.

Fujisawa continued with his diatribe anyway. "Appearances, Okada-san. Appearances. They want to keep this whole enhancer crisis at arm's length. That's what they're calling it, you know—a crisis. My apologies to Mrs. Okada, but we can't sponsor your daughter's little group anymore. That girl who died…"

"*Wakaru.*" George knew his wife wouldn't like the news, but it was understandable, and he was personally indifferent.

"I don't need to tell you, Neuroko XR is built on the same properties that make its predecessor an excellent street drug."

"There's no way the Ministry of Health won't approve Neuroko XR. We'll be fine."

"Maybe, but until then, everything gets done by the book. Speaking of which, did you figure out the discrepancies in the warehouse?"

"Earthquakes," George whispered. "Nothing to worry about."

"Okay, that explains this month, but what about last month, and the one before? Maybe I should look into the matter, myself. Nothing personal. Just remember if you ever become boss, CYA pays your way." It finally occurred to him what was different about George. "Hey…where's your company smartwatch?"

"Lost it."

"No problem. I'll order you another one. Of course, it'll have to come out of your next check." Fujisawa sensed an air of resistance to the idea. "What if I need to find you?"

Unable to hear the rest of their conversation, Izumi lifted her eye patch a bit to afford it a bit of fresh air. The chairman had concluded the meeting, and the sad music of groaning middle-aged managers standing had replaced his melodious voice. While she was disappointed to see the meeting end, her spirit renewed at the thought that there were personnel matters to be addressed.

◆ ◆ ◆

Alice slid open the shoji doors, and a soft breeze carried the smell of spring inside the house. Jack used a straw rake to steady himself as he retrieved a leaf that had drifted inside. The old house was not the type of place Alice would have expected to find a cosmopolitan guy like Jack hanging his trilby hat. "So why here? I mean…you can go anywhere, right? Isn't Vegas more your style. I imagine a place with lots of neon, red velvet curtains, mirrored ceilings…"

"Cute. For your information, I've got digs in France, Singapore, Iceland, and a few I can't even remember. Even had one confiscated because I forgot to pay the taxes, but whoever goes to Dubuque?" There had been one property, in particular, that he had been unable to buy, regardless of money. The issue was hereditary land rights, but he was a patient man. Jack used his rake to draw lines in the gravel meant to symbolize flowing water. Not having enough pebbles to cover the ground, he quickly scraped dirt. Frustrated, Jack let the handle drop. "You think I don't have other places to go? Believe me, I got places to go, but Clement gets his robe all in a bunch if I stray too far from the thread. Maybe he caught me enjoying a pants-free month once. Who can say?" He knocked some dust off a lantern. "You want some advice? Don't get too tied down. People think death is about losing your life, but it's really about losing attachments. What exactly is it that you think we do? We collect the remains because, in the end, that's all that matters."

"Well, I think you like it here."

What the drafty old house lacked in comfort, it more than made up for in charm. She had found her attitude changing one afternoon as she sat with the screen doors open, watching the dragonflies, and eating watermelon they had chilled in the stream.

Jack had his reasons for taking care of Hiro's old villa. "Here's a piece of free advice. When nowhere is home, everywhere is."

Alice assumed he was trying to justify his contributions to her current situation. "There's a pine needle on your gravel."

"So how did practice go? Can you sing yet or still making babies cry?" He picked up the needle and placed it in his pocket.

"No wonder everybody likes you. You always have so many nice things to say." She tossed back a couple of small pebbles that had found their way inside the house.

"I'm yanking your chain. It's how I pass eternity." He blew his nose into his handkerchief. "C'mon, an idol, is basically a geisha with less class and fewer drinking games."

"So why don't you do it?"

"Who says I haven't? Besides, you're doing great." He left it unsaid whether or not he was joking. "Anyhoo, that's not why you're there, is it? You're hip to what the kids are into, and maybe you'll learn something."

"I already know how it feels to be humiliated. I'm a teenager."

Jack had worked the Opium Wars thread back when he was partnered with Hiro. It dragged on for years before they figured out it had less to do with a scented poppy and was more about national pride. "Saul doesn't do trainer threads, and a double-helix is what it feels like we have going on here."

"Double-helix?"

"Two threads, both attached, but...well, that makes about as much sense as killer whales and koala bears."

"I'm sorry, what?"

"One's not a whale, and the other's not a bear." Seeing Alice didn't follow, he added, "Although, if you think about it, koalas are killers—but whales aren't koalas."

"Is part of your job to give me a headache?"

"I'm only saying it's your first time at-bat, and you don't take a new skier on a black diamond run. So let's just stick to the enhancer thread for now. No need to get tangled up."

"We're not already?"

Jack felt like he was picking a scab rather than facilitating closure. "I don't know if I should be telling you this..."

"What?"

"It's probably nothing. I went and had the box read. You know, the one from the car where we met."

"How could I forget?" Sensing stressful news Alice looked around for a chair, but not wanting to sit seiza-style she chose to brace herself mentally. "What did it say?"

At first, Jack picked at a couple of bits of gravel that seemed too large. "Do you remember any pedestrians on the bridge? It said there were kids on the road."

"There was something wrong with the car...my dad was yelling. Keiji and I were playing a game. The glasses were in AR mode so I could see a little."

"Anything yellow? School uniforms?"

Alice's eyes brightened. "Keiji might have. He was facing forward."

Jack found her determination more annoying than plucky. "Now hold on there, pilgrim. I wasn't born yesterday, or even two hundred years of yesterdays ago. Maybe he did see something, but I can look into that myself. Stag."

"Will you listen to me, Jack? Yuki was my best friend, and she didn't even recognize me—much. I'm the only one who would know what to ask him."

"Nopity. Nope. Nope. Personal jobs are risky. This one, I'm doing solo."

"That's not fair, Jack. I'm doing my part...humiliating myself every day."

The samurai armor's menpō had a gap, through which the wearer's eyes once gazed. Jack addressed it like an old friend. "Is this kid a gas, or what?"

Alice kicked Jack's gravel to underline her frustration. "I lost everything. Why can't you understand that? Not just what I had, but everything I ever will."

"Listen, kiddo. A partnership is as much about protecting each other from what we want, as denying others from taking it. The enhancer thread takes priority. If it leads back into your mess, so be it."

"What happened to 'it's a double-helix,' and all that?"

"I was spitballing—like with the koala whales."

"You know where my dad worked, don't you? Tokuji-Tech." She flicked a piece of gravel at him. "Double-helix."

◆ ◆ ◆

"What do you mean they won't support our girls anymore?" Yuki's mom fumed. "Well, first thing tomorrow, I'm going to your work and give Fujisawa-san a piece of my mind. He's not aware that they're about to make a recording. Soon they'll be begging to sponsor us."

"Okaasan, haven't you seen the news? Because of this enhancer epidemic, Tokuji-Tech has a bulls-eye painted on it."

"How is that your fault?"

"They're going with a local baseball team instead. It can't be helped." The last thing he wanted was for his wife to think that there was any hope of procuring additional funds.

"This isn't fair to Yuki. She's only just starting to make friends." Mrs. Okada put enough pressure on the onigiri to produce a starchy diamond.

"The company doesn't need the attention right now. It's a very delicate time. Promise me you're not going to say anything."

"They should punish the doctors and the pharmacists, not our Yuki-chan." Her face was as still as an icy glass of milk.

George presented her with the package of yatsuhashi he had procured as a peace offering. "It's just for a while. Wait until it all blows over, then I'll talk to Fujisawa-san."

"This wouldn't happen if you were the boss."

◆ ◆ ◆

Sho itched the back of his head, a surefire indication that he was being followed. Others in the family spoke of a tingling sensation or an unseen pressure, but he always felt the urge to scratch the indentation where his cleanly shaven head joined his spine. Sho coolly glanced back and discovered that a black car was matching his pace. Its lights blinked as it rolled beside him.

"Hisashiburi, Sho-san. Shall we?" Boss Mori permeated the back seat, his state of mind indecipherable from behind smoky glasses, jaw solid as a giant bluefin tuna.

Sho failed to recognize the driver but understood that disabling any auto-drive restrictions necessitated his presence. Unable to manufacture a justifiable reason to be excused from the impromptu meeting, Sho eased into the front passenger seat across from his kumichō.

"I haven't seen you around the office."

The door sealed with a fatalistic *whoosh*. Because all the safety cues had been silenced, only the sound of rolling tires could be heard as they eased into traffic.

"Mōshiwake arimasen. Recently, I have had many family matters," said Sho. It occurred to him that the Kurome-gumi was the only *family* Boss Mori would acknowledge. "But everything is settled now. Please accept my apology for my absence and any inconvenience."

Boss Mori noticed that Sho's fifth finger still had not been repaired. "There is something I want you to see." The security camera feed from the police impound lot appeared on a screen between them.

Sho did not need to acknowledge what was displayed. He waited to see if the driver twitched, knowing that if the feed contained any unfavorable evidence, that is from where the threat would originate. Unable to resist a glance, he happened to catch when the drone revealed that the car's rear window had been blown out. Sho cautioned himself to appear indifferent.

"This morning, we were able to verify your account of what happened the day we lost Jiro," said Boss Mori. "Normally, you are the one we call upon for such things, but under the circumstances..."

"*Wakarimashita*. I wish there was something I could have done, but it was over before I could react. My sincerest apologies."

Boss Mori tried his best not to display any indication that he had been lied to once again. Sho would receive his comeuppance, but not until it served the needs of the family. He trusted his advisor, implicitly, but his patience was not without limits. "There is some business to which we must attend, a threat to our supply chain. Someone who is in the way of our plans."

"Is this a cleaning job?"

"Yes." Ginza's flashy boutiques blurred outside, where much of Boss Mori's ill-gotten gains were lavished on a mistress with a particularly nasty purse habit. "We're doing some personnel changes, but see that it is done Hokkaido style." The expression was understood to mean a "natural" demise, or not at all.

Sho's phone vibrated, as it received the file. "I'll use a synthetic adrenaline charge." It was a relief to discover he was not the intended target.

"Dissolving needle?"

"Within the hairline. No trace. People will assume it was a heart attack. Stress from work. There will be cameras, I assume?"

Boss Mori's whiskey-infused breath blurred the air between them. "We have someone on the inside. Do it within the time window, and they won't be an issue. Don't let me down this time, Sho-san."

The car glided to a stop, and the door rose, a signal that Sho should excuse himself. It seemed suspicious that Boss Mori had gone to the trouble of acknowledging his innocence, but perhaps that was because he had been acting aloof, as of late. As Boss Mori's car silently rolled away, Sho stayed locked in his bow until long after the car had vanished from sight. Only then did he unfold his phone so that he could better review the file of the person he had been assigned to eliminate. It was a picture of a middle-aged salaryman. Their place of work was Tokuji-Tech Pharmaceuticals.

◆ ◆ ◆

Taka sat outside the rehearsal space like Hachikō, waiting for his master's return. Akari's death had changed the polarity of his existence, but he still longed to be approximal to what remained of her world. Alice's arrival had been a fortuitous opportunity, though he felt a bit guilty for using her to slipstream inside.

Haruto saw Taka sitting beside their rehearsal door, and couldn't help but be reminded of how far he had come since that not too distant age. That was a time when he was driven by a pure love of music; before he realized that the industry was a sausage factory run by cannibals. The only thing Haruto had gotten from the Genki Girls was a series of headaches and not the friendly sort you get from eating ice cream. Seeing Taka waiting so expectantly made him wonder if he could make at least one person's day a little better, even if it not his own. "Hey, Taka. If you're not too busy holding up that street light, maybe you can come inside and give me a hand? I could use some help with one of the room dividers."

At first, the request didn't register. Haruto looked so different, wearing a smile, that he almost didn't recognize him. The Genki Girls' producer usually appeared sallow and pained, bearing the weight of a group that was both unpopular and seemingly cursed. "Hai." Taka gave a short bow and followed him inside, where all his dreams achieved fruition.

Momoko saw Taka lifting a heavy divider and shouted, "Taka-kun! How helpful you are!" Unlike a couple of the other girls, she wasn't surprised to see him hanging out in the rehearsal room.

"Ohayo," he replied, not able to look her directly in the eye.

"Say hello to panda-chan!" she demanded.

"Eh?"

She thrust her purse at him, close enough that its black and white molted fur blurred.

Taka waved half-heartedly. "*Konnichiwa.*"

This seemed to satisfy Momoko, who held the panda up to her ear so she could pretend to hear its whispered approval. "Panda-chan likes Taka-kun."

Unsure how to respond to what was a childish game wrapped in a courtship ritual, Taka noticed Alice, who had arrived looking like she had missed the last train. He had been waiting all morning to catch up with her, but Haruto cut short the reunion.

"Taka, give me a hand with one more of these, and I'll let you stay and watch. Deal?" Haruto was eager to create enough space that the girls could face each other while they sang. Their new song utilized harmony, a first for a group known to sing in the mono-style favored by the talent deprived. "It might be nice to have a fan's opinion."

"Hai," Taka replied. "*Mondainai.*"

As they rehearsed, Alice was irritated to discover that she still couldn't stay on pitch. *Powers of inconvenience—na?*

"You can't sing because it's not necessary," said Jack, in a voice only she could hear. "You're a pop idol. If it were a thread where you were an opera singer, you'd be a straight-up nightingale. I once made some serious bread when I was playing a pro golf thread. Otherwise, sand trap city."

"You're seriously annoying. You know that?" Alice had forgotten that she could be heard, even when Jack couldn't. Seeing Momoko bury her head, in a melodrama of self-pity, she added, "Not you, Momoko. Someone else annoying I was thinking about."

Unable to concentrate over the distraction, Saori fumed. "Maybe this is some kind of joke to you, but some of us are trying to practice. We have this thing called a record deal, and you haven't been here long enough to forget where the door is at."

Before Alice could construct a defense, Haruto cued Ms. Ito to pause the music. His disappointment over his life choices had returned. "Personal conversations," he said, "need to be saved for after we learn the song."

Alice bowed deeply, "Of course, Haruto-sensei. *Gomenasai.*"

"Who does she think she is? She can't even sing." Saori was well aware that Alice had appeared just in time to enjoy the fruits of their labor. She wondered if the record label might have brought Alice into the group because her career had reached its end. The timing seemed a little too convenient. "No way is she natural—genetic mods. I'd bet my life on it. She's faker than Momoko."

Yuki felt unsettled by Alice for her own reasons, but she still couldn't verbalize what was intangibly wrong about their newest member. "She's strange, all right. Like that squid candy, I bought the other day. Just not right."

Having failed her last college placement test, Saori could ill afford the competition. Should the Genki Girls ever have the opportunity to appear in a commercial, only the center would be guaranteed a speaking part. "They better not put her in my spot. No way are they going to parachute in my replacement." Then, Saori became contemplative. "Who am I kidding? We're all disposable. They call us idols, but a better name would be expendables. We're like wrapping paper...appreciated until we're not needed anymore. Then we're torn off and thrown aside."

Haruto slapped Taka on the back. "Taka-san. Thank you for all your help today. *Otsukaresama deshita.*"

Taka radiated the awkward vibe of a boy dragged into a lingerie department by their mom. Being able to hang around his idols should have been the fulfillment of a dream. He had not anticipated that seeing them bickering, and blowing their noses, would strip the veneer right off his fantasy. It was jarring to discover that the Genki Girls were almost as fabricated as the holographic idols they had been created to usurp. The reality was not unlike dancing, great in theory but awkward in practice. "No problem, Haruto-sensei. Tanoshikatta."

One thing Haruto had learned during his record company days was that an artist's core fans were its fuel. They could either take your project to the next level or burn it to the ground. Back in the day, he had a practice of inviting the most rabid supporters of whatever group he was promoting, to the record company to feign interest in their feedback and channel their support. It usually didn't require more than a pizza and a screening of an unreleased video to get them on board. The Genki Girls had only one fan, but that meant Haruto coveted his support one hundred percent. "Say, I had an idea. It might be nice to have a hologram of Akari that the girls could interact with when they perform the tribute song."

Taka had always protected Akari's image, writing Haruto emails when he didn't like something. For a while, Haruto wondered if it was Akari who was berating him. "Eh?" Taka wasn't sure if such a plan was in bad taste or a stroke of genius. "But aren't the Genki Girls supposed to be real idols? The other groups are the illusion. Right?"

It was true that Haruto had created the Genki Girls as counter-programming to the computer-generated singers the industry had been pushing. Creating new songs with artists who had already passed away had become a well-established genre. Algorithms could predict, within three percent accuracy, how an artist would have performed a song in life. Haruto wasn't suggesting going that route, only that a hologram of Akari be included in the choreography. "I thought about putting pictures on a screen, but that didn't seem like enough. It's only one song. What do you think?" Haruto was not very skilled at appearing naïve.

"Ano—I don't know…" Vulnerable to the temptation of access the young producer provided, Taka struggled to object. It was his first formal lesson in compromising his principals, courtesy of the music industry. Unfortunately, appreciating the girls from afar was no longer an option. The only way forward was to become a part of their struggles and successes.

At their sparsely attended performances, Haruto had plenty of time to observe Taka, and there was something he wanted to ask him. "You used to film our shows, didn't you? It's okay. You're not in trouble. I was only thinking…maybe some of that footage might be useful?"

"So that the girls could see how they perform?"

"No, although maybe we should do some of that too. What I meant was, we can use it to make the hologram of Akari. You know…for our little plan."

Having spent most of his free time in Akihabara's otaku shops and cafes, Taka was not equipped to identify the well-practiced manipulations of an entertainment professional. Still, he was able to muster a healthy dose of conviction about the one idol that could never be dragged down in his eyes. "I have a condition."

Being agreeable, only to push back when necessary, was a skill Haruto had used often during his Flavor Beat Records days. "Anything. What is it?"

"I should be the one to put it together." It was not like Taka to make even a modest request. He was a bit embarrassed to realize that his recording of their performances had not gone unnoticed. "It wouldn't be right for anyone else to do it. It has to be me."

"Wakaru, Taka-san." Haruto had seen Taka's fan website, and it was more professional than their official one. The idea of saving money by not hiring a professional service was most appealing. "You can do that? Sugoi."

Taka had once tried on a leather jacket in a thrift store. He felt the same sense of bravado talking about the one area in which he was particularly confident. "I could program every car in Tōkyō to show up at the next Genki Girls performance if I wanted…"

"Really?" pondered Haruto. He took a moment to consider the legality of Taka's hypothetical proposition.

Taka justified to himself that at least it was an opportunity to protect Akari's memory. Any infighting at practice didn't seem to rise to the level of malicious intent. For the first time, he began to wonder if maybe Akari had been her own worst enemy. Perhaps, he was only protecting a fabricated memory of an idol that never really existed.

Aware that it would appear more natural, Alice changed with the others and emerged from the dressing room to find Taka patiently waiting. He seemed uneasy as if he no longer felt comfortable in his clothes.

"So did you see anything?" he asked.

"What? You mean like something that would give you a bloody nose?"

"No. Anything suspicious?" He didn't like Alice talking to him like that. She might have been joking, but it was the way he imagined others felt about him.

"Not really. I mean there's a lot of whining and fighting over who's taken whose makeup, but I don't think any of them would off Akari. Did you ever think that maybe there's something else going on…something you might not have considered?"

For about the last week, he had become increasingly aware that the fantasy he had long nurtured was beginning to die. "You know, I'm starting to think that maybe Akari didn't do herself any favors. A lot of the others seem to think she was the problem. Maybe that's all there is to it."

"Hey, don't give up. You only lose when you quit."

"Whoa. You sounded like a real idol just then."

"*Maji de?*" Alice had a thought. "You know we're probably not going to learn anything at practice. We have to see them in a more natural environment. I was thinking…maybe I should invite the girls to hang out at the VR café. You could even come. Might move the ball forward."

"You're in the Genki Girls. Isn't that like inviting the rest of the herd to a steakhouse?"

Alice knew that Akari had gotten entangled in something more supernatural than virtual, but she had to lead Taka to that conclusion gently. First, it would be necessary to blur the lines between those two worlds; then she would let him get there on his own. More than that, the sooner she uncovered some genuine answers, the faster Jack would take her to see Keiji. "Am I supposed to be one of the cows in that analogy?"

Before Taka could apologize, Momoko bounded up to them like a rabbit and interrupted their conversation. "VR café…*ii jan!* Is Taka-kun coming? Please come. Pretty please." She looked at Taka with large contact-enhanced eyes. "I'm scared, but I never let Akari stop me from having fun, even when she was alive." Momoko knew he was the only boy Haruto would approve having around, which was a bit of a slight. Idols weren't allowed to have boyfriends or go out on dates, lest their fans think they had no chance at winning their affections. Over the years, things had loosened to the point where being with a boy in public wasn't a problem if it were as part of a larger group. Discretion, however, was still advised. For some, that only made it more exciting, and that often led to additional problems. She leaned in close and whispered, "I want to go because I'm scared."

Taka was flustered, though he couldn't explain why. Not that he was strong enough to resist the urging of his favorite idol. "I guess I'd better go too…if it will help everyone."

Momoko squealed excitedly but then frowned. "I almost forgot. Yuki can't come. Her mom won't let her."

Yuki had heard Momoko's shrill voice and had been listening in on their conversation. "Wrong-o. I'm in. I don't think Akari died because of some game. She had issues. I'll tell my mom I'm going to Alice's house." As the phrase rolled off her tongue, she felt a self-inflicted punch to the gut. It was a phrase she hadn't used in some time.

Momoko buried her head in her purse. "But that would be lying, Yuki-chan."

Yuki hated that Momoko never stepped out of character. It made her difficult to relate to, which was probably her intended goal. "Nothing says we can't practice and play at the same time. We'll sing in between matches."

"Are you coming, Saori-chan?" Alice was attempting to be friendly despite the frost Saori projected in her direction.

"Some of us actually care about being ready for tomorrow." Saori sensed Haruto wouldn't approve of their after-practice choice of activity.

"It's too soon, right? I'm an idiot. Gomen. You don't have to come if you don't want to."

Taka took Alice aside. "I don't think it's such a bad idea. When we first started, I was the one urging you to get out of your comfort zone. Maybe I'm the one who needs to be pushed. If something else is going on, we'll never figure it out without stepping outside the box." He had no idea how right he was.

◆ ◆ ◆

Jack wiped the gray dust from his hands and placed the velvet bag in his jacket. He paused to ponder if his personal Zen garden would ever be as sublime. It was unlikely, as the karesansui garden at Ryōanji was the pride of Kyōto with an appropriate-sized staff to maintain it. There was no point bringing Alice, as she had been clear about how rank she found his particular method of gardening.

The carefully balanced tranquility he enjoyed was broken by an annoying buzzing sound near his ears. Anytime he heard such a sound, he automatically assumed it was one of those enormous Japanese hornets that looked like they belonged in a kaiju film. The sparrow bee had stung Jack five times during various assignments in Japan, and he was doing his darndest to avoid a sixth. He swatted indiscriminately and felt something bounce off his shoulder.

"Hey! You broke my selfie-drone!" cried a tourist with a Keep Kentucky Pioneered t-shirt.

Jack looked down at the teeny camera, flailing on the ground. It attempted to limp back into the air before it bounced a couple of times beside him. "No, wait. Hold on a second." He stepped on it with his shoe. "Okay, there it is."

"Hey, bub, what's your problem?" The tourist waddled up as close to Jack as his basketball-shaped belly would permit.

"This is a temple. Try showing some respect dronehole." Jack turned to leave, but his pockets rustled.

"You've got some nerve, pal. Yeah, that's right. I saw you take some of those rocks over there." The tourist smirked in self-conceived vindication. "Souvenir tchotchkes not good enough?"

Jack defensively placed his hand over his pocket, to protect his prize. It was why he made a point of avoiding civilians unless necessary. Though almost all technology made his skin crawl, drones were like hairy-legged spiders to him. A bony finger tapped his collarbone, and he inexplicably found himself face-to-face with the monk he had eluded earlier. This time, however, he was in the company of a police officer. Jack grinned, like the cat that ate the sparrow bee. "Is there a problem officer?"

The sound of the holding cell door as it slammed shut, was but a familiar annoyance for Jack. He had escaped dozens of jails, prisons, and correctional facilities. This one was nothing more than a glorified drunk tank. As he saw it, he would escape the same way as always, just wait until he was alone in the cell, cover up with a blanket, and disappear. It looked like a cheap magic trick, but it was less painful than getting shot while trying to escape.

Jack lowered his blanket and was surprised to find the cell's dingy walls staring back at him. There was a drunken salaryman passing the time on a nearby bench. "Hey, buddy. Can you see me?"

"Hai. Both of you."

"But it makes no sense. Why am I still here?"

The salaryman struggled to articulate a response. "I don't know, but you're scaring me sober." He immediately passed out.

Jack found his answer in the high corner of the room, a small unblinking camera. One of his standing limitations was that he couldn't exert observable supernatural influence. There were exceptions, but rotting in jail was not one of them. It was a problem he faced back in Vegas where there were more cameras than slot machines that paid. *Whatever.* All he needed was a dead spot the camera couldn't see. Over the next six hours, he tried to teleport himself from various locations around the room, but the lens had been well placed.

Eventually, the salaryman was released, but it failed to have an impact on Jack's predicament. "Thank God!" the man cried as they escorted him out. "That guy is a major weirdo."

Finally, a police officer appeared. "Let's go. Your friend came for you."

Jack didn't need a written invitation. "Some partner. About time, she showed. Didn't even notice I was rotting in this godforsaken..." he froze at the sight of Clement, dressed in a white summer yukata. It was the cultural approximation of the toga he usually wore.

"He's a tourist," apologized Clement. "Wholly ignorant of his boorish and uncivilized behavior. Sorry for the inconvenience. It won't happen again...will it, Jack?"

"I didn't know you couldn't take the rocks. I'm just a stupid gaijin."

"Finally, something we can all agree upon," Clement replied.

Jack was uncharacteristically quiet as they left the police station, expectant of the lecture to come. He tried to get a read on the old philosopher, whose lips remained tucked under his white beard. "Thanks for bailing me out, chief. I'm sure you have lots to do. Don't want to keep you, so give my regards to Pallie and Sam back at the office." Clement's silence put him on edge. "I'll say hi to the dame for you."

"Oh, do you mean your partner? The one who's doing all your work? You might not believe it, but I have better things to do than help you make bail." Two pink lines appeared on Clement's forehead.

"They had a camera. A wide-angle job..."

"Of course they did. It's not 1962." Clement gazed up at the heavens for assistance but was only reminded of the futility of his task. "You couldn't do your little hobby at night?"

"That partner you gave me is a little bit judgmental. Maybe you should talk to her?"

Clement's eyebrows wiggled like a pair of gray caterpillars. "You know what it looks like to me? It looks like you think you've found a loophole."

Jack feigned indignation. "A loophole? That is 18-karat crazy."

"To get around me, not letting you fly solo." Though short of stature, Clement's small frame contained twice the piss and vinegar.

"It's called training. You didn't tell Hiro to go easy on me when I was new. I got thrown to the sharks. Literally."

"I didn't know you had it so hard. It must have been difficult those five years you were assigned in Paris."

"How do you think I became such a legend?"

Clement thrust his thumbs inside his obi belt. "Antique and legend are two entirely different things." He wasn't about to tell Jack, but even Hiro had required direction, back in his day. "Also, there is a fine line between providing someone with experience opportunities and hanging them out to dry." They hadn't even breached the actual smell in the chamber pot. "When were you planning on mentioning the actual reason, or should I go ahead and say it?"

"I'm not afraid of him." Jack realized that even answering the question, was a form of admission.

"I didn't say you were. Why should you be? If Solak thought you were a threat, he'd already have taken you out of the equation. That's what he does, or don't you remember?" Clement realized he might have gone a bit far, so he softened his tone. "Listen, Jack. I know you think you're only here because—"

"Hiro cashed his chips in for me?" Hardly a day went by where Jack didn't feel the guilt of not being present the day Solak put an end to their partnership. "He said he could handle it alone. I tried to follow him."

Clement tapped his finger on Jack's chest to punctuate his words. "Keep your priorities straight – train Alice. Collect souls. And don't use your partner as bait. That's what the other side does."

"Hey, I'm the one keeping her from getting hurt. It ain't easy with someone who has more baggage than those carousels; they won't let you ride at the airport." It was one of many adventures Jack had neglected to share. "All things considered, I think she's looking pretty strong out there."

"You know, strength can be measured in many different ways. Capability is power, and what's needed in one circumstance is wholly inappropriate in another."

Jack didn't like getting lectured. It made him question himself, and that could get you hurt. "You know, you are one mixed-up cat. Yeah, that's right. You're the one who threw us into this crazy mess. Would it have killed you to give me a little time to sort out her personal issues?"

"She has skills that are pertinent to what is going on. I was under the impression that you were some kind of legend?" Clement was annoyed Jack was trying to put him on the defensive.

There was no point sparring. "Fine chief. We'll agree to disagree, but don't be surprised if I put something in the comments section of my next annual review. Anyhoo—maybe it's not the right time to ask…"

"Seriously, Jack? What is it now?"

"Did you happen to get back any of my gravel?"

"No, but I did bring you a nice slice of birthday cake."

"Really?"

"No." Clement soaked up Jack's disappointment as his compensation for being inconvenienced. He had a longstanding rule to end their talks while he retained the upper hand. "Now stay out of trouble. If I have to bail you out again, your next thread will be in Antarctica. Something involving penguin guano." There was no goodbye as he walked behind a tree and disappeared.

"Oh, you are cold. No wonder the Greek Empire fell. It was because of meanness." Jack waited until he was sure Clement was gone. "Athenian pain in the gluteus maximus."

"That's another week," shouted Clement.

"Why are you always so sour?"

"Anyone who falls for that definitely needs a partner. Speaking of which. Do you have any idea what she's up to?"

The hairs on Jack's wrist rustled like stalks of wheat, as his beads whirred.

◆ ◆ ◆

A pinging tone notified Alice that she wasn't properly secured in the omnitread. She lifted her headset and checked the safety clip attached to her waist. Solak's offer to help her find Keiji impacted her concentration, but it was Jack who had put her in such a position in the first place. Alice selected the kitsune from the character menu, a fox character that wore a flowing white kimono, and the virtual environment faded into view, a safeguard against disorientation. She was aware that her choice of venue might be inappropriate, but she had already overheard a couple of the other girls admitting that they had returned to their former hangout. Alice wanted a chance to finish her conversation with Solak, but not alone or with Jack.

Alice clutched a katana because while the game featured fantasy characters from Japanese literature, its commitment to reality ended at opposable thumbs. A bushy foxtail peeked from the back of her furisodé kimono. Momoko had taken the neko avatar, a white kitten whose eyes and nose were obscured behind long, white fur that would surely have been the death of any allergy sufferer. Her silk kimono was, naturally, pink, and she wielded a shakujō, a staff favored by warrior monks. Yuki had chosen to play as the type of deer you might see on a class trip to Nara and had a black lacquered crossbow.

Taka brought up the rear rendered as a tanuki. He was readily identifiable by the backpack he always wore, and his paws clutched a chōchin lantern to chase away the shadows. Taka always thought that the raccoon dogs placed outside shops were adorable, with their straw hats and round bellies. At least, until he realized he wasn't wearing any pants. "I might not have thought this through."

The Edo-era post town's crystalline-capped straw roofs shimmered under the harvest moon, abandoned of the weary travelers it had been established to serve. If the environment was intended to provide a summer chill, Alice could not help but be happy to be spending time with an old friend. She even wondered if maybe she might have joined the Genki Girls had Yuki only asked. "Ne. Yuki-chan. What are we playing again?"

"Kappa Carnage." Something about the scenario felt eerily familiar, and it made the hairs on the back of her neck stand at attention. She reminded herself that this Alice had nothing in common with the cherished friend she still missed.

Momoko covered her face with pink-padded paws. "Not kappa. I'm scared of kappa." Her fur quivered.

"Don't worry, Momo-chan," said Taka, his large and trusting eyes reflecting the amber light of his lantern. "Kappa aren't real. They were made up by parents to keep kids away from rivers." He was still a bit naïve concerning her act, but that was what she liked about him.

Alice was equally nervous, but for entirely different reasons. She knew the others would be safe, as long as they stayed away from the gray pills. Jack still might not approve, but they were never going to get anywhere if she wasted all her time asking for permission. Apparently, he had taught her something after all.

"This village is creepy," said Momoko. "I hear kappa drown children and steal their soul."

Taka shone his paper lantern on a stack of old saké barrels. "Everyone stick close. If we survive for five minutes, we get free garlic edamame."

Japanese legend taught that the river monsters, known as kappa, collected the essence of human existence. Alice pondered if she had not turned into something eerily similar. "Taka is right. Let's stick together for now." She turned to see if the others agreed. "Hey, has anyone seen Yuki?"

A small brook divided the middle of the street, with wooden planks laid down as crossing spots. Taka didn't think the water was deep enough to hide one of the mossy river children, but it caused him to shudder. "I don't like the looks of that stream. Maybe we should go around?"

There was a howl in the distance, followed by an oddly recognizable scream. "Yuki," said Alice. "We'd better go."

Momoko's whiskers flattened against her face as Taka put his arm around her shoulder. "I'm scared too Momo-chan, but we'll look out for each other."

"Honto ni?" Momoko gripped her staff and stood tall. "I won't be a scaredy-cat." She bared her fangs. "Kappa is on the menu tonight!"

Taka pulled out the matchlock pistol he had been provided. "Isn't this hat supposed to protect me against trouble. Iku zo!"

Not far from the edge of town, the brook fed into an estuary, where a wooden kōsatsu ordered strangers to stay clear. In the shallows, Yuki wrestled with a kappa that resembled the offspring of a frog and a balding older man. Its webbed hands clutched her arms and attempted to drag her below the surface. Momoko rammed her shakujō into its side, producing a banshee-like screech.

Yuki saw her chance to kick the kappa with her back hoofs and fired a crossbow bolt into its neck.

"A little help?" cried Taka.

Feathered arrows filled the air as web-handed monsters emerged in waves from the slough. The crowns of their heads were indented to hold water and allowed them to retain their power on dry land. Eyes, yellow, and wild, they were able to see through the darkness and the fog. Strong beaks made a sharp *clicking* sound and snapped in anticipation of their prey.

Knee-deep in the shallows, Alice used the business end of her katana to clear the way for the others. A kappa with droopy eyes grabbed her from behind in a slimy embrace and pulled her underwater. Panic struck Alice, as memories of her mortal demise were provoked. As she flailed within the murky dreck, she thought she saw a laughing hannya mask, but mossy bubbles obscured any firm conclusion. Then someone grabbed the back of her kimono and pulled her back up to the fresh air. "Where's Taka?"

Frenzied, Momoko shoved her shakujō into the one-eyed kappa's face. "Taka-kun is dead!" She sobbed. "Those bastards got him!"

"What? Oh, in the game." Alice wondered if Momoko was playing her part a little too well.

"C'mon," screamed Momoko. "We have to save Yuki-chan before it's too late!" She threw Taka's pistol to Alice, who fumbled to catch it with her uncoordinated paws.

On the other side of the village, Yuki left a trail of grayish-green corpses as she backed into a ryokan. She crawled into the corner of the sunken hearth room. A kettle swayed on a pothook, and she could see the outline of something that stalked her on the other side of the shoji screens. It reminded Yuki of hiding from her classmates in the janitor's closet, on the days when she felt like she had a bulls-eye painted on her back. She fired at a shadow, but it was an offset deception. Claws turned the screen beside her to ribbons. The kappa grabbed the lid off the pot that hung from the jizaikagi and used it as a shield. The iron saucer whizzed by her head, but with feline reflexes, she leaped clear, and the lid impaled itself into a wooden beam.

In an abandoned machiya, Alice and Momoko searched for their teammate, pausing in a claustrophobic courtyard. They could hear the muffled sounds of a struggle in the distance.

Momoko sniffed the air for clues. "The wind says that way. I'm sure of it."

Noren curtains parted to reveal a kappa the size of a grizzly bear. It bared its teeth and growled with the sound of a motorcycle clearing its pipes. Alice addressed Taka's matchlock at his chest, but the burning match cord had gone out, and it just produced a heartbreaking click. Fortunately, Alice remembered that kappa could only survive as long as they held life-preserving water in the bowl upon their head. She pretended to offer a respectful, pre-engagement, bow. The kappa, unable to resist, returned the gesture, and its water spilled onto the ground. Immediately, its power to stay on dry land departed; its skin bleached, and it writhed upon the floor.

Thump. Thump. The ground reverberated as if shaken by a mochi-pounding giant. An oni—twice the size of the kappa they had just overcome—smashed an opening into the room beside the courtyard, revealing the woven bamboo infrastructure of the walls as it tore through the connected buildings. Its face was reminiscent of a hannya mask.

"I think we should follow him," said Alice, concluding that she had found Solak.

"But that's an oni," cried Momoko. "I'm afraid of oni."

"You're getting way too into this," replied Alice, aware that there might be an actual cause for concern. They followed the outline Solak made through several buildings, until they found Yuki, held down by the one-eyed kappa, its webbed hands splayed against her throat.

Solak made a casual offer to the river monster. "You can have her liver, but I am entitled to her soul. Are we agreed?"

Alice had no idea whether it was Yuki's time, but she couldn't allow her best friend to be sacrificed needlessly. Perhaps Solak didn't recognize her as a kimono-clad fox. Still, not wanting to abandon the spirit of the game, she decided to split the difference and transformed into a combination of her ghostly maiko manifestation and present avatar. Black makeup ran from her eyes, down to her whiskers. While unlikely to intimidate the shadow demon, it was the best she could do without undermining the virtual environment.

"This one's clean," said Solak, to the kappa. "Children these days. So disappointing."

Alice jumped onto the pothook that hung over the hearth and rode it like a pendulum, splashing Solak with its bubbling gruel. His clawed hand swiped back at her, but he failed to see she had attached the hook to his belt. Clawed feet shredded the tatami mats as Solak charged after her, but the rope she had attached to his belt halted his pursuit. The roof groaned under the tension, then subsequently crashed down upon everyone.

The shadow demon weathered several large wooden beams and clapped his hands together like a sumo rikishi to clear the air of dust. "Alice," he tsked. "And I thought we had an understanding. Is Jack here too?"

"Taka. Turn it off," said Alice, realizing she was in over her head. "Kill the power." She wasn't sure if she could be heard outside of the game or not.

Parts of the straw roof fell upon the cooking fire. The washi paper windows ignited, and the room filled with a potent cloud of black charcoal. No one saw Momoko, pinned underneath one of the roof's fallen support beams, but they could hear her yowl.

"Turn it off, Taka! Turn off the game!" Alice realized she had lost track of Solak until his iron club divided the embers and launched her across the room. Her back slammed into the kappa that held down Yuki, which seemed fortuitous unless the shadow demon's purpose was to remove her from the equation.

"Such a shame. And I was about to tell you the name of the hospital," said Solak, hoping to inflict an internal wound. "Now, you'll never see him." He grabbed the mirror from around his neck and shone it into Momoko's face. "*Moshi.*" He laughed. "Please don't struggle. This isn't what either of us wanted, but you'll have to do."

Everything faded to black, and the café's logo swirled into view. A cartoon mascot held up a sign, but who had earned the highest score hardly mattered. Alice tossed her VR headset aside to find Yuki passed out in her harness. "Taka. Get someone. Now!"

Momoko unlatched her safety straps and staggered upright. "I think I'm going to throw up." Her cheeks inflated. "Yup, I'm sure of it."

"Do you need help?" asked Alice.

Her twintails shook in the negative. "It's okay. I've had lots of practice."

By the time the paramedics arrived, Yuki was groggy but well enough to tell everyone to leave her alone. "I told you I'm fine," she said. "Momoko is the one losing her lunch." For a moment, it looked like she might resist their attempts to place her on the gurney.

"You passed out," said Alice. "It's probably a precaution. You know, tests and stuff. We'll meet you at the hospital."

One of the café's employees saw them talking to the paramedics and came over to return Momoko's purse. "Sorry. Did any of you leave this?"

"It's okay, I'll take it," said Alice. "She's still in the bathroom. I'll make sure she gets it, though."

Taka's allergies had reactivated from all the stress. "You wouldn't happen to have a tissue, would you?" It was an implied admission that the girls, who handed out the free advertising packs on street corners, often neglected him. "I guess we won't be getting the edamame."

Remembering she had seen Momoko blowing her nose at practice, Alice took the liberty to open her stuffed panda's zipper and dig around inside. "I'm pretty sure there's a packet in here somewhere." Her hand found the tissues, but it also discovered something she didn't expect. Within one of its plastic flaps was a single gray pill.

CHAPTER NINE:
GHOSTS IN THE MACHINE

Akari clutched the bathroom counter and splashed water on her face. It didn't feel like enhancer, more like a night of drinking games and other unfortunate life decisions. Her palm slipped on the rim of the sink, and she jammed her finger. It had the positive effect of restoring a bit of her lucidity, but then Akari looked up at the mirror to check her makeup. "Nande?" she cried, not seeing her reflection but that of Momoko. Akari spun around to check behind her, but the bathroom was empty. When she looked forward again, she saw not only a twin-tailed reflection of Momoko but also that of a gentleman in a black suit bedecked in a demonic-looking mask.

"Don't bother to look away," said Solak. He placed his hands on Momoko's shoulders. "I'm only in the mirror.

"Hilarious guys," scoffed Akari. "Nice effects." She ran her fingers along its seams. "I'd have to be pretty stupid…"

Solak reached through the mirror and grabbed her wrist. Akari screamed, but he muffled her mouth. "Do you know why I'm wearing a hannya mask? Is it a face you can relate to?" Seeing that her terror had settled to panicked breathing, he withdrew back inside the glass. I hope you are pleased with your new identity? My eyes were set on another vessel, but I think it worked out well, wouldn't you agree? You've been gone a while, safe in my care." He patted the small mirror that hung from around his neck. "Those who sought to hurt you are very near, though."

"Who are you? Is this supposed to be funny? Why do I look like Momoko?"

"It's not like I could carry your soul around forever. It's quite draining, like working with one hand tied behind my back. Think of it this way. You were a Christmas cake, and I extended your usefulness."

Akari was well aware that, at twenty-one, she was the second oldest member of the group, but with virtual idols staring back at her from every corner in Akihabara, it was still painful to hear. The industry suits that virtue signaled against discrimination, gleefully cast aside such reservations when it came to professional ageism. "Why can't I see myself? Where am I?"

For a pregnant moment, the mask grinned. "Cellular makeup—utterly insignificant. Do you mourn your hair or fingernails when they are cut? What about the form you had as a child, forever lost except in family photos? You are no different. Energy, water, and light made flesh."

Akari looked at her hands, their nails decorated to resemble cupcakes with little bows and pearls. She felt her face, smooth like a polished stone. "I'm Momoko? Why?"

"There are limits under which I bristle. You have agency, something of which I am in short supply. Let me put it this way. The universe is made of checks and balances, and I'm all out of checks."

"Who are you?"

"Names are the only thing less meaningful than flesh. How should I put this? I am the darkness that extinguishes shadow—a hero of lost souls, a phantasmagoric visionary." He leaned forward so that his golden horns broke through the glass. "Call me Solak, and your life is my gift, but I will be well-compensated. Of that, we must make sure."

Akari was used to only being valued for what she could reciprocate. "What do you want from me?"

"You're an artist, are you not? For us to play the same haunting melody."

His offer was too oblique to consider, but Akari had learned how to appear cooperative during her time in the music industry. "I'm supposed to be Momoko, that's what you're saying? Well, if I'm her...what happened to—"

Akari glanced back, if only to gesture, and found herself face-to-face with the frightened ghost of her teammate's unaccounted soul. Momoko's spectral eyes overflowed, and her ghostly hand stretched forth, longing for her physical form. Akari screamed loud enough to make up for when Solak had muted her, clipping the doorframe as she fled outside.

"I think that went rather well," observed Solak.

◆ ◆ ◆

The gyros of Sho's cycle wound to a stop, and a small kickstand scraped the pavement. A 500 yen-sized drone launched from a small door in the back of his motorcycle seat, and the heat signatures of everyone working at Tokuji-Tech Pharmaceutical's corporate offices appeared on his phone. Company-issued smartwatches provided Sho with the specific identification data his task required. *Target Acquired* appeared above one of the heat signatures, so he double-tapped the screen to confirm his selection. *Eliminate target.* Sho favored a drone that gave him three darts at the expense of battery life. Comprised of a variant of speed, it created spasms within the coronary artery that cut off blood flow to the heart. After delivery, it dissolved leaving, no trace of its existence.

The drone whirred to a stop below the large Tokuji-Tech sign that targeted commuters traveling to Kawasaki on the JR line. Usually, Sho would have sent the tiny UAV through the air ducts, but in this case, the factory had a state of the art filtration system that made such transit impossible. Fortunately, the warehouse door opened, and Izumi emerged, taping her self-lighting cigarette and humming a German drinking song. Aided by her eyepatch's blind spot, the teeny quadcopter slipped through the cracked door as she took her final drag.

Immediately, the drone swerved to avoid one of the warehouse's AGVs. Yagi's eyes darted up from his box of cookies; something was amiss in his pallet kingdom. Assuming a cicada had found its way inside, he brushed some crumbs off his navy jumpsuit and went back to his afternoon snack. If it were an insect, the pest control bots that swept the area with ultrasonic frequencies would handle it.

Sho directed the drone to the top of a stack of barrels and eased back the power to its tiny rotors. Seventy meters away, he could see his target surrounded by heat signatures, perhaps engaged in a meeting. An uneasy hour breezed by, as his drone's battery drained to only seven percent. Sho passed the time reading a book of chōka poetry, occasionally stopping to check his messages. It had not been that long since another Tokuji-Tech employee had been eliminated for being too thorough with his job, so discretion was of the highest importance.

Oblivious to the congruence of yakuza and corporate politics, Jack floated into the warehouse adorned in the cryptic vestments he wore for such occasions. He remembered seeing the Tokuji-Tech banner at the Akihabara concert, so it was a good sign that the beads had led him to the company's headquarters. Soon, he would be knocking back martinis in Vegas, ignoring Clement and waiting for his next thread. Jack assumed Solak had shown up out of interest in his new partner, but there was always a chance that more was afoot. The shadow demon had once made a point of turning his show solo. Until he was able to sort out why his old nemesis was involved, there would be no happy hour for Jack. The synchronicity beads were indicating that he had five minutes before his services would be required, and Jack wasn't about to waste them. One of the office ladies walked through him, unaware of his spectral presence and remarked to their friend, "Is it just me, or is it cold in here? I knew I should have brought my sweater." The marketing department had already been creating mock-ups for the expected release of Neuroko XR. The new drug promised improved emotional health along with a list of side effects worse than the condition it proposed to alleviate. Jack didn't have much use for medicine. He metamorphed out of diseases the way some people blew their noses. A heavy door led into a series of clean rooms, where people in white jumpsuits monitored components mixed in large vats. Jack didn't have any idea what all the equipment was for, but he knew that Akari had taken a street drug made from some of the raw materials found in that very room.

On the hill overlooking the factory, Sho watched the heat signals and concluded that the meeting must have ended. Now his job could begin in earnest. He closed his leather-bound copy of the *Early Work of Takuboku Yamamoto* and launched an app that allowed him to assume anyone's identity within the company. Sho sent a message that read, *Could you please come to the warehouse? There is a problem that needs your attention.* To further clear the area, he sent a text to the warehouse supervisor, asking him to report to the executive offices. He reactivated the drone and placed it optimally for his target's arrival. It had been an uncomfortably long wait, far beyond what he had anticipated.

Fujisawa swung open the doors and waited for an AGV, hustling a pallet, to pass. On a previous visit to the warehouse, he had almost been knocked into a tower of boxes. Fujisawa read the urgent message on his watch and shouted, "Yagi-san?" It was strange indeed that he had been called instead of George, which was all that most issues required. This meant that the matter must be severe, and his doctor had warned him to mind his blood pressure. Fujisawa peered down an aisle of neatly stacked barrels. "Yagi-san!" he cried. "Are you back there?"

Sho waited for his drone to indicate that it had successfully locked onto its target. Its crosshairs focused onto a region where Fujisawa's cranium connected to his spine, and he released the safety. Propelled by a small cartridge of air, the dart had to be within two meters to be useful, but closer was better. Seeing his screen flash green, Sho prepared to fire, but the video feed tumbled. Hit by an AGV programmed only to avoid humans, and electronically tagged warehouse equipment, the warehouse's ceiling, and floor traded places. The drone came to rest upside down, bouncing as its blades struck the concrete. Aware of the price of failure, Sho scrambled to right it again.

Yagi returned, surprised to discover Fujisawa milling about his warehouse. "Fujisawa-san? What brings you here? Can't remember the last time I saw you poking around. Couldn't you have sent Okada-san?"

"Are you hitting the saké again? You called me."

"No, I didn't." Yagi looked at his phone, but the message had already cleared. It was very peculiar.

Fujisawa wondered if perhaps he had received a late message from another day. "I swear it was here. Why else would I come?" He decided he might as well not waste the trip. "Since I'm here…did you ever track down the source of that inventory problem we've been having?"

"Etto…you talked to Okada-san, right? He was handling that." Yagi hid his antique watch in the pocket of his overalls.

"Between us, I don't think he's taking the matter seriously. Too many distractions at home, maybe?"

"You could use a few yourself. Say, maybe we should organize a group date for *ojisans*?" Yagi's wife had died several years back, and he was doing his best to raise his daughter alone. "How about we invite Yoshitomi-san in accounting?"

"Don't change the subject. Look. I like Okada-san as much as anyone, but I'm not going to miss a mortgage payment for him."

The drone finally righted itself and gave Sho the green lock signal. The distance was further than he liked, but the extra maneuvering had already contributed to a persistent low battery warning.

"There's cake in the break room," said Yagi. "Why don't you stick around and have some coffee? You seem stressed." As Sho fired, Yagi pushed Fujisawa abruptly. One of the sweeper bots raced by oblivious of the near miss. "Watch yourself and next time grab a hard hat. That one gave me a bruise the other day. Might need a software update."

"Answers Yagi-san. Real ones." Fujisawa was blissfully unaware that Yagi had just saved his life. "If that new drug isn't approved, I'll be applying for one of those politeness positions at the mall, and you'll be in line right there beside me."

Only one dart left, thought Sho. *That's all I need.* At that moment, the battery flashed *zero*, and the video feed went black. Sho stared at his notepad in disbelief and began to consider the possibility of kicking down the door and finishing off the job himself. Success was nothing without subtlety, though his fingers twitched in recognition of the cost.

As he swung open the warehouse doors, Fujisawa heard a *crunch*. Underneath the sole of his loafer was the type of drone perverts used to spy on their neighbors. A tiny lump under its belly suggested it had undergone some sort of aftermarket modification, a peculiar discovery.

Jack whistled a jazzy tune, and though it annoyed Alice that he always repeated the same section, she wasn't around to remind him of the fact. White-collar incidents meant birthday cake. He wasn't sure why the drudgery of office work fueled the need to indulge in a sugar-fueled march towards requiring his services, but the lingering smell of burnt coffee led him to the employee kitchen. There within, as predictable as a rainbow in Hawaii, and accompanied by Beethoven's Ode To Joy, he beheld a pink box, its frosting covered knife heralding the promise of absolute bliss. *Well, happy birthday to me!* Jack reached for the box, but its sugary goodness passed through his spectral hands. Going solid was risky, but it was a sizeable enough company that people would probably assume, he was a contractor or maybe a consultant. He would have to be quick, as everything indicated the need for his services to be imminent. Nothing, however, went better with harvesting a middle-grade executive than indulging in the life-affirming confection that had eluded him, as of late. The effect of baking soda upon flour, sugar, and eggs was magic, even to someone with his considerable powers. *Ah, fiddle-faddle.* Jack went solid, and that is when Fujisawa entered the kitchen, looking for coffee. Seeing his target's blood drain from his face, Jack immediately realized that he had selected the wrong manifestation for cake. The microwave's glass door reflected wraithy robes that sparkled with the embers of funeral pyres, and he realized he was outfitted to give pause to the servants of darkness, not enjoy cocktails at a casino. Fujisawa looked within cindery eyes that reflected the memories of the damned and clutched his chest.

The employee refrigerator shook as Fujisawa stumbled back into its door, bento boxes rattling as if balanced on a snare drum. *Not good. Rule 714,* thought Jack. As Fujisawa's ghost haloed, the cake tumbled to the floor, but Jack wisely bypassed its pleasures to perform his duty. Seeing the drone slip from Fujisawa's fingers, Jack quickly collected it within his robe. His target's smartwatch had already summoned help, so there was but a moment to become transparent before Yagi ran into the kitchen and discovered his co-worker spread out on the floor. Denied sweet indulgence, Jack consoled himself. *Office party cake is never as good as it looks, anyway. It tastes of despair.*

◆ ◆ ◆

"Everything okay? I heard a scream." Assuming it was Momoko, Alice handed Akari her purse.

"Tension release. Had to be done." Akari looked like she had seen a ghost, which was actually the case. "Sorry, I don't think we've met. I'm Akar—I mean, Momoko desu. Hajimemashite."

Taka was immediately concerned. "You don't recognize Alice...your new junior in the Genki Girls? Are you sure you're okay?"

Akari looked at Alice as if she had only just remembered who she was. "What? As if! Sorry, my eyes are still adjusting." She patted her awkwardly. "Okay, then. It's been fun. I'll leave first."

"I don't think so," said Alice. "We're going to the hospital to check on Yuki, and I think you might want to get looked at."

"I'm fine," protested Akari. She searched nervously through Momoko's purse.

"Who's the center of the Genki Girls?" asked Taka.

"I am—I mean Akari!"

"I'll get the cab," said Alice.

◆ ◆ ◆

"It's your boss," said Ms. Ito, an old habit from when they had both worked at Flavor Beat Records. She could tell Haruto was annoyed at the slip, but she handed him the phone, not the least bit chagrined.

Word, no doubt, had leaked out about the accident at the VR café. It might be better if he did still work at the music company, as he would only get yelled at for failing to control the talent. As an independent producer, they could cancel his contract. The second he signed with his old company, they owned his soul far more than when they had their logo embossed on his business card.

"Haruto-san," yelled Genjirō. "Is it true that one of your girls is in the hospital again? Aren't you supposed to be recording?"

"Yes, about that..." Haruto shifted to block the empty studio behind him, wanting to avoid the impression of money flying out the window. "Mōshiwake arimasen." Haruto gave a deep bow but popped up, aware that the vacant space behind him had once again become visible.

There was heavy breathing as if his Genjirō was building up the necessary pressure in his lungs to reveal the full extent of his opinion. "That's absolutely brilliant. I used to think you were soft, but you're the most calculating son of a bitch I ever met. You are incredible."

"I am?"

The A&R exec's narrow-lidded gaze indicated that he was nonplussed. "What? You're going to play stupid? You think I didn't bury a few bodies to get where I am? Why haven't I seen this in the news yet? We need shots of the Genki Girls surrounding her bed. Sisterly affection. Girly crap. You get what I'm saying?"

"Ano…chotto matte kudasai." Haruto fumbled through a file where he kept his press contacts. He pantomimed for Ms. Ito's assistance, only to have her flail back that she didn't understand. "Hai, we're already working on it."

"Well, work faster Haruto-san. Everyone in the department said you didn't have what it takes to survive in this industry. Now we all know what you've been up to. Pigeons," he laughed. "You weren't crazy. You knew what you were up to."

"I did? I mean—of course, I did."

"Just make sure you get that song to us by the end of the week."

The screen went blank. Haruto turned to Ms. Ito and asked, "Which of the girls are still at the hospital?"

"I don't know. No one has checked in."

"Call Saori-chan and tell her to get over there. Don't let anyone leave before they get some pictures."

"The sympathy card?" said Ms. Ito. "That's where we're going with this now?"

"Well, we sure as hell can't play the talent card."

◆ ◆ ◆

"Because Yuki needs you," Mrs. Okada yelled into her phone. "No, she's not hurt. They said they just need to monitor her for a few hours, but she's scared.

They have her hooked up to machines…no, not to keep her alive. Oh, just get over here. I don't care if you have a meeting. What's it about, what toilet paper they're going to use?" Her eyes grew as big as an owl's. "Fujisawa-san died? Oh my god. I can't believe it. This is great! You'll be promoted! I'm sure of it. Yuki can get those modeling shots now." A nurse came by and pantomimed for her to keep her voice down. "Okay, no, never mind. Stay there. I'll take care of everything. Pretend you're in charge. I don't know, act obnoxious." She noticed a few of the Genki Girls approaching the front desk. "Yuki's friends are here. Talk to you later. Bye."

"I can do it myself," Akari barked at the nurse, who helped her into the wheelchair. "I'm fine, maybe a little dizzy and apparently without any sense of fashion." She had not quite yet gotten the handle on imitating Momoko's sugarcoated disposition.

"Hello, Mrs. Okada," said Alice, with a familiarity that did not take into consideration her own identity crisis. "How's Yuki?"

Mrs. Okada had binge-watched one too many dramas. "I just hope she's going to pull through."

"I talked to the doctor, said Taka. "Actually, he said she could go home."

"But will she ever be the same?" Mrs. Okada asked melodramatically.

Alice was similarly distracted by Solak's inference that Keiji was in a hospital. That meant she wasn't going to leave until every last room had been explored. Maybe it was wrong to have used Yuki to draw out Solak, but it never occurred to her that Momoko might be the one using enhancer, not that she didn't feel terrible.

"Momo-chan might have a concussion," said Taka. He thought Yuki also looked a bit tired, sitting upright in her hospital bed. "Yuki-chan—genki?"

"I'll live." Yuki wasn't even sure why she was still there. "I might have blacked out, but the doctor just said to take it easy. No biggie."

"Nyaa-chan will be happy to hear that," said Alice.

"How do you know my cat's name?"

Alice produced a small gasp at her slip. "Your mom called her when I was at your house the other day. Remember?"

"What did I do?" Mrs. Okada entered with a big smile.

"Nyaa-chan," replied Yuki.

"Oh, she's going to be mad. It's past her dinner." Mrs. Okada's eyebrows furrowed. "Well, maybe she shouldn't have snagged my favorite dress."

"Would you excuse me for a minute?" asked Alice. She walked outside to look for a bathroom. Determined to find Keiji, she was ready to tear the hospital apart.

Then, at the end of the hallway, Alice saw what appeared a vagrant, his ratty tunic hanging by a thread, pointed leather boots laced high to his shins. Woolen mittens, cut at the knuckles, revealed dirty fingernails, and yellow teeth gleamed from between his cracked lips. Squatting with his backside almost kissing the waxed floor, his cupped hands tossed a small pile of animal bones, like makeshift dice. He offered no acknowledgment of her presence as he awaited their outcome.

"Hello," said Alice. "What are you doing there?"

The man continued to ignore her as if she was invisible, which she wasn't for once.

"Hello," she repeated. "Is that a game you're playing?"

The man's eyes addressed her like Klieg lights. "Can you see me?" He waved a mitten-covered hand in front of her face. "Do you hear me there?"

"Why wouldn't I?" Alice wondered if she had wandered into the wrong area of the hospital. "Am I not supposed to?"

"You're not dead?" he asked in a thick cockney accent. "I couldn't have missed one. Say...you're not a ghost, are you?"

"No. Are you?"

Now she had the man's attention. "Oh, so you're not mortal. No one told me to expect anyone. Come to relieve me, have you?"

"I don't think so. Are you a harvester?"

The man's face turned sour. "What's that? Are you telling me you're a bloody, sodding harvester? Two hundred years I've been doing this and bugged-boo they put in a child? One hundred and eighty-three thousand souls plucked while I waits for me grease and grime. You've probably only just been dead, am

I right?"

"Look, I'm here to find my friend. I don't care about harvesting or collecting souls, or—"

"You don't want to be a harvester? Is that what you're saying now? Well, isn't that bloody brilliant. Why don't you bugger off and leave me to my bones? I've 'eard enough." He tried to ignore her, but she wasn't to be deterred.

"So, you're a buzzard?"

This was the unfortunate last straw. "What did you call me?" He gestured towards his ear as if he dared her to repeat herself.

Alice realized that she must have misspoken. "Sorry, that's what Jack calls the people who work in hospitals and places like this."

Crusty eyelids rolled up to their stops like window shades. "Jack. Are you telling me that you work for Vegas Jack?"

"Well, it's not exactly like I had a choice…"

"I think I'm going to vomit." The buzzard became taciturn. "Did he tell you what happened to his last partner? No? If he had, you might not be standing there as pleased as a vicar on Sunday."

"What are you doing? What are you rolling those things for?"

His first inclination was to yell, but it was apparent he wouldn't be rid of her until all her questions were satisfied. He pointed his thumb into the room behind his patched pockets. "Lad up to his ears in a comma. He keeps fighting, so I keep tossing these bones. Sooner or later, one of us is bound to stop."

The boy could be anyone, and yet, Alice instinctively sensed where destiny had led her. "Excuse me. I have to check on—I need to see something." In an attempt to be courteous, she made the unnecessary effort of walking around him.

He chuffed like a steam train that had reached its station and rolled again. "Aye, suit yerself."

A taupe, antimicrobial curtain encircled a hospital bed, its synthetic fabric rippling from an overhead vent. There was a weathered green couch upon which rested a stack of unwrapped presents. An unfinished thank-you card sat on a small desk, presumably left by a family member who had run out of time before visiting hours concluded. The gentle hiss of an oxygen machine was periodically interrupted by a reassuring beeping sound. It was not the type of suite used by patients whose time in the facility would be brief. Alice's fingers searched for the seam, but she found herself unable to continue. When her eyes finally found the courage to press inside, she saw the object of her youthful affections, lying pale and attached to enough machines to qualify for a Turing test. As she came to understand the totality of what Jack had been keeping from her, Alice grabbed the curtain in a futile effort to remain upright but tore it free of its hooks as she collapsed beside Keiji.

Yuki had mixed emotions about all the attention she was receiving. On the one hand, the popular girls at school would sneeze tease, and they would be showered with concern from little hypocrites vying to be seen as compassionate. Surrounded by her fellow Genki Girls, Yuki couldn't help but question the sincerity of their interest. "I'm okay…really. My mom is downstairs, checking me out. The doctor said I probably overexerted myself. I'm glad you're all here so we can leave together, though." Yuki started to rise from her hospital bed, but Saori pushed her back so hard that her head bounced against the headboard.

"Not until we get some pictures. Haruto-sensei said we need coverage." Saori threw a bouquet of flowers at her.

"Thank you, but I'm actually allergic." Yuki's eyes became red, and her nose swelled.

"Nice. We can use that." Saori rested her chin between her thumb and index finger. "Now look pathetic. Momo-chan…put your arms around her. Nana. No bunny ears. We're going for sad, but supportive. Perfect."

Akari pushed out her bottom lip, the way she remembered Momoko might, and rested her arm on Yuki's pillow in mock concern. "We care so much about Yuki-chan and her lovely blonde hair that she still hasn't changed." She grabbed her by the wrist and pushed the flowers high into her nose."

"Hai, *cheezu*." Saori snapped several photos. "Okay, let's get out of here. Hospitals give me the creeps."

"Has anyone seen Alice?" asked Taka, who had stepped into the hallway. "She was right behind me a minute ago."

Saori knocked him aside in her rush to leave. "Nande? Am I my idol's keeper? She already missed the photos. Tell her to be at the recording tomorrow or don't. Whatever."

It occurred to Akari that if she was playing the role of Momoko, Saori had clearly assumed her old identity.

"Wakey-wakey." Jack punctuated each word by flicking a card at Alice's forehead. "Someone didn't listen to old Jack's advice."

"Stop it, that hurts. You don't have to be annoying. I can explain." Alice brushed aside an ace of spades that had landed on her forehead. Her wrist rested against something cold, and she realized it was Keiji's bed.

"Aw, why don't you leave her alone," said a voice behind Jack. "She's suffered enough…knowing you and all."

"Stay out of this Buzz. Partner issues. If you hadn't been buzzing about in plain sight, she might not have stumbled onto him in the first place." A curious thought occurred to him. "You did stumble upon him, right?"

Alice wasn't about to reveal that the other team had given her a hint. It was quite apparent that Solak had intended to drive a wedge in their partnership. "He was outside. I can do the math."

"Thanks a lot, Buzz." Jack was pissed at both of them, but one made for a more agreeable target.

"It's Benny, you sad sod. That's not so hard now is it? Why can't you ever call people by their right name? It's disrespectful, that's what it is."

Jack ignored him. "C'mon, we have to get out of here. You're solid. Can't you tell?"

Alice used the bed covers to pull herself up and grabbed Keiji's hand.

"You're not ready for this," said Jack. "You're going to get yourself all tangled up like Christmas lights."

Alice didn't show the slightest inclination to leave. "Is he going to live?"

Buzz threw his bones and examined them like a doctor might a patient's chart. "Uncertain."

Jack was sympathetic but no less resistant to persuasion. "If only I'd gotten here first, but there was this job. Yeah, over at the Tokuji-Tech plant. Some cat named Fujisawa."

"My father's old boss. Is he—"

"I wasn't there to do his taxes."

Alice remembered all the times he had dropped off things after work. "I can't believe it. He used to come over sometimes. I don't think my mom liked him. He was Yuki's dad's boss too. Do you think—"

"Maybe he's next? I don't know, but I wouldn't be planning any vacations if I were him."

"How did he die?"

"This might have had something to do with it." He showed her the small collection of drone parts he had found near the body. "I was going to say we should get this checked out, but we need to start talking. Communication. It's not just for breakfast anymore."

"Fujisawa-san. I can't believe it."

"Yeah, he's probably playing golf with your dad, right about now." Jack seemed genuinely surprised that his little joke wasn't well received. "Ah, you'll laugh in a few years."

Alice held Keiji's hand, which was warmer than she had expected. "Why didn't you tell me? What if I didn't get a chance to say goodbye?"

It didn't please Jack that Buzz was relishing their little drama. Being solo was better; it meant half the issues. "Oh, no. This isn't about me. Don't forget who's the trainer and who's the trainee. I speak. You listen. Capiche?" He was eager to move the conversation outside.

Buzz stopped rolling his bones. "Well, this is curious, isn't it luv? You've been a naughty boy Jack. Naughty. Naughty. I've figured out why that boy's future is so foggy-like. Aye…found the ticket, have I?" He hobbled over and looked deep inside Keiji's ear as if trying to read the wax inside. "This one's supposed to be dead, isn't he?" Jack's uncomfortable silence served as his conformation. "Did it again. Did you? Claimed the wrong soul? Let me guess – a simple wee thread? Can't harvest a pumpkin patch, can you? I'm stuck in this gutter trade while you travel the world, all silver plates, and violins. You can't even do your sodding job right. You're a failure, and you always were. That's why they figured partnering you up with a wee lass to be an improvement."

Jack grabbed Buzz and lifted him off his feet, his bones toppling onto the hospital's polished floor. Cerulean energy rippled around Jack's hands, cutting short the buzzard's metaphysical breath.

"Stop it," said Alice, seeing that Buzz's eyes had begun to bulge. "Jack—enough!" Finally, she cried, "It was my fault!"

"Stay out of this, Alice," said Jack. "I'm teaching this wise guy a lesson." He did not dispute that she should have never tracked down Keiji, but Buzz was the one who had accused him of being incompetent, and one too many times.

"I saw you were coming for Keiji," she said. "I put myself in the way."

Jack loosened his grip and allowed Buzz to drop to the floor. "You what? What did you just say?"

"In the car…the first time we met. I let you harvest me."

◆ ◆ ◆

"Hello, *oniisan*." Akari nonchalantly leaned against Sho's motorcycle, trying not to appear like she was cosplaying in Momoko's skin. The term for older brother was used somewhat loosely, anyway. If anything, it could be taken inappropriately for entirely different reasons.

Sho and Akari had continued to live together after their mother passed, but he was rarely around. When he returned to their apartment, it was usually with blood on his shirt and a look that repelled any questions. Still, he had ensured that she finished high school with a roof over her head and was there in the back row to see her receive her diploma. Akari wondered if Solak would disapprove of the reunion. Perhaps he watched from the spaces between the shadows.

The mobile clinic was little more than a service van that hid in back-alleys staffed by physicians who had lost their licenses and patronized mostly by yakuza. One could get whatever they needed as long as it didn't require a receipt. Sho flexed his new finger and wondered what his sister's former lackey was doing in such a place. It was like Little Bo Peep visiting a brothel. "Get off my bike. Aren't you supposed to be recording, or are you here to get your nose trimmed?"

"What's wrong with my nose?" Akari felt Momoko's face to confirm the lightness of the insult. "Aren't you even going to say hello? Oh, that's right, you don't recognize me. I'm shorter. These clothes…gag. It looks like a nursery rhyme threw up on me."

"Look, I don't have any more pills. I wouldn't give them to you, even if I did." Sho swung his leg over his motorcycle. "I shouldn't have given them to you in the first place. I should have told my sister just to throw them away. Not that she ever listened to me."

Akari had assumed Momoko gave her the enhancer from her own stash. Her brother didn't even make deliveries. "I don't want any more pills. I'm clean." It was something she wanted him to hear, though death had concluded her habit.

"Look, maybe there wasn't a problem with those pills, but if I find out there was…someone's going to die. Not in a nice way either. It's going to be graphic and personal, as in throw my clothes away after I'm done. Is that what you want to hear, or is that too real for you? Anything else you want to talk about, princess?"

Akari's weakened fingers released his handlebar. Telling him her true identity would only necessitate the need for further questions. As Sho drove away, she caught a reflection of herself, looking like a character out of an anime about friendship, set on skid row.

"Don't blame your brother." Solak emerged from the black puddle she had been staring into hopelessly. "He had no more choice than you. Free will is overrated and messy, not unlike cotton candy."

"He knew I was trying to get clean. When he'd find my pills, he'd flush them down the toilet."

"If the family says to make a delivery, he has to make the delivery. Perhaps you should blame yourself for putting him in that position. But it's not the first time, is it? Do you think I don't know why your brother joined the Kurome-gumi? Why do you think I selected you? History. Need we review how your brother's eyes become black? Perhaps his road would be different if he hadn't needed their help."

"That's not fair. Don't you dare put that on me…that was his choice. I could have handled it." She walked through Solak and felt coldness like from the furthest reaches of space.

"You would have gone to jail. Your brother saved your future by sacrificing himself. So noble." Solak stood on the puddle as if it were merely a continuation of the asphalt. "All I want to do is allow you the opportunity to make it up to him, but it might be unsavory. Do you think you're capable of that?"

"I think you know what I'm capable of."

"Indeed, I do."

♦ ♦ ♦

Jack was so upset; he vibrated. "All this time, you let me think I'd screwed the pooch, but you're the one who put yourself in the way? I wasn't just read the riot act; I lived it."

"I was afraid you were going to take him."

"Damn right, I would. Keiji had his time." His beads whirred. "What am I going to tell Clement?"

"Nothing."

"Not a chance, sweetheart. I'm not sticking my neck out for someone I barely even know. I'd trade you for a slice of cake. Not even birthday cake. Sheet cake."

"Go ahead," said Alice. "But say goodbye to retiring. Who knows how much more time you'll get for something like this?"

"Not a day, if I come clean." All his reservations about having a partner had finally come to fruition.

"You'll have to start over again. Or maybe I'll just say we were in on it together. I'll say you wanted a partner you could control."

"I'm dropping you off at the villa, and I'll go talk it out with Clement. He can be reasonable."

"What if I make this work?"

"Make what work?" Jack was ready to cash in, but destiny kept him at the table.

"I'll become a good partner—the best. I'll take it so seriously, just…"

"What?"

"Just leave him alone."

"Keiji? Nope. Don't see that happening." He was surprised to find her

172

pulling on his arm.

"At least wait until the thread is done. I messed up. Don't you think I know that? Didn't you ever make a mistake when you started out?"

Jack had never gotten beyond the making mistakes phase. "What were you doing at the hospital anyway? Didn't I tell you to stay clear of the heartbreak hotel?"

"I thought you'd want to know if Solak could get to anyone without the pills. I didn't know Momoko used. I still wouldn't if I hadn't been in her purse." Alice realized to go forward, one of them would have to risk a little trust. "That's not entirely true. I wanted to see him, Jack, just one more time. And I know if you hadn't been there for me, helping me along the way, I would have never made it this far. You're the reason I'm still around...and I appreciate it."

"Someone must think I'm a turkey, buttering me all up like that." Jack took out his cards and began to shuffle. He couldn't ignore the fact that she had stumbled onto something that he had somehow missed. "But you never actually saw that kid, the one who looked like a rainbow gagged on her, take the pills. Am I right? Did you ever think maybe she might just be holding for Akari?"

"Solak tried to get to her, but he couldn't. The game ended. He probably didn't have enough time."

"What about your friend? She didn't use? You're sure of that?"

"Yuki? Not around me." There were things Yuki had been keeping from her lately, but she was reasonably confident using enhancer wasn't one of them.

Jack lost his concentration, and some of his cards tumbled to the ground. "Then again...maybe you're onto something."

Alice was genuinely surprised he had come around to her point of view. Strangely, though, he seemed to be looking past her. Alice turned to see what might have contributed to his change in perspective and came eye-to-eye with the ghost of Momoko, mouth agape in a silent scream. Her electromagnetic field stuttered, as she ran through Alice and continued down the street.

Seeing Alice about to show some initiative, Jack said, "Cool your jets," having noticed that his beads were as still as a Cumbrian lake. "Something's not kosher. It looks like she's misaligned."

"Misa—what?"

"As in she's not supposed to be dead. A lot of that going around, right?" He was still a bit agitated about the impact Alice was having on his questionable success rate.

"So, we're going to let her run around like that?"

"I'm letting you run about like that."

"Are you?"

"For now…but don't go picking out any china patterns." Jack watched Momoko attempt to get the attention of a police officer that hadn't been able to see ghosts since he was five. "Let's just wait and see if a fleshier version of Momoko shows up for that recording session tomorrow. That could be interesting."

◆ ◆ ◆

The ramen shop was famous for a genetically modified miso base so intensely rich in umami that they were once sued for damaging a patron's taste buds. Taka thought he saw Momoko sulking outside the ramen-ya, but something was amiss. Usually, she could even make a rain cloud smile.

Akari was too embroiled in her stag pity party to notice Taka struggling to catch up with her. She stopped in front of a store that sold vintage idol gear, frequented by the older otaku of Akihabara. With her physical identity gone, nostalgia was all Akari had left. Now she had to deal with the reality that her brother might have contributed to her death. It was painful to think that he might have chosen his yakuza family over his own. Within the shop's display window was the same type of Get Genki! shirt that she once wore.

"I'm probably the only one who ever bought that shirt," Taka said, making his presence known. "I told Haruto-sensei to put the group's name on the front, but he thought you guys should have a slogan."

Akari was shocked at the price tag hanging down from its sleeve. "Nobody will pay that. We're not even famous."

"You are now…well, the reasons might not be great. That'll change, though. You guys deserve it."

"I'm going to buy it," said Akari unexpectedly. It was ludicrously out of character, considering Momoko's style.

"I have one at home," Taka replied. "I need the room in my closet. You can have it if you want."

Akari was surprised he was so cavalier about something he once treasured. It made her feel vulnerable like maybe she'd already been forgotten. "Arigatou," was all she could manage, aware of the changing dynamic between them. "Is it okay?"

Taka assumed Momoko was trying to determine if he was over Akari. He wondered if it meant that something resembling genuine interest had begun to develop between them, but it was complicated. For starters, dating an idol was technically forbidden, and Haruto was starting to treat him like a member of the organization. There was even talk about paying him once the residuals came in from the new recording. It was self-destructive to show any interest, but he couldn't help himself. "She was never real to me…not like you are."

"I'm not so real," said Akari, "but I want to be." She removed the rubber bands that held Momoko's signature twintails in place and pulled off her dolly eyelash extensions. Next, she used wipes from Momoko's purse to remove the makeup she wore thick as a mask, her face naked for his consideration.

Taka wasn't sure what to make of her identity crisis, so he asked the only safe thing that occurred to him. "Up for some bubble tea?"

"You know we can't go alone."

"Right, the whole idol thing. I keep forgetting." It wasn't true, but he wanted to gauge how much risk she was willing to take for him. "Anyway, I've been asked to help out at the recording. Haruto-sensei says I know more about idol music than most record people, but I don't know about that. Maybe afterward, we can get a bite to eat together?" There was an awkward pause, so he added, "With everyone…"

"Sure, Taka-kun. That'd be great."

Nearby, but unseen by Taka's mortal senses, a bluish outline of a girl pulled her twintails as she watched Akari's well-practiced maneuverings. Momoko's ghost passed through the entire color spectrum before her plasma settled on red. A Shibu Inu stopped and let out a short bark before their owner dragged them away. Someone had robbed her not only of her identity but also the first time a boy would have asked her out. It was a bridge too far. She would find out who they were and make them ache, as only a teenage girl could make someone suffer. By the time she was through with them, they would wish they were the one who was dead.

CHAPTER TEN:
NICE BENTO

A lice pressed her mouth against the windscreen but sang barely above a whisper. At that moment, she would rather be fighting the hounds of hell than facing a microphone. Not that she sounded much worse than any of the other melodically challenged idols, but she lacked the hubris to deceive herself.

"You've got to be kidding me," huffed Saori, her words slathered with a veneer of condescension.

Alice assumed that it was her off-key singing that had attracted Saori's ire, but apparently, Momoko had arrived, or at least someone that approximated her in appearance. She was not wearing her usual frilly dress, but a fashionably weathered jean skirt with nary a rainbow or unicorn to its credit. Momoko's trademark twintails were absent, and most alarmingly, she sported the same Get Genki! shirt Akari once wore. It was difficult to tell if it was a tribute or a social faux pas.

"Momo-chan?" asked Taka. "Does it fit okay?" He didn't want to say that it seemed a bit tight in places.

Alice could see Momoko's appalled reflection in the glass of the mixing booth, silently protesting. The spectral princess of kawaii was still committed to the same hairstyle and clothes as on the day Solak had ripped her from her mortal shell, and yes, rainbows were involved.

"Everyone in their places!" shouted Haruto. He turned to Ms. Ito and said, "I suppose I should say a few words, considering the circumstances." Her expression was a summation of her indifference. "A few words? Okay, let's see. How should I say this? Well, we've been through a lot together. Some good, some…well," noting the uncomfortable silence, he added, "let's not dwell on those other times." Ms. Ito took a long sip of her tea. "Maybe it's because I've been under a lot of pressure—that's not an excuse, but I haven't taken the time to encourage everyone and see that you are all reaching your potential." Haruto wished he had planned before starting his soliloquy. "We've all heard other idol groups sing about not giving up, but a hologram can't understand what it feels like to put yourself out there only to fail. I know how it feels; maybe, we all do. We're here today not just to make a record, but to prove all the doubters wrong, especially ourselves. I don't expect anyone here to be perfect. I expect you to be real." Haruto smiled in a bit of a hat tip to Taka. "That's what people like about us. We're all a little bit better than we think. Don't worry if you're a little off-key, or if you sound like you've got a cold. Just make sure that who you are, gets into that microphone. That's all anyone can ask. If they want anything more, they'll have to go through me." Haruto reached for his bottle of water but heard something unfamiliar echoing within the studio. The girls clapped faster until, all at once, a cheer broke out. Having spent much of his adult life in the entertainment industry, Haruto had never experienced authentic gratitude. For a moment, he felt disoriented, as if the temperature within the room was too high. Then he acknowledged their enthusiasm with an abbreviated wave and retreated into the control room. Even Ms. Ito could not help but smile.

As they began to record, tears streamed down several faces, but everyone did their best not to let their voices crack. Alice attempted not to bring the pitch down too much and even made an attempt to enjoy herself. She smiled nostalgically at Yuki, who was a bit weirded out.

They had worked, without interruption, for a couple of hours, when Akari's microphone fell back into her nose. "*Itai!*" she cried. She was reasonably sure she hadn't caused the problem.

"Why are we stopping?" asked Haruto from inside the control room. "Was that you, Momo-chan?"

"It's nothing," replied Akari. "I'm fine. Just a little mic problem."

"Okay, then everyone. Let's focus. Take twelve. From the top of the third verse."

The backing track started, and again the microphone hit Akari in her face. Momoko faced off against her physical doppelgänger, her hand firmly attached to the mic stand.

"Again?" asked Haruto. "Momo-chan, could you please step back a bit from your mic?"

"It's not me!" cried Akari. She could see Haruto's frustration through Momoko's plasmatic outline.

"Okay, one more time. Roll track."

Distracted by the sound engineer, Haruto failed to see the microphone beat Akari like a possessed taiko drum. She fell soundly onto her backside, a red outline of its grill on her forehead.

"*Boke!*" cried Saori, seeing her on the floor. "What is your malfunction today? Your panda purse run away?"

Alice had seen the whole incident and attempted to intervene. "Haruto-sensei, there is definitely something wrong with that microphone. It's not her fault." She looked squarely at the apparition of Momoko, to leave no doubt to whom she was addressing. "I need to use the restroom. Can we take a break?"

Haruto noticed that Sho had slinked into the control room, and hovered behind him like a vulture. He searched around for a clock, even though his phone was next to him. "What time is it? Okay, I guess that's close enough. Taka-san, go ahead and take a look at that mic, would you? All right, everybody, that's lunch."

To obscure his inked-out eyes, Sho wore dark glasses even when indoors. It had the added benefit of making him difficult to read. "Going like usual, I see."

"Sho-san, so glad you could make it. We did some amazing stuff today. You're going to be super-happy. Akari-chan would have loved it."

There was a pounding on the window that separated the mixing room from the studio. Mrs. Okada waved from the other side and held up a stack of bento boxes.

"Alright, Mrs. Okada. We'll be there in a minute." Haruto patted the sound engineer on his shoulder. "Rick, why don't you get some lunch. Yuki's mom made it." He waited until the engineer had left before defending himself to the obstinate gangster. "Look," said Haruto, "I've done everything you've asked of me. I haven't slept in months." It was true that fear had been an excellent motivator.

The stubble on Sho's chin itched. He had an odd way of holding his hand upside down when he scratched it. "This is it, you know. Your last chance to prove I didn't make a mistake when I pulled you out of that prison you called a career." He removed his glasses so that Haruto could see his reflection in the inky oracles through which he considered him. "You would never embarrass my family, would you?"

"Of course not Sho. It's going to be great. Wait and see. You're going to love it."

"Don't make me protect my investment. A personnel change is good from time-to-time."

The yakuza had a long history in the music industry, thanks to the liquidity it provided for money laundering. Legitimate ticket sales, and especially online distribution companies, had put a halt to the party until Boss Mori's predecessor had figured out how to perform an end run around the seat counters. Failure to adapt to changes in technology was why the yakuza had almost disappeared in the first place. Still, they had learned from their mistake. Having the foresight to recruit disenfranchised hackers had re-established the Kurome-gumi as the pre-eminent yakuza clan and saved it from obsolescence.

Mrs. Okada barged into the room, unaware of their conversation. "Haruto-sensei, lunchtime. It has simmered sweet potatoes. Your favorite."

Haruto opened the lid and saw that she had cut the various pieces to resemble the Genki Girls on stage. "Thanks. That's...creative."

Sho started for the door, but Mrs. Okada forced the last bento box into his hands. "Yours is soboro don. I made it myself."

"That's nice, Mrs. Okada, but by the time he gets home, it will be cold," said Haruto.

Mrs. Okada beamed. "It's okay. This type of box maintains the perfect temperature." She tapped its digital readout screen.

"*Domo*," said Sho, taking the bento box as he left.

"He's a bit odd," observed Mrs. Okada.

"Yes. I can't figure him out. One minute he scares me and the next, I think…he's my only friend."

"You can see me?" asked an astonished Momoko, peeking her head into the restroom stall.

"Yes," whispered Alice. "Who is that pretending to be you?"

"I'm scared. I don't want to be dead."

"I know. I get that feeling a lot. Look, maybe we can help each other."

"How?" asked Momoko.

Alice was still trying to figure out the details of the thread herself. "When we were playing that VR game, something happened, and I think you might be the key. You're not supposed to be dead."

"She's trying to take Taka-kun. He wanted to ask me out. I've never been asked out before!" Tears ran down Momoko's translucent cheeks.

"Look, I think you've got bigger problems…"

"Hmm, something about this sounds familiar," said Jack, who stuck his head into the stall. Momoko screamed, not that anyone could hear her.

Alice looked over her shoulder. "You know this restroom is for girls, right?"

"Yeah, but that only applies to live ones, so maybe you're in the wrong place." Jack gave a sapid grin.

"Are you going to help me out or not? Solak put someone into her body. That would seem to be something you should care about." Only Momoko's eyes and the tip of her nose peeked through the door, causing Alice to conclude she must be scared. "Sorry, Momo-chan. This is my—"

"Cousin. I remember him from practice. Why's he—"

"Not alive? Long story."

"Short version…not a ghost," said Jack.

Somewhat reassured, Momoko pressed her way back into the stall. "Who's Solak?"

"Saul?" asked Jack. "He's the guy who 86'd you. Thin. Hannya mask. Maybe he looked different? Firsties, I'd like to get you back into your old shell, if for no other reason than I've already met my quota of muck ups for the month."

"Then, I won't be dead anymore?"

"Well, you're technically not dead now. Not yet, anyway. It's only a separation until…uh, well, how should I say it? Basically, you've got a squatter. Could be another ghost, a demon perhaps? Not sure."

"Solak?" asked Alice.

"Not likely. Maybe a proxy—somebody he's working with."

"In my body?" asked Momoko.

"Hey, this kid is sharp. Question is why?"

"Easy," replied Alice. "He wanted Yuki, but she hadn't taken any pills." Her eyes wandered knowingly in Momoko's direction.

"Ugh, Akari got me started so she wouldn't have to take them alone. I've been trying to stop." Momoko's head completed a full rotation like a clock.

"Now we're getting somewhere," said Jack. "Hang low, will 'ya? The microphone thing was a riot, but now they know you're a problem. We'll be in touch."

Alice waited for Momoko to back slowly through the door and disappear. "Will she be okay?"

"Nothing a little therapy couldn't fix. Relax. By the time we're done, she won't remember a thing."

"Then why do you look so worried? What happens if we don't?"

"When Saul gets what he wants, he'll ice her body, and I'll have no choice but to harvest her. End of story." He could tell that Alice hadn't thought it through by the way her pupils dilated. "But things could go according to plan for once. I'd say I'm due. Probably."

Solak's shadow draped over Akari's lunch like curry sauce. "Keep eating, and don't speak out loud. Just nod." The horns of his mask were so close that they brushed her hair. "They can't see me, but there is one here who can. Can you guess who it is?"

"Alice," whispered Akari, making sure to conceal her mouth as she spoke.

"Excellent instincts well-developed from having to watch your back. I do like working with show business types. So professional and similar to my line of work." He pivoted back to his point. "There's something I need you to do, not as yourself, as Momoko. A little acting job, shall we say?"

"I thought I was," she replied.

"This is decidedly more specific. Solak placed his hand on her phone. "I've added it to your calendar. Also, leave your purse where it can be found."

"Why?"

"Some pills are going to find their way inside. Be sure to bring them to your appointment."

"Why are you talking to yourself?" asked Saori, who had noticed Akari, mumbling. "And why have you been acting so weird?"

"What's it to you?"

"In case you've forgotten, I'm the captain." Saori's glasses smugly bounced on the tip of her nose. "It's my job to—"

"You're just keeping that seat warm for me."

Saori thought she must have heard wrong. "What did you just say?"

"I said, those glasses make you look fat." Akari returned to her lunch, ignoring Saori, who appeared about to burst.

Jack floated into the room; obsidian robes trailing behind him like clouds drenched dark with rain. "Hiya, Saul. Who's that you got there, cause it sure as hell ain't Momoko."

"Another loose one, have we?" replied Solak. "No doubt she's around. People will probably hear her talking when they play the recording backward. Why not go look for her?"

"I'm not going to do your dirty work," said Jack. "I'll harvest her when I'm good and ready. What kind of scam you got here, Saul?"

"Did it ever occur to you I might be a patron of the arts?"

Seeing Alice trying to leave the room to metamorph, Akari grabbed a fistful of her shirt and pulled her back down to the floor. She shoved a bento box into her chest. "Why don't you eat with us Alice-chan?

"Sorry, I'm not hungry." She tried again to stand, but Akari refused to release her grip.

"You really should eat. It might help you stay on key."

Solak was in no mood to catch up with Jack. He held his breath, and as his eyes bulged, the spotlights grew brighter until all at once they exploded.

The sound startled Saori so much that her elbow jerked and knocked over her microphone. It struck Akari square in the face, knocking her to the ground. She took out her cellphone and shone it around the room, but there was nothing left to see. Saori ran over to Haruto, who emerged from the mixing room to make sure that everyone was okay. "Are you sure this place isn't haunted or something?

"I'm beginning to see why time here was so cheap," he replied.

◆ ◆ ◆

George was conscious of the fact that his new office was the one from which he had endured Fujisawa's scrutiny, but now he would make everyone squirm. There would be no more, "Okada-san, you need to double-check the numbers," or "Okada-san, if you don't need a transplant, you're not sick."

"Making ourselves at home, are we?"

George realized he was being watched and looked up to see Izumi in all her ergonomic glory. Her hair was tied back in a tight bun, and her uninfected eye glared. George knocked over his water bottle and scrambled to move several items for her approval. He re-positioned a picture frame as it changed to Yuki's school photo. "There. Exactly like in your memo." He tried not to appear nervous. "I passed it along to the rest of my team." It was a feeble attempt to remind her that he was no longer the low man on the totem pole.

"Looks like someone's made a space elevator out of the corporate ladder. Vice-President."

George coughed. "Yes, well, I can't take credit for Fujisawa-san's bad heart."

"He was popping nitroglycerin pills like raisins, but you've had quite the run of good fortune. People talk, you know." She slid a new smartwatch across his desk, which made an unsettling scraping sound. "Here…it was the last email he sent me."

"Sumimasen," he replied. "I'll always treasure it." Naturally, he had no intention of wearing it longer than she was present.

"Such a shame they outlawed implanting employees with microchips." She adjusted the height of his monitor. "You don't like to follow the rules, do you?"

"I might interpret them a bit differently," George objected, "but I wouldn't say I break them." Trying to prompt her to move on to her next victim, he asked, "So, are we all good here? I placed my chair where you asked. I passed on that memo—"

"That's as important to us as the balls on a fish. I'm here to discuss economics, not ergonomics." She flicked over a glass samurai helmet he had bought on a family trip to Nagahama. "Okada-san, I'm not here to check out your new office. Perhaps you're not aware, but I actually have two bosses, and Fujisawa-san only satisfied one of them. I want to know if I'm going to be having this conversation with someone different in the future."

At first, George didn't grasp the severity of her threat. It hadn't escaped his attention that Izumi was the messenger of people who wished not to be quoted, but her aggressiveness still surprised him. "Look, you can tell whoever sent you…I'm going to do everything I can to see that our new product launch goes smoothly. You can tell your bosses that I'm grateful, and I'm going to do everything I can to live up to Fujisawa-san's example."

Izumi's continence became gray as she walked behind his desk, so close that his chair began to slide. "You've been doing a good job of justifying those N-43 discrepancies. We've been watching you, and you're a man who doesn't let legality inconvenience efficiency. A real family man."

"Now look," George replied. "I'm not sure what you're inferring, but if there is anything wrong with our numbers, I'm happy to have Abe-san look into it immediately."

Izumi gave his face a quick slap. "I don't think you hear what I'm saying. It's unfortunate that none of your predecessors were as morally flexible. Your psychological profile suggests you are someone we can work with. I don't know…maybe because you grew up abroad? You're not rigid. We like that. But people get new titles—new roles, and they change. Never change Okada-san. That's all we ask." The tips of their noses almost touched. "Wakarimashita ka?"

There was a light knock on the door. Mrs. Okada held her husband's lunch up high and waved.

"I'm sorry, okaasan. We're in a bit of a meeting. Can you leave it on my desk?"

"She doesn't need to leave," replied Izumi. "Where do you think we get our N-43? Nice bento box."

◆ ◆ ◆

"Good job, everyone." Haruto unkeyed the microphone and turned to his sound engineer. "Are you sure that's everything? Something seemed off in the third verse."

"Relax," replied the engineer. "I could make a single out of a catfight. Just let me work my magic. I'll add a soft beat—maybe some gated reverb. It's going to be epic."

Haruto already had doubts about doing an Akari memorial song. He was under the impression idol music was supposed to make you happy, not want to call your grandmother. There was nothing he could do now, though, except put his faith in the conclusion that he didn't know what he was doing. "Okay, then. I'll leave it to you. Otsukaresama desu."

Outside, Taka was nursing a bottle of green tea. "Sounded good. I mean, I've never heard one unmixed before, but better than any of the songs you recorded back in the day." It occurred to him that his observation might be a bit raw. "Don't get me wrong. Those were honest. But working with a recording company, it was…well, it's going to be great."

"Yeah, but they're like loan sharks. They'll drive you into bankruptcy, even if the song is a hit. At least I'll have something good to listen to when I'm living in a tent." Haruto rubbed his forehead, a physical reaction to the stress. "What's worse…I've sort of got this silent partner, and he'll want his cut. If this doesn't turn out, I'll be taking 'break a leg' literally."

"What about the concert with Superflat? That's good for something, isn't it?"

"I don't know. I guess they're doing pretty well. They have this song about the pleasures of tanning or something. They even made a couple of commercials. I hear most of their money comes from that. We should be so lucky." Haruto felt like he had been picked out of the water, only for a second chance to drown. "Maybe some of their fans will like us. Who am I kidding? They like Superflat. Oh, I almost forgot. How's the hologram coming?"

"Well, there's only so much I can do at home." Taka looked forward to trying everything out in a more appropriate venue.

"It's okay. I trust you." Haruto patted Taka on the back, like a younger brother. "All right then. Drinking time. Of course, with the Genki Girls, it's always drinking time." He laughed, a bit desperately.

"Need company?" Taka wondered if Haruto might have forgotten that he was old enough to enjoy a glass of saké.

"How am I supposed to wallow in self-pity if you're there, lowering the bar."

As he left, Taka called out, "Haruto-san. Have you seen Momoko?"

"I don't know. She was the first to leave. Acting a bit weird lately, don't you think? But that's like trying to tell if a cat is tired." It occurred to him that Taka might have other objectives. "Wait. Don't forget she's an idol."

◆◆◆

"Can't believe you'd want to come here," said Yuki. "Not many people volunteer to visit a hospital."

Maybe Jack wouldn't have approved of her tagging along to see Keiji, but Alice wasn't about to run it through a committee. The sound of softly whirring machines was simultaneously reassuring and frightening. "Is he still in a coma?" Alice struggled to pretend she wasn't emotionally involved.

"The doctor says it's a miracle he's alive. The trauma to his brain was severe. There was swelling." Yuki thought about her other friend who hadn't been as lucky. "They brought him out of the coma yesterday."

A nurse stopped them at the door. "Oh, hello there. You're Keiji's friends, right? You must have heard he woke up. I don't think he's supposed to see guests yet. We only just removed the ventilator."

"Please," begged Yuki. "We've known each other since, forever. We're practically family."

"I'm sorry, but—"

"Her best friend didn't make it," Alice said, unexpectedly. It was manipulative, but she wanted to show Yuki she could be helpful. "He'll want to see her."

Unable to resist Alice's emotional leverage, the nurse replied, "Look, you two. I'm about to go on break. If you're not here when I get back, I suppose there isn't a problem. Right?" She left the door open as she walked past them.

Keiji lacked the functionality to do little more from his bed than watch TV vacantly. Engrossed, he didn't seem to notice as Yuki placed some flowers next to him, but a blurry outline grabbed his attention. "Alice-chan?" he asked.

The girls looked at each other, hoping the other would tackle the response. Assuming it was her responsibility, Yuki replied, "Keiji, this is Alice...but not our Alice. I didn't tell you, did I? I'm in a group called the Genki Girls. Don't laugh. We're trying to be idols." It was a feeble attempt to circumvent the subject. "I bleached my hair. Do you like it? It was my mom's idea."

"Nice to meet you," said Alice, using a formal introduction to conceal the emotional instability she was experiencing. "How are you feeling? I hear they brought you out of the coma yesterday." She hoped Yuki would assist her with the social pleasantries.

Keiji's eyes were cloudy, and a great while passed before he blinked. "You look different."

"Hai," said Alice. "You understand, right? I'm not the same Alice you knew." She wiped aside a stray tear that must have seemed inappropriate. "I'm not *your*, Alice."

It was apparent that he hadn't yet been told the outcome of the accident. Yuki wasn't sure if it was her place but doubted there would be a better time, and perhaps the waning effect of barbiturates in his system might soften the blow. "You were in an accident," she said. "You were very lucky Keiji."

"Where's Alice? Why isn't she here?"

Alice turned so that neither of them could see her cry in earnest. She didn't feel sorry for herself as much as the fact that he might suffer.

"We won't be seeing her anymore, Keiji," Yuki replied, not nearly as successful in hiding her emotions. "She didn't make it. I am so sorry, Keiji."

This seemed to register as he looked away. Remaining in a medically induced coma was apparently more desirable than being forcibly awoken to the truth.

Alice and Yuki had transitioned the same emotional landscape and were somewhat relieved when Keiji's mother appeared. She looked at her son and immediately inferred why he was upset. "You told him?"

"I am so sorry," said Yuki. "I wanted to lie, but—"

"No, it's fine," she replied. "I'm glad. I tried to tell him last night."

"Is he going to be okay?" asked Alice.

"He needs spinal surgery, but there's an overseas specialist; someone not covered by national insurance. It's way too much money. It would take a miracle."

As the water rushed up from the floor of the car, it had not occurred to Alice that surviving might be the lesser option. At least she had a chance to make a difference now, and that was something. "Maybe we can help."

"I'm sorry I didn't get your name. I'm Keiji's mom."

"Alice desu. Yoroshiku onegaishimasu."

"Oh, dear," she replied.

◆ ◆ ◆

Mrs. Okada watched her husband pick at the egg omelet she had carefully prepared. "Sorry, there's no cookie," she apologized. "They sent me a message saying your glucose levels were off. You know how the toilet in your office checks for such things?" She wrung her hands. "Well, it sent me a text."

George neatly wiped his mouth. He had not uttered a word since Izumi had left, uninterested in their interpersonal drama.

"I'll take the bento box, please."

Something about the request loosened his lips. "That's how you've been getting it to them, isn't it?" George had always been a little embarrassed to be seen having lunch with his wife, but he had decided not to die on that particular hill. What at first, appeared an attempt to recover time lost from his long hours at the office had all been a ruse. It was startling to realize that the source of his inventory fluctuations shared his bedroom. "Do you work for the company? Someone else?"

"I only did it for Yuki…for us. As long as we're needed, we'll be safe."

"Safe? I'm a pharmaceutical executive. What have you gotten us into?"

"I'm saving this family. All you think about is Tokuji-Tech, but it's bigger than that. Much bigger."

There had never been much point arguing with his wife, but he still felt compelled to present his reasoning. "I could have found the money for Yuki's lessons. Why didn't you come to me? Maybe we could have—"

"You don't understand. What do you think happened to the Suzukis? Do you really think that was an accident? And now, Fujisawa-san." She tried to grab his hand, but he pulled it away. "Next time it could be us. Please try and understand."

A glimpse of his new smartwatch led him to consider how he had risen from a low-level manager to vice president in such a spectacular fashion. George remembered Izumi's warning and wondered if even now someone was listening, someone who might not work at the company. For the first time, he honestly considered the look of fear in his wife's eyes. George raised the watch towards his mouth and spoke clearly so that his thoughts could not be mistaken. "Of course, I'll do everything to see that inventory supplies remain steady. If anyone from the PMDA comes by, they'll be more than happy with what they find. Only I can ensure that business continues as usual. It would be unfortunate if anything were to happen to me. Very unfortunate."

◆ ◆ ◆

"It's kind of like a fundraiser," explained Haruto. "It was a couple of the girls' idea. See, they have this friend who needs this surgery not covered by NHI. That's right. They all went to the same school."

There was a pause as Genjirō processed the idea. "Like a charity handshake event. I like where this is going. The high bidder plays VR with some of the girls. We post it online…."

"Or—hear me out, we raffle off a lunch?" said Haruto, not receptive to his former boss' idea, but ready with an alternative suggestion.

"Your girls are known for VR and death. That's your shtick. Embrace it."

Sometimes he didn't understand Haruto at all. "Oh, speaking of which…did you hear the master of the new single yet?"

"Yes. Amazing, right?" Haruto's response would not have differed if it had sounded like cats in heat.

"A freaking miracle if you ask me. Aren't you glad you signed with the best? It drops tomorrow morning. I'll call marketing and see if they can build some interest in this morbid handshake event of yours."

"Actually, I thought it might put the girls in a positive light."

"Maybe one of them could pass out and get admitted to the hospital? Give it some thought. I'm sure you'll come up with something. You always do."

Haruto was in the habit of feigning support. "Right, well, have Wataru-san…" It occurred to him that his former associate was no longer there. "Have marketing get in touch with me. Talk to you later. Jaa na."

◆ ◆ ◆

"So about that assignment, the one at Tokuji-Tech." Boss Mori's office smelled of tobacco and the fear of his visitors.

"I can explain," said Sho. "The warehouse has these forklift bots—"

"I don't care about the particulars." The yakuza boss tossed a packet of gray pills on the table.

Sho had already learned the lesson he was apparently about to be given, but he was relieved that his latest failure might not require his head. He placed his hand upon the desk and readied himself for the appearance of the blade that exchanged flesh for mercy.

"What are you doing?" asked Boss Mori. He took out his decanter and poured Sho a drink. "You're not being demoted." He nudged the pills closer. "This is a special job. The Genki Girls are one of your sideline businesses, right? We need you to slip these into the purse of one of your girls."

Sho pocketed the pills, not understanding why his kumichō thought the matter had been satisfactorily resolved. "So the matter at Tokuji-Tech…"

"Sho-san, what is it you want? We don't give out Employee of the Month awards. Living well is its own reward." Boss Mori noticed Sho's finger had been repaired. "Is there something else?"

"I delivered this week's materials to the lab. There should be enough to complete the shipment. They say we have about a week and a half worth of raw ingredients."

"Soon, we won't have to scrounge around like mice. Remember, Sho-san, a stone in the river, will always be moved in time."

Sho bowed and departed even more confused than when he thought his status was in doubt.

A soft tone indicated an incoming call, and the hologram of Boss Mori's saiko-komon rose from his desk. "Speak of the devil. I was just passing your request on to Sho-san."

"Excellent," he replied. "I also need your signature on the short sell for tomorrow."

Boss Mori considered the document he had been given. "This is for a much larger amount than we discussed. If the stock were to go up, we would be ruined."

"I can assure you that will not happen." The mask was not exactly a conduit of emotion. "Not only will we make money as the shares become worthless, but we will reinvest our profits to solidify our position. You will be most satisfied with the outcome; of that, I can promise."

"I had better be, but what if the damage is permanent? How can you be sure the value to the company will ever return?"

The hannya mask's maniacal grin remained permanently fixed. "We have to destroy everything if we are to own the pieces. Then, we will show people that it was never really broken at all."

"And you think this new amount will be sufficient?"

"Tokuji-Tech will soon be ours. Then we'll no longer need to get our ingredients in a bento box."

◆ ◆ ◆

"We found it near a guy who bought the farm, and I don't believe in coincidence. I believe in convergence." Jack handed Matthew the pieces of the drone.

"A sub-class Z model," observed Matthew, holding it up to his monocle. "Doesn't have to be registered. An apartment drone, and they don't call it a peeping-Tom for nothing. About the right size to fly under staircases, but it's not even the smallest you can buy." He produced his jeweler's tools and unscrewed the casing. "It's as small as you can get with this motor, though. Looks like they upgraded the blades. Made it a bit slower."

"Why would they do that?" asked Alice. Keiji had once let her fly his drone down at the park, but she wasn't what could be called a hobbyist.

"Whoever owned this didn't care about speed. They wanted quiet. These blades cost more than the drone. A lot more." A little metal cartridge fell out.

"What's that? The battery?" asked Jack.

"It's a CO_2 cartridge and a bit of something else." Matthew pulled out some gloves. "This is definitely going to cost you extra. You didn't tell me this thing could kill me." His tweezers held up something almost invisible, lighter than a fiber optic thread.

"What's that?"

"A modified type of speed that uses microspheres to redline your heart. Self-dissolving. Makes it look like the victim died naturally."

"Isn't that how he went?" asked Alice.

"Yeah, guess it must have worked." Jack cracked his neck and shifted nervously in his collar.

"No way to know," said Matthew.

"I said it must have worked," insisted Jack, depositing extra tokens into his account.

Matthew acknowledged the additional funds. "I'm guessing the second shot probably did the job."

"Who do you think could have done this?" asked Alice.

"It's not mine, that's for sure. Only one family has the chemistry department to make something like this."

"Kurome-gumi," replied Jack.

"That'll be double," said Matthew.

◆ ◆ ◆

Frequently, the site of health fairs and other special events, the hospital's parking lot, was rarely used for its created purpose. Most people arrived in automated vehicles, so there was talk about apportioning most of the space in the future to construct a new wing.

"Better than usual," said Haruto, taking note of the turnout.

"Maybe they think it's a farmer's market," said Ms. Ito. She was used to their fan events, only drawing a fraction of what they were seeing.

"And now for the results of our auction." Yuki's voice boomed from the loudspeaker. "A chance to go head-to-head with the Genki Girls to the…" she looked at the verbiage provided by Flavor Beat's marketing department and lowered the microphone. "I'm not saying this."

Saori looked at the script. "It's an expression." She grabbed the microphone from Yuki and shouted, "To the death! Now let's read the winner's name. Chotto matte. Is this right? Is this even fair?"

"He's not technically on staff," said Yuki. "Just read the results."

"And the winner is," Saori dropped any pretense of enthusiasm as she read, "Taka."

Akari did her best Momoko-style cheer to congratulate him on his little victory. "Taka-kun, *omedetou!*" Besides his name, she could see how much he had bid. "But where did you get the money?"

"Let's just say my collection of Akari memorabilia isn't what it used to be."

Realizing what he had sacrificed, she asked, "But I thought you loved those things?"

"Now, I love other things."

Akari's stomach fluttered, or at least the organ she had stolen from Momoko. She wondered if having a different set of eyes was why she had begun to see him in a new light. Even if the intent of his feelings might be for someone else, she found herself hoping that she was the one for whom he was falling. Taka had already proven that he liked her no matter what body she occupied, and that was enough in and of itself.

"And it's for a good cause." Still, Taka saw someone carrying away his favorite poster, and a little piece of him died.

Haruto was relieved the prize would stay within the family, but bad luck had a way of following them, and he was low on insurance. "Omedetou gozaimasu, Taka-san. Listen, I was thinking. Don't feel like you have to go through with it. I didn't order enough merch anyway, so we're probably going to come up short. Anyway, if you want a refund..."

"No, I'd really like my prize," he replied. "It was for a good cause, and something about the way they play is...intense. The hospital has a game room, right?"

"I think it sounds fun," said Akari, pushing Taka through the front doors. "She paused in front of Momoko's ghostly ear and whispered, "Anyway, Taka is kind of cute, and it's not like it's my position I'd be risking." Seeing Momoko fume, she added, "Stay genki!"

"Akari?" As she realized who had stolen her identity, Momoko flashed red like a spectral siren.

"Guess it's not only your body I'll be taking," added Akari.

A nearby poster ripped in half as Momoko vented her rage. Its new owner reacted in horror to find that his prize had mysteriously become worthless.

"I never liked you. Do you hear me? Haruto made me watch you. You'd better not hurt my body!" The only response Momoko received was Akari using her middle finger to draw a long scratch up her leg. "Akari!"

"Did she say Akari?" Jack looked around for Alice. "That can't be right. Alice?"

In the hospital's rec room, Alice strapped into one of the VR rigs used to entertain visitors and patients. No doubt donated, it was an older model than the one at the café, but functional. "So, what are we going to play?"

"It's up to him." Yuki pointed at Taka, who seemed not to have thought his plan out past winning. "He's the one who sold all his old Akari crap."

Saori ducked into the room. "Am I too late?"

"Saori?" asked Yuki, surprised that she would stoop to their level. "Why?"

"What? You don't think I like to have a little fun?" It was apparent that none of the other girls were buying it. "Fine. I'm tired of shaking hands. If I use any more antibacterial gel, my hands are going to crack so hard I'll see bone. Where did all those people come from anyway?"

"I think they only have four VR rigs," said Akari.

Taka was both oblivious and helpful. "There's another one behind the divider. I had my appendix removed down the hall."

"Taka-kun," said Akari. "It's your victory. So what are we going to play?"

"Jetfighter 1946," Taka replied, oblivious to the fact that his companions might not share his taste in games.

"Maybe I should have stayed at the table," said Saori.

"Don't listen to her. You won the auction. We'll play whatever you want." Akari found Saori irritating and not just because her attitude rang familiar.

Yuki dug a bit into Saori. "Haven't you heard that the customer is god?"

"It's Taka-kun. He brings me my lattes."

"Then it's decided," said Alice. Scrolling through the menu, she could tell that the hospital didn't have any of the newer games loaded anyway. Jetfighter 1946 took place in an alternative history where the war had continued long enough for Japan to field its first jets. It was an older game, mostly popular with military otaku, but it had once been reasonably popular.

"The waters off Hokkaido, 1946," said a low, gravelly voice. "The war drags on, but hope comes on aluminum wings. Imperial Weapon No. 2, the Nakajima Kikka, is swift and her pilots brave. All of Japan is counting on you to defend the homeland from the Soviet invaders." Each of the players found themselves in the cockpit of Japan's first jet-powered aircraft, known as the "Orange Blossom." The narrator continued, "The Soviet paratroop corps have successfully taken Hokkaido. It is up to you to bomb their airfields before they can expand their efforts throughout Japan. *Banzai!*"

"Banzai!" repeated Taka, with considerably more enthusiasm than the others.

The catapult on the aircraft carrier released, and Alice felt her Kikka jet surge forward, like the electromagnetic launch of a rollercoaster. The scenery blurred bluish-white as the Niseko Mountain Range passed beneath her fighter jet. "Is that Mt. Fuji?" she asked, seeing a distinctive looking volcanic peak in the distance.

"No," laughed Taka. "That's Mt. Yōtei. This is supposed to be Hokkaido, not Honshu. Head south, and I think we'll find the Soviet airbase. Now listen, everyone. I want my money's worth."

"I'm hungry," said Saori, bringing up the rear. "This isn't going to take long, right? How about ramen? Why don't we ditch in the ocean and do that?"

"Twelve o'clock high," shouted Taka. "Everyone break!" He yanked his yoke to the left and dove for the foothills of nearby Mt. Niseko-Annupuri.

Alice pulled her controller towards her chest and entered into a steep climb. As she did, a Russian MiG-13 emerged from the cloudbank firing its three 20mm G-20 cannons. She was so distracted that she didn't see Jack appear in her cockpit.

"Are you sure you harvested Akari?" he yelled behind her right ear.

She screamed and momentarily lost control of the twin-jet aircraft, performing an unintentional barrel roll. "Don't do that!"

"Let me try that again. Did you or did you not harvest Akari?" He wasn't the least bit concerned with her game.

Alice was having enough trouble piloting the Kikka, without his added distractions. "I thought I did. Now you're asking me? I'm kind of busy." She banked hard in an attempt to aide Saori, who had an enemy fighter at her six o'clock position.

Jack reached over Alice's shoulder and randomly flipped one of the switches. "I would have said something, but I didn't see a ghost, ergo I thought we were copacetic."

"Well, there you have it." Alice flipped the switch back again. "I guess I did." She squeezed the trigger and opened up several holes in the MiG-13's wings. It tore free, and the jet spiraled to the rocky terrain below. Alice banked to avoid the wreckage.

"I see the field," said Akari, her voice distant and scratchy. "I'm carrying a 500kg bomb. Someone clear me a path."

"I'm wingman," offered Taka, pushing his throttle hard to the wall. His speedometer read 600 km/h as he dove to catch up.

"That's her," cried Momoko, her ghost appearing behind Alice's other ear.

"That's Akari!"

Alice screamed, slightly less this time. "This plane is single-crew. Not three. One. Me. Not you," she said to Jack, "or you," she added for Momoko's benefit.

"I'm not even solid," protested Momoko.

"It's not a weight and balance issue." Alice realized her plane was now in an unfavorable position and initiated a climb.

"I told you," said Jack. "This is great. Just great."

Taka saw a MiG sneaking up on Akari's ten o'clock and snipped off the tip of its tail. Unfazed, she dropped her bomb onto the snowy runway below, and there was a pause as everyone waited to see what would happen. A billowy, black, and orange cloud rose into the sky.

"You did it!" cried Taka, following the Soviet plane through the smoke. "Where did it go?"

"I'm shot," said Saori. Smoke peeled from her plane's wings as she flew into the side of the mountain. Metal and snow rained as the MiG revealed itself from behind the wispy fog.

"I guess she's getting ramen, after all," observed Akari.

"I'm on it," replied Alice, applying bottom rudder to tighten her turn and engage the Russian fighter. The MiG-13 flipped onto its back, and that is when she saw its pilot. He wore a white hannya mask with a red star on his forehead. "Solak."

"Son-of-a-gun. It's Saul," said Jack. "Wonder what's his game?"

"Apparently, Jetfighter 1946. Doesn't matter, he's right where I want him," replied Alice, who thought she had found the perfect position, but then he tightened his turn and piloted his plane straight into hers. It happened so fast that there was no time for her to react.

At the last moment, Solak ejected, allowing the planes to collide as he jettisoned to safety.

Before Alice could react, "Pilot terminated," flashed on her screen. She tore off her headset and found herself back in the hospital's rec room. "He did that on purpose."

"You think?" said Jack.

Meanwhile, Taka saw something black streak past him, but it was too fast for him to react. "Where's Yuki?"

Another explosion rocked the airfield. In the excitement, Yuki had managed to release her bomb. "Any questions?"

Solak unbuckled himself from his ejection seat and fell freely towards Akari's plane. Landing on its fuselage, he threw aside his gloves and used his claws to tear it open like a soup can. Wind blinded Akari as Solak threw aside the canopy and relieved her of her duty. She toppled through the air like a ragdoll as Solak climbed inside.

Seeing her plunge to the ground, Taka cried, "I'm coming!" and lowered the nose of his plane. He pushed its two Ishikawajima Ne-20 turbojets to their limits until he was almost beside her. Then, Taka ignited the four gas generators under his seat and ejected.

"Naughty boy," cried Solak, who had regained control of Akari's Kikka.

Taka tucked his arms tight against his chest and fell like a rocket. When he reached Akari's flailing body, he grabbed at her legs, but it was like trying to capture the wings of a fly. It wasn't until Mount Yōtei passed above them that he finally caught her ankle. Taka secured his legs around her waist and pulled his parachute. It jerked violently, and they dangled, limbs entwined, in what appeared a lover's embrace. "You're safe now, Momo-chan." He was unaware that his assistance was neither required nor appreciated. Like the pendulum of a grandfather clock, they dangled against the blue Hokkaido sky.

Akari's eyes opened wide enough for Taka to see the reflection of the white-faced demon firing at them from what was now an open-cockpit fighter. Apricot-sized holes appeared in their parachute, and they began to accelerate towards the ground, a blur that whistled to an inevitable conclusion.

Alice, Jack, and Momoko re-appeared in the game in time to see the plume of snow. As Taka and Akari impacted the brae at the bottom of the mountain, standing near its crest, there was nothing they could do but watch.

"That was supposed to be my romantic death," protested Momoko.

"Relax," said Jack. "It's just a game." He leaned over to Alice. She's not using anymore, right?"

Back in the rec room, Taka removed his headset. He was short of breath from the excitement of what he considered a most epic experience. "Did you see that? I rolled at the last minute so Momoko's character would survive? Did she? I mean, did you?"

Akari hung limp in her VR rig, a physical and transcendental echo of her recent corporal demise. Seeing only Momoko in danger, Taka rushed to help unfasten her safety harness. Alice watched, aware of the situation's resemblance to an earlier one featuring the same players. Taka rested Momoko against his shoulder, but as he did, several gray pills spilled from her hand and pattered upon the floor.

CHAPTER ELEVEN:
CHECKS & BALANCES

I t hardly seemed an appropriate time for Jack to be playing with the samurai helmet. Staring vacantly at the hillside, he wore it as casually as a gardener's hat. Alice had questions of her own, namely, why would Solak attack Akari if he knew she was only posing as Momoko. If intended as an elaborate misdirection, they had already figured out the truth, but perhaps not everything was, as it seemed. "Didn't you say never to touch that?"

"I'm pretty sure its original owner wouldn't mind."

"Solak?" Startled, Alice's leg caught the corner of an antique chest. "Itai!" She had wondered if the silhouette standing in the garden appeared a bit shorter than usual.

"This was once the house of a painter, a poor and tragic figure. He made hanging scrolls for the wealthy families of Kyōto until he fell in love with the daughter of his patron." He wandered over to the kakejiku of the dragon as if it bore some relationship to his story. "His father left him this property, along with a small wheat field, but the man had no ability where farming was concerned."

"Why are you here?"

"I was under the impression you wanted to talk, but we haven't very long. What Jack lacks in intelligence, he makes up for in experience."

Alice rubbed the back of her thigh. One of the benefits of being able to reset her physical state was that she had become uncharacteristically bruise-free. "What did you do to him?"

"Let's just say your likeness sent Jack to a bakery in Ginza…which doesn't sell birthday cake." Solak chortled darkly from behind the helmet's menpō.

"That's cruel."

"Cruel—funny. It's all a matter of where you stand in relation to the joke. Even war is interesting when you're winning."

"Are you winning?"

Solak removed the katana from its stand and executed a vertical draw strike on the orange they had recently added as part of the makeshift shrine. "I suppose by now, Jack knows you didn't really harvest Akari?" He admired the tsuba and restored it to its rightful place on the katana kake. "Perhaps that is my fault. I had other plans for her."

"Why should I care?"

It was the response for which Solak had hoped. "Jack never leaves a thread loose too long. It's why his incompetence is momentarily tolerated."

"Keiji," she whispered.

"He'll wait for the right time, such as when the boy is about to have surgery. Then he'll tie things up. He is, after all, a harvester." He threw half of the orange into Jack's garden. "There is an alternative. I find it hard to believe you feel loyalty towards someone you barely know. Jack's only attachment is to Jack. He probably hasn't even told you he's not from Vegas?" Solak gauged from her reaction that he had struck a vein. "No doubt, he thinks it makes him sound sophisticated and continental."

Alice picked up the other half of the orange. "I don't care where he's from. I'm just—"

"Looking out for the people you love? I respect that. You have honor. So few people in this age do." He paused to appreciate the portrait. "Sometimes, to get the things you desire…you have to become what you hate. We don't have to make this too serious. Think of it as more of a collaboration."

"I don't understand. What do you want from me?"

"Something Jack should have done already…harvest Momoko, the ghost, not the cellular interpretation. There is a haunted house, one of those places people go to as part of their courtship rituals. I'll have everything arranged. You only need to do your job. Tell Jack—" He cocked his head, as if he sensed something, and vanished. The helmet crashed onto the floor.

A pink paper box clutched under his arm; Jack opened the shoji screen door with his free hand. "I don't know who told you that place had birthday cake, but I brought you some macarons anyway. Girl chow, right?" He saw the helmet on the ground, and his nostrils flared. "Hey, I thought I told you never to touch that!"

"I was cleaning…it must have slipped," she lied.

"Why's it on the floor? Ah, c'mon. Look at it." Jack carefully placed it back on its stand. Perhaps there was a new scratch, but maybe he had seen it before. Then Jack noticed that she was holding one of the orange slices. "Hey, those aren't for eating. What's wrong with you? Is nothing sacred?"

"You would know." It probably wasn't the right time to draw the comparison. "I was about to make some breakfast. Can you eat natto?"

Jack was too tired to fight, so he downgraded his temper to annoyance. "Like I said. You might be Japanese, but my underwear has spent more time on this island than you have."

"Really? Do you have to be so gross?"

His overly forced exhale telegraphed that he wasn't interested in staying mad. "Maybe you're right. I keep meaning to generate new ones—"

"Okay. I get it." Alice put wood in the house's traditional kamado, which had a round pot for cooking rice. "So that award-winning sense of humor you have, is that something you picked up in Vegas or somewhere else?"

Jack froze like a cat whose tail had just been pulled. "You've been talking to him, haven't you?"

Alice lit the fire and slowly closed the small iron door.

"Seventy-five years in residence. Good enough? I wasn't born there if that's what you're asking and yet I still put the fun in funeral. What else did he say?"

"Hardly anything. Well…"

"Yeah?"

"How can I trust you? I mean, I barely know you, other than that you killed my whole family."

"I didn't kill them. I harvested. There's a difference."

She began to clean the rice with water she had pulled from their well. "Whatever."

"And no. You can't trust me."

Sensing a moment of honesty, Alice stopped stirring the rice.

"I'm selfish. I'm a scoundrel. I want to be left alone, and if people get hurt in the process, I couldn't care less." He opened the oven door out of concern that she couldn't possibly know what she was doing, only to be impressed that the fire seemed stable. "I've got just one weakness."

"What's that?"

"I always do the right thing. I don't want to, but I just can't seem to break the habit."

"So, how long?"

"How long for what?"

"Breakfast."

"Is that all you have to say? Aren't you concerned that he might have gotten to me?"

"Saul? Look. You either have what it takes to be my partner or you don't. Nothing you say can convince me either way. If Solak got to you, I'll know soon enough, but I don't see that happening before breakfast."

"Fine." Alice poured the starchy water into the sink. "So what do we do now? Is your glorified bracelet telling you anything?"

"All quiet on the eastern front, but maybe we're doing better than we think. For example, now that we know who's in Momoko's body, we can kill her."

"Excuse me."

"Just long enough to get the real Momoko back inside."

"Oh, well, that makes sense, strangely enough."

◆ ◆ ◆

Mrs. Okada could see Sho's silhouette at the turfy knoll's crown, leaning against his motorcycle like a yakuza James Dean. She was slightly out of breath as she passed him the bento box and said, "There's enough N-43 in there for two weeks. There's a government inspector who keeps coming around."

Vapor trailed from Sho's mouth. "What do you think we are, a corner pharmacy? He tapped the box with a black fingernail. "I'm feeling three days—tops. Anyway, the family is making new arrangements." He sensed his words weren't registering. "You hear what I'm saying? Your services aren't required anymore. You're out."

Mrs. Okada dug the heels of her shoes into the grass. "We've all been sticking out our necks for you. No one else can get this much N-43."

"You're not hearing me." He reached for another nicotine cartridge, but his last one was already in his blood. "We're done."

As a measure of last resort, she raised her voice. "But what's going to happen to me—to my Yuki-chan? After everything I've done…"

Kawaisou, thought Sho. He had never seen anything resembling fear in her eyes before and realized he hadn't been treating her like a civilian. "I don't even know what's going to happen to me." With nothing else to offer, he said, "You know how I survive? I make sure I'm one step ahead of everyone else." He placed the bento box inside the small trunk of his motorcycle. "Holding any Tokuji-Tech stock?"

"Only our whole retirement—oh, and we recently received a large grant with my husband's promotion." Her eyes bounced like a table tennis ball. "Yuki's college fund…"

Sho's bike sprung to life as he touched its handgrips. "Yeah, well, that might not be such a good short-term plan."

His tires tore a spot in the grass as he left, leaving her to wonder about the cryptic undertones of what he was trying to express. Any fear of the future had been replaced with an entirely new type of apprehension. She appreciated the correlation between being useful and remaining safe.

◆ ◆ ◆

"Did you get the flowers?" asked Haruto. The practice studio was vacant, so he filled the time by annoying his assistant. It was basically her job description.

Ms. Ito's beady-eyed stare was the one she used to win her weekend card games. "I'm not loaning you any more money. We should have charged admission at that fundraiser. The only people who came out ahead were the food vendors."

"I didn't know so many people would show." He looked under some boxes hoping he might stumble upon some loose change. "Anyway, we can't not get her flowers, especially after we sent them to Yuki, never mind that I'm still paying off the ones for Akari. Maybe they have a point card or something?" He had hoped for more help than Ms. Ito's usual granite façade. "Hold on. Maybe the residuals finally posted. There might be enough for some daisies or some of those weeds that look like flowers." Haruto's phone was two generations old, unthinkable in his industry days. As the app booted, he turned white, as if he had eaten some bad buffet sushi. "I think I've been hacked."

"You're the one always waiting to do the updates." Ms. Ito was starting to wonder if she'd be getting her next paycheck.

He projected the balance on the wall. "Look. I think I'm being trolled. I bet it's that producer from Superflat who hates me."

Ms. Ito didn't handle the accounting for the group, but she knew how to read a ledger. "Who cares? That's over a hundred million yen. Guess I'm getting paid after all." Then it crossed her mind that perhaps it was not their money to spend. "On second thought, better not touch it unless you want to go to jail."

"Don't worry," he said, closing the app. "I'll call the bank and straighten it out." As it closed, he noticed a news website he had left open. "Hey, look at that. Our picture is in the Culture section."

"Oh, great. Who did we lose this time?"

"No one. It's an article about Japan's hottest groups." He pulled up the singles rankings.

Ms. Ito's eyes narrowed. "It says we're number one. Number one?" She joined him in the search for small cameras, or signs that they were being pranked.

"If someone is messing with us, they went to a lot of trouble." Then he froze, as he attempted to process the sudden shift in their reality. "But what if it's true?

Now that I think about it, I thought I heard someone humming one of our songs walking through Shinjuku Station."

"You haven't been able to hear since you scouted out bands for Flavor Beat."

Haruto began to adopt a more optimistic outlook. "No. We're definitely back. The Culture section would never lie!" He gave her a big hug, which she received with the appreciation of a cat. "Where are you going? We have to celebrate."

"To get Momoko some flowers. Have you ever thought about getting a wholesaler's license?"

◆ ◆ ◆

Matthew waited for Jack to finish the transfer of tokens and handed him a small vial of gray powder. "A heart lapse cocktail with enhancer? Pretty freaky stuff."

Jack opened the vial and sniffed it a couple times. "Relax. We're not planning on eighty-sixing anyone. Well…not permanently."

Skepticism was Matthew's resting face. "Reassuring," he said, throwing away the gloves he had been using.

Alice had never wandered far from the anime resellers and maid cafes that lined Chuou-dori, Akihabara's main street. "So, what do we put it in? Do we sprinkle it like salt or something?"

"It's tasteless, so whatever. The enhancer will kick in first. After about five minutes, their esophagus will seize up. They'll pass out, and technically they'll be dead for around two minutes before the adrenaline kicks in. That's why I call it my Zombie Dust. Remember that sumo tournament they said was rigged?"

"Yeah?"

"Well, I don't know anything about that." Matthew gave a cool smile.

"But it works, right?" Alice understood that Momoko had to be paused, but it didn't mean she was entirely comfortable with the plan.

"Most of the time. Not everyone can handle the restart, though. Who exactly are you planning on using this on?

Jack sensed Alice appeared a bit apprehensive. "You've got nothing to worry about. What he's saying is like if somebody already has one foot in the grave. The person we're killing is basically a kid, so…we'll be fine." He rolled the vial in his slender fingers. "Hey, do we still have any more of those macarons?"

"Okay, then," said Matthew. He worked with all kinds, but these two were markedly deranged. From under his desk, he retrieved the black box Jack had forgotten at this booth. "That reminds me. I can't exactly throw this away at the train station."

"Thanks," replied Jack. "I'll toss it in my neighbor's trash."

"So you got it all sorted out, what you wanted to know?"

"Well, not exactly." He sensed Alice's resentment at his lack of progress. "I've been a little busy. I need time to focus on the other thing. Then—right back to the first thing."

"Matthew. Can I ask you a question?" Alice was relieved to have found a reasonable voice.

"Possibly." He tapped his credit counter.

Alice glared at Jack until he started the transfer from his digital wallet. "If you were to hack a car, how would you do it?"

"The hardest part is getting permission. Best to have the person you're targeting do the work for you. I'd enter through an area they weren't expecting like a music file or…"

"A game?" Alice blanched.

Matthew's forehead furrowed, and an eyebrow rose. "Hey—you alright? Didn't get any of that dust on you, did you?"

Alice grabbed Jack with both hands. "Jack. You didn't kill my parents."

"I know. That's what I've been saying. Does this timeline have some kind of delay or something?"

"I did."

◆ ◆ ◆

"I don't even know what I'm doing here," said the reporter. "I cover business, not lifestyle stories."

"Wait a minute." The neatly dressed female reporter next to him became indignant. "I write for Tōkyō Financial Report. I thought I was being hazed when they gave me this assignment. Seriously...idols?"

"If it helps, I write for a medical journal," said a man to their right. "I guess that kind of makes sense since a guy in a tracksuit gave me this at the door." He showed them a small plastic pouch with a single gray pill. "Apparently, from the same batch that put the girl in the hospital."

"I wouldn't even have come," said the first reporter, "but my editor looked scared...like he'd been threatened."

Momoko drifted in through the back wall of the hospital suite, concerned about what further damage Akari intended to do to her reputation. Seeing the sea of cameras, it was apparently going to be something very public.

"Well, it looks like it's go time," said Akari, satisfied that all the reporters had arrived.

"Are you sure you want to do this?" asked Yuki. "Couldn't you just release a statement?"

"I'm only going to say a few words. It's a formality, that's all." Akari was making the most out of her second chance at becoming an actress. "Don't you think we have a responsibility to our fans?"

"I don't know. We've never had fans before. Did you check this over with Haruto-sensei?"

"Like when you colored your hair?"

"What's with you? You sound just like Akari." Momoko had never criticized her in that way before.

Akari raised her bed so that she could better address the assembled media. "I want to thank everyone for your concern." She was loud, but still trying to maintain Momoko's vocal inflections. "I want everyone to know that I feel fine, but there is something that has been bothering me. The Genki Girls have always been about being real, but I haven't been truthful with my fans. I'm in the hospital today because," she bit her lower lip, "I've been using enhancer." She was able to see Momoko's spectral outline intently watching. "Maybe it was my lack of talent or unfortunate need to dress like a four-year-old. I wanted to publically caution all my fans not to copy my sad example and warn them about the dangers of what many think is only a harmless, recreational drug. Not that there isn't blame to go around. Tokuji-Tech Pharmaceuticals used the Genki Girls to market Neuroko. That's the drug people use to make enhancer. Maybe someone in the press should look into that?"

"I'm sorry," shouted one of the reporters. "Which one are you?"

"Momoko," replied Akari, locking eyes with her incorporeal likeness. "Oh—and I'm also a slut."

Unable to contain her rage, the real Momoko flew across the room, her apparition sending shivers through whomever she passed. She wrapped her intangible fingers around Akari's neck, but without the physical substance to support her rage, they slipped through as if she was trying to wrestle a fish.

Aware that the press could not see Momoko's furor, Akari buttressed her comments with malicious glee. "Yes, I have issues. So many."

◆ ◆ ◆

George's old cubicle mate Abe sucked air through his teeth. He was unable to understand how a slacker such as George had risen to become the head of their department. "Chief," he cried, a surreal way to address his former partner in procrastination. He peeked his head inside. "Chief. Have you seen the price of our stock?

Engrossed with his supply reports, George didn't even bother to raise his chin. "I'm kind of busy. Can this wait until lunch?"

"Neuroko XR is going to be delayed. Phase III trials are postponed until further review. All the press is talking about is how enhancer is basically a hack of our drug. Feds want a closer look."

Everyone at Tokuji-Tech knew that to be the case, but no one gave it much thought. Most pharmaceutical companies had a bastardized version of a drug people used for decidedly off-label purposes. "So. What does that have to do with us? It's a street drug." George loaded his stock-tracking app to see how big a hit he had taken.

"A bunch of stories appeared all at once on financial and medical blogs," replied Abe. "A perfect storm. Bad timing. Really bad."

George's sight blurred as he opened the page, and his balance was revealed.

"This can't be right."

"Seriously. It's all over the news. I thought you'd want to know."

"Not that. It says I don't own a single share. What the hell's going on? I better call my wife." He was interrupted by the sound of an incoming call. "Can we do this later? Maybe that's her now." It was, however, an unknown caller. "No, I'm not selling my signed champion Giants ball. I've had that since I was ten years old. Who gave you this number?"

"Knock-knock." Mrs. Okada stood at his office door, beaming.

"I think I might have figured it out. Sorry to disappoint you. No. No need to call again. How much? Seriously? That much, huh? Etto…no, sorry, I can't." George smashed the disconnect icon to cement his resolve. "Do you know anything about my signed Giants baseball being for sale?"

"Probably just a wrong number. So, I'm taking care of some financial matters. You know, home issues. Things you wouldn't care about. Would you be a dear and sign here…and initial in these three spots."

George took out his stylus and began to sign. "You know, I love that ball." She handed him his encrypted hanko stamp, which he activated with his fingerprint. "So, you're saying you don't know anything about it being for sale?" He digitally stamped wherever his wife pointed. Then he recalled what he had been worried about before he was distracted. "Wait, that reminds me. I was looking over our stock balance." His eyes lingered too long on one of the documents, but she hurriedly closed the file. "Hold on. What were those for again?" It was difficult to be suspicious of anyone in a bunny apron, but everything had been going sideways since he woke up.

"Oh, that?" she said with a twinkle in her eye. "We just sold the house. No lunch today. Gomenasai. Much too busy—lots to do." She vanished before he could fully process her last statement.

"We what?" His desk shuddered as his knee caught its bottom. He started for the door, but the president of Tokuji-Tech appeared on his monitor.

"Emergency meeting in the conference room Okada-san, all hands on deck. Apparently, your daughter is tied up in it. Call your family and tell them you're going to be home late."

"That's not a problem. It looks like I'll be sleeping at the office anyway."

◆ ◆ ◆

"Haruto-san." Flavor Beat's SVP of A&R had a face that perpetually appeared like he was sucking on a grapefruit. Years of legal human trafficking will do that to a person. He stared down his former protégé like a principal might someone who had pulled the fire alarm.

Momoko's makeshift press conference was actually done without Haruto's knowledge, but that was worse than if he had known. It represented his lack of control as a producer. Idols got mixed up in dating scandals, not drug stories.

"Haruto-san," said Genjirō, a bit more evenly. He always parsed out his words when he was about to dress down his former subordinate. Apparently, old habits died hard. "That press conference."

"Hai?" Haruto reverted to the submissive posture he had always assumed whenever the hammer was about to fall.

"The one people are saying single-handedly destroyed a pharmaceutical company…"

"Hai," Haruto repeated. He never dreamed that accepting such a token sponsorship from Tokuji-Tech would lead to such complications of association.

"Genius."

"What?"

"You no longer needed them, so you burned them to the ground and danced in their ashes."

"Sorry?"

"Your song had slipped to number four in the charts, but look at it now." He brought up the top hundred singles chart on his monitor. "Back on top. I'm just glad you left Flavor Beat before you came gunning for my job. Even I'm not cruel enough to bring down an entire company."

"Yeah," said Haruto, unconvincingly. "That's me. That's…apparently who I am."

"You do know what this means?"

"Um, well…no." Haruto hadn't the slightest such instincts to draw upon.

"We need another song. Now. By Friday."

"I can do that."

"Not you...the other guy, your secret weapon."

"My secret weapon?" He realized he was talking about the lyricist who had written their last song, but only Sho knew his actual identity.

"The hired gun you used to write the lyrics to the last song. The guy with actual talent."

Haruto had hoped that he could go back to writing everything they recorded. It was the only reward for the other menial tasks he had to endure. He had even saved up a few ideas, including one about making anime real. "If I don't have talent. Why exactly am I here?"

"Honestly? You scare the shit out of me."

◆ ◆ ◆

"Hello, Keiji."

"Not my Alice," he replied, beaming at his visitor. "How have you been? You can tell how I'm doing." Keiji sounded a bit like Yuki, whom he had been spending quite a bit of time with lately. It was apparent that her sense of humor was starting to leave its mark, not unlike a pencil rubbing.

Alice couldn't help but wince at the nickname he had adopted for her. "Do you ever feel like you only exist to ruin everyone's life?"

"Aren't you supposed to be making me feel better? I thought Yuki said you were an idol. I don't think this is how these hospital visits are supposed to go."

"Sorry. I know you've got your own problems."

"What are you talking about," said Keiji. "I'm obviously doing great."

Alice almost laughed, but she felt somewhat responsible. "Well, I was in the area, and I thought I'd see how you were doing." It was the best excuse she could fabricate, seeing as they were supposed to barely be acquainted. She also wanted to ask him what he had seen when they were on the bridge, but it was difficult to imagine how that might work its way into the conversation.

"I'm going to have the operation. The specialist is coming from America."

"That's great." She was surprised, having heard from Yuki that they had fallen short of their fundraising goal. "How?"

He wasn't really sure, but he assumed his parents had come up with the balance. "Does it sound stupid to say I'm scared? It's not like they could make me any worse. I guess they could break the top half." He wondered if his joke was inappropriate, seeing that his guest looked like she was about to cry.

"Keiji. When you were in the accident—"

"I thought I heard someone." Yuki came out of the bathroom in a way that made it plain she had been listening. "Alice, what brings you by…the hospital food? I hate to tell you, but that's not real crab."

Alice sensed somewhat of a protective vibe coming from her old friend. "Just thought I'd stop by and see how he's doing."

"You should have called so we could come over together. I had to get out of the house, major drama on the home front. Apparently, my mom sold our house without telling anyone, and everyone's looking at me funny."

She noticed that Yuki had brought a package of chicken onigiri. "Oh, he'll love those. They're his favorite. Mine, I mean."

"Hey, we have a lot in common." Keiji laughed.

"More than you know." Alice coughed and attempted to change the topic. "So Keiji says they can afford the operation now."

"Apparently someone anonymous stepped up. My mom won't say who it was, though. Maybe she doesn't want me to feel bad."

Keiji groaned as he placed the rice ball on the table. Both girls ran to help, almost knocking each other over.

"You're probably stiff from being in bed," said Yuki. "Would you like a massage?"

"Sure," replied Keiji, more than happy to take advantage of her offer.

It was undeniable to Alice that the chemistry between the two had changed. Such borderline non-platonic touch would have been unthinkable between her and Keiji. "Well, I'd better be going. I'll see you two later. I'm sure everything's going to be okay. *Ganbatte.*"

"*Arigatou,* Not My Alice."

Down the hall, Alice saw Buzz rolling his bones outside some unfortunate person's hospital suite. "Buzz," she whispered. "Psst. Hey, Buzz."

"Well, if it isn't the twist and twirl who stole my job. So nice to see you again—not."

"Look, Buzz. I had no control over that, and you know it." Alice was starting to think there was a conspiracy of people out to destroy her life.

"Whatever. I'm going to hang tenner. Don't wait around."

Seeing Buzz making his exit, she stepped forward to block him, but he passed right through her with a rancid smell that nearly caused her to vomit. "Wait, Buzz. Just one thing." Seeing he had no intention of stopping, she yelled. "It'll piss off, Jack."

Had he been physical, his patchwork leather boots would have squealed. "This ought to be a tin bath. Well, spit it out. What is it?"

"Do you know who paid for Keiji's surgery?"

"What's that have to do with the price of tea in China?"

"What I mean is…did you see anyone?"

"I see lots of things. I'm not some plonker, you know." He waited to see if they were in agreement on that fact, but Alice only appeared confused.

"Okay, then. What did you see?"

"Just some dome-headed bloke with dark glasses. What's that to Jack?"

"Nothing. I couldn't think of anything else that would make you stop. Do you hate me?"

"Not any more than before."

"Gomen ne. If there's anything I can do for you…"

"Kill, Jack."

Alice appeared to consider his request. "Get in line."

◆ ◆ ◆

"Yamamoto-sensei. What was that? I can't hear you." Sho had experienced a rare moment of doubt as he attached the carabiner that secured his favorite poet to the spire of the 500-meter-tall Nakai Tower. Gale force winds immediately swung Yamamoto over the edge, but the tautness of the rope indicated that it still held. "Was that a yes?"

The national treasure and reluctant lyricist of the current number one ranked song in Japan hung upside down, his face red from being hung like a side of beef over the twinkling lights of Tōkyō. A blast of wind sent him almost horizontal to the platform, causing the antenna to groan ominously. "Put me down! I won't do it. I don't care how high you suspend me!" He glanced down into infinity, and his resolve cracked.

"You didn't want to do it last time and look how well it turned out. Did you know it's become this year's graduation song? Too bad no one knows it was you."

"Good. I hate it. It's everywhere I go. At the mall, the grocery store—my proctologist's office…"

"You shop for your own groceries?" The dome-headed gangster struggled to imagine his hero shopping for dairy and seasonal vegetables.

"No, but my maid told me about it."

Sho wrapped the end of the rope around his forearm and swung Yamamoto far outside the rooftop's periphery. The antenna shuddered as its metal frame began to bend. "You're making me look like the bad guy here. Did you ever think I might be helping you stretch as an artist?"

Yamamoto, who had a well-established fear of heights, began to scream hysterically. "Pull me back. Please. I'm begging you."

"So, you'll do it?" Sho had started to doubt his talents of persuasion. He wondered if his admiration for Yamamoto was interfering with his work.

Back over the platform, however, Yamamoto's resolve steeled. "Not even if you drop me to the sidewalk."

"Have you ever seen that sport where the guys in skirts…they have this heavy ball, and they spin it around on some kind of wire. Have you heard of that?"

"If you are referring to the Scottish version of the hammer throw, the spherical weight is attached with a wooden handle."

"But it should work with this climbing rope, right? I'm not sure about that antenna, though. Seems a bit shaky, don't you think? I didn't have time to check its weight capacity." Sho added some slack and proceeded to whip Yamamoto in a large circle that extended well outside the rooftop's perimeter. The poet's screams could only be heard when the circumference of his journey brought him back around again. "Yamamoto-sensei. Please save your voice. I don't think anyone can hear you. Maybe that plane that just passed below us." He removed the play in the rope, and Yamamoto dangled before him upside down. "I'll tell you what. Just do me this favor, and no one will ever learn about our little association."

Only whimpers could be heard coming from the poet.

"It would make quite a good story," said Sho, "hearing that 'Remembrance' was written by Yamamoto, Takuboku. I doubt they'd even *remember* you for anything else."

"Okay."

"What's that? Is there something you'd like to tell me?" Sho placed his hand over his ear, struggling to hear over the wind that whipped his trench coat.

"I'll do it. Just put me down. I'll write whatever you want."

Sho released the rope, and Yamamoto jerked barely short of having his head cracked open on the platform. Sho shoved a thick envelope into his mouth.

"What's this?" mumbled the poet.

"Residuals from the last song," replied Sho. "We're not monsters."

◆ ◆ ◆

"Alice-chan, thanks for helping us out," said Taka. "You know how it is. Momoko and I can't go anywhere alone, or someone will say it's a date. Idol rules."

"Is there like a handbook I should be referring to or something?" asked Alice.

"Very funny. Don't forget I know you're an expert in these sorts of things, and if you could maybe give us a little room, that would be even more awesome."

Momentarily annoyed, Alice wasn't there to help them with their love lives. Solak's motives were clear enough. He wanted to remove the real Momoko so that Akari wouldn't have to vacate her body. Under other circumstances, they might even have aligned purposes. Alice remained concerned about Keiji, and it was true that Jack represented the most immediate threat. Solak's manipulations were readily apparent, but it was rather brilliant how he had used the restrictions against dating, to force a group outing. "So, where are we going?"

"The Haunted House at Odaiba." Taka had been there before, but never on a date.

"Isn't that place, kind of seedy?"

"Momo-chan says she likes to be scared. I wouldn't have thought she went for that sort of thing. She's not at all how you'd think."

"That's for sure."

"I am not okay with this," said a voice in Alice's ear. The ghostly Momoko seemed eager to prove that unrequited love could be both physically and emotionally imperceptible. "She probably wants to be scared, so she'll have an excuse to grab hold of him."

Alice pulled Taka aside. "Did you bring anything? You know, like a gift? Girls like that, you know."

Taka blanched. "Is that really a thing? Idiot." he smacked himself on the forehead.

Alice produced the package of macarons. She had attached a bow so that it resembled more a gift than leftovers. "I thought you might need some help."

Seeing that Akari had arrived, he decided to forgo the usual practice of pretending to refuse. "Arigatou. *Yasashii desu.*"

It wasn't that Alice didn't feel guilty, but she had decided she could live with herself if it could save Keiji. Jack wasn't about to let two mistakes go unanswered. Even if Solak had gotten into her head, she had decided it was still right to take the risk.

Akari appeared less committed to maintaining appearances, as she had abandoned any attempts at dressing like the person whose vessel she had appropriated. Physically she might have passed for Momoko, but it was like when your favorite band put out an album where their new sound was utterly unrecognizable.

"*Tsumaranai mono desu ga…*" said Taka, presenting Akari the macarons.

Akari removed one from the sleeve and offered it to Alice. "Thanks for coming, Alice-chan. Hungry?"

"No, thanks," she replied. "There are only four now and, as you know, that represents death and seeing as we're going to a haunted house—"

"I can't imagine why you'd be concerned," replied Akari. She noticed

Momoko flickering nearby and directed a green-eyed jeer in her direction. "I can think of someone else who should be..."

"Okay then," said Taka, oblivious to the undercurrent of their conversation. "Let's go have some fun. They even gave me a coupon for downloading the app."

"How frugal." It was typical Akari, but her words lacked the bite for which she had once been known.

Built on an artificial island in Tōkyō Bay, Odaiba had once been the go-to place for Tōkyō couples to court. After the 2027 earthquake, however, it had never fully recovered. More sophisticated options in the area had stalled any major redevelopment plans, contributing to its reputation as a hangout for derelicts and losers. The haunted house had started out as a summer attraction to help people shiver away the oppressive Tōkyō heat, but due to its popularity, it had become a year-round attraction. Initially an abandoned hospital-style terror attraction, it had been converted to a VR walkthrough to avoid having to pay teenagers to pop out at guests. Hanging from the ceiling was a grid of rails that small bots sped along, spraying water and tapping people on the shoulder.

Seeing Taka occupied at the ticket machine, Akari turned to Alice and whispered, "Just do your job, and no one will get hurt. Today we're on the same team, but that can change." She watched Taka collect the VR headsets. "And keep Taka out of it."

It occurred to Alice that Akari might actually be falling for him. "There's no way to make it work, you know." She was preaching to herself as much as anyone.

"Maybe not if you're on the side that follows the rules." Akari could tell she had landed a blow by the face Alice made.

"Here you go." Taka handed them their wireless headsets. "There's a small room where we'll get the rundown. Hopefully, not zombies today."

"Wait," said Akari, wiping a crumb off his mouth.

"Taka," said Alice, starting to panic. "Did you eat one of the macarons?"

"Why? Was I not supposed to?"

Before Alice could wholly react, the environment's narrator started to recite the backstory in their headsets.

"Once there was an architect who became infatuated with the daughter of a local butcher. To win her hand, he promised to build a beautiful mansion, as proof of his affections. It was mostly complete when he went mad from handling the roof shingles, which were made of lead. Overcome by delirium, he attacked his beloved and was slain by her hand. Having lost all reason, she began to kill the visitors to the nearby shrine for their bones and personal items, which she used to complete the last remaining expression of their love. Tonight, you must find your escape, lest you become part of the house yourself."

"This is your idea of a date?" asked Alice.

"Quiet, wheel," said Akari. "Limit any comments to how jealous of us you are."

The doors to the play area opened, and they were greeted by obsidian shadows. A path directed them through a tunnel of closely spaced torii gates, their black bases creating the illusion that they floated under the oscillating moonlight. Brass lanterns creaked beneath vermilion arches inhabited by spiders whose webs served as a form of architectural embellishment. A small fox emerged from between the posts and beckoned them with its snout. Then it disappeared between the glistening orange gates that led up the hill into the forest.

"Well, I guess we're supposed to go this way." Taka switched on the plastic candle each of them had been given, which allowed the VR equipment to better track their hand movements. "Go ahead. Turn yours on."

Alice flicked the switch of her plastic torch and held it up to a patch of darkness between the torii gates. A wild boar jumped out and ran past her with a banshee-like scream. "People pay for this?"

"Good, right?" At least, Taka seemed to be enjoying himself.

"Come on," said Akari, wanting to go further up the hill. "Let's go."

Taka didn't want Alice to feel left out, but it was apparent Akari was eager to ditch their chaperon. "Do you mind?"

As much as Alice didn't like being left alone, even in a virtual haunted house, she wasn't in a position to refuse. "Hey, those 'no dating' rules were created to protect people like you."

"What do you mean people like me?" Taka had already started to forget his otaku past. He had taken to dressing like Haruto, and his hair now had more gel than several of the girls in the group.

"Nothing. You guys have fun. I'll be fine."

"Why are you helping them?" the real Momoko asked. She watched Akari take Taka's hand as they passed out of sight. "This is supposed to be my date. She's stealing him from me!" Her spectral outline vibrated.

"I'm not helping them. I'm trying to get you your body back." Alice was aware that she had her own interests to consider. "I slipped a type of special dust into Akari's macaron."

"What kind of dust?"

"Something that stops the heart...I don't really understand it, but she'll be kind of dead. Temporarily."

Momoko immediately grasped her relationship with Alice's plan. "You're going to stop my heart?"

"Do you want to be alive again or not?" She had hoped that Momoko wouldn't dwell too much on how the sausage was made. "Seriously. What do you have to lose?"

Momoko twirled one of her twintails nervously. "Is it safe?"

"Safer than staying dead." Alice hadn't expected to debate the body's original owner. "Can you keep Taka busy long enough for me to deal with Akari?"

"I can do that."

"There's one more thing."

"What?"

"Taka ate one too."

Momoko's ghostly face was incapable of appearing any less flush, but she let out a silent scream as she flew in the direction they had last been seen headed.

Akari slipped her fingers into Taka's hand and led him to where the torii gates concluded beside an oily pond drenched in pale green moonlight. Teetering stone lanterns flickered within her eyes. "I like you, Taka." Akari's newfound vulnerability meant that, for the first time, she passed for Momoko in a way that wasn't merely physical. "It took a while to figure out. Please don't hold the way I acted in the past against me."

Unaware that she was speaking as Akari, Taka could only think that Momoko had never been anything but kind. "But you're an idol. Isn't it forbidden?"

"True." Akari's thoughts lingered on the prohibition. "But maybe that's what makes it fun?" She grabbed the back of his head and pulled him into a long kiss.

Momoko arrived in time to see her likeness, lips locked to Taka's; only it was Akari who felt his mouth pressed against hers and the warmth of his hands on her back. No longer constrained by the physical world, Momoko became a flash of illuminated acrimony and slammed into Akari, knocking her against a stone torii gate. They rolled on the ground, grabbing each other's hair, and throwing anything within reach.

"Alice. Have you decided?" asked the fox, pleased to have found her alone. His ears were arced in the same manner as the horns he usually possessed.

"Solak?"

"I see all the pieces are set. I ensured that, but I wonder the motivations of the players."

"Mine hasn't changed," she replied.

"Good." He swished his tail. "Momoko was easy enough to attract. Jealousy is the sweetest of snares. Now, will you stand for the one you love or the one you tolerate?"

There was an ear-splitting scream, and an apparition of an old woman ran through Alice. She continued up through the rows of torii gates, causing the temple cats to scurry.

"That actually wasn't me," said Solak. "It's a haunted house."

Alice watched the fox scamper away, relieved that he had chosen a less offensive form, but unsure if he understood her complete meaning.

Momoko attacked Akari with the ferocity of a heartsick tantrum. Taking advantage of her compromised lucidity, Akari tucked her legs tight against her chest and flung Momoko over the pond. Like a rubber band, Momoko came back, right foot first, knocking Akari into a pile of wooden torii gates. Nearby, the enhancer had begun to take effect, and a perplexed Taka watched his date engage in a battle with her own ghostly likeness that, for once, he could actually see.

"Stay away from him," yelled Momoko, emphasizing her point with a solid uppercut.

Hearing the commotion, Alice ran up the hill to find that Momoko had already vanished, leaving Akari to nurse her wounds.

"What was that?" asked Taka. "Maybe they have the game's difficulty turned up too high? Do you want me to tell them to pause and reset?"

Akari wasn't leaving until her future was assured. "I can handle myself."

The fox waited where the vermilion gates dissolved into woodland, slyly looked back, then sped up the path into the thicket where the tunnel of gates reached their conclusion. A drop of water made Taka question the touch upon his shoulder. He turned and was startled by a specter of a woman who shrieked, then vanished.

"She's the one who attacks travelers on this road," said Alice, trying to help maintain the storyline. "She feeds the feral cats that live beside the torii gates."

"Come on," said Akari. "The fox seems to know which way to go."

Around the bend, they came upon a dilapidated Victorian manor with some decidedly Eastern roof titles. Once grand, it carried the same patina of neglect shared by the abandoned homes that littered the Japanese countryside. As people moved to the cities, such buildings passed into decay, forsaken even by their caretaker's progeny.

"Why is it—chunky?" Taka held up his candle to examine the wooden paneling better and discovered the house to be made almost entirely of discarded pieces of everyday items like baby carriages, lanterns, and umbrellas. Spotting a femur, he understood how the old lady had acquired the materials to finish her home. "Being here…might not be the best idea we've ever had."

Alice saw an apparition peering from a termite-infested window, and though she didn't know if it was part of the game, remembered that Taka had eaten one of the tainted macarons. Vulnerable to the more supernatural elements within the game, there would be little she could do to protect him. "Taka, maybe you should stay here, and I'll come back after everything's—"

"As if," protested Akari, grabbing his arm. "We can't leave him here. It wouldn't be fun."

A shriek echoed from someplace within the grisly dwelling. Taka gulped, unsure if he should be more nervous of Akari, or what might await him inside.

The house's interior reflected the style of European elegance that had grown to prominence during the Meiji era, an unsettling reminder of lives whose time had already passed. Its furnishings were peppered with dust, and the peeling wallpaper was dulled by decades of oxygen and light. Drapes held together more out of habit than strength, allowed the moonlight to creep inside.

"Do you hear that?" asked Alice, reacting to popping sounds coming from the next room. "That crackling sound…"

Inside the drawing room was a marble fireplace, with a gaping mouth that harbored a gradually dying fire. Taka used an iron to poke the contents of its firebox, and when he pulled it back, something was attached to its hook. "It's a yukata. Why would anyone burn that?"

"A victim. Materials to complete the house," concluded Alice. She wondered if Solak had chosen such a disturbing venue to put her off-guard.

Deep within the fireplace, there was a low gurgle, like the house's stomach had become unsettled. From between the iron teeth of the firebox, a wave of body parts, soot, and clothing retched, and threatened to fill the room. Taken by surprise, Alice braced to withstand the black deluge but was knocked off her feet. A multitude of hands and legs began to pull her under the sludge.

"Taka, come on," yelled, Akari, who pulled him into the next room. Before Alice could fight her way free, she slammed the door and fastened its brass lock.

Taking advantage of her newfound privacy, Alice transformed into her ghostly maiko manifestation and directed her obi to latch onto a chandelier. As she was pulled towards its plaster ceiling medallion, the disembodied arms and legs lost their grip. Freshly unencumbered, she sent the kimono sash racing up the chimney's smoke chamber like a delicately embroidered serpent, to clog the flue. *Powers of convenience*, she remembered. She recalled it back and used it to ride the wave of sludge through the door, which broke free of its hinges. On the other side, the fox waited with a wicked grin.

"Alice? You're a bloody mess. Is this really what you signed up for?"

In the house's library, Akari felt exposed for entirely different reasons. "Taka, there's something I need to tell you."

"Have you seen this wall? What is it made out of exactly?" He felt the patchwork of dresses, feathers, broaches, and jewelry that had been placed about in a helter-skelter fashion. His candle revealed the framing to be made of bones tied together with sinew, similar to how bamboo was once used.

"When I said that I liked you, well, there's something else you should know. There are going to be people, others who try to get between us. We can't let them. We're going to have to fight…"

Before she could finish, Taka clutched his chest, and the marbles in his eye-sockets shook. Akari lowered him slowly to the floor as he convulsed.

"Taka, what's wrong?" she cried. "Can you hear me?"

Alice wafted through the wall, and seeing Taka, her first instinct was to rush to his side. However, it was not possible, as Akari had protectively positioned herself over him, having no doubt who was behind his condition.

"Solak warned me you couldn't be trusted," said Akari.

Using her plastic candle, Alice summoned a ribbon of flame and cinched Akari's arms to her waist. "I can be trusted," she replied. "Just not by you."

The luminous braiding held, but Akari used it to hurl Alice through the wall and outside into the conservatory. The cracking of bones, as she passed through the outer wall, was most gruesome to hear. Before Alice could pull herself back together, Akari's foot sent her through the greenhouse's ornate glass roof.

"Maybe we should form a sub-unit with only people who are dead. We could even get Momoko to fill out the team."

"I'm not afraid of you," replied Alice. "I harvested you before."

"Not from what I heard," said Akari. "You're even worse at that job than being an idol."

Alice grabbed a sizeable stone lantern and swatted Akari deep into the garden. *The dust isn't working,* she thought. *Why isn't it working?*

Taka had begun to separate from his body and floated above his gangly frame. What surprised him most, though, was the concerned ghost of Momoko who hovered nearby. "Momoko?"

"Lie back into your body," she instructed him. "If you don't, you'll end up like me."

Akari picked up a tombstone and hurled it at Alice, who used the long sleeves of her kimono to form a shield. "I knew you'd never help us. I'll be done with this body when I'm good and ready. Then again…maybe, I'll take yours." She dug into the soil and pulled out what appeared to be Alice's corpse.

"You're not going to be around long enough to choose lunch," said Alice.

Akari grabbed a bronze sword from a funerary statue and lunged at Alice, who summoned a wall of wooden markers to block her way. Akari tried to force her way through, but as she cut down the last one, everything turned black.

The lights in the warehouse flickered, and Alice returned to her physical form. Removing her VR headset, the attraction's industrial infrastructure was revealed along with Taka, who flopped like a trout as his heart restarted. Alice saw Jack's hand attached to the breaker for the facility and was both relieved and embarrassed.

"I hope everyone was playing nice?" Jack asked. "But then I wouldn't have been called here, I suppose."

The animatronic arm, above Akari, continued to slap her repeatedly as if it had malfunctioned. "Stop it. I swear I'll pull you from your socket."

"Please don't," coughed Taka, having successfully passed through the defibrillation stage of the chemical cocktail. "I'll lose my deposit." He rubbed his eyes. "Why am I so sweaty? My chest is killing me. Did somebody punch me?"

"Well, that was fun," said Alice, attempting to maintain a base appearance of normalcy. "And I had heard dating could be stressful."

Akari grabbed Taka's hand and pulled him off the ground. "I want to go home. I don't care if we're caught alone."

"See you at practice," said Taka, as Akari dragged him outside. Having a weak hinge, the door slammed behind them with an echo that filled the warehouse.

Jack looked as pleased as a monkey in a banana farm. "So, you did the right thing. I guess you're more like me than you'd care to admit."

"No one wants to admit that. Wait a minute. Was this your test or Solak's?"

"Does it matter?"

"Say, you're not as dumb as you look." She remembered the shadow demon's warning. "Keiji's about to go into surgery. You're not going to touch him, are you?"

"Haven't you learned anything? Partners don't betray partners."

"So, are we really partners?"

"Apparently."

♦ ♦ ♦

Unable to see around the box he was carrying, the man in the Tokuji-Tech jumpsuit kicked George's ankle, dangling over the couch's side. Fortunately, George had been asleep, so he only felt a slight throb as he wiped the crust from his eyes. It was the fourth night he had slept in his office. Though his vision was blurry, he still recognized the glass pyramid that rested atop the pile of papers the man was carrying. "Wait. What are you doing? That's my award."

The moving man adjusted his grip on the box. "Sorry. We have orders to get you out of this office by noon."

"Chotto matte. Nobody's talked to me. Is this because of my daughter? I already explained she didn't know anything. Please…just give me a second. Let me call HR."

"Problems at home, Okada-san?" Izumi's hair was tied back so tight it was giving her a facelift. She picked up an empty ramen container and threw it in the box the man carried out the door.

Immediately, George sat up and began to pull himself together. "You can't let them fire me, Izumi-san. I'll make her quit."

"Who…your daughter? Didn't she help collapse our stock?"

"It was the other girl. Not my Yuki-chan. She was only there to support her, and besides, I had no idea. How could I, Izumi-san? I'm always at work. You know that."

Izumi smiled coyly, sorry she had to let him off the hook. "You haven't seen the news, have you?" It was apparent George hadn't even bathed in seventy-two hours. "A reporter took one of those pills apart, and it wasn't based on anything we make."

"How's that possible? But I thought enhancer—" He grabbed his phone and opened his news app.

"It wasn't enhancer."

Maybe it was due to work exhaustion, but George didn't get what Izumi was trying to tell him. "What was it based on?"

"Our competitor's drug...Sakco Pharmatech. The press is calling it mindwipe. It's basically, enhancer, but made with their components. Our stock has almost entirely recovered. The financial markets decided it had to punish everyone or no one. The PMDA might still have something to say, but we can deal with them."

George watched as the mover removed the last box from his office. "But then why are they taking away all my stuff?"

"You've been promoted again. Apparently, when the stock tanked, new investors took control of the company, and for some reason, they like you...Senior Vice President."

◆ ◆ ◆

Holograms of the Kurome-gumi patriarchs appeared around the conference table. Next to Boss Mori appeared the avatar of his saiko-komon, a hannya mask better known outside the yakuza world as belonging to Solak. The author and orchestrator of their latest achievement projected an expression that could be interpreted as joyful or maniacal.

"With the acquisition of Tokuji-Tech," began Boss Mori, "we have achieved our long-standing goal. Legitimacy. Our supply problems are now behind us. We can expect explosive growth in the months ahead. Thanks to my leadership, and the advice of my saiko-komon, we are now unstoppable."

"What is this I hear about some new type of enhancer?" Kazuyo, who led his own family, was not a fan of Boss Mori's advisor, who acted a bit too much like he pulled the clan's strings. "Is it true we have competition now?"

"Nothing more than a one time experiment," said Solak. "A bit of misdirection necessary to restore value to the stock by showing that Tokuji-Tech wasn't the only pharmaceutical company with this particular illicit association. Enhancer will continue to be made with N-43, especially now that we control the sole means of production. The other drug's recipe has already been disposed of, and the chemist had an unfortunate accident, or so I hear."

Kazuyo was not in the least impressed. "But what about the government? I hear they're still breathing down our necks."

Solak knew his solution was not one that a boorish and materialistic instrument could comprehend. "Rome wasn't built in a day, and neither was our empire. Being free of governmental restraints is, shall we say, a work in progress."

"From what I hear, we don't even completely control the company. What is to keep us from suffering the same shortages as last year?"

Boss Mori was unable to thoroughly understand the financial ballet his saiko-komon had performed, but he had seen enough to earn his trust. "We recently made an alliance with an investor who controls seventeen percent of the stock. That gives us effective control and an unbreakable majority."

"What did you say? An outsider? Who is this person? How can we trust them if they aren't even a member of the family?" Kazuyo's paranoia had saved him from three assassination attempts, and he wasn't about to relinquish it now.

A holographic flicker appeared in the last empty chair, and a flour brushed bunny apron oscillated into focus. Mrs. Okada's closed-eyed smile obscured her customarily twinkling eyes. "Hello. Ohayo. Sorry, I'm late, everyone. I had to get some cookies out of the oven. I had hoped to send a dozen over, but the day got away from me. Dear, oh, dear."

"First, let me congratulate you on placing your buy order exactly when the stock bottomed." Solak would have preferred that he had been able to purchase a controlling stake, but her order had caused a bump in the price. "Your timing was…remarkable."

Mrs. Okada sneezed from the presence of some flour on her nose. "I just knew it had to bounce back. My husband is doing his best with the new drug.

Everyone is working so hard. Of course, I had to sell our house, liquidate our savings—our retirement, take out some unconventional loans, but it all worked out."

"We have already seen that your husband has been amply rewarded, as per our agreement. However, perhaps you could address some here who are concerned about our alliance." The hannya mask pivoted towards Kazuyo, to underline the intended direction of his comment.

"Goodness me. As I said earlier, if you protect my family, I'll protect yours. Oh, and one more thing. I understand you have a financial interest in the Genki Girls. I want my Yuki to be the center. Like I said, this is all about family. Surely, you understand?"

"Agreed," said Boss Mori, not caring in the least about such an inconsequential detail. "For those of you who do not know, Mrs. Okada was critical in helping us get through our recent materials shortage. We consider her an honorary member of the family, so I hope that addresses any lingering concerns. Now let us raise our glasses in recognition of our latest collaboration."

Mrs. Okada looked around for something, not within sight of her camera. "Oh, sorry. Would it be okay if I use milk?" She took their bewildered expressions as tacit approval. As she raised her glass, freshly baked cookies cooled in her massive new kitchen, one larger than a typical Tōkyō apartment. Being a primary stakeholder in a major pharmaceutical company, and yakuza associate, certainly had its perks.

CHAPTER TWELVE:
EVANESCENCE

White smoke swirled within Alice's nostrils, a gaseous blanket of what had once been wood and straw. Lured by sleep's pleasures, Alice was unaware of the toxins that slithered into her lungs. When, finally, a reflexive cough jolted her awake, it revealed the room to be pallid and gray. "Fire! Jack! The house is on fire!"

The soft thud of her partner running across the wooden planks was immediate, but she could only hear his voice. "Grab the samurai helmet. I'll get the sword." Forced to remain physical, Jack choked on soot as he felt his way outside.

Alice's hip discovered the corner of the tansu chest, which produced a much-needed dose of adrenaline. She followed the cabinetry's metal fittings until her hands found an appropriately shaped object. Satisfied, she snatched its strap and ran outside. The Kyōto Fire Department's drones had already arrived to spray silica nanoparticles in a heroic attempt to save the villa. Steam rose from the thatched roof as she waited for Jack, who had been taking a rather long time to appear.

Rolling down the steps, and black as a chimney sweep, Jack bounced short of Alice's feet and coughed up some rather unattractive black phlegm. "Cover me," he gasped. "Smoke inhalation."

Alice pulled the blanket over him, and when she drew it back, there wasn't even a spot of soot on his face.

"Too close. You know if I die, you finish this thread alone?"

"Don't tempt me. What were you thinking?"

"That wasn't just any sword; it was Hiro's. A blade contains the warrior's soul…at least that's what he used to say. Then again, he once broke my favorite Miles Davis record. How about you? Did you get it?"

Alice held up the hannya mask she had mistakenly grabbed. "Sorry. It felt about right."

Jack snatched the mask and stared at it in disbelief. "He burned down my house? It's against the rules. My house!"

"I'm sorry, Jack. Well, I guess we have his attention."

Jack hurled the hannya mask far up the hillside. "Nice of Saul to leave his calling card." He watched the firemen gathering up their equipment, leaving the roof of the house looking like a marshmallow from all the suppressant foam. "He doesn't know it, but he might have just tipped his hand. Think about it, where did your dad work?"

"Tokuji-Tech."

"And who makes enhancer?"

"Not Tokuji-Tech. That's the yakuza, but didn't you say my dad's old boss was killed by—"

"Well, that would seem the logical conclusion," said Jack, shifting uncomfortably, "but people are fragile. Did you know you could die from eating bananas?"

"Bananas?"

"Potassium poisoning. You'd have to eat about forty trees worth…but it's possible."

"Have you run into a lot of banana cases?" Alice thought Jack had been acting a bit evasive about his solo trip to the Tokuji-Tech warehouse.

"A few. Mostly falling ones. Bushels, actually."

Akari's brother was yakuza, so maybe it wasn't a waste of time to be at practice after all. A grain of sand might not seem important, but pile enough of them together, and they formed a beach. No matter how insipid, the Genki Girls stood at the center of the thread.

"Back in the day, Saul couldn't sneak up on me like that," said Jack. "I would have been waiting for him at the front door. Maybe I'm going soft?"

"Well, at least you didn't download a virus into your family's car."

"How long are you going to beat yourself up over that?"

"How long have I got?"

Jack was in no position to talk. He had accumulated a couple of centuries' worth of regrets that he flogged himself about regularly. "At least you've still got time to turn it around. I'm a museum piece. And not even a good museum...one of those small-town ones where they don't even bother to charge. You're going to visit a lot of those in this job, by the way."

Alice didn't think it helped Jack to lose his starch. "You know museums are where they keep the things worth saving."

He tossed a charred kimekomi ball at her. "You're okay, kid, but why do you think Buzz hates me? I'm buzzard quality at best. Everyone knows I'm a fake."

"What are you talking about? They all wish they were you. Buzz. Solak. I mean, c'mon. You speak a hundred and twenty-seven languages. You're kind of from Vegas...you know interesting facts about fruit. Maybe you just need to believe in yourself."

A sarcastic motorboat sound came from Jack's lips. "Look who's starting to sound like an idol."

"Doesn't mean it's not true," she replied. "You're the one who said we're getting somewhere. Someone who puts a shadow demon on their back foot doesn't sound like buzzard quality to me."

Perhaps she had stiffened his spine, or at least he had decided to put his sparsely attended pity-party on hold. "Okay, hotshot, since you're on such a roll. Everything was in the villa. What do we do now?"

Alice took out the vial of Zombie Dust from her pocket and shook it for emphasis. "You're not the only thing I saved."

Jack didn't even bother to argue that he wasn't a thing.

◆ ◆ ◆

The animated folder titled, *Family Photos*, hovered in front of Sho. He blinked twice, and a picture labeled, *Our Apartment, May 5th, 2032*, lingered in the foreground of his home screen. His palm held the last pill from the batch that had killed his sister, his final chance to assuage his guilt. The new drug that the press was fixated on was nothing more than a fabricated misdirection, so his clan could manipulate the price of Tokuji-Tech's stock.

Usually, Sho didn't touch anything harder than shōchū, but there was no better way to understand what his sister had encountered than to experience it himself. He tapped the floating icon that represented a family photo, and it immediately rendered as a fully immersive VR environment. Not sure where he had left his beer, and with the outside world blocked by his headset, Sho hard-swallowed the last remaining pill. If anything were wrong with the chemical composition of the drug, he would soon know.

The last apartment Sho had shared with Akari was in San'ya, a neighborhood known both for despair and a homeless population that outnumbered its vending machine. Enhancer had always been the preferred crutch of the middle class, who had the means to afford both the equipment and the drug. There was actually a VR cafe in San'ya, but its patrons usually had to cut their pills in half and make up for any loss in potency with alcohol.

Sho touched *animate* on the menu and walked around the living room he had known during his last year of high school. One of the first toy drones he had ever modified rested atop his mother's end table. His mother hated how he left his projects strewn about the house, but she wasn't eager to upset him since his dad had run out on them.

"Oniisan?"

A twelve-year-old Akari looked up at him, a mere stick figure of the young woman she would later become. Her school uniform was dirty from having climbed a tree to avoid some particularly mean girls in her class. It was a regular occurrence. "Akari-chan?"

"Oniisan…you took the pill? Why? Why, oniisan?"

"You can tell? How?" He grabbed his head, feeling slightly dizzy.

She walked over and socked him on his arm. "Feel anything?"

"Hai," he replied, rubbing his shoulder.

"You want to know if it's different? Is that it? Well, it's not the pills you should be afraid of." Akari socked him again. "Ne. Let's get out of here. We can go to the park and feed the swans. Remember? I wanted to go to the movies, but you said we didn't have the money. We don't need it here. Ikimashou ka?"

"Wait," replied Sho. "I don't feel right." The walls of the room stretched like rubber. The rendered snapshot of their comingled memories started to blur. In a final moment of lucidity, he asked, "Akari-chan. I gave you the pills. Why? I could have thrown them away. I could have—"

"Gone to war with the family?" She led him over to a family portrait from before his head was shaven, and his eyes inked black. "That's your problem. You never look out for yourself."

"Is it really you, Akari-chan? Where am I?"

"Why this photo, oniisan? You know what happened. This was not a good day."

"I should have been here…not out playing chinpira. Maybe I can…"

"Change things? Nothing can change. Not the things we want." Akari looked afraid, concerned they might be overheard. "Ne. I want to tell you something. Something secret."

Before she could finish, the wallpaper contorted within dark shadows from which emerged a set of horns that terminated in a knife-like chin. "What a lovely home. Is this where the two of you grew up? Your mother must have made some unsavory sacrifices to put such an almost acceptable roof over your heads."

Sho was surprised to see the dark figure he had fought at the police impound lot attired in the same black suit and white hannya mask. He clenched his fist, prepared to fight.

"Oniisan. You know him?" asked Akari.

"We may have crossed paths," replied Sho. He was not interested in reviewing the circumstances.

"We have something in common," Solak replied. "Well, other than you. We're in the same family. Your brother lacks the rank to have associated with me, but I am his kumichō's chief advisor."

Sho had heard that the family's saiko-komon wore a Noh mask, but he had assumed it only an avatar. "You're the family's saiko-komon?"

"In the flesh, well not really. And what is this…a family reunion?" Solak could see Sho weighing the advantages between fight and flight. "You're wondering if I remember you? You still don't get who I am? Knowing everyone's secrets is what I do. Keeping them depends on you."

"Oniisan." Akari tugged on Sho's sleeve. "Let's go to the park. We don't need to stay."

Solak knew that Sho had taken the pill from the moment it had traveled down his throat. His shift in consciousness was a signal flare to the immaterial world. "You're hardly a concern to me, but even the smallest pebble irritates when it crawls into your sock. What is it you hope to find here? Do you think you can change the past? Perhaps the time has come to accept the truth or at least my version of it."

"And what's that?" asked Sho.

"Your sister was nothing but a junky…like your whore mother."

Sho was more than capable of transforming self-loathing into anger, and his reaction was immediate and without thought of consequence. He tried to tackle Solak but instead found himself flying through the living room wall as if he was nothing more than a sack of rice. The faucet in the kitchen sink dug into his side like an anchor. Sho landed with a *thud* on the tile floor. Next to him laid a pair of baggy construction pants in a dark crimson pool. Akari stood over the body, her small fingers clutching one of their mother's kitchen knives, eyes wild.

"I suppose this was the family's fault as well?" asked Solak.

"I don't want to see this."

Akari dropped the knife, as if unaware how it had found its way into her hand. "Oniisan. Please don't tell. I had to. He tried to…." She wiped red streaks on her dress. "Don't tell mama."

Sho grabbed a towel and started to clean her hands. "I'll take care of it. You don't have to worry. I'll handle everything. You did nothing wrong."

Solak's eyes reflected genuine pity. "But you couldn't really clean this up, could you Sho-san? Not without the family's help, the same one you now question. That hurts. Is loyalty too high a price to pay for keeping your sister out of prison? Perhaps I should ask Jiro?"

"I don't want to see this anymore," cried Sho. "Make it stop."

"Don't look for answers if you're afraid of what you might find," said Solak. "Have I made myself clear?" He grabbed Akari by the wrist and dragged her from the room. "Don't go looking in the past. It's all an illusion, anyway."

"Oniisan!" Akari cried as the scene collapsed behind her.

Sho threw off his headset and attempted to fight himself sober. Unable to differentiate between technology, materiality, and the realms beyond human understanding, Sho could only hypothesize the extent to which the family was aware of his doubts.

◆ ◆ ◆

"Okaasan, have you seen my briefcase?" George collapsed on the foot of the bed. It was the most he had said to her since he had received a cryptic message containing the address of the new Okada residence, and an inconsequential question about dinner.

"It's in the office," replied his wife. She powdered her nose in front of a 19th Century French gilt mirror she had acquired from an antique shop in Ginza.

"Never mind." His voice bounced off the marble floors and echoed within the high ceilings.

"Aren't you going to get it?" She assumed it was a passive-aggressive attempt to get her to stop what she was doing.

"No."

"Why not?"

"I don't feel like going all the way downstairs." He looked for his phone, but seeing it across the room; he decided not to exert the effort. "Where's Yuki?"

"At the hospital." She stood within the frame of the doorway and modeled a silk robe her eye had been set on since last Christmas. "We're alone tonight."

George's eyes closed as if he had fallen asleep. He knew what she was up to, and he wasn't that easy. It was apparent how she planned to put an end to any lingering animosity between them.

"You're punishing me for saving this family. I don't regret it. They can't touch us now and just look at this place." She was honestly surprised that he was going to be difficult.

"I could have handled it without dragging either you or Yuki into any of this. You should have at least come to me." Perhaps it was an unrealistic request considering he couldn't even stand up to her, never mind the yakuza.

"I didn't see you turning down any of those promotions." She immediately regretted her observation. "Never mind. Did you see all the space in our closet? I put some new shirts in there for you."

"What was wrong with our old house? Who are you trying to impress?" No matter how nice, it wasn't worth the compromises they had been making lately.

"It wasn't safe." She drew the belt of her robe tight.

"It was before."

Months, and many justifications, had led her to this moment. "You don't know what they're capable of. They need us now. That's all that matters."

"I never wanted any of this. I only wanted to take care of you...of Yuki, to lead a quiet life. Now they'll never let us go."

"Don't you know why enhancer exists?"

"It's a street drug. Do you know how many of those there are?"

She refused to believe he was as naïve as he pretended. "Your company has one product. How many people with that particular neurological condition are there?"

"We're working on XR." It was true that there had been whispers of lay-offs, but that was always the case. "There are other companies. Maybe that opportunity in Fukuoka I told you about." George wasn't particularly interested in relocating again.

"Investors expect growth. Why do you think one of enhancer's side effects causes people to end up on your drug?"

"Are you saying we planned that? I think I'd know if that were true. I go to enough meetings."

"The Kurome-gumi knows who they can work with and who they can't. Do you want us to end up like the Suzuki family?"

"That's not fair."

"People are cheap, and so was the price of Tokuji-Tech's stock when it collapsed. I bought just enough to make sure we'll always be safe...if they want to stay in control."

It hadn't escaped George's attention that his wife had always gone too far when it came to protecting their daughter, but then, she had been the product of a difficult pregnancy. "Tell me one thing. How long ago did they get to you?"

His wife untied her robe and allowed it to drop to their polished marble floor. She turned off the lights and from the nightstand, produced a small UV light. Its purple glow revealed that from the nape of her neck to the small of her back, she was covered with yakuza tattoos. Fluoresced, for his consideration, was a pair of carp that struggled up a stream beside a weeping cherry blossom tree. When the light turned off, they vanished, leaving only her naked vulnerability and his doubt.

◆◆◆

Pigeon-toed, Alice stood outside Taka's apartment. She would have crawled into a hole if not for the hope that he would chalk up the previous day's disaster to a mixture of enhancer and haunted attraction effects. Jack wasn't about to let her risk a blowout at practice, so he had suggested that she go and feel out the situation. Alice gave three quick knocks, and Taka appeared wearing an expression that indicated everything was not cool between them. "You haven't been answering my texts."

"You poisoned me," he replied.

"Not on purpose. Can I come in?" Alice was glad to receive a passive-aggressive invitation, in the form of his back and a slightly open door.

Taka's apartment had certainly changed since her last visit. No longer decorated in hikikomori-chic, it reminded her of the set of one of those TV dramas where the CEO was unrealistically young. The Akari stalker montage was now a bookshelf lined with foreign-language novels. "Sugoi! Kakkōī." She hoped her enthusiasm for what he had accomplished would mute any negative vibes.

Sitting cross-legged on the edge of a new leather sofa, Taka looked like he'd stepped out of a men's fashion catalog. Loosely draped over his black t-shirt was a scarf that gave him the appearance of either a producer or a barista. "I trusted you."

There was no way for her to explain adequately. "It was an accident. I swear I didn't know. You haven't told anyone, have you?"

"It all makes sense. Akari died. You show up out of nowhere. How could I have been so stupid?" He slammed his laptop shut. "Well, that was the old me."

"Taka-kun. Please. It's not what it looks like."

"You killed her, didn't you? You killed Akari and passed it off as an accident. Why? So you could join the group?"

"That's not what happened. I know how it looks, but hear me out." She was starting to understand what Jack meant when he said that being completely dead was the less complicated option.

"Then you poisoned Momoko, Yuki…and now me."

She stumbled to find the right words. "You weren't supposed to eat them. I was afraid if I told you, you'd say no. Besides, I knew they wouldn't kill her…permanently. Look at you. Very genki."

"You're jealous of her, aren't you?"

"Who?" Alice was genuinely confused.

"Momo-chan. She told me why you gave us those laced cookies."

Alice burst out laughing. "She's not even Momoko."

Taka's face caved like a sandcastle. "What?"

It occurred to Alice, she had revealed too much. "Never mind. That was stupid."

"No, actually, I'd like to hear what you were about to say."

"You know, I used to hang out in Akiba. Every weekend. When all the other girls were shopping for cute clothes and makeup, I was in the arcades or the manga shops. Do you know why? Because with all the different hobbies and things you can find, everyone was into the same thing…imagination. I could never understand why people thought it was so uncool to dream. Maybe I wasn't popular, but I always had at least one person who believed in me. When you said Akari didn't die naturally, who believed in you? Who tried to see beyond what everyone else saw? Maybe you could believe in me a little bit too."

Taka may have appeared world-weary, but he still struggled to read the air. "You know Alice; there's already someone I kind of like."

"What? No. I'm asking that you give me a little time to prove you were right."

Taka seemed a tad injured not to be caught up in his first love triangle. He reached into the drawer and set the fan of cookies on his desk. Four out of the five macarons remained. "When I died, I saw something."

"What?"

"Momo-chan, only different, and it wasn't my imagination. My chest still aches." He rubbed his ribcage. "You're right. You went along with me when everyone thought I was sketchy. I'll give you a day."

"You won't regret it." Alice held her palms together. "Um, Keiji is about to go into surgery. I might need a little more time. Two days?" She eased her way back slowly towards the door; hands pressed together.

Taka was generally surprised at how she had managed to negotiate through his anger. "Alice."

"Hai."

"If that isn't Momo-chan…then who is it?"

"Akari." Alice slammed the door before he had time to construct any follow-up questions.

◆ ◆ ◆

"You were about to tell him, weren't you?" asked Solak. His mask concealed the totality of his disappointment, but his annoyance penetrated its carved wood.

"He's my brother," protested Akari. "I see him all the time at practice, and he treats me like a total stranger. Why can't I tell him? He can be trusted." She flung herself onto Momoko's ruffled pillows, not that any display of exasperation could affect the shadow demon.

"Your brother is yakuza, not the type to ponder Cartesian dualism. How could he possibly understand?"

"He thinks he killed me. How am I supposed to live with that?"

The mask's nostril holes whistled, as Solak formulated his next thought. "I gave you a new life, a new body, and you couldn't even get one silly girl harvested."

"Alice was going to take care of her, that's what you said. She wasn't supposed to come after me." It would make things slightly awkward at their next practice, were it not in their mutual interest to maintain appearances.

It was inconceivable to Solak that Alice and Jack had fostered enough of a bond to impede his goals. "I don't think you understand the gravity of your failure. Now they will hurry to place Momoko back into her body – the very one you've been inhabiting."

Akari felt her arms and was reminded that the skin she occupied had been borrowed. "How?"

"They'll take you to the point of clinical death, place her ghost inside, and bring her back. I'm not saying it will be easy, but one of them has been doing it since before Queen Victoria."

"And what will happen to me?"

"Well, they don't call them harvesters for nothing."

There was a knock on the door, and Momoko's dad, Mr. Yagi, walked into her bedroom. He picked up the hannya mask Solak had dropped when he abruptly disappeared. "Hey, did I hear you talking to someone?"

"Just hung up." Momoko's dimples had a reality distorting effect that Akari had grown to appreciate.

Mr. Yagi admired the old mask. "Say, where'd you get this?"

"Antique market," Akari lied. "A little creepy, right?"

Momoko had never offered to shop for antiques with him before, so he was both pleased and surprised. "I thought you didn't like things that were old."

Realizing she had stumbled into an area of Momoko's background where her knowledge was deficient, she changed the subject. "Is that a new watch?"

Pleased, Mr. Yagi held out his wrist. "Nice, huh? See, newer isn't always better. Here—listen." He sat next to her on the bed and held it to her ear for a moment. "I guess as you get older, you learn to appreciate the things that have been around for a while. It's comforting to think that this watch will be here long after I'm gone."

"No, I totally understand," said Akari. "I don't want to be replaced either."

◆ ◆ ◆

Yuki listened to the nurse give directions about what Keiji could eat after the operation, not that she was responsible. She used the rail of the gurney to support herself. "I went to Shiba Daijingū shrine this morning," she said and pressed an omamori into Keiji's hand. "Everything's going to be fine, but keep this with you. Just in case." She tied the silk amulet around his wristband.

Keiji's head rose as much as he could manage. "I wasn't worried before, but I am now." His attempts at humor increased as his surgery drew near. Keiji had never been that way with Alice, but he had also never been so scared before.

"We should go." The nurse politely directed Yuki aside. "They're waiting for us."

As they rolled him away, Keiji called back. "What are you doing next weekend?"

"Why?" asked Yuki.

"I was thinking we could go hiking." He laughed nervously.

"That's not funny," said Yuki, "but we'll go—somewhere. Someplace fun."

"You figure out where and I'll worry about learning to walk." Keiji watched the holes in the hospital ceiling tiles blur past as they rolled him towards the operating room. He didn't get to see Yuki's eyes expand like opened umbrellas as she realized that she had just been asked out.

"Tuff break mate," said Buzz, appearing next to Alice, who watched unseen nearby.

"*Urusai*," replied Alice. She noticed that Buzz was headed after Keiji. "Buzz, where exactly are you going?"

"I'm on da job. Awright?" He searched his pockets the way middle-aged men often do. Right in front of the operating room door, he trespassed through a heated discussion Sho was having with Keiji's surgeon.

"The kid makes it, right?" Sho's finger poked the surgeon's chest harder than might be appropriate.

"There's a good chance he'll never walk again. The translator app put the surgeon's words into Japanese as fast as they were spoken but stripped them of any veneer of compassion.

Sho's hands dug into the pockets of his trench coat. "But you're good, right? They said you were good."

"Sometimes it's better to be lucky…but if there's anything that can be fixed, you'll get what you paid for." The surgeon stepped around Sho and disappeared inside where both Buzz and luck waited.

There was no time for Alice to parse any meaning from the exchange. Within the surgical suite, Buzz had already set up in the corner and was fast at work rolling his bones. "Don't you have somewhere else to be?" she asked, appearing beside him.

"Wright' ere," replied Buzz. "Fancy that."

"He's ready for you, doctor," said the anesthesiologist, oblivious to the supernatural disagreement occurring beside her.

"Butcher's hook," said Buzz. "He's already under. That's why yer 'ere, right? To get 'side his head, yeah?" Seeing Alice mesmerized by all the tubes and wires, he added, "Luv a duck! You do know yew can get 'side his dreams?"

It hadn't occurred to Alice that Keiji's unconscious state represented an opportunity. "Sure," she replied. "I knew that. Why do you think I'm here?"

Buzz knew a liar when he saw one, and a poor one at that.

Alice could tell that Keiji's anesthesia-induced dream occurred on a school day. She rarely wore her uniform on the weekend, and the last time they met, she had actually selected a summer dress. A sakura petal brushed her nose, and she realized the dream's source.

Keiji swung his wooden stick high with a two-handed finish. "It was just a dream, right?"

"What?" asked Alice, realizing that she had arrived within the discussion that would permanently alter their relationship.

He rested on the bat's knob. "Never mind," he said and picked a stray flower out of her hair.

"It's really good to see you. The last time…well, maybe you weren't really there."

The sight of the old tree triggered Keiji's memory. "I remember now. You told me something…" Realizing it was when she had confessed her feelings, he was too embarrassed to complete his thought. "What happened? What did I say?"

There was no way to explain the distance that had grown between them like a well-nourished weed. It was more than a change in circumstances. Neither of them was the awkward soul that had stood beneath the sakura tree near their school.

"You still want an answer," said Keiji. "I didn't tell you…"

Alice was somewhat relieved that he had finally taken some initiative. "Onegaishimasu." It was a slightly formal way to respond.

"Gomen," he replied. "It's hard to explain, but every day, when Yuki-chan visits me, it's the happiest I've ever felt. I really like her."

"I see—of course." Alice had prepared herself for the possibility of rejection, but not in favor of her best friend. It was apparent that Keiji and Yuki had grown close, but she had hoped that it was merely a reaction to the stress of the accident.

"I just want to see her laugh again," said Keiji. "She's been through a lot."

"Sorry," said Alice. "Forget I said anything. I was kidding. So, how did you do on the math test?"

It occurred to Keiji that this was the first time he had seen Alice in quite some time. "You went away. Where have you been?"

"I never stopped looking for you," replied Alice. There was a soft beeping in the distance. "I wanted to see you…but I couldn't."

"What is that? Did you hear something?" Keiji wondered if, perhaps, a truck backed up nearby. Then his legs collapsed, as the reality of his injuries reached his subconscious. His stick cracked as it struck the pavement beside him, and Alice attempted to help him back onto his feet, but his limbs bent like straws. "I'm sorry. I can't…" He passed out before he could complete his thought. Beeping bled into a tonal screech, but Alice was helpless to interfere. The bright pink of the cherry blossoms, the black of the asphalt, and the blue of the sky chromatically bled like a spilled easel.

Disgorged onto the operating room floor, Alice did not need to read the monitors to understand Keiji's condition. The formerly implacable surgeon worked in a sweat-fueled frenzy beside the alarm's source. Buzz squatted in the corner, frantically rolling his bones and mumbling in a cockney dialect that Alice couldn't understand. There was but one thing to do. She grabbed Buzz's bones and hurled them down the hall with all her might.

◆ ◆ ◆

Occupied, with their morning zazen practice, Jack assumed that none of the monks would be around to give him any trouble. The tourists, well, they wouldn't show up for another three and a half hours, so he was reasonably confident that he could go about his business undisturbed. He scooped up a fistful of moist gravel and immediately felt a tap on his shoulder. Behind him, arms folded, was the very same monk that had previously pursued him into the bamboo grove.

"Aces and spades. You're everywhere," said Jack sheepishly. "Firsties, it's not how it looks. See, I'm onto something, and I'm running out of time. You know how that is, am I right…because you're old?" The only sound was the chirping of a group of Japanese wagtails that watched from a nearby branch. "I'm dying here. Okay, how about this. My house caught fire. There's a big hole in the roof—water damage. A scoop or two, that's all I'm asking." He opened his palm, and a couple of pebbles dribbled from his hand. The monk offered nothing but aged eyes, held down by a pair of bushy eyebrows. "Look, I get how you see this, but if you knew what I was actually trying to accomplish, you'd dig what I'm doing. Seriously. It's right up your alley, very spiritual. Very Zen."

The monk tossed a small bag of gravel at Jack. The kabuki stare that accompanied it indicated that his feelings hadn't warmed, however.

"For me? That's nice. You didn't have to do that. It's not actually how it works. Not sure I can explain…" Jack searched for some indication his thoughts were getting through. "I'm being rude. You're trying to help me—or get rid of me. Anyhoo, no point in dissecting the transcendental at five in the morning, although you're all about that, am I right? Never mind." Jack shook the bag as if to acknowledge the gesture. "Thanks. I'll get it somewhere else. You've been super. Never change."

"What are you?" asked the monk.

The question took Jack by surprise. "Oh, so you can tell. Right. Of course, you can. You're super spiritual, so you picked up on my vibe. You've probably known all along. Am I right?"

"No," replied the monk. "Are you," he took a moment to gather his English, "an idiot?"

Jack was nonplussed. "Laugh it up, cue ball. You won't be in two years and seven months." He shook the bag, but then turned back as if something had occurred to him. "Oh, and maybe take it easy on the fried tofu."

◆ ◆ ◆

As the requirements for attending a live event became increasingly onerous, an opportunity had been created for a drug that made you question whether you had even gone. There was no need to use a proximity app or share your health status if you opted to drop enhancer and catch the performance from home. Only idol groups, and niche performers, had fans loyal enough to fill a small auditorium. Even then, most viewers simply paid to watch the VR live stream.

Saori looked over Taka's shoulder and watched him make a few last-minute adjustments to the Akari hologram, alternating between a headset and his laptop. "That's not her at all," complained Saori.

Taka took a moment to see if there was anything on the monitor worthy of criticism. It was difficult to account for the inherent variations in all the mediums in which the concert would be consumed. "Looks fine to me. I took that capture myself." He tried to hand her his headset but was rebuffed.

"Where's the resting bitch face...the 'I'm the reason you're all here' condescension? The patronizing haughtiness."

"Someone's been studying for their exams," replied Taka.

Saori wasn't through, though. "She treated you like a foot does a rug. The best thing that ever happened to you was when she went away." She pointed to the hologram with her vanity glasses. "Now look what you've done. You've brought her back."

"It's not his fault," said Akari, who had been watching from behind a rolling garment rack. "Maybe she never had the chance to get to know him. Sometimes you just need to be given a slightly different perspective."

Assuming she was talking to Akari's former lackey, Saori rolled her eyes so far back she could see the frontal lobe of her brain. "But she didn't. And what about you? She only let you hang around so she could use you...and you let her."

Akari couldn't deny what was obviously true. "Maybe she didn't know how to be a real friend? Maybe she'd been hurt before."

"You two are pathetic. Akari did nothing but make you miserable, and now she's like the patron saint of idols."

Eager to change the subject, Taka said, "Saori-chan. I just remembered. I heard Haruto-sensei was looking for you."

Akari waited until Saori had stomped away. "Haruto-sensei wants to talk with Saori?"

"No, but we have an agreement. It keeps us sane."

She glanced over the hologram, but it felt like she was looking at a complete stranger. "So, how's it going?"

"It's not quite there yet, but I'll get it."

She puckered her lips like a duck, imitating how Momoko might gather a thought. "I had fun the other day. It was...interesting."

"Yeah, sorry if I've been distant. It's just, I've had so much going on, with the concert and everything." He put down his stylus. "Your birthday is coming up, though, right?"

"Um...right. Taka-kun remembered! Ne. Are you getting me a surprise?"

"Maybe. You know your favorite animal—" Taka waited for her to fill in the blank.

Akari struggled for a moment but then remembered Momoko's purse. "Panda-kun?"

"Might have something to do with that." He made a few more adjustments to the software and tried to appear too occupied to continue the conversation.

She made sure no one was watching and kissed him on the cheek before skipping away. Nearby, the real Momoko expressed her jealousy by causing the lights to flicker momentarily.

"She already had her birthday," Taka said, to himself. "And Momo-chan likes cats."

Surprised that Taka remembered so much about her, Momoko's spectral outline returned to blue. The purse had been a gift from her grandmother, who viewed her grandchild's maturity through the same lens that she did. Anyone who had paid attention to Momoko's interviews knew her real preferences.

Though she knew there was no way he could hear her, Momoko whispered, "See Taka-kun. Alice was right."

"Maybe Alice was right," Taka repeated, though not entirely sure where the thought had originated.

The sight of his sister on the monitor drew Sho in for a closer look. "Hey, Taka. What the hell? Can't you see? The sync is all off. Look at her mouth moving. Right there."

Taka realized that this time his critic was the follicly challenged gangster. "I'm having a bit of trouble," he stuttered. "I used old concert footage, but it's for a different song. Written before…"

Sho shoved him aside, opened the source code, and started to make corrections. He restarted the program, but his annoyance increased. "What's this?"

"The new song."

"Those aren't the lyrics I brought him. What is this? Some kind of joke?"

"Haruto-sensai thought it would be a good idea to have your sister's hologram appear for both the tribute song and the new one."

"Yeah, well, those aren't the lyrics. I've suddenly got a craving for Hokkaido crab. Where is he?" Sho stormed off without waiting to hear Taka's insufficient reply.

"What have you done with my lyrics?" Though Sho hadn't written them himself, securing Yamamoto to the Nakai Tower's decorative spire had been a sort of contribution, motivation being an artist's most valuable collaborator.

"Sho-san. How are you today? Big night, right?"

"Do you know how much trouble I went through to get those lyrics for you?"

"They don't make any sense. Where did you even get them? A science journal?" Haruto quoted the only line he could remember. "Your love is a white hole, spacetime my heart cannot enter."

"So?"

"What does that even mean?"

Sho had spent a few hours looking it up. "It's about general relativity. The kids are going to love it."

"Our fans aren't in the Nobel Prize Committee. The chorus was literally a mathematical formula."

"Yamamoto-sensei is a national treasure." Sho wondered if his reluctant lyricist might be intentionally trying to put an end to their association.

"Takuboku Yamamoto? *The* Takuboku Yamamoto?" Haruto was both taken-aback and impressed. Still, his gift was knowing what the audience wanted, and there was no way he was putting lyrics too advanced for a science journal out as a single. "Bonus track." he blurted out. "We'll pretend like it's a secret message. That's kind of cool, right?"

The gangster's black eyes reflected no indication of acquiescence.

"So…are we good?" asked Haruto. Hearing nothing, he added, "I'm going to take that as a yes."

"Something else," replied Sho. "Yuki's now the center."

Haruto found himself hanging from the fiery hoop he thought he had just cleared. "What?"

"You heard me. Yuki is now center."

"I can't do that. Saori would kill me."

"Would you like to hear the alternative?"

Haruto realized that he would not receive as respectful a treatment as the poet whom Sho admired. "Interesting idea, but hear me out. I know you've considered it kind of a hassle to have this little operation in your portfolio, especially now that your sister…well, I thought you might want to wipe your hands clean of this situation. Am I right? The last single did pretty well, so I can pay you back, and maybe even a little extra—"

"This isn't about the money. The family has its reasons."

Haruto looked at him, stunned. "What else could they possibly want?" He knew that success often brought more problems than it resolved.

"You've been important to the family's plans. You didn't really think you were the unluckiest producer in Japan, now did you?"

"Yes." Haruto reflected. "I honestly did." The revelation wasn't reassuring. "What if they ask you to take care of me? You wouldn't hurt me, would you?"

"About Yuki—"

"Our new center?"

Sho pulled a piece of hard candy out of his pocket and popped it into his mouth.

Mrs. Okada was so engrossed watching Sho and Haruto's exchange that she squeezed the o-nigiri she was holding like a stress ball. Seeing the gangster about to leave, she stepped in front of him to force his attention. "You probably think it's silly, but you don't have a daughter. I just want what's best for my Yuki-chan. The girls at her school can't laugh anymore. She's the center—popular. Isn't that what you wanted for your sister?"

"I wanted her to be safe. Maybe I wasn't as good at it as you."

Mrs. Okada wondered if he'd ever address the recent inroads she had made into his other family. "Sho-san. Why did you warn me? You didn't have to do that. I had time to get loans—make arrangements. I don't know where we would have been…"

"I don't know what you're talking about. You just got lucky."

"Or maybe, you understand what's it's like," said Mrs. Okada. "Maybe we're more alike than you'd care to admit."

"Are we through?"

Mrs. Okada realized that she no longer felt afraid. It was as if she finally understood what it meant to be the recipient of such a significant change in fortune. "I'd say we're just getting started."

Saori was astonished that Momoko couldn't seem to remember any of her moves. Maybe it was pre-concert jitters, but when they reached the part where the center ran between the other girls, Momoko completely missed her mark and slammed into her shoulder. "Is one of those fuzzy earrings stuck in your brain? What's your problem today?"

"Nothing I couldn't take care of," replied Akari. When she had been in the center position, she was always downstage of Momoko, so she had no choice but to fake her way through the choreography.

Saori pushed her glasses back onto the bridge of her nose. "You better not have given me a bruise. When we hit that mark, you're supposed to be in the center-left position."

"Maybe you're not meant to be near the front?" The old Akari had returned.

"Say that again," replied Saori. She had endured more than enough of Momoko's recent attitude.

Seeing it looked like the two might come to blows, Haruto placed himself between them. "I'm going to settle this fast. Yuki's now the center."

"Like hell she is," said Saori.

"Over my dead body," replied Akari, unintentionally self-referential.

Haruto smiled. "See...it worked already. Nice to see everyone in agreement."

Saori did not find his little joke amusing. "I'll..."

The young producer had seen her try this ploy before and waited to see if she would complete her threat to quit. "Look. No one stays center forever, and it's not as bad as you think. There's going to be an audience vote at the concert anyway."

"A what? Nobody told me anything about a vote."

"I didn't tell you? Yuki gets to be center for now, but we're going to let the audience decide who it's going to be for the next single. So rather than argue, you might want to start practicing, juicing up support on social media. Whatever it is idols do. All right, everyone. The concert is tomorrow. Get plenty of rest."

Ms. Ito intercepted Haruto on the way to get his tea. "A vote? Why didn't you say anything about this?"

"How could I? This is the first I've heard of it."

◆ ◆ ◆

Jack was aghast at the hole the firefighters had hacked into the side of the villa. It looked like maybe two or three months of repairs to him, but it was a job for specialized artisans and lots of handholding. If it were any other house, he'd tell them to mail him a bill, but this wasn't like his condo in Miami. He might have stared at it all afternoon had he not felt a telltale tickle on his wrist.

"Thanks for the heads up. Where is he? Inside? Super."

Jack ducked through the hole to find Clement brushing ash off a lacquer tea caddy.

"I don't know if Hiro would be pleased with what you've done to the place," said Clement, in his usual acerbic tone. "He always took such good care of things."

Jack snatched the caddy back. "Well, it's not my fault. I've got proof and if the mask fits…"

The philosopher gathered his robes to sit, but seeing that the tatami mats were covered with a thick layer of soot, he decided to stand. "Well, it's not an official rule, so I suppose he can do whatever he wants, something you appear to think you have in common." He taped on Jack's pocket. "What's that rustling sound I hear?"

"Nothing. Some poker chips."

"Really?" Clement reached into Jack's pocket and removed the velvet bag. "You don't think I came here because of the fire, do you? I've noticed you've been running up quite a tab lately." He held up one of the pebbles, and then flicked it off Jack's forehead.

"What do you care? More time for you, right?" Jack snatched his pouch back and spread the gravel onto his garden before Clement could object. "Or maybe that's what you're afraid of?"

Clement stroked his bushy beard. "I see. So that's what you've been up to…"

"You think I haven't figured out how everyone wants to put me out to pasture? That's why you were so hell-bent on hooking me up with the kid, right?"

"Oh, no. You did that entirely on your own." This did not seem like the Jack that Clement had grown to love and tolerate. "It's true, we don't always see eye-to-eye, but honestly…I thought you wanted to retire."

"I do. I don't. It's hard to explain. I don't know if I even understand it."

"What's really bothering you, Jack?"

"Saul found a way to crack open the door. Asleep. Awake. It doesn't matter. It's like the Opium Wars all over again, but worse."

"Mortals always try to push the limits of their reality. I remember somebody complaining about television. And then, when they went to color..." Clement had sensed that there might be something eating away at Jack. He wondered if he wasn't afraid of losing his already shaky identity or hoping to patch up past mistakes. "How is this time any different?"

"Free will."

"Yes, I know what free will is."

"Like heat from an old light bulb, it has secondary effects."

"Such as..."

"What keeps the boogieman at bay? It's the unbreakable rule. If normies can't tell what's real and what's not, then goodbye shackles. There's no telling what Saul can do with an opening like that. Don't you get it? That's what this has been all about."

Clement hadn't seen Jack acting like a country preacher in a while. "I see. Well, that is monumental. Maybe this is a job for a specialist. Virgil is available—I think. Perhaps I could call in a few favors. Possibly get him a transfer."

"Hey, old man, hold your dice. I haven't been breaking into temples to buy time for nothing. You're not pulling me off this one. We've got everything under control."

"Did I hear someone say 'we' for once? Are you saying a has been, and a pop idol, can take on Solak, who has dispersed three of our best harvesters?" The philosopher's gray eyes considered the debris-strewn room. "Hiro thought he was strong enough to meet the storm head-on. Look what happened to him. What makes you any different?"

"Because, unlike Hiro, I know I'm not enough."

◆ ◆ ◆

"Akari's brother. Hey, I want to talk to you." Alice knew his name, but she didn't want to appear that she had been taking undue notice of him.

Generally, Sho failed to return even a cursory acknowledgment to any of his sister's former colleagues, so he avoided rewarding her with even so much as a backward glance.

"Keiji's going to be okay." Alice knew her arrow had hit when Sho's leather shoes stopped in their place. "You paid for the rest of his surgery. Why?"

"Maybe, I'm just a nice guy." He pushed the door open with his foot.

"Maybe you felt guilty?"

"What's that supposed to mean?" Backlit, his trench coat made him appear more shadow puppet than human.

Perhaps being direct wasn't the right approach, but there was no option left but to shake the tree. "You were there, weren't you? The day of the accident…when Keiji was hurt on the bridge."

At first, it seemed that he wouldn't bother to reply, but then he said, "So what if I was? Maybe I tried to help."

"Did you?"

"I don't kill kids." He reversed direction and placed his face so close to Alice that she could almost listen to him with her teeth. "Who told you to ask me that?"

"Why were you there?"

"*Shinitai desu ka?* Don't ask questions like that…not if you want to live."

"I don't think you were there to help," said Alice. "I think you're the reason he needed that surgery."

A sound came from within Sho that could best be described as a growl. "You don't know me, and you'd be safer to keep it that way." And yet, for some reason, he felt the need to justify himself. "Who do you think pulled him out of the water?"

Fear, rage, and gratitude collided within Alice like she was standing in the eyewall of a typhoon. If Sho had been the poison, then he had decided to become the antidote. He must have understood that even one decision of selflessness could prove fatal in a morally indifferent world, yet he had acted nonetheless. Alice wanted to excavate his reasoning further, but Sho had already taken advantage of her confused state, to kick open the door and leave.

CHAPTER THIRTEEN:
THE VIOLENCE OF POETRY

Maybe Jack would be cross that she had cornered Sho, but Alice had the patience of a teenager, and his two-century advantage didn't seem to contribute to his maturity.

A nail in his mouth, Jack could only acknowledge her return with a brief grunt before his hammer missed, collapsing the wall outside. He spat the nail on the ground. "Good as new."

"*Tadaima*," said Alice, prepared to be blamed for his apparent lapse in concentration.

"So, how was practice?"

"Same," replied Alice, helping Jack push the wall back against the house. "Well…there was one thing, but it's really nothing."

"What?"

"Remember, Akari's brother…"

"Bald. Dark glasses. Permanent scowl like someone just stole his Christmas presents. I'm actually the one who told you to watch him." Jack set his hammer down. "You know, you're not just there for the dancing lessons. What'd you find out?"

Alice picked up the hammer and put a nail in the wall. "Don't let it go to your head, but maybe, you were right. I had to push, and now—maybe I wish I hadn't."

"I'm not following. Am I supposed to be mad or not? Clement always seems to know the right way to land."

"Sho was at the bridge. He saved Keiji, but…"

"Ah, our hero type. I did not see that coming." Jack snatched his hammer back. "Of course, I didn't get a very good look. I was kind of busy…well, that's all water under the bridge." He put another nail in his mouth. "Still too soon?"

"He paid for Keiji's surgery. Why would he do that?"

"The yakuza do these kinds of things from time to time, helping out after earthquakes…handing out candy during Halloween. If you change manifestations, you can go back as many times as you want." Jack started to lean against the wall, but he lacked confidence in his work and pulled his hand back. "Don't get me wrong; ulterior motives are always involved. It's not like they're running a charity. Why do you think Sho did it?"

"I don't know. He looked cornered, but like he wanted someone to know."

"Everyone breaks a few eggs, but what's different about our side, is that we make omelets. Maybe Sho's more like us than we thought."

"I don't know. I'm just really confused. How am I supposed to go back knowing what I do?"

"Well, I guess this is when we find out if I actually taught you something, 'cause if this is just a job, then honestly, it doesn't make sense to go back. But if you even have some inkling of what it is we're trying to do here…then nothing, and I mean nothing will stop you. That reminds me." He retrieved a small box from under a floorboard.

"What's is it?"

"Everything you'll need if something happens to me, deeds for properties, crypto wallets, a few incriminating photos…"

"Why would I need any of that?"

"Saul's found his key. He's not going to let a minnow, like me, get in the way of his plans. Don't get me wrong, I'm not going down without a fight, but I'm no Hiro. I'm just a guy who can make one heck of an omelet. No need to get choked up or anything. I'm fine with it—probably not the retiring type anyway."

At first, Alice made an attempt to refuse, but Jack wrapped her hands around the box and stepped back.

"But you're Vegas Jack. Maybe he beat all those other guys because it wasn't you. Did you ever think of that?"

"Yeah, well, I know something about odds, and the house always wins."

"Then let's burn it down," replied Alice. "Together."

◆ ◆ ◆

The folding table was festooned with homemade signs outlined with tinsel, a look more high school fair than music industry. Akari nibbled on her ice cream and watched five fresh-faced girls set up their booth outside the train station. Before the Genki Girls, such groups were as rare as trashcans in Tōkyō, but their success had encouraged others to crawl out of Akihabara's electrically illuminated woodwork. Akari knew she was looking at the future, but with no idea where she stood.

Taka handed her a bottle of water. "Checking out the competition? Don't worry. They're at least a year or two behind us."

"Was that how we looked?"

"Are you kidding? You guys were never that cool." Taka laughed, knowing her slow-burn stare merely reflected participation in his joke. "They'd probably be excited to know you're here. Let's go over and say hi."

Akari enjoyed her last bite of ice cream, aware that Momoko's body had a slightly better metabolism. "I wouldn't know what to say. They probably saw how bad we were and figured they could do better."

"I bet they wish they had a concert coming up, like someone else I know." Such dark introspection was out of character for Momoko and made Taka wonder if Alice might be on to something. "You always knew what you wanted. Not everyone is so lucky."

One of the girls shook an awkward otaku's hand vigorously, and Akari was reminded of the first time she had met Taka.

Such events had long-standing historical precedence that made it difficult to subject them to contemporary standards. The cultural loophole had allowed for the return of an activity that fulfilled a basic human need, actual human contact. Some even said that it had helped fuel the reappearance of real idols, even more than the music.

"The first time you shook my hand...it changed my life," he said, unexpectedly. "I didn't even care how fast you reached for your sanitizer gel."

No one had ever told Akari that she made a difference, and her face became flush. "You know you were supposed to use the anti-bac spray first. Didn't you see the rules?"

"Actually, I think it was Akari's hand I shook, wasn't it?"

"Really? I can't remember. There were a lot of people. Three or four, maybe." She laughed defensively but was caught off-guard. The smiles on the girls at the booth seemed sincere, but she knew differently. "I only want to be the person you think I am, but I keep changing."

Taka didn't even recognize himself when he looked in the mirror. A hairstylist in Roppongi was partly to blame for that, but he had grown in other ways. Now he saw more than skin-deep, and it was clear that this was not the same idol he had once known. "I know what you mean."

"C'mon," said Akari, tucking her wrapper in the pocket of her skirt. "Let's go, say hi."

◆ ◆ ◆

"Hey, Keiji. It's me. Alice." She couldn't tell if he was sedated or merely asleep. At practice, Yuki had mentioned that the pain had increased as his nerve endings came back online. "I just thought I'd stop by. I'm not sure how much longer I'll be around. My life has become – really complicated, but I still think about you; every day." She watched his heart monitor, wishing she understood what the squiggly lines indicated. "Yuki says you'll be walking again in no time. I wish I could see that." Keiji gave no indication of comprehension, which bolstered her confidence. "I can't believe how everything has changed. When you're just focused on school and your friends, you assume your life will always be about the same things...the same people. Remember that day I told you I liked you? It's not that I didn't mean it, I did, but I guess I've learned a few things since then." Alice brushed the hair from his forehead. "Do you know what love really is about? Do you know what it taught me? When to think about others…and when to let go." She realized that confessions were as much about loss as hope. "Last time, I didn't get to say goodbye—oh, I almost forgot." From her pocket, she produced the angel necklace he had given her for her birthday and tucked it into his hand. "For good luck." She heard footsteps in the hall. "Goodbye, Keiji. Ganbatte."

Yuki was sure that she smelled perfume, but the room was empty. "Hello? Anyone here?" It was a familiar scent that she couldn't quite place. Keiji appeared to be sleeping, so she whispered. "Hello?" She was relieved to see that the color had returned to his cheeks, which was a good sign for sure. Sunlight eased its way through the blinds, causing something to glimmer in his hand. Yuki gently pulled the silver chain that peeked from between his fingers, and immediately recognized the necklace Keiji had given Alice for her birthday.

◆ ◆ ◆

There was a glimmer in Izumi's unpatched eye as she threw open the door to George's office. She tossed a file on his desk and placed her right foot on the arm of his office couch. Forearm on her knee, she looked like a pirate, which was not entirely a false impression.

"About all that stuff I ordered on the company account," stammered George. "Those golf clubs are for entertaining clients." The folder scanned his iris and opened. "What's this?"

"My monthly report on all of your employees. For security, this is how you'll receive it, but it bricks in twenty minutes. Read fast."

Perplexed, George was still trying to process the possibility that, on this particular occasion, he was not the source of her ire. "I don't understand. Why give it to me?"

"You tell me. You're the one who masterminded your way into this office, or was that your wife?" She itched under her eye-patch, in defiance of her doctor's orders.

It was unfair but accurate enough that George could hardly protest. "What exactly am I supposed to do with this?"

"Remember how you felt when you were looking over your shoulder?"

"Yes," replied George. "Yes, I do."

She waited until he absorbed her meaning.

"Oh. I see, but...I just don't know if that'd be right." Izumi reached for the folder, but he placed his hand on it. "Maybe a glance couldn't hurt."

The brevity of his moral conundrum was everything she had seen in him. If there were any doubts, they wouldn't be having the conversation in the first place. "You'll get it every Tuesday," she said, retrieving an e-cigarette from her pocket. She blew a cloud of vapor in his face and left him to appreciate the change in the scenery.

George struggled to even look down at the file until finally, he allowed himself a glance. "Abe-san has internal hemorrhoids? I thought he had bone spurs." Then he recalled his numerous visits to the company doctor. He still had an unfinished model of a battleship from when they had assigned him a hobby. "What am I doing?" he said and threw the report into the trash.

◆◆◆

The auditorium had been repurposed to capture VR performances, but occasionally, enka and classical concerts were still held at the facility. Twenty years earlier, anime characters slowly replaced physical artists, which led to the dominance of publicly staged holographic VR concerts. When they started inserting the viewers' names into songs, in real-time, it made regular performances seem impersonal by comparison. People began to marry their holographic idols, often several to the same one. Actual conflict in the physical world resulted and even crimes of passion. Haruto had decided to position the Genki Girls as representing a nostalgic throwback to a time before such complexities. *Natsukashii* was the word most people said upon seeing the girls in person for the first time. Next, would invariably follow a debate over whether they were actually there or merely the product of, particularly good animation. Giving a live concert would satisfy both skeptics and fans.

Outside the artists' entrance, Alice psyched herself up to enter the venue.

Jack had already metamorphed into his harvester manifestation, although the action had yet to commence.

"You know, you're not helping," she told him.

"What?"

"Dressed like that. I'm nervous enough. I can't believe I actually miss Vegas Jack."

"We're about to stand in the way of a shadow demon's dinner. They don't tend to like that. I want to be prepared."

"Great. Now I'm not worried about being off-key."

"That's why I'm here."

Saori had arrived to find Alice, apparently talking to herself. "Nervous?"

"Just going through the lyrics." She tried to smile, but her face resembled the sort of awkward photo your friends tended to post online.

"If you can't remember them, just mouth 'watermelon.' Don't worry. The bar is so low you can step over it. Half the people coming only want to say they've seen us. The other half...were dragged here by those people." She patted Alice on the head, in a way that was oddly supportive and went inside.

"Was she just nice to me?" Alice started to pace. "Okay, now I'm really nervous."

"Like I was saying. I'll run interference," said Jack. "Something tells me Saul's after something bigger tonight than a flock of otaku." A light appeared to go off within his head. "Say, great band name."

"What if I can't harvest Akari? What if there isn't an opportunity?"

"You've got to stop worrying about failure. I don't."

"I know. That's why I'm here."

◆ ◆ ◆

Taka tried to focus on the many things that had to go right for the concert to be a success, but the more he tried to brush off the idea that Momoko might be Akari, the more it made sense. His near-death experience had broadened his perspective, like acquiring thermal vision or a wide-angle lens. A thousand-meter stare indicated he wasn't entirely focused on the VR camera he had just locked down.

"Doesn't the set look amazing?" asked Haruto, slapping Taka hard on the back.

Taka nearly jumped out of his skin, but there was one question that had been on his mind. "Where did you get that huge lantern sculpture? It must have cost a fortune."

"A gift from one of our investors. You didn't think those tracksuits putting them together worked for the union, did you?" It seemed apparent that the Kurome-gumi clan had liberated the crown jewel of his set dressing from this year's Aomori Nebuta Matsuri.

"Something tells me they didn't pay for them."

Haruto was aware some gifts were best not refused. "Are they hooked up yet?"

Taka flipped a switch and the five-by-nine meter sculpture of a samurai fighting a kabuki-esque oni illuminated. Colorful washi paper stretched over a massive bamboo frame made it appear like an anime sculpture brought to life.

"We had a couple of cameras that were out of alignment, but it's all sorted out now."

"And the hologram?"

"I tried to test it earlier, but there were already people in the room. Sorry, I tried to get them to leave. Superflat groupies." Taka thought that even if nothing worked, the concert was still going to be more impressive than anything they had accomplished before. "What do you think Akari would say if she could see all of this?"

"What's Yuki doing in my place?"

They both laughed because they knew it was true.

The red, gold, and blue glow that emanated from the float made Haruto appear profoundly introspective. "You know…I don't actually like idol music. Flavor Beat used to give that genre to the kōhai of the department. Why do you think I always bugged you? I couldn't tell if we were good or not. It all sounded like crap, as far as I was concerned."

Taka had so many questions. "Then what do you really like?"

"Bluegrass."

◆ ◆ ◆

Kurome-gumi clan business often took place at Boss Mori's private residence, but lower-level decisions were generally handled in a separate office in Akasaka. All the buildings surrounding the estate had been demolished so that a rice field could be planted. This served as both a physical buffer and to highlight the traditional aesthetics of the Meiji era buildings, an unimaginable extravagance.

Sho was greeted at the front gate by Kazuo, whom he had known since first joining the family. Boss Mori had many bodyguards, but only a few carried handguns smuggled in from Korea. Those who wore tracksuits did little more than pour tea and run errands.

"Sho-san. Hisashiburi. I haven't seen you around in a while," said Kazuo, who dressed more like an office worker.

"Well, I've been busy."

"I hear that idol front company of yours has brought plenty of value to the family. Between us, I never hear about Jiro anymore."

It made Sho uncomfortable to revisit the subject, so he waited silently for the conversation to take a more agreeable direction.

Kazuo realized that he might have misspoken. "Don't worry. He was like a snake in the tall grass. I was always afraid I might step on him. Good riddance."

"Is the kumichō home?" asked Sho, eager to change the subject.

"Sure. Is he expecting you?" Kazuo took out his security wand.

"Probably," replied Sho, opening his jacket.

Kazuo searched Sho for weapons, but with minimal enthusiasm. "Okay, you're clean. Good to see you, Sho-san."

"Arigatou. Otsukaresama desu."

A simple stone path, made of single, uneven stones, led across a pond that contained Boss Mori's prized collection of kasane sumi koi fish. It encouraged the need to focus and added a layer of security. Sho waited for Kazuo to close the gate before taking out his phone. A small drone dropped from the sky and landed on Sho's shoulder. Because it was official Kurome-gumi clan property, no alarms were triggered, not that it would matter. Sho oversaw the clan's drone security and personally signed off on any changes in the software. The garden was serene, but would not be for long.

◆ ◆ ◆

Ms. Ito adjusted the bow on the back of Yuki's skirt. "Don't forget. Now that you're center, you hold the fist pump at the end of the song."

"Great. Now I have something to live for."

There was enough backstage drama that Ms. Ito didn't bother to acknowledge Yuki's sarcasm. Nana was crying over a missing brush, Saori was yelling at Nazomi, and Haruto awaited his pre-concert update. She swallowed a matching pair of aspirin and sent Yuki on her way.

"So are they ready?" asked Haruto.

"Define ready."

"They're dressed?" It was all that he could reasonably expect. "I want to thank you. You didn't have to leave the record company. You had it pretty good there." He waited to see if she would provide him any additional insight into her behavior, but she only offered him her trademark iron stare. "I mean…we were never that close. Were we? I couldn't tell."

Ms. Ito took a long sip of tea. "I just wanted to be there when you failed."

Haruto chuckled nervously. "Well, sorry to disappoint you."

"Who says I was disappointed?" It was difficult to tell if she was joking, but she lifted her cup to conceal something behind its rim.

Haruto felt a tap on his shoulder and turned to find Saori, arms folded, her foot moving like a speed metal band's bass drum pedal.

"Haruto-sensei. We need to talk."

He was pretty sure he knew what she wanted to complain about, but it wasn't like he could negotiate with the yakuza. "It's a company decision. My hands are completely tied. There's nothing more I can do."

"Not that. Yuki can be center for all I care." She showed him something on her phone. "I got in. I'm going to college!"

As happy as he was for her, he was more relieved not to have to hear about who could wear a special train on the back of their skirt. "That's great! You finally did it…I mean, fantastic, Saori!"

"I couldn't have done it without you."

It moved Haruto to think that he might have been a small part of her accomplishment. He wondered if being an idol producer might be about more than profiting off the psychological deficiencies of otaku.

"You showed me the need for an education."

"Why is everyone insulting me today?" Haruto couldn't help but wonder if someone had placed a glitter-festooned sign on his back.

Saori handed him an ornate envelope. "This will be my last performance as a Genki Girl." She bowed deeply. "Honto ni arigatou gozaimasu."

Haruto was as touched as he was concerned. He wanted to thank her for providing the group with leadership since they had lost Akari, but Saori had already joined her teammates backstage. "Wait. Saori-chan. You have to do a graduation concert!"

Momoko drifted—as if underwater—to where Taka fiddled with some last-minute adjustments to the holographic projection equipment. "I wanted to wish you good luck," she said. "It's okay if you can't hear me. When you held my hand, even if it was Akari, I kind of felt it. Is that weird? I'll be cheering you on, whether you can see me or not. Ganbatte, Taka-kun. Do your best." To her surprise, his chin rose. "Taka-kun? Can you hear me? Snap your fingers, or raise your hand. Blink."

"Hey. How are you feeling?" Alice still felt terrible about what she had put Taka through, even if it had been somewhat of an accident. "Sorry if I've been freaking you out lately. I seem to be doing that a lot to people lately."

"I've been thinking over...you know, that thing we talked about. Something tells me you might believe what you're saying. Do you?" Taka remained unaware of Momoko's attempts to get through to him.

"I wish I had something less crazy to tell you. In my defense, you were the one who started all this."

"Sou desu." Taka rubbed his forehead. "I asked Momoko some questions, easy ones. Not even one answer right. Not one."

"Sorry. I'm not trying to look like a freak. It must come naturally."

"I get why you think it's not her, but that doesn't mean she's possessed or anything. I mean, c'mon, let's be rational. There could be lots of reasons."

Alice could see Momoko beside him, her spectral face glowing expectantly, and decided to abandon any attempt at subtlety. "What if I told you she was standing next to you?"

"I'm trying to be serious."

"Maybe it's breaking some kind of rule, but I don't know them, so here goes. If you have a question, go ahead…ask. I'll tell her, and you can decide for yourself."

Alice appeared sober enough that Taka figured he might as well play along. "Okay, ask her what Haruto-sensei originally rhymed with 'doughnut' in the third verse of the Doughnut Song. Back when they performed konbini stores and animal shelters." He knew that the question pre-dated Alice's involvement with the group.

Momoko whispered something into Alice's ear. "No," said Alice. "*Magi ka?*" She reluctantly turned to Taka. "She says, 'peanut.' That can't be right. Peanut? How does that even make any sense?"

Taka was momentarily stunned, but then he remembered something. "Chotto. You had an idol blog. Of course, you would know. You love the Genki Girls. You told me yourself."

Caught in her own cover story, Alice replied, "Fine. You caught me. Ask me something else."

"Okay. Ask her where she was sitting at the first handshake event I ever attended…the first time she shook my hand." Taka looked over at the many projects he had yet to finish. "Well, what did she say?"

"She says she didn't shake your hand. She wanted to, but Akari monopolized all your attention." She waited for Momoko to add something. "She sat to Akari's right—your left. You probably didn't notice, but she was wearing pink and blue ribbons. I don't see how that matters."

"Sugoi," said Taka, astonished. "But maybe you saw a photo. Maybe somebody told you—"

"We can do this all day," replied Alice. She was starting to wonder if there was any point in trying to convince someone of something they didn't want to believe.

"Tell him he sleeps on his stomach and snores like a chipmunk," said Momoko. "It's really cute. I've been watching him every night."

"Do you even want him to like you?" asked Alice.

Taka couldn't hear their conversation, but if Alice was acting, she was way more talented at it than being an idol merited. "Wait, what is she saying?"

"She says you keep one of Akari's gum wrappers in a box in your closet, and she wishes you would throw it away."

For a moment, Taka's heartbeat rattled his throat. "Let's just say, for a moment, that I believed you. What exactly is it you want me to do?"

Alice presented him with the vial of Zombie Dust she had saved from the fire.

◆ ◆ ◆

The president of Tokuji-Tech was not usually inclined to take a call from a yakuza patriarch. Still, since the Kurome-gumi had, for all practical purposes, assumed control of his company, he would have to take his medicine. "Inspections are a part of doing business," he explained. "It's not like we can tell them no. Our books are entirely in order. I'm confident that you have nothing to worry about."

Boss Mori downed his whiskey, which cost more than the president's suit. "I've heard that one of the drug investigators is particularly troublesome, but we have studied his background and interests, most thoroughly."

"Ah…well, I'm sure he'll be more than satisfied. I've spoken with all the division heads, and everyone has assured me that everything is in order. It can be a challenge, but government regulations being what they are…"

"I don't like regulations; I like flexibility. Maybe being headquartered in Japan has outlived its usefulness?"

The president had family in Tōkyō and no interest in moving their facilities, especially when corporate ownerships could be fluid. "No. No. We're fine. You make a lot of good points. I'll be sure to bring your concerns up with the board. Okay, then. Jaa. *Dewa mata.*"

The screensaver returned to the family seal, and Boss Mori's thick finger resumed rolling the ice ball in his glass. Something buzzed near his ear, which he attempted to swat away. At first, he thought another dragonfly might have found its way in from the garden, but then the wakizashi flew off its stand behind him. It landed in the outstretched hand of Sho, who was outlined by a vermillion sky. The drone pulled off its sheath, leaving the blade naked and determined.

"Sho-san. I hope you did not return to dishonor yourself."

"How strange you should say that. Honor is exactly why I'm here."

Boss Mori's hand moved to the underside of his desk, where he kept a handgun secured by a rare-earth magnet. "I know you killed Jiro. How can you have any? See, even with what I have learned, you are still here. If I had wanted you dead, you would already be nourishing my rice field."

"Don't worry. Soon I won't need your charity."

Boss Mori seized his pistol, but before he could bring it over the desk, Sho sliced through his hand. The black lacquer desk acquired the appearance of red enamel. Boss Mori grabbed Sho with his other fist, by which he ruled Honshu, but Sho locked his grip and used it as leverage to walk up the wall behind him. When Sho came back down, he drove the wakizashi through Boss Mori's back, piercing his stomach, and exposing his soul to be devoid of virtue.

"It always tastes blood. Isn't that what you used to say?"

Sho heard the sound of guards running on the engawa's wooden floorboards, Grabbing Boss Mori's gun; he fired twice for each tracksuit that had the misfortune to appear. Sho felt more for them than their boss, who had never even bothered to learn their names. It proved a challenge to liberate the wakizashi's blade from the dead kumichō's chest, but he knew it would serve him better than its former master. Sho wiped it clean under his left shoulder, and for the first time, since he had graduated from the apartment in San'ya, he felt liberated.

Sho's mirror-like gaze absorbed the reflection of a guard running across the small stone islands that broke up the courtyard pond. He used his last round to introduce him to the koi and then, seeing a shadow, hurled it through the paper screen door, producing a groan.

Boss Mori's bodyguard, a former sumo wrestler, named Masaru, emerged rubbing his head. "Sho-san. If I find our kumichō hurt, I cannot go gently on you."

"*Kyōdai*, there is nothing for you to see here. You are about to have a new boss – one surely grateful for the service I've rendered." Sho was reasonably sure that whoever ascended would not show him any leniency, no matter how much they profited. It was a matter of honor.

Such political considerations were beyond Boss Mori's bodyguard, who charged Sho as if a gyōji had turned his war-fan. He only paused at the discovery that a short sword had been driven into his shoulder, but still managed to toss Sho against a stone lantern breaking one of his ribs. Sho winced as he threw the top of the lantern back at him, but it was easily swatted aside. Unfortunately, the lantern's shaft made an excellent bat, which Masaru used to launch Sho into a pile of rocks below a small waterfall. The wakizashi landed nearby, so Sho tossed a handful of pebbles, a distraction the bodyguard did not fully appreciate until the muscle within his belly parted.

Sho's body ached, but he was determined to stumble towards the gate, though he painted red lines upon the vibrant moss along the way. Blocking his passage to the civilian world was a pale hannya mask with surprising patience. There was no point turning away, as one's back makes for a weak impression.

"What a mess you've made of our garden," said Solak, neatly attired in a freshly tailored suit. "Should we defile the rice-field as well? Then I can be assured you will not see paradise."

◆ ◆ ◆

"Izumi-san? You like this sort of thing?" George was surprised to see his ergonomic inquisitor searching for a seat, like any other otaku fan. He never imagined she might have interests other than tormenting her co-workers.

"I assumed your wife told you…we're an official sponsor again."

"Is that a good idea?"

"As long as we never speak of it." The lights in the arena dimmed, and a deep thumping shook the seats. George noticed that the black lights had illuminated something on Izumi's leg. She adjusted her sock, but not before he caught a glimpse of the Kurome-gumi crest on her ankle. "Who are those idiots supposed to be?" She was unmoved by Superflat's pectoral display of rhythm.

"The opening act? My daughter Yuki-chan says they're on the same label. Must be a contractual obligation."

Izumi saw that Mrs. Okada had arrived carrying snacks and took it as her cue to excuse herself. "Sorry for the intrusion. I'll leave you both to enjoy the concert." She held her bow as she exited backward.

"Isn't this exciting?" said Mrs. Okada. "Can you believe our Yuki is going to be center?"

"Yes," replied George, quite matter-of-fact. "Yes, I can. Wouldn't it be better if she did it on her own?"

"If that were possible, I wouldn't be needed." It seemed a logical enough conclusion, from her point of view.

"I think I could have been happy."

"Well, now you have power—and that's like happiness with wings."

"Who are you?" he asked, though, for the first time in their marriage, he truly understood.

◆ ◆ ◆

Taka tapped the vial, and a gray powder filled the holes of the windscreen. "Momoko," was written on the microphone's housing, but Alice had created enough doubt in that assertion that he had tentatively agreed to her plan. Though confident that the powder wasn't lethal, his hand still shook, and for a moment, he considered dusting the windscreen off, but then he had an unanticipated visitor.

"Isn't that a little beneath you?" It was Momoko's voice, but who exactly stood behind the words was rather in question.

"What?"

"Checking the mics? Isn't that at little below your pay grade?"

"Are you kidding? I just serviced the bathroom. Well, I changed out the toilet paper. The last guy must have forgotten…"

Akari sniffle-laughed, as was Momoko's habit when she was nervous. "Taka-kun is so funny."

"They aren't even real mics. They're props. I guess it's supposed to look retro or something."

"With you looking out for me tonight, I'm sure it'll be awesome." She closed the distance to such a degree that it would be problematic if someone saw them. "Maybe afterward, we should talk about a more permanent arrangement." Before he could object, she gave him a quick kiss and ducked behind the curtains.

Consumed with guilt, he leaned against the microphone stand and asked himself if it would not be better to embrace ignorance. The elation he had felt had been real enough. If the truth was love's oxygen, he was about to smother it, along with his happiness.

◆ ◆ ◆

Within the flooded rice paddy that surrounded the Mori Family estate, yellow kodai-mai stalks saluted the combatants. Black sludge clung to Sho's feet, and water penetrated his pant legs. Maintaining the field was a form of indoctrination for new members. Once, when they attempted tanbo art, Sho had helped author the security program that dealt with the increase in drone activity the picture attracted. It had elevated his standing in the family, despite Boss Mori's disappointment that their family crest would no longer be appreciated by passing planes.

"I don't really have the time for this today, but in honor of your sister, I'm going to kill you myself." Solak sincerely felt he was doing Sho a favor, like providing him an autograph signed in blood.

Sho addressed his wakizashi towards the rice, and orange light glistened upon its steel folds. His breathing was steady, and the muscles in his shoulders were strung as tight as a bow.

"That grip is better for enclosed spaces." It disappointed Solak not to have a more worthy adversary. At least the encounter would be brief, if not satisfying.

"You don't have a weapon," replied Sho. "We'll be fighting at close range." He wiggled his fingers, an unintended cue that his opponent nested inside his head.

Though unarmed, Solak felt no urgency to await his own weapon's arrival. "I suppose you are right. Well, then...shall we?"

"First, I need to know something. Did you kill my sister?"

"She's much freer now. Will that allow your spirit to be at rest?"

Solak's feet struck the water like the skin of a drum. He noticed that Sho had switched to a jōdan-gamae stance, but as Sho cut downward, Solak grabbed his wrists and locked his joints. Having seized his wakizashi, Solak hooked Sho's leg and sent him onto his back with a loud splash.

As he looked down with pity, the shadow demon observed, "That stance is really not meant for a short sword." Then, he pierced his stomach as if taking care of a centipede, rotating the wakizashi handle to ensure that any nearby organs would not be left to chance.

"Who are you?" asked Sho, his black eyes becoming dull, and blood running from the corners of his mouth. "What did you do to my sister?"

"I am the puppeteer," replied Solak, rather matter-of-fact. "Your sister? That's the ironic part. She's never been better."

Kazuo had finally arrived with Solak's katana, only to find it unnecessary. "Is that Sho-anaki?"

"He's not going to make it," said Solak, sliding the sword he had liberated from Jack's villa through his belt. "I forget. Is today burnable or recyclable? You'll sort it out, won't you?"

◆ ◆ ◆

Alice's face became flush at the sight of Yuki wearing her necklace. "Did Keiji give that to you?"

"Hai. When I saw him at the hospital." She noticed the rise in Alice's temperature. "How did you know?"

"Well, you just came from seeing him, right?" She blinked rapidly and was relieved to see Haruto get up on a chair about to speak.

"Okay, that punishment you're hearing is Superflat's last number. Assuming there is still an audience, there'll be a short break while they reset the stage." Ms. Ito interrupted Haruto to show him something on her phone. "This just in.

Listen up, everyone. Are you ready? Our new song is at number one!" He waited for the cheers to subside. "And 'Remembrance' is back at number three. You know what? I don't even care. There's better news. Saori got into college. Isn't that amazing?"

Everyone cheered, including some of the crew who stopped to applaud.

"Is that supposed to be an insult?" asked Saori, removing her glasses.

"No, not at all. Seriously. I'm grateful – and not just for Saori's unbelievable accomplishment, but for everyone. I know what you all went through, not just in the group but also at home and school. Years from now, well, you'll always remember that you were a part of the number one idol group in Japan. Whatever happens, no one can take that away from you." There were murmurs of recognition as the reality of what he was saying was absorbed. "Now, go out there and show everyone what that means." Accustomed to losing, Haruto hardly knew how to enjoy success, but he was willing to learn.

◆ ◆ ◆

At first, the only thing Sho felt was pressure from within his abdomen. He clenched his jaw more from anger than pain at the realization that he had faired worse than in his last engagement with the leering hannya mask. When the extent of his injury finally manifested, it arrived full-force like a shinkansen through an unscheduled station. His ears rested below the rice paddy's waterline, so his cries were muffled. The next wave of pain pushed him to the very edge of unconsciousness. All he saw was white, like the robes of the kimono he would soon receive.

A crimson Rorschach test formed in the water around the fallen yakuza, who had lost everything but the poetry that served as his talisman of civility in a world of violence. "Our life," he recited, "is the light of the moon passing behind a cloud at dawn." The sky spun overhead, the earth tumbling upon its axis. Memories achieved equity with his fading consciousness, and, once again, he saw the apartment he had shared with Akari. She clutched a boning knife covered with blood that tumbled from her adolescent hands as they embraced. "It is as lasting as morningtide's tears or a waning crescent." In a back room in

Ikebukuro, a needle moved towards his eyes. A burly man with Bushidō code tattoos held up a mirror so that he could see his irises were perfectly black. "Yet the night is not overcome by the stars." From across the street, he watched Haruto get tossed out the front doors of Flavor Beat Records. Covered in pigeon droppings, he bore a sheepish smile as he looked to him for approval. "Nor the day absorbed by the mire." Refusing Sho's protests, Jiro slammed the dark-blue car with shadows too small not to be innocent. Diving into the water, Sho left Jiro slumped over the steering wheel, a bullet hole above his temple. "What jealous cloud undertakes to deny belies concealment." On the floor of his apartment, Sho collapsed amidst the many belongings that shared his brokenness. A monitor displayed, "News at 10: Death of an Idol."

Back in the rice paddy, Sho's breathing slowed, and his face became as blanched as the mask that had slain him. His words, little more than a gasp, reflected the totality of his journey. "What the sun bids to outshine is nary overcome." Ocherous light permeated the field as he breathed his last upon the cursed earth. "Day nor night obscures the shadow that endures."

CHAPTER FOURTEEN:

HAVING YOUR CAKE

The auditorium's stage held all the welcome of a guillotine platform. Jack played the role of supernatural executioner, his coal eyes pulsing as Alice worked up the courage to join her teammates. She had already concluded that performing was like public speaking, but with singing and dancing added to the equation.

"What are you waiting for, Christmas? Time to saddle up." Jack hadn't anticipated stage fright in the equation. There was an infinite amount of other things his partner could be concerned with, and a glorified talent show wasn't one of them.

An impatient Saori waved aggressively for Alice to take her place between Nana and Yuki. Fists against their waists in the start position, the other girls awaited the rise of the curtain. Yuki bugged out her eyes in an attempt to nonverbally compel Alice to take her first step onto the stage.

"This was a bad idea."

At first, Jack wasn't sure to which mistake she was referring. "I've seen you at practice. There are at least three girls worse than you. Okay, maybe two."

"This is the real thing," she replied.

"Real? What does that even mean? Were things more real before or after we met? AR? VR? How about now?"

"Why did I think I could do this? I can't even remember the lyrics to songs I actually like."

"So, you're afraid. Is that what this is about? Fear is that voice telling you now is different from the last time you won. Bind, gag, and drive it out to the desert. For the record, it's absolutely critical to do it in that order."

"Maybe everything is easy for you, but I'm not Vegas Jack. I'm the girl who was too afraid to join the yearbook club."

Jack's beads were spinning like a prayer wheel, so he covered them with the sleeve of his robe. "You don't think I get scared?"

"No."

"Well, that shows how little you know. Maybe I just show it differently." He considered materializing, so he could give her a proper shove. "Maybe, I become a bit of a jerk."

"So, you're always scared?"

"Hysterical. Look. Timid Alice is over. She's gone. Never liked her." He could see that she was about to deliver her usual go-to remark, so he beat her to the punch. "And I didn't kill her. You did. You're stronger than she was, and frankly…a bit scary now."

Alice tugged her ruffled skirt into place and adjusted her chocker to allow for one last deep breath. "You make a lot of sense for a Halloween reject."

"I know. It's part of my charm."

Being convinced by Jack was more unnerving than any ghoulish manifestation, she might be forced to face, but he wasn't entirely wrong. "So, you'll hold off Solak while I take care of Akari?"

"Rock and roll," said Jack, who disintegrated into ash and wafted into the back of the auditorium.

"I knew I should have picked the other door."

◆ ◆ ◆

From Los Angeles to Lisbon, Budapest to Singapore, windows cracked open so that delivery drones could toss dime bags of enhancer inside. Around the world, fans watched the Genki Girls logo slowly rotate inside their headsets, and awaited the start of the concert's live stream. In Japan, unseasonably hot spring weather made the wait uncomfortable until the drug's synthetic glutamate coaxed the user's brain cells to release reality's hold upon their consciousness. N-43 had been developed using seaweed as its foundation, and it worked intracellularly within the brain, to ensure that signal transduction in the central nervous system could be manipulated with absolute precision. Whether in Columbia or Madagascar, anyone who took the drug sincerely believed that they were in an auditorium in Tōkyō. As they waved their light stick in time with the intro music, nothing could convince them it was all a technological illusion.

◆ ◆ ◆

Bad chill in the air, thought Buzz. *Nuff said, right?* He dusted himself off and skipped towards the hospital's rec room. "Duty calls, yeah? Hands full and all that." He could feel it in his bones. Tonight there would be work enough for everyone in the incorporeal essence collection business. Later that evening, the hospital staff would comment on how unusually quiet the evening had been for them. Scientific training did not inhibit postulations on whether the cycle of the moon affected their workload. What could not occur to them was that the buzzard had flown his coop for more international pickings. And if he could only succeed in making his mark, he might never return.

◆ ◆ ◆

The flashing lights, and projection mapping effects, made it difficult to see anything beyond the stage. Jack was out there somewhere, and Alice knew Akari must have sensed it by the way her eyes searched the auditorium. She had caught herself doing the same thing, though she tried to play it off as nothing more than an attempt to connect with the audience.

"Dreams are the wishes of your hopes and ambitions," sang Alice, focused on Akari, who was faking her way through Momoko's moves. "My fantasy *hanabi* with you."

Projection mapped fireworks exploded behind the lantern sculptures. The matsuri set was appropriate for songs centered on love confessions, and its many tropes.

For the first time, the choreography placed Akari next to Alice. "What's your friend up to Alice? I know he's out there."

"Nothing. Just watching me perform."

"In harvester form?" Akari was insulted by Alice's apparent lack of candor. "Momoko's not coming back. She might as well get used to being in my shadow...not that anything's changed."

The lights flashed in time with the strumming of Spanish guitars, and their second song, "Ganbatte Olè," started. Alice spotted Jack, but he was distracted by a message he had received. He appeared to acknowledge a new set of coordinates and then dove into a nearby VR camera. Alarmed to find herself without any backup, Alice missed her mark and stumbled into Saori.

"Focus," yelled Saori. Her clenched teeth made it clear that her plastered on smile was for show.

"Gomen," replied Alice.

"Don't apologize. Sing."

Akari crossed behind Alice and elbowed her hard in the back. "Stay genki."

◆ ◆ ◆

The chief investigator for the Pharmaceuticals and Medical Devices Agency, or PMDA, had a well-established reputation as being a ballbreaker during office hours. In his free time, however, he pursued the passion he had embraced for the past twenty-five years. A well-aged idol otaku, he no longer felt comfortable attending concerts in person, but fortunately for him, that wasn't necessary. Thanks to advances in VR technology, he could enjoy everything from the comfort of his apartment. More than that, his job gave him access to the medicinal means to erase the distance between his couch and the front row. Untouchable to bribes, he reasoned that taking an occasional sample from his busts was no more harmful to society than a police officer that broke the speed limit from time-to-time.

If he had been sober, he might have seen the katana Solak raised behind his neatly trimmed neckline, the gleam of its steel unseen from within his headset. Perhaps if he had been more corruptible, it would not have been necessary to provide him with such an early retirement. His closest subordinate at the PMDA had large tabs at three of the family's gambling dens, which made him a more flexible alternative. Solak brought down his blade, but a charred beam of wood appeared and arrested its progress.

"Jack." Solak didn't need to confirm the source of his aggravation. "I actually care about this one. Kindly step aside."

"They're all important to me." The blue veins on Jack's blanched hands throbbed as he struggled to hold the sword at bay. Using the beam's weight, he drove Solak's katana into the floor and then brought it back up into the shadow demon's chin. "That's for burning down my house. Here's the rest in change."

Jack opened his sleeves, and blasted Solak with the stored debris from the villa fire, sending him through the sliding glass door and over the balcony. Stepping over the broken shards of glass, Jack discovered Solak clinging to its edge by his fingertips. He brought down his boot, only to have Solak grab his heel and pull him into the fifty-two stories of air below. As the pair tumbled, they grappled for advantage until the ground arrested their fall, at which point they found themselves in London.

"Isn't this where you're really from, Vegas Jack?" Solak adjusted his mask, which had become askew during their tumble. "Just a poor, uneducated textile worker who died protesting the future. The one I'm creating can't be avoided. Not in this world or the next."

"Neither can this." Jack grabbed a light pole and swung it at Solak, who leaped clear. "That doesn't make me wrong."

"You can't close this door. They've opened it most willingly." Solak ran through a nearby collection of row houses, its inhabitants unaware that a preternatural apex predator was in their midst. He stopped next to a teenager whose plastic smile was a telltale sign of enhancer's handiwork.

"Whatever happened to spirit boards?"

"So nineteenth century Jack—just like you, Luddite." Solak jumped into the teen's headset and re-emerged in a Chinese medicine shop in Hong Kong.

Jack materialized between a mountain of ma huang, làngdàng, and seaweed. A brass scale measured the weight of a red powder that rose from its base like a well-stacked pyramid. "Is this supposed to rattle me?" He stuck his pinky into a bottle of snake wine and gave it a taste. "What are you trying to say?"

"Take a hint, Jack. It's a brave new world. This is where I found the missing ingredients. Don't you remember?"

"To make enhancer?"

"Every new house needs a key. Haven't you ever heard about quantum physics? How is this world any more substantial than the one I'm about to conquer?"

"Better graphics?"

"It's all energy, Jack…positive and negative, zeros, and ones. Reality is a contrivance."

"Yeah, but it's all we've got." Something about Solak's philosophizing felt familiar, like a sweater he had outgrown. "If nothing matters, then why try and ax that guy in the apartment?"

"A gatekeeper who thinks he can stop the future. A bureaucratic speed bump…we failed to come to an understanding, something I will soon rectify."

"I don't like rules either, but at least I know when to bend them." Jack exploded the jars of dried jujubes, lotus seeds, and anise. A torrential whirlwind of seeds, peels, and roots filled the shop.

"Now, Jack. Do you really think I dragged you all the way here to waste time fighting? The same reins hold us both back. Don't make the very mistake you made attacking that textile mill." Nearby lay the pickled snakes from some broken wine jars. Solak threw them onto Jack, and the serpents animated and ate their tails. Arms and legs cinched, Solak tipped him over with a gentle push. "Within every atom is a tornado of energy within which exists nothing—and yet everything that matters. Have fun in Hong Kong, Jack. You always did your best work here." Unable to bring balance to their differences, the shadow demon stepped into the kaleidoscopic cyclone of medicinal compounds and left his longtime hindrance behind.

◆ ◆ ◆

The Akari hologram emerged, as if from a trapdoor, to the delight of her loyal fans. "Remembrance," the haunting single popular with friends moving on in life poured from the speakers. Off-stage, Taka made a couple of final adjustments to the refresh rate and wiped a tear that had breached his professionalism.

The real Akari considered her holographic likeness with mock nostalgia. "I miss me." She waited for the lights to flash in the eyes of the audience and grabbed Alice by her hair. "Solak told me why you're here." She dragged her to the ground and dug her nails into her neck. "He also said you're weak when you can't transform, and if you die, I win."

Alice grabbed a decorative chain sewn into Akari's dress and smashed their foreheads together. "I'm not that weak."

Dazed, Akari stood and swung wildly, but missed and accidentally knocked Saori's glasses off her face. Annoyed, Saori pushed her into Yuki, and a shoving match ensued.

From off-stage, Haruto sensed something was wrong. "Taka-san. Why is no one on their mark?"

Taka reached for the auxiliary control panel and moved the Akari hologram in an attempt to block the audience's view of the skirmish. He raised his voice to be heard over the growing roar of approval within the auditorium. "Um, they appear to be fighting—worse than usual."

"Pretend that it's part of the show." Haruto pinched his nose, regretting his life choices. The hologram was the only member of the group he could control. "They told me never to work with animals or idols, and did I listen?"

"You've never used animals," replied Taka, using the strobe lights to make it appear that the skirmish was an unbridled form of choreography.

As programed, the microphone stands rose from under the stage. Alice reached for the one that Taka had dusted. Comprised of synthetic and natural toxins found in frogs native to South America, it would send its victim into immediate cardiac arrest. Having seen Taka shake it onto her windscreen during rehearsal, Akari thrust it back towards Alice.

"I'm not dying again!" cried Akari.

"You're not even supposed to be alive," replied Alice.

"Hypocrite." Akari forced the windscreen within a hairsbreadth of Alice's lips, but then her grip relaxed. The foundation of everything she has rested her grievances upon had shattered.

Sho's head was neatly shaven, but his eyes were no longer black. It was as if death had removed the stain of his many past indiscretions. Crystalline, incorporeal, and pure in form, he floated onto the stage; right palm held outward. "Akari-chan. Stop."

"Oniisan?" Instantly comprehending what seeing him in such a state implied, she asked, "Who did this to you?" The full wrath of her gaze bore into Alice.

Emerging from the VR camera, in a manner not unlike a spider, Solak re-appeared in the auditorium. He knew Jack would only be temporarily delayed, and when he re-emerged, it would undoubtedly be to check on his partner, a weakness upon which the shadow demon could take advantage. Once Solak was satisfied that there would be no further interruptions, the matter with the PMDA inspector could be concluded. To his surprise, however, Sho was there; finger thrust accusingly in his direction.

Like the snap of a puzzle piece, Akari immediately comprehended Solak's role in the tragedy of her life. She jerked the microphone away from Alice, stage lights dancing wildly in her eyes, and defiantly licked the windscreen. Akari's eyes rolled back as she collapsed on stage, a puppet that had willingly severed its strings.

"Fool!" cried Solak.

Unseen, Jack emerged from the camera and blasted Solak with grave dirt. "What did I miss?" His cindery eyes followed Sho's lucent gaze to where Akari lay. "Hey, Saul. I don't think she's going to walk that off. It might be time to look for a new partner."

Solak coughed from the dust. "Unlike you, I can work alone."

"That doesn't make you stronger." Jack unfolded a stack of femurs from within his robe to form a ghoulish spear. Unfortunately, the blade intended as the weapon's conclusion became stuck at a ninety-degree angle. Jack glowered. "Ah, for the love of...you're going to do this to me now?" He shook it a couple more times in an attempt to make it properly extend. "Seems to be stuck. It's not a scythe, really. Seriously, the end is stuck." He pounded it against the ground, aware of whom he now resembled. "Son of a biscuit! She's never going to let me live this down."

The stage lights pulsated as Alice readied to restore Momoko's soul to her body. "Chotto matte," said Alice, seeing Momoko eager to leap back into her own skin. "Akari's still in there. You might find it a bit crowded. I need to transform." There was no way that was possible, surrounded by concerned teammates who believed Momoko had passed out.

Alice searched expectantly for Jack, but he was occupied with Solak, keeping him at bay with his bladed staff. Supernatural flashes of light, and tentacles of fire, lit up the back of the auditorium, but she could not determine how her partner faired.

Seeing Momoko, spread out on the floor of the stage, Taka panicked and killed the lights. With the aid of darkness brought on by his face-saving maneuver, Alice was able to transform and harvest Akari's soul. To her surprise, she found it most willing to be removed from its mortal coil.

"Stay genki," said Alice. "And thanks."

Momoko lay back into her old body and soul rejoined flesh. Her recent memories dissolved as her consciousness was restored. Bewildered to discover herself on stage, Momoko assumed that she must have collapsed in the middle of the concert and sprang to her feet.

"She's okay," yelled Saori, waving off the EMT. "Bring back the lights!"

Taka restarted the program, and the girls scrambled to their marks. The audience cheered so loudly that it overwhelmed the music. Taka's relief at seeing Momoko back in her position turned to alarm as he realized someone else had gone missing. "Seven. Eight. Where's Alice?"

Then, the auditorium was enveloped with the gasps of people reacting to the Nebuta Matsuri lantern sculpture coming to life. The section that comprised the giant oni broke free from the set and stood high over the stage, an illuminated woodblock print come to life. It wielded the katana liberated from the villa, leaving no doubt concerning the cause of its animation.

"That's my sword," said Jack, trying hard not to appear intimidated.

"Is it? Possession is nine-tenths of the law." Solak laughed and took a swipe at him.

"You may have a point," said Jack, taking control of the other sculpture, that of a fierce samurai. Holding up its considerably more fragile weapon, they faced off, much to the delight of the audience.

Solak brought down his blade, slicing open Jack's chest. The float flickered as the wiring debated whether or not it would yield. He attempted a counter-strike, but Solak grabbed his arm and tore it from its frame. Alice tried to come to his aid by throwing her fans, but the two large tears in Solak's sculpture only bled light. Enraged, the shadow demon sliced wildly at Jack, sending washi paper flying like confetti. Having beaten him to the ground, Solak held his katana high over his head and remarked, almost regrettably, "Goodbye, Jack."

Before Solak's sword could descend, he found himself blinded by several small flashes. "Oni *wa soto!*" Get out, demon! Alice yelled as she threw several exploding beans. She used the distraction to wrap her obi chords around Jack's waist and pull him high into the rigging above the stage.

"Setsubun, right?" noted Jack, pleased that she had finally caught on to how their powers worked. "Nicely done."

Alice's obijime cords retracted. "Was that a scythe you were using?"

"Not. One. Word."

Solak grabbed a rope line and started to pull himself up to the rafters. The matsuri float allowed him the freedom to work in the real world, but if it became any more disfigured, the audience's free will would put the breaks on his performance. Jack opened his sleeves in an attempt to unleash brimstone, but the context was wrong. Such a limitation was Solak's primary consideration when he had chosen his manifestation.

Alice threw her fans and sliced the ropes just above Solak's hands. At first, he fell towards the stage, but then he managed to grab hold of the counterweight rigging and dangled barely above where they performed their final number.

Realizing she had to work within mortal expectations, Alice assumed a lantern float version of her maiko manifestation. She kicked at Solak's face as if a giant leg had appeared from the rafters, but he caught her ankle and pulled her towards the stage. Alice used her foot to cave in his sculpture's head.

Taka watched the set props, engaged in battle, and exclaimed, "That's the most incredible effect I've ever seen!"

"Kurome-gumi," replied Haruto. "My silent partners. Must have cost a fortune. I'm sure I'll see the bill."

Saori saw her teammates losing focus and yelled, "Eyes forward. Not on the stage dressing."

"Careful. That's not any sword." Jack cast a chain of clasped gravestone hands from the folds in his robe and pulled Alice back towards him.

Alice returned to her regular form in time to avoid a close swipe at her legs. Looking around the rafters, she spotted the pyrotechnic effects intended for the concert's grand finale. "Jack. Lighter."

He flicked its spark wheel, and for once, it came alive. Alice animated her obi cords and snatched the firework canon, allowing Jack to light its payload. Silver sparks showered down upon the washi-covered float, igniting its colorful skin. Its demonic expression burned away to reveal Solak, as the ghost within the machine. Billowing flames bubbled the white and gold paint of his hannya mask, and its straps burned away, causing the mask to hang loose until he pressed it back against his face.

Jack gazed inside the float in disbelief, unable to accept the form that stared back from within the ocherous abyss. "Hiro?"

"You never get anyone's name right."

If it was merely a distraction, it carried weight enough to still Jack's hand. "But why?"

As the mask blistered and blackened, from behind its wooden fangs, could be heard, "Darkness extinguishes shadow."

Then the shadow demon released his grip and fell within the pyre of washi and wire, the horns of his mask visible until the theater's fire suppression system obscured their opposing perspectives. When the smoke cleared, nothing remained of the illuminated matsuri float or its possessor.

Having regained his composure, Jack drifted down from the rafters to retrieve Hiro's sword, which had fallen tip-first into the stage. Flashing lights filled the room with a vibrant haze. Akari's hologram continued to perform, though her breathing teammates had already scattered. Sho watched in quiet contemplation, a kinship of ethereal energy, one of spirit and the other science.

"What was all that about?" asked Alice.

"No time to explain." Jack flicked Sho's ear to gather his attention. "C'mon. Let's go."

Once upon a time, Sho might have killed a man for less, but he simply asked, "Where?"

"The hospital. We need to get you undead. I'd like to do better than one out of two for a change."

♦ ♦ ♦

Buzz skittered about the world looking for his fifty pieces of silver. Beijing. Seattle. Düsseldorf. There was nothing to be had, not even crumbs. He wasn't above being fluid with his allegiances, but not if he gained absolutely nothing for his co-operation. If he were ever to graduate from being a buzzard, he would have to show his worth, so when the shadow demon spoke of mutually beneficial circumstances, he listened. Something had gone wrong, though, as the party had ended much too abruptly, and his money was on Jack. Maybe that annoying partner of his had been involved, he wasn't sure. The last stop on his itinerary was a residence that belonged to a mid-level government official.

"Well, where is he?" asked a perturbed Solak, who had already arrived to find a recently abandoned headset. "Weren't you supposed to take care of him if I was delayed? I believe that was our arrangement." It was Solak's way of ensuring that the PMDA investigator would never see the rising of the sun.

Buzz was taken aback at Solak's scorched and broken hannya mask. It spoke of an evening that had not gone according to plan. "Lickety-split. That's how I came. Honest. I figured you had it tight as a bow. And what of Jack? Right as rain is he? Wasn't how that was supposed to go now, was it?" The damaged mask did have the advantage of better revealing Solak's displeasure. Buzz stopped short of saying that he was not the one who had neglected their deal.

Too fatigued to waste time on a buzzard, Solak took his leave without even offering a dismissive wave. He could not understand why Jack or Alice had failed to act in their interests, especially when survival was the only virtue he understood. Despite the more romantic musings of history, loyalty was not the way of the warrior so much as winning. *Then why have I lost?* He tried to convince himself that he was not so much defeated, as delayed. Self-deceit was a mask impervious to both flame and foe.

◆ ◆ ◆

Jack looked at Sho's hospital chart. "A close shave. Looks like someone named Kazuo brought you here…and in the nick of time."

"We worked together back when we were chinpira. He's a good man and a reliable friend." Though clinically dead, the hospital's machines had done an admirable job of preserving Sho's body. It was unsettling to endure such a lucid out-of-body experience, but it beat the alternative.

For his part, Jack was grateful for a second chance to set things right, if for no other reason than to keep Clement guessing. "Relax. I'll have you back inside your old shell in no time. It'll be as if nothing ever happened."

Sho looked at his well-ventilated body, animated more by machines than physical will, and said, "I'm not going back. There's nothing left for me. No one to protect."

Alice assumed his sister was the source of his hesitation. Perhaps choosing the course of one's exit was something that ran in the family. "You'll see her again. Won't he, Jack?"

Though typically cagey, Jack's answer didn't inspire confidence. "What? Of course, he will. Odds being what they are…maybe."

"But not until I die, right?" Sho had a talent for seeing through people's attempts at misdirection. It was an occupational talent. Everything he had fought for was gone, and he saw no point in delaying the inevitable, not to be rejoined with his former self.

Chasing Sho's ghost around Tōkyō would certainly impede Jack's appointment with the roulette wheel back in Vegas. Anyway, it was apparent that this was where the thread was going to be tied. Every rotation of his beads confirmed it to be the case, and he wasn't in a mood to argue. "Now listen, Sho. It's not time for you to cash out. C'mon, I bet you've got people who owe you money…maybe a hostess club that needs managing? Someone, you need to shake down?"

"Sometimes—to be whole—you've got to allow the space for who you're supposed to be. I'm not going back."

Voices in the hall made it clear that someone, presumably hospital staff, was getting closer.

"People in the hallway, Jack." Alice understood Sho's reticence. She was familiar with having your world burned to ashes only to discover that you liked what grew out of it.

Sensing she was empathetic to his plight, Sho added, "Haven't you noticed? My eyes aren't black anymore."

Alice peered deep within his soul and saw that Sho had reached the end of his journey, even if it wasn't the original destination. Lacking time to disseminate her revelation, Alice transformed, and before Jack could object, harvested Sho where he stood.

Jack's beads conveyed the consequences of her unilateral decision with the utmost of urgency. "Great googly moogly!" Aware his course of action had been determined; Jack drew Hiro's blade from its sheath and drove it deep into Sho's chest. The bedside monitor trumpeted its protest with a singular, yet recognizable tone.

"Oh my god, Jack. What have we done?"

"Relax kiddo. Destiny is never a mistake."

When later written, the police report would say that the victim had been one of the most feared yakuza ever to come out of San'ya. What those who could not see beyond the veil failed to record was that Sho had found a way to safeguard others from within his faults. His eyes clear and bright, like the moonlight at dawn that belies concealment; he had become not a shadow, but a light.

◆ ◆ ◆

"I can explain," said Haruto, who had been too busy evacuating the auditorium to kill the video feed to the record company.

Genjirō quietly burned into the screen for what seemed a very long time, but then he brightened. "Brilliant! That show was brilliant! Everyone here is talking about it."

"They are?" Haruto couldn't be sure he heard correctly over the cleaning bots gathering up the pieces of what had passed for their grand finale.

"Simply amazing. People watch the Genki Girls because they want to see a train wreck. Well, mission accomplished."

"I thought we were pretty good in a few places. Did you see the Latin number?"

"Mediocre at best." Genjirō looked up from his desk toy. "The lantern sculptures coming to life...not entirely bad, but that number where we thought the girl died. Genius! It was like musical theater for drug addicts. You certainly know your audience."

"Well, maybe next time you should come by in person and see for yourself?" Haruto wasn't sure that there would be a next time, which made the offer relatively safe.

"See the Genki Girls? Not on your life. I've got people who take those kinds of blows for me."

The call concluded abruptly, and Haruto discovered that Taka and Momoko were waiting to share a word with him. Momoko handed Haruto an ornamental envelope and bowed deeply. Her signature twintails pointed towards the ground in sincere contrition.

"Momo-chan. What's this about?"

"Haruto-sensei has been so kind to me," she said, "and I'm extremely grateful for everything you've taught me, but I regret I must step down. Taka and I..."

This was Taka's cue, so he handed Haruto his own envelope. "Thank you for everything. You gave me a great opportunity, and I'll never forget it," he took Momoko's hand and said, "but this is one I can't pass up."

Haruto felt a vibration from inside his pocket. "Hold that thought—those must be the results of the voting." His eyelids drew wide open. "I wondered if this might be the case. You won Momoko. You're going to be the new center!"

"I what?"

"People loved that part when you fainted. I told you guys never to lock your legs, but people must have thought you were acting."

"Gomen," apologized Momoko. She was equally ignorant as to what had actually occurred. Her memory had been completely erased when her soul had been restored.

"I guess people really do want someone they can root for," said Haruto, a metaphorical hat-tip to Taka. Before he was independent, he had only thought on behalf of the company, but he had started to consider artists as actual people. "You know, I've been thinking about making a few changes."

"What kind of changes?" asked Taka.

"That whole 'no dating' rule. Who came up with that? How can you sing about love if you don't even know what it is?"

"So I can stay?" asked Momoko, her face radiating more than when she had been spectrally aligned.

"Well...I can't lose my new center." Haruto put his arm around Taka. "Or the guy who saves me from paying four positions. Mister Assistant Producer."

◆ ◆ ◆

Solak's hannya avatar hovered beside Boss Mori's empty chair, but he had become a grotesque version of his former self. Cracked and charred, the mask's lower jaw was attached with leather strings. "You might have noticed a few new faces here today," said Solak, having assumed control of the meeting. "In their zeal to ensure that our patriarch would have a suitable successor, Bosses Shinjirō, Nakai, Yamauchi, and Ishinomori joined our beloved leader in permanent retirement. I'm afraid that in the explosion, Ishii-san was also gravely injured."

"You know why we're here," said Kazuyo who, due to the personnel openings, appeared to be unopposed. "Who is the new kumichō? That's what we want to know."

"My position as saiko-komon was due to aligned interests and was never meant to be permanent. Regrettably, I cannot continue in this position due to other obligations. Fortunately, though, it provides me with some degree of neutrality."

"So we've got to replace you as well? Isn't that what all these power grabs are about? What if the Ankōshoku clan decides to get involved? You're not planning on leaving without ending this war over succession?"

"I have already found a solution, one that will forestall any further bloodshed," said Solak. "Legitimacy has always been the goal of this family, and now that we have a controlling interest in one of Japan's largest pharmaceutical companies, we need a different type of leader, someone who is beyond reproach. The time has come for this family to start to act like a corporation. In the samurai era, mutually advantageous marriages were often arranged to ensure interdependence and encourage stability. My solution is unconventional, but in line with that way of thinking. The next patriarch will be someone with connections in both worlds." Murmurs erupted as the heads of the families tried to decipher his meaning.

Boss Mori's chair creaked as its latest occupant eased into its leather. "As I see it," said Mrs. Okada, her hair trimmed just above her jawline, "my job is to ensure that everyone gets along. From this point on, we're all going to act like one happy family. Rest assured, I know a thing or two about discipline. As you know…I'm a mother." The gentle murmur of the air-conditioner was the only reply. "Oh—would anyone like some fresh cookies?" A tracksuit-wearing attendant placed a tray on the conference table. "Sugar is the real drug, don't you know?"

◆ ◆ ◆

Yuki pushed Keiji's wheelchair around the hospital garden, though it could do so unattended. The afternoon ritual was something they both cherished, and the grounds lifted both their spirits. With no small amount of regret, she observed, "So tomorrow you're finally breaking out of this place?"

"That's right," said Keiji. "I'm hoping you'll be there to send me off. I'll attend your next concert – not that I haven't suffered enough."

She hit him playfully, but a little harder than intended. Before she could apologize, her watch buzzed. "Oh, time to get you back inside. I promised the nurse I wouldn't be late again."

"*Mondai nai*. I can walk." Keiji rose from his wheelchair and stretched out his arms as if he had just performed a magic trick. "*Jan-jan!*"

"What? Why, you!" Yuki was only mad for a moment before she burst out laughing.

Then Keiji stumbled forward and grabbed hold of her. "My physical therapist told me not to do that, but I thought it was funny." He wrapped his arms around her neck, and she eased him back into his wheelchair. "Worth it, but please don't hit me again."

Yuki was happy to see that he was making progress, even if he couldn't actually walk. "Well, I'll check with your mother about the time. *Mata ashita.*"

Alice had been watching from a nearby bench and decided to speak up rather than wait to be discovered. "Florence Nightingale believed in gardens. Looks like it's working."

"How long have you been there?" Yuki was more embarrassed than surprised, but at least Alice didn't creep her out anymore. "It's nice that you visit Keiji, but you don't have to pretend why. I know you like him."

Alice was quick to brush off any such speculation. "We barely know each other." If it was a lie, there was at least some underlying truth to the notion. "Besides, I know you like him. A real friend would never do that."

"Are we really friends?"

"More than you know." Regardless of how she had felt about Keiji, love meant not trying to force open a door that had already closed. "I think you two would be great together. Don't worry about me. Really."

If they weren't in competition, then Yuki was relieved, but even unopposed, she lacked any confidence in her chance for success. "It probably doesn't matter. Pushing him around the hospital was the only game I had. Soon I won't even have that. We could go see fireworks – no, that's not until summer."

"Play Smash Jumpers with him," said Alice. "He likes that. On second thought, better not. I hear it's riddled with viruses."

"Wait a second." Yuki unfastened the angel necklace from around her neck and handed it to Alice. "I think you're supposed to have this."

"Arigatou," replied Alice. "You're a good friend."

"Better than I knew."

◆ ◆ ◆

"Have you ever seen anything so beautiful?" Sakura petals collected within the golden bow of Alice's yukata, the remainder drifting to the river below where they gathered atop the water like textured fabric. Alice noticed how Jack wore his and laughed. "You're not supposed to wear it right over left. Haven't you ever been to a funeral? That's only for people who are dead." Mindful of the look Jack was giving her, she added, "I'll change mine later."

"So, back to your old body?" Jack's rakishly draped hat gave him a relaxed demeanor that sharply contrasted what he usually wore to the office.

"I would have changed in Tōkyō, but – maybe it doesn't matter. I think Yuki kind of figured it out." She rubbed the necklace that had been restored to her neck.

"Doubt is our real power of convenience, kid. Thinking you know isn't the same as knowing." He blew a pink pedal off his nose. "Remind me. Is that how you looked when I found you?"

Alice thought about it for a moment, and a dimpled grin revealed that even she couldn't remember. "There's something I've been meaning to ask."

"Shoot."

She became very quiet. "When you took me from the car that day, was I going to heaven or hell?"

"Hell." Jack drank in her horror; then began to laugh. "Relax princess. They don't tell me that sort of thing, but I will tell you something."

Alice expected another of Jack's famous smart-ass observations. "Yeah, what?"

"I don't care if Solak was Hiro."

"You don't?" She waited for the punch line.

"Nah. I already have a partner. Yeah, that's right. You're not a trainee anymore. There's no certificate or anything." He grabbed a handful of sakura petals and tossed them at her. "Mazel tov."

"But you're retiring soon, right? Then what am I supposed to do?"

"With all my demerits?" He patted his pocket, which bulged with gravel. "I'll go when I'm good and ready." Jack already had a plan to return his inappropriately borrowed souvenirs, but only when the time was right.

Alice realized there was a lot she could learn from him about gaming the system. "So what about Sho? Is he with Akari now?"

"Well, I did just get a nasty message from Clement." He lifted his wrist to reveal that his beads jerked about most unpleasantly. "Be glad you can't read this." Apologizing for things he didn't regret was the cornerstone of his personality. "In other news, one of the Genki Girls' songs is up for a Nobel Prize, some sort of math formula on one of their B-sides. Maybe idol music is deeper than I thought."

"I guess." Her Mona Lisa smile had returned.

"Well, I'd say it's about time to wrap up this clam-bake. Was there anything you needed to do while we're still in town? Someone you wanted to see? Might be a while before we get back around this way again."

Alice wondered if it was possible to lose everything only to find out you had more. It occurred to her that somewhere along the way, she had stumbled across the answer. "Actually, I think I'm good. Oh, that reminds me." She reached into her silk handbag and produced a pink box. She unfastened the tabs and removed a small ice pack.

"What's that?" asked Jack, his nose wrinkling.

"A little something to eat while we watch the cherry blossoms. Haven't you ever done this before?" There was a piece of cake and two forks.

"Don't mind if I do."

Alice rested her head on the bridge's railing and watched the pale pink and white flowers drift dreamily upon the river below. "Why can't there always be sakura?"

"Because then, who would need us?" Jack didn't intend to be both creepy and deep; it just came naturally. "Say, this is pretty good."

Fluttering petals twinkled in the whites of Alice's eyes. "Ne. You know what today is?"

"Saturday. So? What of it?"

"It's my birthday," she replied coyishly.

A spilled coffee grin spread across Jack's face. "You mean this is…"

They toasted with their forks.

GLOSSARY

Akihabara (秋葉原): A district in Tōkyō, also called "Electric Town," known for selling electronics and catering to manga and anime enthusiasts, the center of otaku culture.

Anata (あなた): Translates as "you," but is used as a term of endearment between husbands and wives, considered rude between less familiar people.

Aniki (あにき): An honorific meaning "older brother." Used when addressing someone who is your senior within a yakuza family.

Anime (アニメ): Animation of Japanese influence or design. Often highly stylized and adapted from a manga source material, the source of many internet memes.

AGV: An AGV is an automatic guided vehicle, or mobile robot, typically used to transport resources around a commercial facility.

AR (Augmented Reality): The enhancement of reality through the imposition of a digital overlay. Often viewed through augmented glasses or the monitor of a smartphone, the computer-generated data or images are superimposed on what the viewer would see in their natural environment. Not to be confused with the ideological lenses most people wear.

Autonomous Moral Hierarchy (AMH): A list of pre-programmed values an autonomous machine can call upon when making decisions and judgments.

Autonomous Vehicle: A driverless car, or vehicle, that can guide itself to a predetermined destination with minimal human interaction and an improvement over most drivers.

Buchō (部長): A boss or head of a department.

Buzzard: A low-ranking harvester assigned to soul collections that do not require a high level of discretion. Often found on battlefields, hospitals, or fast-food restaurants.

Center (Idol): The center position of an idol group is often voted for by the fans or won in a game. A critical position as the center usually serves as the spokesperson during television appearances. No less meaningful than other titles, people come into conflict over.

Chinpira (ちんぴら): Often seen wearing tracksuits, these young yakuza are in training and little more than street thugs, excellent preparation for a career in the army or a large corporation.

Edo Period (江戸時代): The era in Japanese history between 1603 and 1868 in which the Tokugawa shogunate and regional daimyo primarily ruled Japan. The Edo period ended with the restoration of imperial power under Emperor Meiji.

Enhancer: A designer drug that turns off the part of your brain that interferes with one's suspension of disbelief. Apparently, most of Hollywood has already taken this pill.

Enka (演歌): A sentimental type of Japanese music popular during the twentieth century. Themes often are about regret, loss of love, and longing, mostly used for drinking rather than actual enjoyment.

Fusuma Panel: Sliding doors meant to separate rooms in traditional Japanese homes. The washi paper is often highly decorated.

Geisha (芸者): A highly trained female artist who entertains through their mastery of the traditional Japanese arts, in Kyōto geisha are called geiko (芸子). A maiko (舞妓) is an apprentice geisha, and they are particularly renowned for their colorful appearance with kimono, obi, and hana-kanzashi that reflects the seasons.

Genki (元気): To have energy, spirit, or vigor. It can also mean to have good health but is without an exact English equivalent. In the future, it is often used in a slang context that differs slightly from present-day usage.

Genki Girls: A group created as a counter-punch to the trend of holographic idols in the music industry. Current and past members have included: Alice, Akari, Keiko, Moe, Momoko, Nana, Rie, Saori & Yuki, and in point of fact, no worse than most popular music.

Ghost: A spirit that was not harvested in the appropriate allotment of time and is trapped between the material and celestial dimensions.

Gomen/Gomen-nasai (御免): Japanese for "sorry." Not as formal as moushiwake-arimasen, which is closer to meaning, "my actions cannot be justified, and I apologize."

Gyōji (行司): The referee of a sumo match who helps coordinate the initial charge and rules on the outcome. The Gyōji also purifies the ring, announces the matches, and keeps the results.

Hajimemashite (はじめまして): Roughly translated as, "It's the first time I'm meeting you."

Hannya (般若): A demonic mask of a female filled with rage and jealousy. Among other things, this horned image indicates that its wearer is unforgiving, evil, or haunted by their past; basically, how many people view their exes.

Harvester: A harvester is an unintentionally deceased human who assumes the role of transporting the souls of the dead to the celestial dimension. Not to be confused with a grim reaper, unless your intended goal is to annoy them.

Heisei (平成): The era that corresponds to the reign of Emperor Akihito, starting on January 8, 1989, to April 30, 2019.

Hikikomori (引きこもり): Adults who pursue a lifestyle of intensive isolation from society. As a result of worldwide lockdowns, what was previously seen as primarily, a Japanese issue became a global phenomenon that technology and shifting norms have enabled. Such voluntary confinement has become one of the twenty-first century's greatest social threats but is a writer's regular lifestyle.

Holograph/Hologram: Most artificially created idols of the mid-twenty-first century actually result from volumetric display technology (technology that can display 3D graphical images that appear to hover in space). However, due to misuse of the terms holograph and hologram, the meanings are commonly misunderstood. For convenience, the term holograph shall be taken as referring to the technique of capturing 3D images, while hologram shall be considered shorthand for volumetric display technology.

Honorifics: In the future, Japanese honorifics remain popular in workplace environments. Western honorifics, however, have snuck into daily life. As a result of American film and television, Japanorifics eventually led to the use of both eastern honorifics such as -san and sensei along with Western ones such as Mr. and Mrs.

Idol/Idol Group: A boy or girl pop group. Dance and singing ability are often secondary to rooting-interest. Fans enjoy encouraging their favorite member and often vote to see them rise to the coveted "center" position. The center idol receives the most attention in choreography and is one of only a few members allowed to talk during television interviews. Idol music themes often center on confessing your love and doing your best. Particularly noteworthy as it is the last musical genre in which the artists are allowed to smile.

Kakejiku (掛軸): A hanging scroll meant for decoration. Often a display of calligraphy, or painting, mounted on silk. A rod at the bottom allows it to be rolled up for secure storage.

Kakkoii (格好いい): A Japanese word with the approximate meaning of "cool" or "good appearance."

Karesansui (枯山水): Commonly referred to as a Zen garden in the West, a Japanese dry landscape garden.

Katana Kake (刀掛け): A stand, intended for displaying Japanese swords and often made of wood and lacquer.

Kendama (けん玉): A traditional children's game where you catch a stringed ball, with a hole, in one of three cups or on a spike — a popular pastime of weeaboo.

Kawaii (可愛い): Japanese for cute, and the most common word in the Japanese language.

Kobun (子分): A yakuza member of low-status, like a trainee. The literal meaning is "child status."

Kokuhaku (告白): Confession of love or sins, an acknowledgment. In a romantic context, this somewhat formal scenario either signals the start of a relationship or a downward spiral into depression.

Kōsatsu (高札): A sloped-roofed wooden signboard for official edicts and laws.

Kumichō (組長): A yakuza head boss, similar in meaning to oyabun, which is also used in addressing the family head.

Kyōto (京都): Japan's former capital, a position it held for a thousand years. The city where the author spends most of his time working on DIY projects and eating kakigōri, a shaved ice dessert topped with flavored syrups and condensed milk. Apparently, it also has many sites of historical and cultural importance.

Manga (漫画): Digital or printed graphic novels of Japanese influence or design.

Machiya (町家): A traditional Japanese townhouse, a style of dwelling especially popular in Kyōto. The reason the author spends all his time in Kyōto on DIY projects.

Marubo-Dekka (マル暴デッカ): A yakuza-world detective.

Media Interactivity: A particular medium's ability to facilitate the properties necessary in an ideal conversation. A theory the author published before his brain began to decline.

Meiji Restoration (明治維新): The period in Japanese history when power shifted from the Tokugawa Shogunate to the Emperor. A time of rapid technological change, as Japan ended approximately two centuries of isolation.

Meiji Era (明治): The era that corresponds to the reign of Emperor Meiji starting on October 23, 1868, to July 30, 1912.

Menpō (面頬): The faceguard of a samurai helmet.

Metamorph: Transforming from a physical into a metaphysical manifestation.

Nande/Nandeyanen (何で): Japanese for "why/what?" Nandeyanen is Kansai-ben, dialect used in that region to say something approximating, "what the heck?"

NHI: The abbreviation for Japan's National Health Insurance.

Oni (鬼): An oni is a type of troll, or demon, from Japanese mythology. Typically red or blue, they are often pictured wearing a tiger pelt loincloth and wielding a spiked iron club   the subject of the greatest song ever written about pants.

Omamori (御守): A good luck amulet, and usually made of colorful cloth, that people buy at shrines or temples.

Otaku (オタク): Once a derogatory term for the subculture obsessed with anime and manga, it is now often embraced by fans of many interests.

Oyabun (親分): A yakuza boss. The literal meaning is "parent status." If you call your actual parent this, you might have larger problems.

Psychopomp: A guide of deceased souls into the afterlife. A standard fixture in most cultures, some well-known psychopomps might include Anubis (Egypt), Mercury (Rome), Daena (Persia), banshees (Gaelic), the Grim Reaper (West), and shinigami 死神 (Japan).

Reiwa Era (令和): The period in the Japanese calendar that corresponded with the reign of Emperor Naruhito began on May 1, 2019. The author would not provide the end date, as he would be expelled from Japan.

Ryokan (旅館): A traditional Japanese Inn.

Salaryman (サラリーマン): A Japanese businessman who works long hours and defers his identity to his company, often used in a derogatory sense. Almost universally seen in a dark suit, white shirt, and tie.

Seppuku (切腹): "Cutting One's Belly" or hara-kiri. While self-disembowelment is often seen as ritualized suicide in the West, it was often a form of imposed execution. Also known as hara-kiri (腹切り), the stomach is cut open to reveal the character of one's soul.

Shadow-demon: A human or otherworldly entity that assumes the role of being a demon's surrogate. This position is not unlike the moral compromises many mortals willingly accept in their normal lives.

Shatei (舎弟): Younger brothers, under the supervision of their oyabun, within a yakuza family.

Shingiin (審議委員): A high-ranking yakuza advisor, similar to consigliere in the mafia.

Shishi-odoshi (鹿威し): A bamboo water fountain designed to scare away animals and a common sound effect in samurai movies. Gravity causes the bamboo tube to drop, dumping the water and creating a knocking sound.

Shōji (障子): Lattice wooden framed doors with translucent washi paper that allows light to filter into a room. The reason the author now has to open soy sauce packets in the kitchen.

Syabu (シャブ): Methamphetamine produced by the yakuza and especially popular in the post-war years.

Synchronicity Beads: A harvester tool that uses subtle signals to communicate directions from the tenth dimension. They can also take the form of a necklace or charm, depending on the user. They are often criticized for being vague or imprecise due to the limitations of the mortal realm.

Torii Gate (鳥居): A traditional gate found at the entrance to a Shinto shrine. They can also be found individually or positioned in a row within the shrine, often vermillion in color, and intended to denote passage into an area that is considered sacred.

Tsuka (柄): The hilt of a Japanese katana.

Tympanum: An architectural feature often found in religious architecture. Usually, a semi-circle or triangular shape found above an entryway that contains sculptures or ornamental elements that reinforces the purpose of the structure.

Votaku: A blending of VR and otaku, an enthusiast of VR technology and gameplay. A term the author invented that he hopes will catch on.

VR (Virtual Reality): An interactive medium that creates sensory experiences, often through the use of accompanying peripherals, to interface within a simulated reality.

Wakizashi: A short sword, often worn as a pair with a longer katana. Samurai used their wakizashi for close-range fighting and in the ritual act of seppuku.

Yakuza (ヤクザ): Japanese organized crime organizations with origins in the Edo period. Involved in a variety of rackets, they often see themselves as fulfilling samurai traditions and values. The "extreme path." There are many in Kansai, so the author will refrain from making any impudent remarks.

Yankii: A style especially popular in the late twentieth century, that involved gangs of young people who wore similar outfits and had a passion for customized cars and motorcycles. Often associated with delinquency, the yankii style of squatting called "yanki zuwari" (ヤンキー座) allows you to rest your elbows while in a squat.

Yatsuhashi (八つ橋): A type of cinnamon cookie well-loved in Kyōto.

Yokozuna (横綱): The highest rank in sumo.

Yubitsume (指詰め): The yakuza ritual of cutting off one's finger, at the joint, as an act of contrition.

Yūrei (幽霊): Quite similar to the Western notion of a ghost, but with slight differences. Usually pictured floating, and with no legs, dressed in white burial clothing, with long black hair, worn down, as if for burial. The reason the author no longer enjoys hiking Inari Shrine at night.

Zetsuenjō (絶縁状): Excommunication from the yakuza world.

ABOUT THE AUTHOR:

(The Author In Kyoto, Japan)

When not restoring his old house in Kyoto, Fernando Torres enjoys shopping at temple markets and early-morning walks in many of the locations featured in the story. With roots in the United States and Japan, an unusual contrast of environments influenced the writing of this book, along with time spent in the entertainment industry.

"When no place is home, everywhere is."
- Fernando Torres

Commercial Inquires And Reader Feedback:

Comments@fivetowerspublishing.com

Authorfernandotorres.com
&
fivetowerspublishing.com

The Author humbly requests your favor, either through a review or referral. With a million books published every year, your support could not be more essential.

Also By The Author:

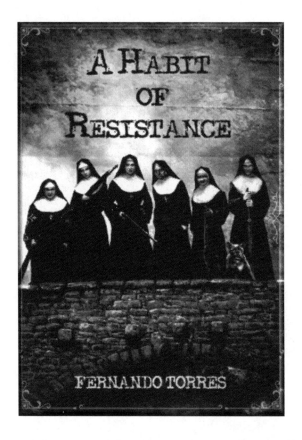

How will a quirky group of nuns stand up to history's most evil tyrants? A Habit of Resistance is the humorous story of a most unorthodox gang of nuns who join the French Resistance during WWII. Set in provincial France, A Habit of Resistance is Fernando Torres' poignant illustration of obtaining love's victory through denial, sacrifice, and redemption.

Also by the Author:

Ian MacDonald lived a solitary, but agreeable existence, in his small Scottish town, until he discovered a mysterious globe that transported him into the multiverse. Little did he realize that in a world where medieval and rococoesque civilizations struggled for supremacy, he had awakened creatures that sought to right past transgressions, using the ink of men's blood. Some would declare allegiance with dragons, while others would sacrifice their lives for honor. For within the darkness, if but a shadow remains — there is light.

Made in the USA
San Bernardino, CA
02 July 2020

74639506R10190